Palgrave Studies in Literature, Science and Medicine

Series Editors
Sharon Ruston
Dept. of English and Creative Writing
Lancaster University
Lancaster, United Kingdom

Alice Jenkins
School of Critical Studies
University of Glasgow
Glasgow, United Kingdom

Catherine Belling
Feinberg School of Medicine
Northwestern University
Chicago, Illinois, USA

Palgrave Studies in Literature, Science and Medicine is an exciting new series that focuses on one of the most vibrant and interdisciplinary areas in literary studies: the intersection of literature, science and medicine. Comprised of academic monographs, essay collections, and Palgrave Pivot books, the series will emphasize a historical approach to its subjects, in conjunction with a range of other theoretical approaches. The series will cover all aspects of this rich and varied field and is open to new and emerging topics as well as established ones.

More information about this series at
http://www.springer.com/series/14613

Elsa Richardson

Second Sight in the Nineteenth Century

Prophecy, Imagination and Nationhood

palgrave
macmillan

Elsa Richardson
Strathclyde University
Glasgow, United Kingdom

Palgrave Studies in Literature, Science and Medicine
ISBN 978-1-137-51969-6   ISBN 978-1-137-51970-2 (eBook)
DOI 10.1057/978-1-137-51970-2

Library of Congress Control Number: 2017938578

© The Editor(s) (if applicable) and The Author(s) 2017
The author(s) has/have asserted their right(s) to be identified as the author(s) of this work in accordance with the Copyright, Designs and Patents Act 1988.
This work is subject to copyright. All rights are solely and exclusively licensed by the Publisher, whether the whole or part of the material is concerned, specifically the rights of translation, reprinting, reuse of illustrations, recitation, broadcasting, reproduction on microfilms or in any other physical way, and transmission or information storage and retrieval, electronic adaptation, computer software, or by similar or dissimilar methodology now known or hereafter developed.
The use of general descriptive names, registered names, trademarks, service marks, etc. in this publication does not imply, even in the absence of a specific statement, that such names are exempt from the relevant protective laws and regulations and therefore free for general use. The publisher, the authors and the editors are safe to assume that the advice and information in this book are believed to be true and accurate at the date of publication. Neither the publisher nor the authors or the editors give a warranty, express or implied, with respect to the material contained herein or for any errors or omissions that may have been made. The publisher remains neutral with regard to jurisdictional claims in published maps and institutional affiliations.

Cover illustration: Old Paper Studios / Alamy Stock Photo

Printed on acid-free paper

This Palgrave Macmillan imprint is published by Springer Nature
The registered company is Macmillan Publishers Ltd.
The registered company address is: The Campus, 4 Crinan Street, London, N1 9XW, United Kingdom

ACKNOWLEDGEMENTS

This book is the product of journeys north and south. It began when I took the path trodden by many of the Lowland Scots featured in this book and moved to London in search of broader horizons. There I joined the History Department of Queen Mary University of London (QMUL), where I started this research, worked in a bookshop, taught bright undergraduates, got lost on night buses and eventually completed a doctorate. Then last year, horizons sufficiently broadened, I retraced my steps northwards to the calm of a wet Glasgow summer and to the quiet needed to finish this book.

Along the way, my work has benefited from the generous input of colleagues, from the patience of friends and from the support of family. Special thanks to Rhodri Hayward and Thomas Dixon for granting my membership to the Centre for the History of the Emotions at QMUL where, as an English literature student with itchy feet and interdisciplinary tendencies, it was a relief to find myself among the similarly afflicted. The Centre was a hugely stimulating environment in which to undertake a PhD and my research was greatly influenced by the astute, rigorous scholarship pursued by its members. I owe a substantial intellectual debt to Rhodri, my primary supervisor, mentor and friend, without whom this project would never have come into being. It has been a pleasure to learn from such an original thinker, whose criticisms, multiple read-throughs and countless acts of kindness have proved invaluable. To find my own wildly diverse interests not only matched but bested by my supervisor was a remarkable stroke of good luck. I am grateful also to Johanna Cohen for her clear-headed guidance; to Catherine Maxwell for her advice at a formative stage; to Barbara Taylor for advocating for my work; to Christine Ferguson and Roger Luckhurst for reading the manuscript in its nascent form and for offering sound advice on how to improve it; and to Tiffany Watt-Smith for her friendship and keen scholarly insight.

Libraries and archives have, of course, played an essential role in the success of this research. Much of this book was written in the library at the Wellcome Collection, a quiet space in the centre of London with well-stocked shelves and well-informed librarians. Special thanks to Ross MacFarlane for pointing me in the direction of useful material and for indulging my interest in malevolent Highland fairies. I also spent a good deal of time in Senate House Library, where a number of knowledgeable archivists helped me to steer a path through the supernatural immensity that is the Harry Price Collection. Further acknowledgements are due to the patient archivists at the University of Kent and to the custodians of the Pitt Rivers Museum who allowed me to access their vast storehouse of curiosities. This research was made possible by the long-term financial support of the Carnegie Trust and the Wellcome Trust, and by small grants from the Stirlingshire Educational Trust and QMUL.

Lastly, I am indebted to my wonderful friends for cooking me dinner, keeping me sane and offering endless encouragement. Special thanks to my old housemate Elaine Tierney for her editorial prowess and scholarly enthusiasm; to Rosie Eveleigh for understanding how one does judge a book by its cover; and to Laura Guy for seeing it through. My deepest thanks are reserved for my parents, Eileen and Alistair Richardson, for their unwavering support, kindness and wit. I dedicate this book to them.

CONTENTS

CHAPTER 1

Introduction

On 23 August 1894, the *Dundee Courier* printed a short report that detailed a tour being taken through the West Highlands and Islands by several members of a London-based organisation called the Society for Psychical Research (SPR). The purpose of their trip, we are told, concerned 'that peculiar faculty said to be possessed by many people, especially in the Highlands, and popularly known as "second sight"'. Accompanied by a small white terrier, two of the organisation's 'lady members' were making their way through the small fishing villages and farming communities of Tiree, Iona, Eriskay, Barra and Portree in search of people in possession of this special ocular capacity.[1] Writing in *Cock Lane and Common Sense* (1894), Andrew Lang, a Scottish writer and prominent member of the SPR, described the hallmarks of the phenomenon under investigation:

> In second sight the percipient beholds events occurring at a distance, sees people whom he never saw with the bodily eye, and who afterwards arrive in his neighbourhood; or foresees events approaching but still remote in time. The chief peculiarity of second sight is, that the visions often, though not always, are of symbolical character. A shroud is observed around the living man who is doomed; boding animals, mostly black dogs, vex the seer; funerals are witnessed before they occur, and 'corpse-candles' (some sort of light) are watched flitting above the road whereby a burial procession is to take its way.[2]

© The Author(s) 2017
E. Richardson, *Second Sight in the Nineteenth Century*,
Palgrave Studies in Literature, Science and Medicine,
DOI 10.1057/978-1-137-51970-2_1

Described in Gaelic as the *An-da-shealladh* or the 'two sights', this intuitive vision was said to thrive among the Scottish Highlanders. Unlike the doctrinal revelations of the religious prophet or the nation-forming proclamations of the oracle, the premonitions associated with second sight trafficked in quotidian experience. To give an example, in one account recorded by the SPR an island woman delays packing for a trip to England because of a vision in which a 'messenger came on horseback with a letter' telling of a death in the family; two days later, just as she is confessing this 'foolishness' to her husband, the letter arrives exactly as forecast.[3] Arriving unsought, such predictions detailed everyday events in the lives of people living in remote communities: the death of a neighbour, the unexpected arrival of a relative, the wrecking of a fishing boat or the success of a harvest. From the late seventeenth century onwards, these mundane prophecies began to attract the attention of scientists, antiquarians, travel writers, artists, novelists, folklorists and eventually, psychical researchers. This book is, in part, an examination of these varied enquiries and an attempt to understand how the odd portents of a remote people came to occupy a prominent position in the British imagination.

Second sight was an object of fascination for many English-speaking observers, drawn north in search of symbolical visions and eerie prophecies. Writing in *A Journey to the Western Islands of Scotland* (1775), the lexicographer and essayist Samuel Johnson avowed that his travel narrative would really have 'little claim to the praise of curiosity' if it failed to address the question of second sight among the Highlanders. Describing it as an 'impression made either on the eye, or by the eye upon the mind', Johnson finds that the premonitions associated with second sight feature set narratives: such as, a man 'on a journey far from home falls from his horse' and is seen 'bleeding on the ground' by a relative working miles away from the accident, or a seer 'driving home his cattle' is surprised by the sudden appearance of a spectral 'bridal ceremony or a funeral procession' blocking his way.[4] These visions are, the writer explains, the spectral imprints of distant or future events seen as 'if they were present', that are brought about by a 'superadded' power of sight.[5] Having encountered 'many tales of these airy shows' and carefully weighed their evidentiary value, Johnson departed from Scotland unconvinced but 'willing to believe' in the possibility of supernatural foresight.[6] The measured tone of this conclusion, grounded in empirical observation and probabilistic reasoning, is typical of the investigative cultures examined by this book. In his history of ghost-seeing from the Reformation to the twentieth century,

Shane McCorristine uses the term 'Enlightenment-agnosticism' to describe the peculiar approach to the supernatural that emerged as an 'uncanny reflection of positivistic scientific practice'.[7] When, in 1882, a group of Cambridge University scientists and philosophers came together to found a society dedicated to the 'organised and systematic' study of anomalous phenomena, they did so as part of an established intellectual tradition.[8] Though over a century separates Johnson's tour through the Highlands from the expedition undertaken by the SPR, the two share in a desire to expose the extraordinary visionary capacities rumoured to proliferate among the Gaelic people to the scrutiny of empiricist observation. With the financial backing of a sympathetic laird and the practical assistance of a local priest, through the closing decade of the nineteenth century psychical researchers worked to gather a corpus of individual testimony pertaining to the nature and prevalence of second sight. This data then formed the basis of several formal reports made to the SPR in London and reprinted in the organisation's proceedings, the *Journal of Psychical Research*: an alchemical transformation that, like Johnson's erudite rationalism, worked to convert uncanny foresight into a form of scientific knowledge.

The principal focus of this book lies in the nineteenth century with the enquiries made by several nascent investigative cultures, including spiritualism, anthropology and psychical research, into the subject of second sight. The Victorian supernatural has been described as having a 'protean quality of being a cause, a place, a kind of being, a realm, a possibility, a new form of nature and a hope for the future'; an amorphous multiplicity that has long attracted scholars working in the humanities.[9] There has been, however, a shift in the focus of this attention away from literary treatments of the ghost story or social histories of superstition, towards the interdisciplinary study of spiritualism, mesmerism, mysticism and the occult. Scholars such as Jill Galvan, Christine Ferguson, Roger Luckhurst, Pamela Thurschwell and Sarah Wilburn have explored the complex patterns of information sharing that took place between orthodox and heterodox practices, technology and the occult, science and popular literature.[10] In doing so they have unearthed metaphoric interstices capable of upending any easy division of natural and supernatural, science and religion, rational and irrational. Methodological and disciplinary differences aside, these treatments all share in a desire to challenge a disenchanted reading of modernity, first made famous by the sociologist and political economist Max Weber, in which rationalisation

and intellectualisation are credited with forcing magic, religion and spirituality from the public realm.[11] Historians have chipped away at the idea of
disenchantment to reveal the magical imagination at work in the operations
of capitalism and the structures of modernity itself.[12] Prominent in this area
of study, the work of Michael Saler and Joshua Landy have disassembled
Weber's thesis by exposing the close relation of secularisation to multifarious forms of modern enchantment.[13] The examples that Saler and
Landy use to illustrate the concept of re-enchantment come, almost exclusively, from elite culture; modern magic lies, for these authors, in the
discourses of literature, philosophy and aesthetics. Along similar lines,
historiographical treatments of the Victorian supernatural have, with a few
notable exceptions, tended to formulate their arguments in relation to the
experiences and written reflections of the highly educated.[14] They have
done so with good reason, as studies into the magical beliefs of educated
elites have permitted historians to map out important interconnections
between the cultural modalities of the supernatural and developments in
science, medicine and so on. What this approach necessitates, however, is
the jettisoning of beliefs, stories and customs associated with the illiterate,
the poor and the marginalised.

The history of second sight demands a different approach. Strongly
associated with the Highlands of Scotland, a region that remained economically, politically and linguistically peripheral through the nineteenth
century, second sight existed as part of a culture situated on the fringes of
British society. Since the seventeenth century, English-speaking observers
have tried to make sense of this peculiar power by gathering first-hand
accounts, conducting surveys and translating oral testimony into written
evidence. In the process, they have transformed customary and peripheral
knowledge into data to be processed, instrumentalised and eventually
assimilated by discourses operating at the imperial centre. The SPR's
inquiry was, for instance, undertaken with the aim of amassing data in
support of a new theoretical framework for understanding the supernatural, based on the idea of thought transference or telepathy. This is clear
in an early report on the progress of the investigation, in which stories of
second sight are described as running along lines 'with which we are all
familiar' and as constituting clear examples of 'thought transference—
information subconsciously acquired'. No matter then that such terms
are 'quite unrecognised by the seers themselves'; their mysterious prophecies must now be recognised as only the work of 'memory and unconscious observation'. Assured of a common conceptual language, that 'with

which we are familiar', their accounts are re-formed by the epistemological heft of new psychical theories of mind.[15] Through the nineteenth century, tales of second sight were used to bolster the claims of a number of burgeoning investigative cultures, and this book attends to the ways in which previsionary narratives were colonised by educated discourses. In doing so, it diverges from dominant historiographical narratives of the Victorian supernatural by pointing to the presence of myths, customs and lore, harvested from marginalised communities and put to work in the forming of elite knowledge at the metropole.

The appeal of second sight, the factor that distinguished it from other supernatural phenomena for outside observers, was its geographical specificity. Though presentiments and prophecies were by no means exclusive to the Highlands and Islands, the idea of second sight entered the cultural imagination as a peculiarly Scottish faculty. This strange faculty certainly precedes and exceeds the English naming of it, but the tradition of second sight that begins to appear in antiquarian miscellanies, scientific studies, travel narratives and novels from the late seventeenth century onwards must also be recognised as a product of the demands and intentions of those particular texts. The meanings attributed to the prophetic vision arise, then, not from the Gaelic-speaking communities in which they are said to take place, rather they are imposed by outside observers. Read as one of Eric Hobsbawm's 'invented tradition[s]', as a 'set of practices, normally governed by overtly or tacitly accepted rules and of a ritual or symbolic nature, which seek to inculcate certain values and norms of behaviour by repetition, which automatically implies continuity with the past', second sight exemplifies the problematic relation of the study of folk customs to the politics of representation.[16] This 'invented tradition' owes its existence to the intellectual traffic between Scotland and England, where the fabled augury served as a complex and contested marker of national identity. Recent histories of Scottish literature and culture after the Acts of Union propose post-colonial theory as the most appropriate analytical model for describing the transformations wrought by that decree. Whilst conceiving of Scotland as a marginalised nation is complicated by its oscillation between the subject positions of coloniser and colonised, studies such as Matthew Wickman's *The Ruins of Experience* (2007) and Silke Stroh's *Uneasy Subjects* (2011) have claimed post-colonialism as a suitable critical frame in which to consider the experience of Gaelic communities in a newly unified Great Britain.[17] Where the Lowlands became apprentice to England's imperial ambitions, Highland territories remained linguistically, politically and religiously other.

Britain's northernmost regions were called upon to signify preliterate, primitive culture. Where, depending on the nature of their ideological investment, the observer might find the comforting survival of a traditional way of life removed from the destabilising forces of industrialisation or an equally affirming reminder of the reprehensibly savage state from which modern civilisation has evolved. Building upon readings of the 'Celtic fringe' as composing a kind of proving ground for colonial discourse, this book places questions of nationhood in close proximity to those posed by the supernatural, and asks what power relations the demarcation of second sight as a peculiarly Gaelic superstition might expose.

One of the stories that this book tells, then, concerns the processes of appropriation and colonisation at stake in the construction of second sight as an 'ancient' Gaelic tradition. This story is complicated, however, by the often disruptive influence exercised by these prophetic narratives. Psychical researchers, for instance, found the evidence associated with second sight remarkably difficult to assimilate into the development and elucidation of new theories such as telepathy. To give an example, one account gathered during the inquiry tells of a fishing trip around the Western Isles and a dinner below stairs, during which a member of the party known to 'possess the gift of second sight' observes a young crew member covered in a strange 'phosphorescent light'. From this the seer concludes that the 'young man would soon be drowned', but his companions assure him that this was highly unlikely, given that the 'weather was fine' and they expected to 'reach the island of Skye' by morning. The tragic prophecy is fulfilled, however, when the doomed boy leans 'against the railing of the gangway, which could not have been properly fastened, for it gave way: he fell overboard, and his body was never recovered'.[18] Secondhand, undated and without corroboration from other witnesses, such testimony as this failed to match the veridical conditions set by other studies undertaken by the SPR. More problematic still is the symbolic content of the vision, where it is only by an act of decoding that the seer is able to identify the dire import of the 'phosphorescent light'. Encrypted in form, second sight was rooted in a world to which the English-speaking, London-dwelling members of the SPR had only limited access. Writing on the subject, the Lowland-born Andrew Lang hazarded that though the power was apparently very prevalent throughout the remote communities of northern Scotland, 'the tourist or angler who has no Gaelic is not likely to hear much about it'.[19] This linguistic barrier encodes an even greater problem for psychical research, as Lang cautions that though second sight might be 'now *called* telepathy' this denomination does 'essentially advance our knowledge of the subject', because the faculty connotes 'a belief and system' that precedes and exceeds the boundaries of this categorisation.[20] In line with critical interpretations of folklore as posing an alternative and unsanctioned opposition to institutional culture, this book engages with the troublesome and upending potentials of an extraordinary form of vision predicated on privileged, local knowledge.[21]

Second sight is primarily, but not exclusively, associated with the eyes, and many historical accounts of the phenomenon share in a desire to unmask the complex processes of perception and reflection involved in the production of extraordinary foreknowledge. Samuel Johnson described it as a 'mode of seeing, superadded to that which Nature generally bestows'; a correspondent of the antiquarian John Aubrey reported in 1693 that those bestowed with the special power 'see these things visibly; but none sees, but themselves'; in the early decades of the eighteenth century, a Scottish travel writer detailed the physicality of the experience where 'at the sight of a Vision, the Eye-lids of the Person are erected, and the Eyes continue flaring until the Object vanish'; and in the late nineteenth century, psychical researchers gathering testimony in the Highlands characterised the second sighted as remarkably 'strong visualizers'.[22] The value of historising vision and in particular, what composes visual 'reality', has been adeptly illustrated by Norman Bryson, who argues that 'vision is socialized, and therefore deviation from this social construction of visual reality can be measured and named, variously, as hallucination, misrecognition, or 'visual disturbance'.[23] Some theorists, for example Jonathan Crary, have examined the impact of new technologies such as the camera and the stereoscope on the visual imagination, while some historians, for example Chris Otter, have explored how new developments in medical science shift the boundaries of what constitutes 'normal vision', and others, such as the literary critic Kate Flint, have queried the role of visual perception in popular genres of fiction.[24] What makes second sight such a useful subject for the history of vision, is the way in which it is called upon to both participate in and subvert the functioning of ocularcentrism. On the one hand, accounts of prophecies among the Scottish Highlanders were typically made by those invested in a model of perception that elevated the eyes as rational arbitrators of exterior reality. But on the other, the subject of these investigations—remarkable feats of foretelling and far-seeing—tended to frustrate, rather than confirm, scientific certainties regarding the nature of our perceptual experience. Borrowing the term 'ocular-eccentricity', which Marin Jay has employed to describe alternative modes of visual engagement, this book explores how other ways of seeing—prophetic, previsionary, inner, extra sensory—might be said to have interrupted, punctured or complicated the epistemological privileging of sight as a superior route to truth.[25]

The philosophical and cultural significance of the eye has already proved to be a particularly rich field for humanities scholarship and this book is not intended to contribute to an already abundant area of research. Rather, it makes a new intervention by excavating a specific set of relations, between the predictions and visionary foreseeing of the second sighted and the writing of history. Part of what this project examines are the ways in which seemingly miraculous events are folded into coherent historical narratives. This can be observed most clearly in the application of historicist methodologies to the question of the supernatural. Published with varied intentions, from debunking to defending the existence of witches, ghosts and, occasionally, Scottish auguries, the nineteenth century oversaw the production of a vast and varied literature on the history of supernatural belief. In a more complex manner, the second-sighted vision is not only an object of history, it is also a participant in the historiographical process. The prediction of a seer, whether reproduced by oral or textual formations, is itself a form of historical narrative, which refuses linear formations of time to conflate the present with the future, so that the effects are ascertained before their cause comes into existence. Following Hayden White's description of the work of the historian as a 'poetic process', a 'fusing of events, whether imaginary or real, into a comprehensible totality capable of serving as the object of representation', this book is interested in the new and potentially disruptive narrative structures that premonitory tales help to create.[26] Where the Highlands of Scotland were written into a teleological account of historical order, in which the region and its people were called upon to signify a kind of pre-modern primitivism, the prophecies of the region's fabled seers offered up a quite different understanding of historical process. Distinct from the doctrinal revelations of the religious prophet or the nation-forming proclamations of the mystic oracle, second-sighted visions typically gave over a micro history of the neighbourhood: the death of a neighbour, the unexpected homecoming of a loved one or the arrival of strangers into town and so on. Against the universalising gestures and grand narratives of dominant historiography, the histories produced by second sight attend to the local and the quotidian. Working with Diana Basham's description of prophecy as constituting 'a threat and a challenge to existing laws and paradigms of reality' because it 'indicates weakness in the existing law' by forcing 'that law to consider what has been pushed outside', this book asks what unruly potentials the mundane predictions of the second sighted might embody.[27]

Though the primary focus of this study lies with the modality of second sight in nineteenth-century culture, it is necessary to acknowledge an earlier period during which the tradition was first instituted as an object of study. Beginning with the enquiries made by the Royal Society chemist Robert Boyle in the late seventeenth century and closing with the publication of Walter Scott's debunking of the supernatural in *Letters on Demonology and Witchcraft* (1830), Chapter 2 considers the grounds on which a canon of writing on the subject was first established. Early studies of second sight are significant because not only were many of them reprinted and recirculated through the nineteenth century, they also established a methodological and philosophical framework emulated by later scientific investigations of supernatural. The texts covered by this chapter—which include scientific treaties, travel narratives and historical fictions—find commonality in their application of empiricist standards of evidence to a phenomenon positioned on the margins of the natural realm. Jumping forward to mid-nineteenth-century Edinburgh, Chapter 3 charts the migration of second sight through the new heterodox sciences of craniometry, phrenology and mesmerism, and into middle-class parlours, theatres, lecture halls and medical schools across the country. Specific attention is paid to Catherine Crowe, a novelist and disciple of the phrenologist George Combe, who was made famous by her best-selling defence of the supernatural, *The Night Side of Nature, Or Ghosts and Ghost-Seers* (1848). Crowe occupied a prominent role in the literary life of the Scottish capital and partook in an astonishing range of intellectual pursuits. Her biography opens up unrecognised connections between individuals and subject areas, while her calls for the scientific treatment of phenomena such as second sight engaged in contemporary debates concerning the reliability of ocular perception and the possibilities of inner vision.

Chapter 4 considers the rise of modern spiritualism alongside the institution of modern anthropology, an intellectual tradition that transformed tales of exotic tribes and customs, superstitions, ghosts and myth into schematic visions of human development.[28] Reading these seemingly distinct discourses as, at times, dependent upon one another, this chapter considers how second sight begins to be pressed, by both spiritualism and cultural anthropology, as a kind of inheritance. Whether written into the biographies of famous mediums, as an example of where civilisation has progressed from or alternatively might journey to, or as a part of an archaeology record uncovered in the remote regions of Britain, the idea of second sight was subsumed by an expansive evolutionary narrative that plotted the world's cultures and their peoples, past and present, along a scale from primitive to civilised. Key to this history are the figures of Edward Burnett Tylor, the founder of comparative anthropology and a vocal opponent of spiritualism, and William Howitt, a Quaker reformer and early convert to the new religion. Remaining with the subject of popular evolutionism, Chapter 5 reads second sight through the prism of the late nineteenth-century romance revival in British fiction, alongside the founding of the Folklore Society and the Society for Psychical Research. Centred on the Scottish polymath Andrew Lang, this chapter considers second sight as subject for and producer of the popular romance. This involves attending more closely to the narrative components and generic framing of previsionary narratives—as folklore, personal anecdote, fiction and so on—as well as to the cadence of non-embodied or prophetic vision as a form or analogue of creative inspiration. Respecting the suggestion made by the novelist Robert Louis Stevenson in his 1884 essay 'A Humble Remonstrance' that the fantastic in literature 'appeals to certain sensual and quite illogical tendencies in man', this chapter examines the relationship between questions of literary form or production and evolving psychological understandings of the imagination.[29]

The last chapter returns the book to where it began, with the SPR's investigation into second sight. Led by Ada Goodrich-Freer, an elusive and somewhat controversial figure, the inquiry has been largely written out of the society's institutional history. This is perhaps unsurprising given that, despite a promising start and the financial backing of a wealthy benefactor, the research team was disbanded after a couple of years, with no coherent account of their findings published. This chapter excavates the story of this failure and examines the cultural context in which it was first initiated. The inquiry into second sight cannot be read outside a broader resurgence of interest in Celtic themes, and though the SPR did not contribute directly to those debates, its work was prompted, framed and informed by the resurgence of Celticism in *fin-de-siècle* Britain. Finding a corollary in the contemporaneous Celtic Revival, this chapter reads the SPR's ill-fated tour alongside the rediscovery of Scottish folk culture and mysticism being undertaken by this broader cultural movement. More specifically, it spends time with William Sharp, a Scottish born lawyer and published poet, who also wrote poetry and prose under a female pseudonym, Fiona Macleod. A key participant in the Scottish Renascence flowering in the Edinburgh literary scene, Sharp was also a member of the Hermetic Order of the Golden Dawn, an elite magical society that provided adepts with training in the practices of tarot divination, astrology, geomancy, scrying and astral travel. Drawing together psychical researchers, revivalists and occultists, this chapter examines the modality of second sight in these elite discourses. It considers the transformation of this folkloric trope into a common feature of the psyche, a unique creative mode and, finally, a magical visionary technique.

Seeking out the Scottish seer in nineteenth-century culture, this book makes the case for this folkloric figure as a valuable subject for historians of science, psychology and popular culture. Refracted through the eyes of English-speaking observers, we will observe the second-sighted augury called into the service of multiple investigative regimes: phrenology, mesmerism, spiritualism, anthropology and psychical research. In her essay 'Forging the Missing Link: Interdisciplinary Stories', Gillian Beer situates the value of interdisciplinary methodology with its potential to track the 'circulation of intact ideas across a larger community', while at the same time bringing into 'question the methods and materials of differing intellectual practices'.[30] This study is similarly invested in the stories that emerge from this method: when anthropology is forced into conversation with spiritualism, or psychology is made to reflect upon the romance novel, the epistemologies of these disciplines reveal themselves in a state of flux, out of which new connections and possibilities arise. Stretching Beer's argument to its limits, it posits second sight as itself an 'intact idea', one that forces us to reflect upon the smudged areas of nineteenth-century history, in which seemingly distinct discourses and realms of experience collide.

NOTES

1. "Second Sight"' in the Highlands', *Dundee Courier & Argus*, 24 August 1894. ('Second Sight' . . . 1894)
2. Andrew Lang, *Cock Lane and Common Sense* (London: Longman & Green, 1894), p. 228. (Lang 1894)
3. 'Second Sight in the Highlands: The Second Report of "Miss X"', *Borderland* 3 (1896) 57–61 (59). ('Second Sight' . . . 1896).
4. Samuel Johnson, *A Journey to the Western Isles of Scotland* (1775) (London: A. Strahan and T. Cadell, 1785) p. 248. (Johnson 1775)

5. Ibid.

6. Ibid., p., 256

7. Shane McCorristine. *Spectres of the Self: Thinking about Ghosts and Ghost-seeing in England, 1750–1920* (Cambridge, 2010), pp. 11–12. (McCorristine 2010)

8. 'Objects of the Society', *Proceedings of the Society for Psychical Research* 1 (1882–1883), 3. ('Objects of the Society' ... 1882–1883).

9. Nicola Bown, Carolyn Burdett, and Pamela Thurschwell, 'Introduction' in *The Victorian Supernatural*, eds. Bown, Burdett, Thurshwell (Cambridge: Cambridge University Press, 2004) pp. 1–19 (8). (Bown et al. 2004)

10. Jill Galvan, *The Sympathetic Medium: Feminine Channeling, the Occult, and Communications Technologies, 1859–1919* (Ithaca: Cornell University Press, 2010). (Galvan 2010), Christine Ferguson, *Language, Science and Popular Fiction in the Victorian Fin-de-Siecle: The Brutal Tongue* (Aldershot: Ashgate, 2006). (Ferguson 2006), Roger Luckhurst, *The Invention of Telepathy: 1870–1901* (Oxford: Oxford University Press, 2002). (Luckhurst 2002), Pamela Thurschwell, *Literature, Technology and Magical Thinking, 1880–1920* (Cambridge University Press, 2001). (Thurschwell 2001) and Sarah Wilburn, *Possessed Victorians: Extra Spheres in Nineteenth-Century Mystical Writings* (Aldershot: Ashgate, 2006). (Wilburn 2006)

11. Max Weber, 'Science as Vocation', *From Max Weber: Essays in Sociology* trans. and ed. H.H Gerth and C. Wright (Oxford: Oxford University Press, 1946) pp. 129–156. (Weber 1946)

12. Owen Chadwick, *The Secularisation of the Human Mind* (Cambridge: Canto, 1990). (Chadwick 1990), Christopher H. Partridge, *The Re-Enchantment of the World: Alternative Spiritualities, Sacralization, Popular Culture, and Occulture* (London: T&T International, 2004). (Partridge 2004) and Michael Saler, "Clap If You Believe in Sherlock Holmes': Mass Culture and the Re-enchantment of Modernity, c. 1890–c. 1940', *The Historical Journal* 45.3 (2003), 599–622. (Saler 2003)

13. Joshua Landy and Michael Saler eds., *The Re-Enchantment of the World: Secular Magic in the Rational Age* (California: Stanford University Press, 2009). (Landy and Saler 2009)

14. Karl Bell, *The Magical Imagination: Magic and Modernity in Urban England, 1780–1914* (Cambridge: Cambridge University Press, 2012). (Bell 2012) and *The Legend of Spring-Heeled Jack: Victorian Urban Folklore and Popular Cultures* (Woodbridge: Boydell, 2012). (*The Legend of Spring...* 2012), works to uncover the supernatural experiences and magical imaginary of the urban working-classes, using the popular newspapers and magazines, accounts from folklore, street ballads and 'penny dreadfuls'.

15. 'Second Sight in the Highlands', *Borderland: A Quarterly Review and Index* 3 (January 1896) 57–61 (59). ('Second Sight' ... 1896)

16. Eric Hobsbawm, 'Introducing: Inventing Traditions', *The Invention of Tradition*, eds. Hobsbawm and Terence Ranger (Cambridge: Cambridge University Press, 1992), p. 2. (Hobsbawm 1992)

17. Matthew Wickman, *The Ruins of Experience: Scotland's 'Romantick' Highlands and the Birth of the Modern Witness* (Philadelphia: University of Pennsylvania Press, 2007). (Wickman 2007), Silke Stroh's *Uneasy Subjects: Postcolonialism and Scottish Gaelic Poetry* (Amsterdam: Rodopi, 2011). (Stroh 2011), Mark Toogood 'Decolonizing Highland Conservation' in *Decolonizing Nature*, eds. William M. Adams and Martin Mulligan (London: Earthscan Publications Ltd, 2003). (Toogood 2003), Ania Loomba, *Colonialism/Postcolonialism* (New York: Routledge, 1998). (Loomba 1998), Saree Makdisi, *Romantic Imperialism: Universal Empire and the Culture of Modernity* (Cambridge: Cambridge University Press, 1998). (Makdisi 1998) and Katie Trumpener, *Bardic Nationalism: The Romantic Novel and the British Empire* (Princeton NJ: Princeton University Press, 1997). (Trumpener 1997).

18. 'Second Sight in the Highlands', *Borderland: A Quarterly Review and Index* 3 (January 1896) 57–61 (59)

19. *Cock Lane and Commonsense*, p. 247

20. 'Andrew Lang 'Introduction' to Robert Kirk, *The Secret Commonwealth of Elves, Fauns and Fairies* (1691) with comment by R.B. Cunninghame Graham (Eneas MacKay: Stirling, 1933), p. 55. (Lang 1933)

21. Jan Harold Brunvand, *The Study of American Folklore: An Introduction* (New York: Norton, 1986), p. 4. (Brunvand 1986)

22. Johnson, p. 205, letter from Dr. Ja. Garden, Professor of Theologie at Aberdene to Mr. J Aubrey Concerning the Druid's Temples. (Bodleian Library, Oxford, MS, Aubrey 12, fol. 122, repro. Michael Hunter ed., *The Occult Laboratory: Magic, Science and Second Sight in Late 17th Century Scotland* (The Boydell Press: Woodbridge, 2001). (Hunter 2001), 'Second Sight in the Highlands', *Borderland: A Quarterly Review and Index* 2 (January 1895), 56–59 (59) ('Second Sight...' 1895).

23. Norman Bryson, 'The Gaze of the Expanded Field', in *Vision and Visuality*, ed. Hal Foster (Seattle: Bay Press, 1998), p.91. (Bryson 1998).

24. Jonathan Crary, *Techniques of the Observer: On Vision and Modernity in the Nineteenth Century* (Washington MA: MIT Press, 1992). (Crary 1992), Kate Flint, *Victorians and the Visual Imagination* (Cambridge: Cambridge University Press, 2000). (Flint 2000), Chris Otter, *The Victorian Eye: A Political History of Light and Vision in Britain, 1800–1910* (Chicago: University of Chicago Press, 2008). (Otter 2008) and See also Daniel A. Novak's *Realism, Photography and Nineteenth-Century Fiction* (Cambridge: Cambridge University Press, 2008). (Novak 2008), Srdjan Smajic, *Ghost-Seers, Detectives and Spiritualists: Theories of Vision in Victorian Literature*

and Science (Cambridge: Cambridge University Press, 2010). (Smajic 2010), Jonathan Crary, *Suspensions of Perception: Attention, Spectacle and Modern Culture* (Washington, MA: MIT Press, 1990). (Crary 1990)

25. Martin Jay, *Downcast Eyes: The Denigration of Vision in Twentieth-Century French Thought* (Berkeley CA: University of California Press, 1994) p. 591. (Jay 1994)

26. Hayden White, *Tropics of Discourse: Essays in Cultural Criticism* (Baltimore: John Hopkins University Press, 1978). (White 1978), p. 125. Also relevant here is Rhodri Hayward's *Resisting History: Religious Transcendence and the Invention of the Unconscious* (Manchester: Manchester University Press, 2007). (Hayward 2007)

27. Diana Basham, *The Trial of Woman: Feminism and the Occult Sciences in Victorian Literature and Society* (London: MacMillan, 1992), p. 51. (Basham 1992)

28. Alex Owen, *The Darkened Room: Women, Power and Spiritualism in Late Victorian England* (Chicago: University of Chicago Press, 1989), p. 70. (Owen 1989)

29. Robert Louis Stevenson, 'A Humble Remonstrance', *Longman's Magazine* 5 (1884), 139–147. (Stevenson 1884)

30. Gillian Beer, 'Forging the Missing Link: Interdisciplinary Stories' in *Open Fields: Science in Cultural Encounter* ed. Gillian Beer (Oxford: Clarendon Press, 1996), pp. 115–145 (115). (Beer 1996)

REFERENCES

Basham, Diana, *The Trial of Woman: Feminism and the Occult Sciences in Victorian Literature and Society* (London: Macmillan, 1992), p. 51.

Beer, Gillian, 'Forging the Missing Link: Interdisciplinary Stories' in *Open Fields: Science in Cultural Encounter*, ed. Gillian Beer (Oxford: Clarendon Press, 1996), pp. 115–45.

Bell, Karl, *The Magical Imagination: Magic and Modernity in Urban England, 1780–1914* (Cambridge: Cambridge University Press, 2012).

Bown, Nicola, Carolyn Burdett and Pamela Thurschwell, 'Introduction', in *The Victorian Supernatural*, ed. Nicola Bown, Carolyn Burdett and Pamela Thurshwell (Cambridge: Cambridge University Press, 2004), pp. 1–19.

Brunvand, Jan Harold, *The Study of American Folklore: An Introduction* (New York: Norton, 1986), p. 4.

Bryson, Norman, 'The Gaze of the Expanded Field,' in *Vision and Visuality*, ed. Hal Foster (Seattle, WA: Bay Press, 1998), p. 91.

Chadwick, Owen, *The Secularisation of the Human Mind* (Cambridge: Canto, 1990).

Crary, Jonathan, *Suspensions of Perception: Attention, Spectacle and Modern Culture* (Cambridge, MA: MIT Press, 1990).

Crary, Jonathan, *Techniques of the Observer: On Vision and Modernity in the Nineteenth Century* (Cambridge, MA: MIT Press, 1992).

Ferguson, Christine, *Language, Science and Popular Fiction in the Victorian Fin-de-Siecle: The Brutal Tongue* (Aldershot: Ashgate, 2006).

Flint, Kate, *Victorians and the Visual Imagination* (Cambridge: Cambridge University Press, 2000).

Galvan, Jill, *The Sympathetic Medium: Feminine Channeling, the Occult, and Communications Technologies, 1859–1919* (Ithaca, NY: Cornell University Press, 2010).

Hayward, Rhodri, *Resisting History: Religious Transcendence and the Invention of the Unconscious* (Manchester: Manchester University Press, 2007).

Hobsbawm, Eric, 'Introducing: Inventing Traditions', in *The Invention of Tradition*, ed. Eric Hobsbawm and Terence Ranger (Cambridge: Cambridge University Press, 1992), p. 2.

Hunter, Michael, ed., *The Occult Laboratory: Magic, Science and Second Sight in Late 17th Century Scotland* (Woodbridge: The Boydell Press, 2001).

Jay, Martin, *Downcast Eyes: The Denigration of Vision in Twentieth-Century French Thought* (Berkeley: University of California Press, 1994), p. 591.

Johnson, Samuel, *A Journey to the Western Isles of Scotland 1775* (London: A. Strahan and T. Cadell, 1785), p. 248.

Landy, Joshua, and Michael Saler, eds., *The Re-Enchantment of the World: Secular Magic in the Rational Age* (Stanford CA: Stanford University Press, 2009).

Lang, Andrew, *Cock Lane and Common Sense* (London: Longman & Green, 1894), p. 228.

Lang, Andrew, 'Introduction', to Robert Kirk in *The Secret Commonwealth of Elves, Fauns and Fairies* (1691) with comment by R.B. Cunninghame Graham (Stirling: Eneas MacKay, 1933), p. 55.

Bell, Karl, *The Legend of Spring-Heeled Jack: Victorian Urban Folklore and Popular Cultures* (Woodbridge: Boydell, 2012).

Loomba, Ania, *Colonialism/Postcolonialism* (New York: Routledge, 1998).

Luckhurst, Roger, *The Invention of Telepathy: 1870–1901* (Oxford: Oxford University Press, 2002).

McCorristine, Shane, *Spectres of the Self: Thinking about Ghosts and Ghost-seeing in England, 1750–1920* (Cambridge: Cambridge University Press, 2010), pp. 11–12.

Makdisi, Saree, *Romantic Imperialism: Universal Empire and the Culture of Modernity* (Cambridge: Cambridge University Press, 1998).

Novak, Daniel A., *Realism, Photography and Nineteenth-Century Fiction* (Cambridge: Cambridge University Press, 2008).

'Objects of the Society', *Proceedings of the Society for Psychical Research* 1 (1882–3), 3.

Otter, Chris, *The Victorian Eye: A Political History of Light and Vision in Britain, 1800–1910* (Chicago: University of Chicago Press, 2008).

Owen, Alex, *The Darkened Room: Women, Power and Spiritualism in Late Victorian England*, (Chicago: University of Chicago Press, 1989), p. 70.

Partridge, Christopher H., *The Re-Enchantment of the World: Alternative Spiritualities, Sacralization, Popular Culture, and Occulture* (London: T&T International, 2004).

Miss X [Ada Goodrich Freer], 'Second Sight in the Highlands', *Borderland: A Quarterly Review and Index* 3 ((January 1896) 57–61) (59).

Miss X [Ada Goodrich Freer], 'Second Sight in the Highlands', *Dundee Courier & Argus*, 24 August 1894.

Miss X [Ada Goodrich Freer], 'Second Sight in the Highlands: A Provisional Report by Miss X', *Borderland: A Quarterly Review and Index* 2 (January, 1895), 56–59 (59).

Miss X [Ada Goodrich Freer], 'Second Sight in the Highlands: The Second Report of "Miss X"', *Borderland* 3 (1896), 57–61.

Saler, Michael, 'Clap If You Believe in Sherlock Holmes': Mass Culture and the Re-Enchantment of Modernity, c. 1890–c. 1940', *The Historical Journal* 45.3 (2003), 599–622.

Smajic, Srdjan, *Ghost-Seers, Detectives and Spiritualists: Theories of Vision in Victorian Literature and Science* (Cambridge: Cambridge University Press, 2010).

Stevenson, Robert Louis, 'A Humble Remonstrance', *Longman's Magazine* 5 (1884), 139–47.

Stroh, Silke, *Uneasy Subjects: Postcolonialism and Scottish Gaelic Poetry* (Amsterdam: Rodopi, 2011).

Thurschwell, Pamela, *Literature, Technology and Magical Thinking, 1880–1920* (Cambridge: Cambridge University Press, 2001).

Toogood, Mark, 'Decolonizing Highland Conservation,' in *Decolonizing Nature*, eds William M. Adams and Martin Mulligan (London: Earthscan Publications Ltd, 2003).

Trumpener, Katie, *Bardic Nationalism: The Romantic Novel and the British Empire* (Princeton, NJ: Princeton University Press, 1997).

Weber, Max, 'Science as Vocation,' in H.H. Gerth and C. Wright (trans. and ed.), *From Max Weber: Essays in Sociology* (Oxford: Oxford University Press, 1946), pp. 129–156.

White, Hayden, *Tropics of Discourse: Essays in Cultural Criticism* (Baltimore, MD: Johns Hopkins University Press, 1978), p. 125.

Wickman, Matthew, *The Ruins of Experience: Scotland's 'Romantick' Highlands and the Birth of the Modern Witness* (Philadelphia: University of Pennsylvania Press, 2007).

Wilburn, Sarah, *Possessed Victorians: Extra Spheres in Nineteenth-Century Mystical Writings* (Aldershot: Ashgate, 2006).

Second Sight and the Creation
of the Highlands

Contemplating the 'years 1660 to 1850, or so', Andrew Lang, writing in
1897, condemned the 'cock-sure common sense' of the age that
'regarded everyone who had an experience of hallucination as a dupe, a
lunatic or a liar', as having severely retarded the serious scientific consideration the supernatural now being undertaken in earnest by the Society
for Psychical Research.[1] Where the author seems uncertain of where to
end this long period of destructive scepticism, '1850, or so', he has no
doubt as to where it began: in 1660, the year that the Royal Society of
London was founded. Instituted by royal charter, the society counted
architects, economists and scientists among its early members, and was
founded to promote the investigation of the natural world through careful
observation and experiment.[2] For Lang, engaged at the end of the nineteenth century in an attempt rethink the value of supernatural evidence,
this pivotal moment in the history of science also marked the beginning of
a new and ultimately disastrous approach to unexplained phenomena.
Excluded from the realm of proper scientific inquiry, apparitions and
strange visions were divested of their claims to objective reality, to be
condemned instead as the products of individual pathology. In his classic
study, *Religion and the Decline of Magic* (1971), Keith Thomas argues
that by the beginning of the eighteenth century science and religion had
conspired to expunge witchcraft, divination, apparitions and magical healing from civilised society, so that though 'men went on seeing ghosts' they

© The Author(s) 2017
E. Richardson, *Second Sight in the Nineteenth Century*,
Palgrave Studies in Literature, Science and Medicine,
DOI 10.1057/978-1-137-51970-2_2

were now taught 'not to take them at their face value'.[3] Yet the elite investigative cultures formally inculcated at the close of the seventeenth century were never uniformly dismissive of strange phenomena, folk beliefs or magical thinking. Rather the fixed understanding of reality seemingly established by texts such as Isaac Newton's *Principia* (1686–1687), arguably promoted the study of invisible or immaterial forces by investing these with the power to reveal hidden secrets about the orders of God and nature, and there existed among scientific thinkers a broad spectrum of belief. What is more, the founding of the Royal Society also signalled the beginning of an intense and prolonged period of interest in the prophecies of the second-sighted Highlander.

Through the late seventeenth and eighteenth centuries rumours of second sight attracted the attention of numerous scientists, travel writers, antiquarians, artists and novelists. From the tentative enquiries made by the Royal Society chemist Robert Boyle and the bolder pronouncements ventured by Samuel Johnson, to the obscure tales collected by the antiquarian John Aubrey and the folk legends popularised by the novelist Walter Scott, second sight was made the subject of manifold interpretations. Despite their differences, these early enquirers shared in a desire to apply empiricist standards of evidence to phenomena positioned on the margins of the natural realm and to transform strange visionary experiences into test subjects for incipient methodologies. This is important because once these experiences were instituted as valid objects of study, reports of prophetic sight once dismissed as isolated aberrations could coalesce around the idea of a distinct tradition. It is not that the phenomenon had no anterior existence, but rather that the accounts given in dedicated annuals, antiquarian collections, imaginative fictions and travel journals over this period produced a particular and enduring imaginary of second sight. One that pressed the unsought and often ominous nature of the visions, along with the unschooled charm and poetic sensibility of the, usually male, seer and his remote habitation. Foundational to the construction of this shared narrative was the demarcation of second sight as a peculiarly Scottish wonder, and though some observers continued to note similarities with reports of prophetic sight gathered elsewhere, a growing consensus insisted upon the distinctly national attributes of the strange visionary ability. So much so that interest shown in the extraordinary visions of men living in remote northern communities came to reflect upon broader shifts in the nation's political and cultural character. Specifically, the tradition was one delineated and formalised in relation to the increased intellectual and creative traffic between England and Scotland in the years leading up to and following the Acts of Union in 1707. In this ongoing dialogue the premonitory faculties of the Highlander constituted a far from neutral topic, with investigations into the subject frequently overlaid with overt and contested political, cultural and religious meanings. Though the predictions of the second sighted were usually confined to everyday events in the seer's community—deaths, the arrival of unexpected visitors, the success or failure of a fishing trip and so on—in their retelling they accumulated broader resonances. Investigations into the phenomenon of second sight engaged and tested not only scientific methodologies, but also vexed questions of national identity.

By the close of the eighteenth century, Scotland occupied a position of extraordinary cultural authority, with philosophers and scientists such as Francis Hutchenson, John Millar, Thomas Reid, Adam Smith and David Hume developing a new synthetic accounts of human nature, historical process and social formation, and university cities such as Glasgow and Edinburgh emerging as key intellectual contributors to a wider European Enlightenment.[4] Yet within its borders the country also housed the seeming antithesis to these modern values. The Highlands and Western Isles presented a society linguistically, culturally and religiously removed from the dominant Lowlands, where something like colonial conditions—cultural repression, military occupation and economic underdevelopment—prevailed. How this particular geographical area came to be known as a repository for ancient superstition in an enlightened age, or as Michael Hunter has it, a 'cockpit where the reality of the preternatural could be soberly and scientifically tested', is the subject of this chapter.[5] If, as Hugh Trevor-Roper and Malcolm Chapman have argued, the time-honoured customs and ancient traditions of the Highlands are largely fabrications of the late eighteenth century, then stories of second sight collected in and around this period must communicate similar cultural and literary appropriations.[6] The imaginary of the region produced by English-speaking culture, as at once barbarous and Edenic, beyond civilising and under threat from civilisation, as vulgarly superstitious and anciently wise, engaged the tragic seer beset by foreboding visions as an essential contributor to its dichotomies. It is during the period covered here that a canon of writing on the topic of second sight was first established, texts and guiding tenets that would come to form the basis of future investigations. Retold and re-published through the nineteenth century, works like John Frazer's

Deuteroscopia (Second Knowledge); Or a Brief Discourse Concerning Second Sight (1707), James Macpherson's *Treaties on Second Sight* (1761) and Theophilus Insulanus's *Treaties on Second Sight, Dreams and Apparitions* (1763) provided the foundation for studies undertaken over a century later. Even Andrew Lang, so disparaging the years '1660 to 1850', relies in his own writings on second sight upon the examples and insights offered up by a relatively small set of texts all published during this period.[7] The following chapter will explore the authoring of a second sight tradition, as undertaken by historians, scientists, traveller and writers from the late seventeenth century onwards, and consider the kinds of work to which this tradition was put.

SECOND SIGHT AND HISTORY

In 1685 a Sunday sermon in the village of Kildonan on the Isle of Eigg was interrupted by the frantic prophesising of a local tenant, who urged the congregation to abandon their homes and the island as soon as possible. In front of an increasingly astonished audience the man recounted details of terrible events to come. The island, which lies south of Skye in the Inner Hebrides, would soon be occupied by a hostile foreign force, one willing to use violent and ungodly means to subdue the native population; women would be raped and the village would be burned to the ground. The assembled worshippers were largely unmoved by these revelations, and Father O'Rain—into whose service the seer had interjected—urged the man to recant his false prediction. The seer died four years later, in June 1689, unrepentant despite years of ridicule. Just two weeks after he passed away, his dark vision of death and destruction finally came to pass when, as part of an attempt to crush the Jacobite uprisings that were erupting across the Highlands, troops loyal to William of Orange landed on the island. Led by Major Robert Ferguson, the invading force enacted a brutal campaign of violence, rape, abduction and looting against the inhabitants of Eigg, in retaliation for the murder of a government soldier by local men. The second-sighted vision of these dire acts, once confirmed, dictated the manner in which these events were remembered; bringing the prophetic warning, which conflates the present with the future so that the effect is ascertained before its cause comes into existence, to bear upon the creation and circulation of an historical narrative.

Within a few years of the invasion, this tale of the much-maligned seer and his terrible prediction had attained an audience far beyond the

Small Isles. It was first set in print by a native of Skye, Martin Martin, who included an account of it in his widely read and much anthologised *Description of the Western Isles of Scotland* (1703), and from here news of the remarkable vision travelled quickly.[8] Four years later, the Reverend John Frazer, minister for the neighbouring isles of Coll and Tiree, featured a retelling of the story in his book *Deuteroscopia (Second Knowledge); Or a Brief Discourse Concerning Second Sight* (1707), and in 1763 the prophecy appeared again in a popular treatise on apparitions written by another resident of Skye, the Reverend Donald Macleod. Taken up and retold in print, a prediction once confined to events occurring in a small and fairly isolated community gained a national audience. This is important because it represents only one instance among many in which local prophecies concerning family deaths, the arrival of unexpected visitors, the success or failure of a fishing trip and so on performed distinctly political functions in their retelling. Specifically, the tenant farmer's vision of invading Williamite forces contributed to a mass of prophecies that clustered around the tumultuous and divisive events of the Jacobite Risings that took place between 1688 and 1746. The atrocities on Eigg were carried out as part of a broader military campaign against forces loyal to the House of Stuart, who were attempting to return the descendants of James VII to the throne with the martial support of many of the Highland clans. Retold and circulated in print, second-sighted premonitions of invading English forces, famous battles and extraordinary feats of bravery could be transformed into highly effective works of propaganda. As Juliet Feibel has remarked, it is not insignificant that many early investigations into second sight were undertaken by scholars with averred Jacobital allegiances, and that the stories included in their studies tended to invite a sympathetic reading of the defeated rebellions. Following a standard narrative pattern, a 'Highlander predicts the appearance of English military forces, who then arrive to wreak havoc on those suspected of supporting the Stuarts'; these recorded visions publicised instances of Hanoverian brutality and recast the events of war under the guise of detached antiquarianism.[9] Like the frenzied seer who interrupts the calm of a Sunday sermon, the power of second sight is a disruptive one. It uncovers hidden meaning in the smooth surface of the everyday by forcing the future to coexist with the present, a glimpse of trouble to come, a sighting of Stuart victory perhaps or the flickering image of a Catholic monarch restored to the throne.

Bringing second-sighted visions to bear, even obliquely, on the historical record raised questions regarding the viability of seership as a reliable method for witnessing and reporting. Though put to effective use as a form of Jacobite propaganda, the case for prevision as a trustworthy form of testimony was initially made in a rather different context. In the late seventeenth century, members of a recently founded scientific body enquired into the second-sight tradition with the intention of exploiting rather than exploding its supernatural elements. For theistically minded associates of the Royal Society, such as the Anglican divine Joseph Glanvill and the chemist Robert Boyle, the existence of strange phenomena such as second sight could be harnessed as proof of forces and worlds operating beyond the realm of the visible, material world.[10] In the opening pages of his hugely successful pamphlet *Saducismus Triumphatus: Or, Plain Evidence Concerning Witches and Apparitions* (1681), the Anglican divine Glanvill made clear the pressing need for such proofs: 'there is no one, that is not very much a stranger to this world but knows how atheism and infidelity have advanced in our days, and how open they dare to show themselves in assorting and disputing their cause'.[11] According to Glanvill, the inescapable end point of the fashionably sceptical attitude to apparitions and magical belief being popularised through London's network of coffee houses and validated through 'Hobbesian and Spinonzian principles', was a denial of the resurrection itself and, by extension, of the immortality of the human soul; or as the philosopher Henry More summarised, 'No Spirits, No God'.[12] In answer to this materialist threat, Royal Society members complied case histories of alleged metaphysical experiences, developed theoretical frameworks and sought out new methodologies for exploring the margins of the natural world. Assured of the innate piety of empiricism, they sought to expand the scope of objective and scientifically orientated observation into the realm of the immaterial. These forays produced some of the first attempts to systematise second sight, through the collation of first-hand testimony, the identification of characteristic features and development of classificatory methods; empirical modes of observation borrowed from natural science and applied to the seemingly supernatural.

The remarkable feats of prevision said to take place in remote island communities supplied ideal material to the kind of investigative work undertaken by the Fellows of the Royal Society. Ideal, in part, because with a few exceptions second-sighted visions forecast everyday and often banal events, such as the early arrival of a visitor or the quiet death of a family member. Such visions, neither fantastical nor diabolical, were open to scientific recuperation where the dark rumours and deathly covens associated with witchcraft were not. Beyond the relative mundanity of their content, the structure of these localised prophecies also encoded a kind of predetermined verifiability. A vision that claims to forecast future events is, after all, remarkable only after its version of the future is confirmed. While it would be indeed credulous, Martin avowed in his 1707 study, to believe 'implicitly, before the thing foretold is accomplished' it would also be against 'Senses or Reason' to deny the veracity of a prophecy once it comes to pass.[13] Studies such as Theophilus Insulanus's *Treaties on Second Sight, Dreams and Apparitions* (1763) feature only fulfilled prophecies, typically relayed through a fixed narrative sequence that begins with a premonition of events to come and closes with their inescapable enactment. In one account a servant is beset by the apparition of 'her master wrapped in a winding sheet, laid on a bed close to the fire side, with a piece of linen from under his chin tied to the crown of his head'. The symbolism of the vision, the ominous shroud, signposts imminent death and the case ends with the sad completion of the prophecy, as in a 'few weeks he sickened, but lay in a back house till the last night of his life, where he expired under the circumstances related'.[14] Recounted in simple, unembellished terms, the story is framed by a number of authenticating gestures: not only is her name and occupation given, the reader is also assured that 'Christine McKinnon' is 'a woman of good report'.[15] In recompense for the lack of primary documentation and empirical evidence, early studies of second sight relied upon what Samuel Johnson described as the 'force of testimony' attendant on the subject.[16] Using Theophilis Insulanus as a pseudonym, the Reverend Donald McLeod collected 'upwards of a hundred instances' from his neighbours on Skye and around the Western Isles, so that if his reader remains unconvinced as to the veracity of an individual story, the sheer bulk of evidence may still persuade them.[17] There are, Glanvill assures the reader of *Saducismus Triumphatus*, 'Innumerable Stories' related to the second-sight tradition, and in the majority of these 'there is nothing, either improbable or unlikely'.[18] Co-opted into a wider epistemology that explicated preternatural happenings as the further evidence of God's omnipresence, the strange visionary powers of the Highlander could provide particularly compelling evidence for the claims of natural theology.

As English researchers such as Glanvill and Boyle were rarely able to claim direct knowledge of the phenomenon, the truth of second sight was typically predicated on the apparent guilelessness of the rustic subject and the untutored nature of the gift itself.[19] Unlike witchcraft or related methods of divination, second sight was commonly presented as an entirely uncultivated faculty, and most early reports on the subject are prefaced with assertion of the seer's good character and a guarantee of the unsought nature of their strange ability. For instance, in an early study by a Scottish correspondent of Robert Boyle, the University of Glasgow's George Sinclair, we learn that though the power may originally have arisen 'by a compact with the Devil', those who have inherited it 'by succession' are 'innocent and have this *Sight* against their will and inclination'.[20] Along similar lines, Martin concluded that the 'Seers are generally illiterate, and well-meaning People, and altogether void of design, nor could I ever learn that any of them made the least gain by it, neither is it reputable among them to have that Faculty', while the antiquarian John Aubrey recorded in 1696 that 'the thing is very troublesome to them that have it, and would gladly be rid of it. For if the object be a thing that is so terrible, they are seen to sweat and tremble, and shreek [*sic*] at the apparition.'[21] Aubrey's chapter on second sight given in *Miscellanies* (1696) is one of the first accounts of the subject published in English and is formed of the replies the author received to eight questions that queried the origin of the strange faculty, the content of the visions and the character of seers.[22] What he found was that premonitions typically occurred at random without volition and commonly featured sad or distressing events, while the power itself was more often described as a curse rather than a gift. The mechanism of second sight, in Aubrey's account and in those that followed it, came to embody a kind of sel-evident, self-affirming truth, through which the seer was affirmed as a passive and objective register of information. This model of trustworthy witnessing relied upon the construction and constant reiteration of the second-sighted as by nature unknowing, simple and entirely without artifice. However, the extolling of the Highland sage as a kind of animated *tabula rasa*, a blank slate onto which events and data impressed themselves, did not render that figure ideologically neutral; rather it placed him in conflict with the oppositional understandings of causation and linear process in broad circulation by at least the beginning of the eighteenth century.

Returning briefly to the Isle of Eigg and the terrifying vision of an invading enemy force, it is important to note that the narratological alchemy by which this prediction was solidified into historical record also worked to establish the seer, briefly and problematically, in the role of historian. To claim premonition as a form of history, one that represents the past through prophecies of the future or revivifies the spectre of a violent past in the present, is to read against the conditions of western historiography. Where a work such as David Hume's *History of England* (1754–62), that sweeps from the 'invasion of Julius Caesar' to the 'Revolution of 1688', exemplifies the conjectural ideal of a progress-driven, forward-looking grand narrative, the second-sighted vision is antithetical to linear formations of time, conflating the present with the future, so that the effect is ascertained before its cause comes into existence. Moreover, the prophetic capabilities of the Highlander not only produced accounts radically out of step with the rationalist progressivism of this intellectual climate, they also elevated persons usually barred from this literary culture to the lofty position of historian. At stake here, then, is not only the question of what constitutes history or what is the proper subject of the historian, but also who is qualified to write it. For a particular eighteenth century sensibility, one that valorised the ability to map the passage of time as a key distinguishing factor between civilised and savage races, the illiterate crofter or fisherman could not easily be accommodated as a contributor to that process.[23] Considering the crucial role of letters in Enlightenment conceptions of civilised life, the apparent absence of Gaelic literature or civic records called into question the ability of such a race to reflect accurately upon their own lives. Samuel Johnson, on his 1773 trip through the Western Isles, observed a peasant population whose daily struggle for basic survival prevented them from reflecting upon or recounting their shared history, and commented that as such 'we soon found what memorials were to be expected from an illiterate people, whose whole time is a series of distress'. Because he is unable to write his own history, the islander also lacks the capacity to analyse, learn from or influence events. This exclusion is conceptualised in terms of vision, as in nations where there 'is hardly the use of letters, what is once out of sight is lost forever'.[24] The Highland peasant, according to Johnson, has no past and no future, being only a creature of the present buffeted by forces outside his control.[25] This reading was, of course, only made possible by discounting the kinds of knowledge transmitted through oral traditions such as storytelling or in customs passed from one generation to the next. An English speaker immersed in the world of letters and print, the lexicographer was unable or unwilling to recognise the presence of a rich Gaelic culture thriving in the Hebrides.

Space is given in *A Journey to the Western Isles of Scotland* (1775) to a lengthy discussion of second sight, where Johnson offers a fairly balanced assessment of its veracity, avowing that the power is only 'wonderful because it is rare' and really 'involves no more difficulty than dreams'.[26] Where the faculty seems plausible in the abstract, when the author finally encounters a seer on Skye he finds that the man is little use as a witness, being 'gross', 'ignorant' and unable to speak English.[27] What this antipathy reveals, aside from Johnson's renowned dislike of the Scots, is the political and ideological resonance of oral tradition in relation to the written word. His marked hostility toward the illiterate world inhabited by the seer reveals the importance of what was at stake in literary culture, namely the legitimacy of the British state. Where the written word remains affiliated with the rule of law, the intellectual world of the academy and governmental power, the spoken word is conversely allied to story-telling, rumour, embellishment, memory, conjecture and fantasy. To base the history of a nation on such material, on the predictions and exaggerations of uneducated peasants, would be to disrupt the foundations on which the authority of the state is built. More threatening still was the challenge that second sight posed to the idea of universality, a tenet central to Enlightenment philosophy, in the way that it privileged local and restricted knowledge. As Johnson's frustrated interview of a seer with 'no English' reveals, the meaning of a premonition was usually far from self evident and often restricted to those with native knowledge. Thus seers only appear to be passive receivers of data, when in fact they are engaged in complex processes of decoding and reconstruction, as it is only through the correct appreciation of a vision's peculiar symbolism that its significance may be ascertained. The Welsh antiquarian Edward Lhuyd provides an example of the coded nature of these minor prophecies when he notes that 'men with the second sight see a man with a light like the light of the glow worm, or with fish [scales] over his hair and clothes', an uncanny vision that only takes on meaning—that the man is 'to be drowned'—for those capable of decoding its symbolism.[28] Visions of Jacobite victories and English insurgencies were similarly open to occulted readings. Functioning as a kind of ghostly revenant, revisiting its earthly habitation to right injustice or mete out revenge, second-sighted accounts of the uprisings promised to resurrect a true history of events, one erased from official records and unsanctioned by dominant narratives. Respecting Silki Stroh's assertion that 'postcolonial discourse patterns can temporarily co-exist with colonial ones', it is possible to read these prophecies as having contributed to something like a political counter-discourse.[29] Importantly, the acknowl-edged participation of the second-sighted Highlander in creating stories and legends that attended upon and influenced significant nation-shaping events, cast that figure as not only an object of historical study, but a producer of historical narrative.

As a rhetorical trope, second sight was also called into the service of anti-Jacobite propaganda: a pamphlet titled *The Young Pretender's Destiny Unfolded: Being an Exact Account of Several Prodigies Seen in the Highlands Before the Breaking Out of the Present Rebellion* (1745), for instance, purported to be the record of several soon-to-be-fulfilled predic-tions regarding the triumphant capture of Bonnie Prince Charlie and the glorious defeat of the rebels. Along similar lines, in the early eighteenth century claims to prophecy were also made on behalf of the recently forged and still precarious Acts of Union (1707). In the pro-Union pamphlet 'The Second-Sighted Highlander, or The Scots New Prophecy' (1712), widely thought to be the work of the novelist Daniel Defoe, the author lays claim to the strange 'Celestial' ability to 'discern of things to come' before applying it to predict the country's bright and united future.[30] Whether placed in service of the rebellion or taken up in support of the Union, prophecies attending to the uprisings contributed to a wider cultural obsession with these events in the latter half of the eighteenth century. The Battle of Culloden marked not only the final defeat of the Jacobite rebellion that had at one point threatened London and occupied Edinburgh, but also a turning point in the relations between Britain's newly constituent nations.[31] Though its significance has perhaps been overstated, it remains arguable that the finality of the 1746 defeat and the draconian laws that followed in its wake precipitated a dramatic change in wider perceptions of Highland society and culture. In the immediate aftermath of the Hanoverian victory, measures were taken to bring the north under the jurisdiction of centralised British authorities: traditional forms of dress and music were banned, landowners who had pledged allegiance to the Stuarts lost their titles, prohibitions against bearing arms were enforced and permanent military garrisons were estab-lished. Though by 1782 the Highland population was deemed tame enough to wear plaid once more and elements of the Acts of Proscription were duly repealed, this softened legislative attitude was paralleled by the institution of a programme of increasingly violent forced evictions. Empowered by the collapse of the old feudal system and justified by a rhetoric of improvement, the Clearances saw crofters moved off the land to make way for more profitable sheep farming, an aggressive upheaval that precipitated waves of mass emigration to the colonies.

The repercussions of these severe laws and the rapid depletion of the populace precipitated a significant shift in how the Highlands were represented in English-speaking culture. After the rebellion, as Hugh Trevor-Roper acerbically has it, 'Celtic barbarians who so recently had been denounced and feared as vagabonds, thieves, blackmailers and rebels, but were now found to be helpless and impotent, gradually acquired the romantic charm of an endangered species'.[32] Transformed from a site of pagan savagery and backwardness to a mythologically powerful representation of an ancient and noble culture under imminent threat from the forces of modernity, the Highlands increasingly served as a point around which broader narratives of Scottish history and identity could form. Walter Scott, a novelist and prominent cultural figure, played a prominent role in the imaginative reconstruction of the national character in a post-Union context. Charged with stage-managing the tartan pageantry of George IV's visit to Edinburgh in 1822, during which the newly anointed 'Jacobite' king was garbed in the red plaid of the Stuarts, Scott was emblematic of the Unionist nationalism that came to dominate political discourse in Scotland.[33] In the early decades of the nineteenth century Scott published a series of historical novels that played on the romantic pathos of the Jacobite defeat by returning readers to the chaos, violence and intrigue of the rebellions. His hugely popular *Waverley: or 'Tis Sixty Years Since*, published anonymously in 1814, charts the progress of its English-born hero Edward Waverley as he journeys from the civilised south to the wild north on a commission from the Hanoverian army, where he crosses paths with a group of Highlanders loyal to the Jacobite cause. Eventually won over by the courage and fidelity of the Clan Mac-Ivor, Waverley sides with the Jacobites and fights at the Battle of Prestonpans. The novel closes with Edward, having saved the life of an English colonel and thus escaping retribution for his rebellious activities, marrying Rose Bradwardine, an aristocratic Lowland Scot. As several critical readings of the text have asserted, in the marriage of Edward and Rose the novel consecrates the long troubled union between Scotland and England by smoothing over a destructive and tumultuous history.[34]

In *Waverley*, the fictionalised return to the battlegrounds of the last Jacobite rebellion encodes both mourning for an extinct past and a desire to forge a redemptive narrative from this history. This recuperative project rests on the careful negotiation of the image of a modern country, newly united, with the supernatural lore and ancient customs of a redeployed Highlands. The novel adapts the labyrinthine plotting, atmospheric settings and intense subjectivities of the gothic novel to historicist themes, but its uncanny tropes are largely contained by one character: Fergus MacIvor, chief of the Clan MacIvor and representative of an old feudal order. Near the beginning of the story Fergus greets Edward on his arrival into Edinburgh by exclaiming, 'Said the Highland prophet sooth? Or must second-sight go for nothing?'; a jocular salutation that foreshadows the darker prophecy to come. In possession of the second sight, Fergus is visited by the *Bodach Glas*, a grey spectre who tells of him of his own approaching death and of the inevitable downfall of his clan.[35] Though the legitimacy of this vision is supported by the novel's plot—all that is prophesied eventually comes to pass—the reader is nonetheless encouraged to view this supernatural prediction with some scepticism. This rationalist position is voiced by Edward, who attributes the apparition of the *Bodach Glas* to the 'exhausted frame and depressed spirits' of the ghost-seer, and is supported by the detached tone struck by the author regarding the tale's stranger elements. Adopting the role of a cultural historian, Scott embeds the novel with paratextual material: extensive editorial footnotes, poetic fragments, found manuscripts and collected superstitions. This rationalising retrospect is particularly evident in the collected edition of his *Waverley Novels*, published with notation between 1829 and 1833, in which the novels' supernatural incidents are tempered through the addition of measured editorial commentary. The narrative distance this creates works to reframe the power of second sight and its Jacobital practitioners as objects of academic interest and, perhaps, nostalgic affection.

Where we have previously observed the second-sighted prophecy as itself a form of history making, Scott captures the tradition as an object of history. In a note on *Rob Roy*, for instance, the author discusses at length a seventeenth-century treatise on Scottish fairy lore, Robert Kirk's *Secret Commonwealth of Elves, Fauns, and Fairies*, and recounts the strange circumstances of the author's death: 'he is believed himself to have been taken away by the fairies, in revenge, perhaps, for having let in too much light upon the secrets of their commonwealth'.[36] Incredulous but nonetheless fascinated by the traditions and 'high spirit of a people, who, living in a civilised age and country, retained so strong a tincture of manners belonging to an early period of society', the author confines such outmoded customs to an uncivilised and superstitious history.[37] The lesson

Waverley teaches its readers, as James Buzard suggests, is 'not that romance must be rejected or outlived in favour of "reality" but that it must strictly sequestered as culture', in which the supernatural comes to signify a feudal, Catholic and superstitious past opposed to the present occupied by the reader.[38] With regard to second sight, which also appears in *Guy Mannering* (1815), *The Lady of the Lake* (1810), *A Legend of Montrose* (1819) and *The Antiquary* (1816), this temporal remove allows Scott to incorporate the tradition into a broader imagery of picturesque and antediluvian Highland manners, and in the process undermine its power to unsettle and upend. This is most evident in a note given in *The Minstrelsy of the Scottish Border*, a collection of ballads published between 1802 and 1803, which states that according to his 'learned and excellent fiend, Mr. Ramsay of Ochtertyre' a man named 'Macoan', residing in Appin, was the 'last person eminently gifted with the second sight'.[39] No longer disruptive speech or disquieting insight, under Scott's antiquarian gaze second sight comes to signify only a lost past, rendered affectively accessible through fiction and poetry.

HIGHLAND GEOGRAPHIES

In *Waverley* Walter Scott's Englishman completes a journey, later repeated in *Rob Roy* and *The Antiquary*, that sees him travel from the imperial metropole through the cultured Lowlands of Scotland and on to remote and undomesticated northern regions. Overcome with 'wild feelings of romantic delight' on first glimpsing the vast mountainous terrain, the hero is soon lured away from the 'sober reason' that governed his behaviour in London by unruly passions that will eventually lead him foolhardily into battle, passions that seem to originate in the landscape itself.[40] Crossing into the Highlands, the wandering aristocrat encounters a 'picturesque and romantic country' inhabited by a poetic and noble race, distinct in character and custom from their southern counterparts.[41] Fascinated by the region's natural beauty and captivated by the 'ancient traditions and high spirit' of its inhabitants, Edward commits treason to join the Jacobite army. There the spell that the untamed kingdom has cast on his senses is finally broken, as he observes the 'wild dress' of his compatriots, hears their 'whispers in an uncouth and unknown language' and wishes to awake from what suddenly appears as like a 'dream, strange, horrible and unnatural'. Roused as if from a trance, he comes to comprehend the foreign nature of the landscape and people that surround him.[42] Absolutely distinct from the modern world, the territory emerges as a richly imagined site of sentimental Jacobitism, superstitious fancy, lost heroism and romantic unrealities, of ancient manners and customs on the brink of imminent destruction; it is embodiment, to use Tzvetan Todorov's term, of 'alterity'.[43] Following the stadial systems of social development proposed by Enlightenment philosophers such as Adam Smith and Alex Ferguson, the Highlands solidify here as a contemporary remainder of a savage past, set apart from the civil present spatially embodied in the industry and institutions of the south.

What is significant is that simultaneous with *Waverley's* imaginative portrayal of the Highlands as a wild and isolated place governed by elemental forces and held in the sway of primitive customs, the novel also functions as a blueprint for exploration. The journey Scott drama- tised for his readers, from the cultivated worlds of London and Edinburgh into the wild and barren north, was one being made by an increasing number of travellers. Newly constructed military roads, improved coach services and post-Culloden policing made travel safer, while the Napoleonic wars raging on the continent had, by the 1790s, vastly expanded the market for domestic tourism. By the time of its publication, the arduous and potentially dangerous expedition that *Waverley* recounts had been transformed into a leisurely journey, undertaken by tourists rather than hardened explorers. Through the latter decades of the eighteenth century publishers met the demands of this new market by producing guidebooks such as *Scotland Delineated* (1799) and *A Traveller's Guide to Loch Lomond* (1792), which pro- vided maps, directions, lists of landmarks and recommendations of the most scenic spots. Visitors might also avail themselves of a pocket-sized 'Tourist Edition' of the poems, short stories and novels of famous writers such as Walter Scott. Commenting on the popularity of these, Katherine Grenier has suggested that the experience of visiting Scotland was one often mediated through fiction, where guidebooks commonly 'provided sightseers with the Scott associations of any given sight or attraction' to 'evoke the proper atmosphere'.[44] Furnished with portable abridged copies of *The Lady of the Lake* or *The Lord of the Isles*, English travellers were taught to view sites such as Loch Katrine or Ardtornish Castle through the prism of historical fiction.[45] This is not to suggest that visitors mistook fiction for fact, but simply that popular novels such as *Waverley* helped to set the terms of their readers' investment in the country's landscape, customs and history.

Attempts to map and explore northern territories were significant on two fronts. On the one hand, journeys undertaken through this 'wild' landscape were increasingly mediated through travelogues, histories and antiquarian studies; all of which endeavoured to guide the observer to 'what is worth looking at, how it looks, and perhaps most important of all, how it should be looked at'.[46] Reflecting on the development of tourism in this period, Peter Womack has attempted to draw a clear distinction between the kinds of observation implicated in the act of 'travelling', which is alike to reading history with the advantage of witnessing 'antiquities, fields, paintings, for oneself', and the 'holiday', which is not an 'inquiry into the world, but a playful refusal of it'.[47] Though this demarcation articulates something of what was at stake in the opening up of Britain's remoter regions to a broader portion of the population, it fails to allow for the possibility that while 'holiday-makers' may not have actually partaken in the kinds of 'information'-gathering activities Womack associates with travel, perhaps choosing to pack a 'Tourist Edition' of *Waverley* instead, this did not stop them from imagining their trip in precisely these terms. The appeal of the Highlands and Islands to English visitors was not that of the leisure offered by the Georgian resort towns of Bath or Brighton; rather it lay with discovering the odd customs, antiquated manners and foreign tongue of a strange people. The observatory practices of the tourist were allied to those of the antiquarian, so that visitors were encouraged to seek out the remnants of a feudal clan system and the remainders of superstitious beliefs, on the assumption that these would soon be eradicated by the march of progress. Confined to what Ina Ferris has termed 'the most unsettling modality of the almost', the Highlands came to embody an ancient way of life preserved for the attentive traveller, but under threat from the civilising forces of modernisation and improvement.[48]

In search of ancient rituals, feudal clans and wild landscapes, tourists to the Highlands sought an encounter with an archaic and undeveloped world. As the essayist James Boswell explained in his *Journal of a Tour to the Hebrides* (1775), such places as the isolated Western Isles offered the opportunity to 'contemplate a system of life almost totally different to what we had been accustomed to see; and, to find simplicity and wildness, and all the circumstances of remote time or place, so near to our native great island, was an object within the reach of reasonable curiosity'.[49] Popular travel narratives, republished through the late eighteenth and early nineteenth centuries, catered to a growing interest in the region.

Chief among these was Martin Martin's *A Description of the Western Isles of Scotland circa 1695*, the first edition of which appeared in 1707, before being republished in 1716, then reproduced in John Pinkerton's *A General Collection of the best and more interesting voyages and travels in all parts of the world* in 1809 and again in *Miscellanea Scotia* in 1819. A native Gaelic speaker, Martin's account of his travels through the Outer Hebrides was intended as a riposte to what he condemned elsewhere as the 'modern itch after the knowledge of foreign places' and a means of encouraging others to explore the far reaches of their own 'nativity'.[50] His travelogue details the topographical features of the archipelago and the peculiarities of its people, their agricultural practices, living conditions, religious affiliations and manners. In a lengthy chapter devoted to the subject, the author also revealed himself to be an authority on the power of second sight, which he found to be fairly commonplace on the islands. Describing it as a 'singular Faculty of Seeing an otherwise invisible Object, without any previous Means used by the Person that sees it for that end', Martin recounts the first-hand testimony of several seers and underlines the unsought nature of their visions.[51] Most interesting to the travel writer was the practical function that the strange powers appeared to serve in binding isolated communities together, as while the 'Inhabitants of many of these Isles, never had the least contact by Word or Writing' and are separated by 'forty or fifty Leagues' they can connect through shared visionary experiences.[52] We learn that as Martin travels slowly from one small island to the next, the details of his journey are forecast by seers; he writes that these auguries 'had never seen me personally, and it happened according to their Visions, without any previous design of mine to go to those Places, my coming there being purely accidental'.[53] Imagined as a kind of communication network linking geographically distant sites, this special foreknowledge becomes tied to the workings of the travel narrative itself, providing uncanny continuity from place to place. Woven into a thickly detailed depiction of Hebridean society, the strange faculty appears borne of the topographical features and unique demands of island life.

As a young boy Samuel Johnson received a copy of *A Description of the Western Isles* from his father and when, in 1773, he embarked upon a similar tour of the Hebrides with his Scottish biographer, he carried the book with him.[54] Inspired by Martin's account and against the assurances of his Lowland correspondents that the belief no longer prevailed, Johnson made enquiries into the mysterious power of second sight on the grounds that his travelogue 'should have little claim to the praise of curiosity' if it failed to address the question of its veracity.[55] Having heard 'many tales of these airy shows' and finding that seers have 'no temptation to feign', he eventually ceded a 'willing[ness] to believe' in the possibility of extraordinary foresight. Despite its measured tone, this avowal exposed the respected writer and moralist to charges of credulity. An article from 1808, for instance, reflected that few of Johnson's 'eccentricities have excited so much ridicule as his defence of Scottish Second-Sight; a gift that has always been considered by every well-bred Englishman as a proof only of the ignorance and vanity of the Caledonians'.[56] Crossing into the Highlands and courting an encounter with that 'peculiar and discriminative form of life' constitutes a betrayal of the stolid rationalism of his Saxon heritage.[57] Unacknowledged in this caustic assessment is the fact that, in the main, the *Journey* does not dissolve but rather upholds and reifies the division of 'ignorant' Scot from 'well-bred Englishman'. Critics then and now have recognised that the tour showcases Johnson's deeply antipathetic relation to his northern neighbours: as the painter John Knox complained in 1786, the lexicographer crossed the border 'under incurable impressions of a national prejudice, a religious prejudice and a literary prejudice'.[58] Tales of miraculous prophetic vision did not challenge but confirmed these prejudices. Having described the 'manners' of the Hebrideans he has encountered as 'commonly savage', Johnson proposes that rather than being only the result of an inherited predisposition 'derived from their ancestors', their unrefined comportment is likely the consequence of geographical, political and cultural circumstance. Just as their martial nature is rendered explicable by a long history of intra-clan warfare, so too is the seemingly 'useless' faculty of 'seeing things out of sight' understandable only in a local context.[59] Where there is certainly no place for second sight in the civilised south, the lonely mountains and windswept valleys of the north might produce a peculiar cast of mind open to such visions.

The imagined confluence of mind and landscape is typical in writings on the subject of second sight. In an attempt to explain the prevalence of this superstition in isolated areas, James Beattie, in his *Essays on Poetry and Music* (1779), describes a 'lonely region, full of echoes, and rocks and caverns' the spectral appearance of which can not help but impact upon 'persons of lively imagination', while in 1780 Jacob Pattisson concluded that second sight is 'much more believed [in] proportion to distance, or obscurity of the place, and the consequent ignorance of the people'.[60] Elsewhere, in J.S. Forsythe's *Demonologia* (1827), the author makes clear that is only because of the 'obscurity of the place' that the inhabitants of northern regions retain a belief in the operation of supernatural forces. Where in England's great towns the 'hurry and dissipation that attend the opulent, and the little leisure the poor have' do not allow space for the supernatural, in the Highlands the populace has 'little to do, or see done' and consequently 'when any thing of the above nature occurs, they have the leisure to brood over it, and cannot get it banished from their minds'.[61] As well as being generally more inclined to credulity—the author assures his reader that 'no people on earth are more addicted' to the 'belief in spirits and apparitions'—the topography of the landscape itself contributes greatly to this particular disposition. The 'whistling of wind among the heath, rocks and caverns, a loose fragment of a rock falling from its top, and in its course downward bringing a hundred more down with it, so that it appears like the wreck of nature', ensure that even the most enlightened among the Gaels fall prey to superstition.[62] A ghostly and ancient landscape of mountains, glens and towering crags produces an hallucinatory condition of mind in which supernatural beliefs can take hold and flourish.

The second-sight tradition also embodies its own geographical co-ordinates. It is strongly tied to a sense of place, so that even when the seer is not named recorded accounts always name the location in which the vision is said to have taken place; and what is more, seers are said to lose the ability if they stray too far from their homeland. Martin, for instance, recounts the case of a seer from Harris who made a new life in Barbados and found that he was no longer troubled by premonitions.

In a more abstract manner, the power was also called upon to mark a point of topographical tension, to demarcate a borderland between wild and civilised locales, where the rational and the supernatural are drawn into an encounter with one another. In an early tract on second sight, circulated in manuscript form from the end of the seventeenth century and published by Walter Scott in 1815, this boundary is conceived of as a very real one dividing the human world from the realm of the faeries. A self-taught Gaelic speaker and Minister of Aberfoyle, Robert Kirk was enlisted to help with Robert Boyle's evangelising translation of the Bible into Gaelic for distribution among the un-Reformed Highland population. What this seeming deference to Christian orthodoxy belied, however, was Kirk's commitment to the absolute reality of another world of faeries, brownies and elves that he believed to exist in parallel to our own, the details of which are described in his treatise *The Secret Commonwealth of*

Elves, Fauns and Fairies. In depicting this faery land, Kirk worked with a Neo-Platonist conception, common to that pursued by other seventeenth century thinkers such as Thomas More, of a world infused by innumerable astral bodies and 'intelligent studious spirits'.[63] In *Secret Commonwealth* only those in possession of the second sight can perceive these 'light changeable bodies' and interact with beings who are of a 'middle nature between Man and Angel'. Acting as an emissary to this occulted realm of the faeries, the *tabhaisder* or seer functions as a kind of ethnographic observer, describing the social structure, strange customs and habits of this twin world. Writing in *Folklore and the Fantastic in Nineteenth Century British Fiction* (2008), Jason M. Harris has described the 'metaphysical contact zone' typically exploited by folk tales, which situates supernatural 'intrusions' at boundaries that are perceived as simultaneously geographical and psychological.[64] Something similar can be noted in the way that *Secret Commonwealth* maps the supernatural onto the landscape itself, so that a barren mountain side or a silent forest is enlivened by the invisible actions of armies of magical beings.

First published by Walter Scott at the height of the Romantic period, the *Secret Commonwealth* contributed to a broad turn, visible in poetry, painting and philosophy, toward a new mode of engagement with the natural world. A number of literary historians have described a late eighteenth-century revolution in the relationship between art and the natural world: Ian Whyte credits this with having explored a unique 'mysticism of place', while Sasha Handley describes 'the intimate and sometimes subconscious connections drawn between the idea of ghosts [and the] landscape' and John Hedley charts the transmutation of values attributed to the landscape itself; so that while Samuel Johnson finds the Highlands marred by 'hopeless sterility' in 1775, William Gilpin compliments the same rugged topography as being 'entirely in a state of nature' in 1794.[65] This engagement with nature, particularly in the picturesque mode, has also been theorised as a process of aesthetic detachment whereby the viewer removes himself from the concrete particularities of place in a 'nostalgia-tinged attempt' to 'recapture the freedom, simplicity, and intensity of experience associated with childhood and past times'.[66] The power of second sight, so intimately connected to mountainous terrain and windswept moors, took on new meanings under this increasingly subjective appreciation of landscape. In her *Recollections of a Tour Made in Scotland 1803* (1874), Dorothy Wordsworth recounts her party's encounter with a Gaelic-speaking boy, who she describes as a 'text' containing 'the whole history of the Highlander's life—his melan-choly, his simplicity, his poverty, his superstitions, and above all, that vision-ariness which results from a communion with the otherworldliness of nature'.[67] This startling image, where the truth of a nation is glimpsed in the fleeting image of plaid-clad youth, reveals something of a shift in the terms on which the second-sighted subject was permitted to enter educated discourse. Where antiquarian and scientific literatures of second sight treat the phenomenon as an object of study, almost always distinct from the experience of the educated investigator, Romantic writers incorporated the fabled power into their theories of creativity, imagination and the soul. In his 1812 notebook, for instance, Samuel Taylor Coleridge, who had joined the Wordsworths on their 1803 tour through Scotland, speaks of his own 'second sight' that permits him to see a vision, which is 'not as one given to me by any other Being but as an act of my own Spirit'.[68] Written into a developing philosophy of the imagination, at the turn of the eighteenth century second sight retained an almost mystical connection to the land-scape, ancient custom and local mythologies, but it also began to take on the appearance of a poetic resource—accessible through the exploration of altered states of consciousness. In the same moment that second sight was marked out for destruction by the opening up of the landscape to improve-ment and industry, a nascent Romantic movement identified the prophetic mountain dweller as its eternal muse.

VISIONARY IMAGINATION

Second sight is, in the main, a visual experience, in which pictures of events to come—weddings, funerals, happy reunions and tragic accidents—flit momentarily before the eyes of the seer. Common to every extended treatment of the faculty, whether framed as travelogue, demonology, scientific study or literary exploration, is a concern with the processes of perception and reflection involved in the production of these images. Johnson described the method as 'an impression made either by the mind upon the eye, or by the eye upon the mind by which things distant or future are perceived, and seen as if they were present', a neat formula-tion that expresses something of the quite complex negotiation of time and presence at stake in these mundane prophecies.[69] Such visions are not evoked; rather, glimmers of 'sad and dismal' events impress them-selves, unsought, on the senses.[70] According to the antiquarian John Aubrey, visions of future events are 'acted before their eyes; sometimes within, and sometimes without-doors as in a glass', but these sudden glimpses threaten to disappear in the blink of the eye.[71] On observing a seer in the midst of such a premonition Martin recalls its disquieting physical manifestations, whereby the 'Eye-lids of the Person are erected, and the Eyes continue flaring until the Object vanish', so much so that after the vision has ended the 'inner part' of the eyelids must be drawn back down with the fingers.[72] It is significant, perhaps, that initial attempts to systematise the phenomenon and collect evidence in its favour often pause to remark on the manner in which a subjective experience, one in which remote scenes are imprinted briefly on the eyes, is played out in the physical movements and gestures of the seer. As we have seen, early investigations into second sight were usually undertaken under the banner of empiricism and often with the intention of demonstrating the remarkable scope of the natural world to materialist sceptics; to awaken, in the words of Henry More, 'benumbed and lethargick [sic] minds' to the knowledge that 'there are other intelligent beings besides those clad in heavy earth or clay'.[73] Second sight, from the late seventeenth century onwards, was dragged into a number of boundary disputes taking place in natural philosophy and elsewhere over the nature and meaning of perceptible reality.

Writing in the 1690s, as his friends in the Royal Society were beginning to make enquiries north of the border, Robert Kirk proposed that the faculty of second sight might best be understood as simply an extension of normal ocular capacity, alike to the 'artificial helps of Optic Glasses (prospectives [sic], Telescopes, and Microscopes)'.[74] Plucking it from the realm of the miraculous and the diabolical, he compares the power to the kinds of enhanced perspective enabled by scientific devices, before speculating that a proper investigation of this strange capability might prove a discovery comparable to navigation, printing or gunnery. Pursuing the comparison with modern optical devices makes possible the objective reality of the faerie realm described in the *Secret Commonwealth*: just as the tiny particles made visible by the microscope remain invisible to the naked eye, so too are the 'light changeable bodies' of the *sidths* only perceptible to those in possession of second sight. That some elements of the world are not visible to all people at all times does not make them, the author asserts, any less 'real'.[75] In the same moment that the superiority of the eye is reaffirmed, however, its ability to distinguish between the real and the illusionary is called into question. For Kirk, faeries composed part of a larger Neo-Platonic world peopled with not only humans, but a myriad of other forms whose nature is 'betwixt man and angel' and who can guide or malevolently manipulate the processes of perception. Stuart Clark's recent work on models of sight during the Renaissance period is illuminating here. He writes that 'objects in the world gave off resemblances or replicas of themselves (*species*)' and that, broadly speaking, the 'mind had direct access to accurate pictures of the world', but at any stage of this cognitive process diabolic or angelic agencies could intervene to manipulate either perceived objects or interior perceptions.[76] Where Kirk, working at the end of the seventeenth century, draws heavily upon this Aristotelian theory of vision to describe the mechanism of second sight, in a slightly later treatment of the subject the meaning of *species* has undergone a telling etymological shift. Discussing second sight in *Deuteroscopia* (1707), John Frazer falls in with an early modern understanding of perception when he describes how when the 'Brain is in a Serene temper' the 'Species' keep 'their Rank and File, as they were received'; in other words, normal vision maintains uniformity between exterior action and interior perception. His account moves into new territory, however, when it lights upon instances in which the 'Brain is filled with gross and flatuous Vapours', so that 'Spirits' and 'Humours' and 'Ideas' become 'multiplied as an Army in the mist: sometimes magnified; sometimes misplaced; sometimes confounded by other Species of different objects'.[77] At stake here is something close to a psychologised understanding of perception. Though Frazer does not suggest that the 'Species' perceived by the second sighted are entirely products of the imagination, he does propose that a 'natural constitution and temperament' particular to the seer permits him to observe what remains invisible to most. This move from exterior to interior action was, as the eighteenth century progressed, realised as part of a larger relocation of uncanny happenings from an objectively structured outside world to the realms of subjective mental experience. [78]

The primary instigators of this new visual regime are usually identified as the Protestant Reformation and the mechanist philosophy pursed by René Descartes; the former having done away with the doctrine of purgatory and with it the ghosts of the departed, while the latter's pursuit of natural law dispensed with the notion of divine intervention. Reflecting on this, Keith Thomas has argued that the 'notion that the universe was subject to immutable natural laws killed the concept of miracles', weakening belief in the 'physical efficacy of prayer' and relegating spirits, 'whether good or bad, to the purely mental world'.[79] Recent scholarship has attempted to moderate this position by arguing that this top-down approach overlooks the role that supernatural customs continued to play in marginal communities and the continued relevance of magical beliefs for those situated outside elite intellectual culture.[80] Further, as we have already seen, the revolutionary epistemologies Thomas charges with having precipitated a decline in magical belief—namely those of mechanistic philosophy—also served as the primary impetus for investigations into phenomena such as second sight. That is to say, the scientific methodologies pursued by figures such as Robert Boyle did not do away with interest in the supernatural, but they did reframe the conditions under which anomalous occurrences were to be judged. Though the empiricist regime instituted by organisations such as the Royal Society endorsed vision as a crucial source of knowledge about the world, it also encouraged a fascination with unseen and invisible forces. Contemplating the ocular cultures of the sixteenth century, Clark has described how the world came to be characterised by 'visible signs of indeterminate meaning', which increasingly marked out human vision as a site of 'profound disagreement'.[81] Originating in the early modern world, phenomenological debates over the limitations of ocular knowledge rested on the perceived direction of flow between the perception of an image and the construction of that image: does the eye faithfully record reality or does it help to create that reality?

In the early decades of the nineteenth century this dispute played out in a flurry of polemics on the subject of apparitions and ghost-seeing. Treatises such as Samuel Hibbert-Ware's *Philosophy of Apparitions* (1825) and Joseph Taylor's *Apparitions; or, The Mystery of Ghosts* (1815) aimed to debunk superstitions by situating supernatural experience firmly in the deluded eye or misled mind of the beholder. In an *Essay Towards a Theory of Apparitions* (1813), for example, John Ferriar argued that ghost-seeing is akin to a waking dream, in which apparitions appear as a 'renewal of external impressions' by which a vaguely remembered image is stirred in the mind and appears before the eyes as if new. Working in the same tradition, Samuel Hibbert held excessive passions and a morbid cast of mind to blame for spectres, and later in the century David Brewster attributed ghost-seeing to a superstitious misreading of natural occurrences, such as retinal after-images and blind spots.[82] The visions associated with second sight took place within a broader ghost-seeing culture and were impacted by a pathological model of hallucination that recast preternatural foreknowledge as the result of a confused sensorium. This is observable in the geologist John Macculloch's denigration of second sight in 1819 as an ability confined only to the 'doting old woman or the hypochondriacal tailor', and later in Robert Macnish's contention that

'What is called the Second Sight, originated, in most cases, from spectral illusion; and the seers of whom we so often read, were merely individuals visited by these phantoms.'[83] What this easy dismissal belies, however, is the complex position second sight held in relation to the reality or fallacy of ghosts. Investigations into the Highland tradition found the mechanics of premonition framed by the language of the spectral. Samuel Johnson, for example, notes that in Gaelic the faculty is described as a *taisch*, a term that signifies both a spectre and a glimpse of future events. Another term, *tainbh*, denotes the spectral double of a living person that is presented to the eyes of the seer during the vision. When, for example, the image of a still-living neighbour wrapped in their winding sheet appears to the seer, this is acknowledged as a ghostly reflection forecasting death rather than an apparition of someone returned from the dead.[84] Instances of second sight subverted the hallucinatory model staked out by supernatural debunkers, because the ghosts associated with that experience were, in a sense, already contained within the imagination of the seer.

In the closing passage of his *Letters on Demonology and Witchcraft* (1830), Walter Scott avows that given that 'most ordinary mechanic has learning sufficient to laugh at the figments which in former times were believed by persons far advanced in the deepest knowledge of the age', perhaps the 'present fashion of the world seems to be ill suited for studies of this fantastic nature'.[85] This oddly self-effacing conclusion to a collection of superstitions and legendary ghosts composed from the author's own library captures the increasingly ambiguous positioning of the supernatural in Britain. *Letters on Demonology*, in common with the heavily annotated *Waverley Novels*, sees the author negotiate a space for the uncanny or the folkloric at an historical remove from the reader; the 'grosser faults of our ancestors' being now 'out of date'.[86] But the force of this rationalising retrospect is circumscribed by Scott's own acknowledgement of the psychological universality of supernatural experience: 'Who shall doubt', he asks, 'that imagination favoured by circumstances has the power to summon up to the organ of sight, spectres which only exist in the mind of those by whom their apparition seems to be witnessed?'.[87] This seeming contradiction, whereby the supernatural is threatened with extinction in the same moment that its absolute universality is assured, is best accounted for in terms of what Terry Castle has described as the 'invention of the uncanny'. The dismissal of the supernatural as the result of a disordered sensorium did little, Castle has argued, to diminish the affectivity of that experience. Instead it resulted in the 'spectralization' of inner space: the rationalisation of spectres and spirits as psychological aberrations produced the mind itself as haunted.[88] What is more, the internalisation of the supernatural speaks to a broader evolution in the idea of the imagination: through literature, aesthetics and philosophy, the imagination was increasingly held to be the defining feature of human experience, with dreams and hallucinations held as routes to understanding consciousness and the mysterious workings of the psyche.

One of the writers best attuned to the gothic potentials of this 'spectralization' was Scott's friend, collaborator and Border compatriot James Hogg. The narrative possibilities of the haunted mind are most fully explored in *The Private Memoirs and Confessions of a Justified Sinner* (1824), a story whose dualistic and conflicting narration binds the language of superstition to emerging psychological theories. Set in Edinburgh, the story concerns the various misdeeds of Robert Wringham, a fanatical Calvinist convinced of his pre-election and lured to commit heinous acts by his diabolical double Gil Martin, as told first by a sceptical narrator and then by Robert himself. The motif of the double, that duplicitous and eerie other self, encodes the thematics of multiplicity and uncanny sympathy which were at stake in literary Romanticism.[89] In line with Ian Duncan's characterisation of Hogg's fictions as typically affirming 'the potency of rural culture [as] outside terms of explanation, a final, opaque otherness', his use of the double also calls up the tradition of Scottish second sight.[90] In the *Secret Commonwealth*, Kirk recounts how 'Some men of the exalted sight [...] have told me they have seen at those meetings a double-man, or the shape of the same man in two places, that is, a Superterranean and a Subterranean Inhabitant perfectly resembling one another in all points.'[91] These otherworldly doubles appear in the visions of the seer, acting out phantasmal scenes and prophetic pictures, shadowing the actions of the living. Often these spectral selves are fatal to the first self, as a story recounted by Martin reveals. In *Description of the Western Isles* he recalls a 'Woman in *Skie*, who frequently saw a Vision representing a Woman having a Shroud about her up to the middle but always appeared with her back towards her'. The distressed seer eventually discovers a means to trick the spectre into revealing its identity, but after it finally presents 'itself with is Face and Dress looking towards the Woman' she is horrified to find that it 'proved to resemble her self in all points', and she is reported to have died a 'little time after'.[92] Writing at about the same time, Frazer reports that the seers on the island of St Kilda often describe being haunted by an apparition of themselves that 'walks

with them in the fields in broad daylight', mimicking their every movement and foretelling their imminent demise.[93] Wringham's horror on
'perceiving that [Gil Martin] was the same being as myself' is, in one
sense, a revivification of second sight's uncanny potentials that brings
rural lore to bear upon evolving models of the self.[94]

In the early nineteenth century, the creative possibilities of the *doppel-
ganger* bound the poetic ideals of Romantic writers to emerging theories
of mind being worked through in the fields of philosophy and psychology.
Reflecting on its literary manifestations, Karl Miller has proposed that the
'story of the modern double starts' when 'Animal Magnetists went in for
the experimental separation of the second self'.[95] First coming to prominence in eighteenth-century Vienna, through the work of Franz Anton
Mesmer, animal magnetism, or mesmerism as it came to be known, was
based on the idea of a invisible natural force that could be manipulated for
healing purposes. As a new theory of mind, magnetism's appeal lay with its
evocation of unseen energies and connections unexplainable by physical
laws; or as Jenny Ford describes, 'it posited the influence of psychological
powers, particularly those of the imagination, and possessed a mysterious
aspect which could not be matched by theories of association'.[96]
Privileging altered states of dreaming, reverie and trance as sites in which
the mind is empowered to transcend the familiar and the commonplace,
this nascent theory promised to illuminate new connections between
psyche and body, soul and nature. What is more, it was at the intersection
between Romanticism and a growing body of literature on animal magnetism that second sight discovered a new context.[97] Sparked by a broader
interest in the landscape and history of Scotland, through the latter half of
the eighteenth century a number of canonical works on the subject of
second sight were translated and anthologised for a new European audience. The fabled seer held special appeal to readers primed by such works
as the Ossian cycle, a series of epic poems supposedly created in the third
century that were complied and translated by James Macpherson in 1760.
The publication of *Fragments of Ancient Poetry, Collected in the Highlands
of Scotland, and Translated from Gaelic or Erse Language* occasioned a
storm of debate concerning the true origins of this newly unearthed Celtic
Homer and the collection went on to enjoy international success, with
translations produced in nearly every European language and paintings
depicting scenes from the poems exhibited widely. In addition to cement-
ing the image of the Highlands as a misty and heroic otherworld, the
blindness of Macpherson's Gaelic bard also strengthened connections

between creative inspiration and the question of extraordinary vision. In the poem Ossian's physical sightlessness is identified as a source of both poetic and prophetic insight, and this confluence bound second sight to models of inspiration developing through the period.[98] Reflecting on this merging of the figure of the seer with that of the poet, Peter Womack has argued that under the 'nostalgic and affective' gaze of Romanticism, second sight was transformed into a 'vehicle for imagining the imagination'.[99] Situated at the intersection between animal magnetism and aesthetics, the previsionary abilities of the Highlander were now brought to bear on theorisation of creativity and the unconscious mind.[100]

Writing in 1838, Baron Dupotet de Sennevoy, a leading French mesmerist, claimed to have solved an 'ancient' riddle: 'The somnambulic faculty of clairvoyance, or the power of seeing events passing at a distance, affords a solution to the mystery of what, in the north of Scotland, is called second sight.'[101] Envisioned by its proponents as a revolutionary scientific paradigm, the theory of animal magnetism promised to explain what had been unexplainable. Reflecting on the interconnections between Romantic visionary aesthetics, *naturphilosophie* and the 'mystery' of prophetic sight, the historian A.J.L. Busst has concluded that, by the close of the eighteenth century, second sight had ceased to operate as a discrete phenomenon, having been explained by and assimilated into a more dominant magnetic discourse.[102] For Busst the Highland tradition was only taken up by mesmerism as a 'means of conferring respectability' and a sense of precedence to their claims, but the engagement with its history and mechanisms by German Idealists such as Georg Wilhelm Friedrich Hegel, F.W.J. Schelling and G.H. von Schubert suggests an interest in the phenomenon itself.[103] Despite being framed by a new language of mesmeric sensitivity and magnetic receptivity, the prophetic powers long associated with the inhabitants of mountainous regions and barren isles remained exemplified by those romantic figures. In her *Essays on the Superstitions of the Highlands of Scotland* (1811), for instance, the poet Anne Grant argued that though the second-sighted vision is brought about by involuntary 'shuddering impulse, a mental spasm', the faculty is itself the product of characteristics found in the Gaelic people. Using the example of second sight as a means by which to valorise the 'sensitivity' of the Highland people, the author situates this foresight firmly within the imagination of the seer, which must 'be awakened, and the mind stored with images, on which to feed in deep and silent musing, before these shadows can occupy'.[104] It is not 'in the coarse and vulgar mind of apathy, that the imaginative faculty thus predominates'; rather it involves 'the habits of deep meditation and sensitive and fantastic feeling, which nourish this creative faculty'.[105] In this reading, the supernatural does not exist as an agency exterior to the individual and second sight is not produced by the machinations of faeries or spirits; rather it is the product of a uniquely creative interior feeding from its own imaginings: 'visionary modes of thinking' are simply part of the national character.[106] Where once second sight constituted an object of the observer's imagination—as a topic for scientific or antiquarian inquiry, as well as a source of poetic inspiration—here the visionary power resembles something closer to a system for describing and understanding the imagination itself.

—

In his *History of English Poetry* (1774–1781) Thomas Warton voiced the perennial concern of his age that with the development of civilisation and vast material improvements: 'we have lost a set of manners' more attuned to the 'purposes of poetry, than those which have been adopted in their place. We have parted with extravagances that are above propriety with incredibilities that are of more value than reality.'[107] Throughout the eighteenth century poets, writers and seekers of the supernatural looked to the Highlands of Scotland to provide exactly this type of imaginative resource. Pictured as the geographic embodiment of an earlier stage of human development replete with ancient customs, the region was marked to English-speaking tourists, writers and scientists as a site in which unfamiliar superstitions and antiquated manner still held sway. Implicated in the identification of its history, myth and folk culture as a creative resource was the knowledge that these acts of appropriation signalled the death of this primitive arcadia. Respecting Michel de Certeau's description of the historiographical operation—'Writing speaks of the past only to inter it'—it is remarkable that attempts to observe and record Highland life appear to almost 'inter' the present.[108] In a strange temporal negotiation, accounts of this 'ancient' people present them both as exemplary of an earlier stage of cultural development and also on the brink of historical erasure. Writing in 1822, David Stewart is typical in his assertion that 'much of the romance and chivalry of the Highland character is gone. The voice of the bard has long been silent, and poetry, tradition and song, are vanishing away.'[109] This dying away is realised, like second sight, along both temporal and geographic lines, so that travel narratives often encode elegiac lamentations for imagined geographies or histories in decline. In his *Journey to the Western*

Isles, Johnson regrets that 'We came thither too late to see what we had expected, a people of peculiar appearance, and system of antiquated life.'[110] When Johnson and Boswell set out in 1773, the image of the Highlands as an antediluvian world transitioning to the modern was already a well-established trope. Precipitated by the breakdown of the clan system and waves of mass emigration, this sense of eroding tradition was also a product of the travel narrative itself. Freshly constructed military roadways and improved coach services made exploring the north easier, and post-Culloden policing made travel safer: mapped and subjected to new statistical surveys, the Highland landscape was one made increasingly familiar as the eighteenth century progressed. The second-sight tradition is formulated by and read through the prism of this narrative of decay: in the same moment as it is identified as a discrete subject its imminent dissolution is predicted, as if the reticent seer cannot be captured by the full glare of an inquisitive gaze.

NOTES

1. Andrew Lang, *The Book of Dreams and Ghosts* (London: Longmans, Green & Co., 1897), p. ix. (Lang 1897).
2. See Michael Hunter, *The Royal Society and its Fellows: The Morphology of an Early Scientific Institution* (Stanford: British Society for the History of Science, 1994) (Hunter 1994).
3. Keith Thomas, *Religion and the Decline of Magic: Studies in Popular Beliefs in Sixteenth and Seventeenth-Century England* [1971] (London: Penguin, 1991), p. 590. (Thomas (1991).
4. George E. Davie, *The Scottish Enlightenment* (London: Historical Association, 1981). (Davie 1981).
5. Michael Hunter, *The Occult Laboratory: Magic, Science and Second Sight in Late 17th Century Scotland'* ed. Michael Hunter (The Boydell Press: Woodbridge, 2001), p. 9. (Hunter 2001).
6. See Malcolm Chapman, *The Celts: The Construction of a Myth* (London: Macmillan, 1992). (Chapman 1992), *The Gaelic Vision in Scottish Culture* (London: Croom Helm, 1978). ('*The Gaelic Vision*'... 1978), Hugh Trevor-Roper *The Invention of Scotland: Myth and History* (London: Yale University Press, 2008). (Trevor-Roper 2008), and Ian Donnachie and Christopher Whatley, *The Manufacture of Scottish History* (London: Palgrave Macmillan, 1992). (Donnachie and Whatley 1992).
7. In *The Making of Religion* (1898) to give an example, Lang leans on the work of Henry More, Joseph Glanvill and Robert Boyle to provide a British context for his discussion of the topic (41–46).

8. M. Martin, *A Description of the Western Isles of Scotland* 2nd edition (London: A. Bell, 1716), p. 332. (Martin 1716).

9. Juliet Feibel, 'Highland Histories: Jacobitism and Second Sight', *Clio* 30:1 (2000), 51–77 (65). (Feibel 2000). See also Geoff Holder, *The Jacobites and the Supernatural* (Gloucestershire: Amberley House Publishing, 2013). (Holder 2013). Feibel also notes that Scottish clerics like John Frazer and Arthur Ross were stripped of their offices during the Glorious Revolution 1688 for refusing to swear allegiance to William of Orange and both went on to investigate the phenomena of second sight.

10. See Steven Shapin, *A Social History of Truth: Civility and Science in Seventeenth-Century England* (Chicago: Chicago University Press, 1994). (Shapin 1994).

11. Joseph Glanvill, *Saducismus Triumphatus: Or, Plain Evidence Concerning Witches and Apparitions* (London: J. Collins and S. Lownds, 1681), p. 3. (Glanvill 1681) 'Sadducism' meaning skepticism or disbelief regarding the veracity of supernatural witnessing or experience.

12. George Sinclair, *Satan's Invisible World Discovered* (1685), (London: T.G. Stevenson, 1871) p. ixxx. (Sinclair 1871) and Henry More, *An Antidote Against Atheisme* (London: Roger Daniel, 1653), p. 64. (More 1653).

13. *A Description of the Western Isles of Scotland*, p. 309.

14. Theophilus Insulanus, *Treaties on Second Sight, Dreams and Apparitions* (Edinburgh: Ruddiman, Auld and Company, 1763), p. 3. (Insulanus 1763).

15. Ibid.

16. Samuel Johnson, *A Journey to the Western Isles of Scotland* (1775) (London: A. Strahan and T. Cadell, 1785), p. 254. (Johnson 1785).

17. Insulanus, *Treatise on Second Sight*, p. 135.

18. Glanvill, p. 53.

19. Early investigations into second sight were carried out primarily through letters sent between English savants and aristocratic Scots. Robert Boyle, for instance, corresponded with and eventually interviewed George Mackenzie, Lord Tarbat on second sight in 1678, while the antiquarian John Aubrey wrote to the Professor of Theology at the University of Aberdeen in search of information on the subject, and Samuel Pepys sought out tales of prophetic vision in his letters to Lord Reay. Many of these documents are reproduced in Michael Hunter, *The Occult Laboratory: Magic, Science and Second Sight in Late 17th Century Scotland'* ed. Michael Hunter (The Boydell Press: Woodbridge, 2001). (Hunter 2001).

20. George Sinclair, *Satan's Invisible World Discovered*, p. 21.

21. M. Martin, *A Description of the Western Isles of Scotland*, 2nd edition (London: A. Bell, 1716). (Martin 1716), p. 309, Samuel Johnson, *A Journey to the Western Isles*, p. 254 and John Aubrey, *Miscellanies Upon Various Subjects* (1696) (London: John Russell Smith, 1857) p. 184. (Johnson 1857).

22. Aubrey's chapter 'An Accurate Account of Second-Sighted Men', extracted and re-published in several later studies: John Beaumont's *Historical, Physiological and Theological Treatise of Spirits, Apparitions, Witchcrafts and other Magical Practices* (1705) and Theophilus Insulanus's *A Treatise on Second Sight, Dreams and Apparitions* (1763).

23. See Mark Salber Phillip's *Society and Sentiment: Genres of Historical Writing in Britain 1740–1840* (New Jersey: Princeton University Press, 2000). (Phillip 2000).

24. *A Journey to the Western Isles,* p. 89.

25. Ibid., p. 79.

26. Ibid., p. 137.

27. Ibid., p. 138.

28. Edward Lhuyd, *A Collection of Highland Rites and Customs: copied by Edward Lhuyd from the manuscript of the Rev. James Kirkwood (1650–1709) and annotated by him with the aid of the Rev. John Beaton* (1699–1700).

29. Silki Stroh, *Uneasy Subjects: Postcolonialism and Scottish Gaelic Poetry* (Amsterdam and New York: Rodopi Press, 2011), p. 21. (Stroh 2011).

30. Daniel Defoe, 'The Highland Visions, or The Scots New Prophecy' (1712) quoted in *Bardic Nationalisms,* p. 98. (Defoe 1712). Trumpener also discusses the publication of *The History of the Life and Adventures of Duncan Campbell* (1720), an account—usually attributed to Defoe—of a 'Highland clairvoyant who created a London sensation' (98).

31. Charles Wither, 'The Historical Creation of the Scottish Highlands' in *The Manufacture of Scottish History,* eds. Ian Donnachie and Christopher Whatley (Edinburgh: Polygon, 1992), pp. 143–156. (Wither 1992).

32. Hugh Trevor-Roper, *The Invention of Scotland: Myth and History* (New Haven and London: Yale University Press, 2008), p. 84. (Trevor-Roper 2008).

33. Hugh Trevor-Roper, 'The Invention of Tradition' in *The Invention of Tradition* eds. Terrance Ranger and Eric Hobsbawn (1983). (Trevor-Roper 1983).

34. See Leith Davis, *Acts of Union: Scotland and the Literary Negotiations of the British Nation, 1707–1830* (California: Stanford University Press, 1998). (Davis 1998), and Peter Womack, *Improvement and Romance: Constructing the Myth of the Highlands* (London: Macmillan, 1989). (Womack 1989).

35. Walter Scott, *Waverly; or, 'Tis Sixty Years Since* (1814), ed. Claire Lamont (Oxford: Oxford University Press, 1986), p. 261, 372. (Scott 1986).

36. Walter Scott, *Rob Roy* 2 vols. (Edinburgh: Cadell, 1830), vol. 2 p. 179. (Scott 1830a).

37. Walter Scott, *Letters on Demonology and Witchcraft addressed to J. G. Lockhart Esq.* (London: Murray, 1830), p. 14. (Scott 1830b).

38. James Buzard, *The Beaten Track: European Tourism, Literature and the to 'Culture' 1800–1918* (Oxford: Clarendon Press, 1993), p. 51. (Buzard 1993).

39. Walter Scott, *The Minstrelsy of the Scottish Border: Consisting of Historical and Romantic Ballads Collected in the Southern Counties of Scotland' with a Few of Modern Date, Founded upon Local Tradition* (1802–1803) 3 vols. (Edinburgh: James Ballantyne and Co., 1810), p. 159. (Scott 1810).

40. *Waverley*, p. 75.

41. Ibid., p. 24.

42. Ibid., p. 340.

43. Tzvetan Todorov, 'The Origin of Genres', *New Literary History: A Journal of Theory and Interpretation*, 8.1 (1976) 159–167. (Todorov 1976).

44. Grenier, *Tourism and Identity in Scotland*, p. 81. (Grenier 2005).

45. See also David Inglis and Mary Holmes, 'Highland and Other Haunts: Ghosts in Scottish Tourism', *Annals of Tourism Research* 30.1(2003), 57–61. (Inglis and Holmes 2003).

46. Lorraine Daston and Peter Galison, *Objectivity* (New York: Zone Books, 2007), p. 23. (Daston and Galison 2007).

47. Peter Womack, *Improvement and Romance: Constructing the Myth of the Highlands* (London: Macmillan, 1989) pp. 150. (Womack 1989).

48. Ina Ferris, 'Melancholy, Memory, History', in *Scotland and the Borders of Romanticism*, eds. Leith Davis, Ian Duncan and Janet Sorensen (Cambridge: Cambridge University Press, 2004), pp. 77–93 (82). (Ferris 2004).

49. James Boswell, *The Journal of a Tour to the Hebrides with Samuel Johnson* (1775) ed. Mary Lascelles (New Haven: Yale University Press, 1971), p. 161. (Boswell 1971).

50. Martin Martin, *A Late Voyage to St. Kilda, the Remotest of all the Hebrides or Western Isles of Scotland* (London, 1698), p. xi. (Martin 1698).

51. *Description of the Western Isles of Scotland*, pp. 296, 298, 305.

52. Ibid., p. 312.

53. Ibid., p. 303.

54. James Boswell, *The Life of Samuel Johnson* vol. 1 (1791), (London: J. Davis, 1820), p. 204. (Boswell 1820). See also Thomas Jemielity, 'Samuel Johnson, the Second Sight and His Sources', *Studies in English Literature, 1500–1900* (Summer, 1974), 403–420. (Jemielity 1974).

55. *Journey to the Western Isles*, p. 248.

56. *The Satirist*, 3 (December 1808), 483–491.

57. *Journey to the Western Isles*, p. 256.

58. John Knox quoted in Malcolm Andrews, *The Search for the Picturesque: Landscape, Aesthetics and Tourism in Britain 1760–1800* (California: Stanford University Press, 1989), p. 198. (John Knox 1989).

59. Ibid., p. 95 and 252.

60. James Beattie, *Essays on Poetry and Music* (Edinburgh: William Creech, 1779), p. 169. (Beattie 1779). and Jacob Pattisson, 'A Tour through part

of the Highlands of Scotland in 1780', National Library of Scotland, MS. 6322, p. 24.

61. J.S Forsythe, *Demonologia; or, Natural Knowledge Revealed, Being an Expose of Ancient and Modern Superstitions* (London: A. K. Newman and Co, 1833), p. 199. (Forsythe 1833).

62. Ibid., p. 199.

63. Robert Kirk, *The Secret Commonwealth, An Essay on the Nature and Actions of the Subterranean (and for the Most Part) Invisible People, Heretofore Going Under the Name of Elves, Fauns and Fairies* [1691], with comment by Andrew Lang and an introduction by R.B. Cunninghame Graham (Enemas MacKay: Stirling, 1893), p. 60. (Kirk 1893).

64. Jason Marc Harris, *Folklore and the Fantastic in Nineteenth-Century British Fiction* (Aldershot: Ashgate, 2008), p. 103. (Harris 2008).

65. Ian D. Whyte, *Landscape and History Since 1500* (London: Reaktion, 2002), p. 120. (Whyte 2002), Sasha Handley, *Visions of an Unseen World: Ghost Beliefs and Ghost Stories in Eighteenth-Century England* (London: Pickering & Chatto, 2007), p. 178. (Handley 2007). and John Brewer, *The Pleasures of the Imagination: English Culture in the Eighteenth Century* (London: Harper Collins, 1997), p. 507. (Brewer 1997).

66. John Glendening, *The High Road: Romantic Tourism, Scotland, and Literature, 1720–1820* (New York: St. Martin's Press, 1997), p. 7. (Glendening 1997).

67. Dorothy Wordsworth, *Recollections of a Tour Made in Scotland 1803* (London: Edmonston and Douglas, 1874), p. 43. (Wordsworth 1874).

68. Samuel Taylor Coleridge, *Notebook* 1812 (4166), quoted in Gregory Leadbetter, *Coleridge and the Daemonic Imagination* (London: Palgrave, 2011), p. 43. (Coleridge 2011).

69. *Journey to the Western Isles of Scotland*, p. 309.

70. Aubrey, *Miscellanies Upon Various Subjects,* p. 185.

71. Ibid., p. 184.

72. *Description of the Western Isles of Scotland*, p. 298.

73. Henry More to Joseph Glanvill, cited in *Saducismus Triumphatus: Or, Plain Evidence Concerning Witches and Apparitions*, p. 16.

74. *Secret Commonwealth*, p. 94.

75. *Secret Commonwealth*, p. 45.

76. Stuart Clark, *Vanities of the Eye: Vision in Early Modern European Culture* (Oxford University Press, 2007), pp. 2–3. (Clark 2007).

77. Frazer, *Deuteroscopia*, p. 9.

78. Jo Bath and John Newton, 'Sensible Proof of Spirits": Ghost Belief during the Later Seventeenth Century', *Folklore* 117: 1 (2006), 1–14. (Bath and Newton 2006).

79. Keith Thomas, *Religion and the Decline of Magic: Studies in Popular Beliefs in Sixteenth and Seventeenth-Century England* [1971] (London: Penguin, 1991), pp. 769–70. (Thomas 1991).

80. See for example, Alexandra Walsham, *The Reformation of Landscape: Religion, Identity, and Memory in Early Modern Britain and Ireland* (2011), Joshua Landy and Michael Saler, *The Re-Enchantment of the World: Secular Magic in a Rational Age* (California: Stanford University Press, 2009). (Landy and Saler 2009) and Lorraine Datson and Katherine Park, *Wonders and the Order of Nature, 1150–1750* (New York: Zone Press, 1998). (Datson and Park 1998).

81. Clarke, p. 2.

82. John Ferriar, *Essay Towards a Theory of Apparitions* (London, 1813), p. 95. (Ferriar 1813), Samuel Hibbert-Ware's *Sketches of a Philosophy of Apparitions; or, an Attempt to Trace Such Illusions to Their Physical Causes* (Edinburgh: Oliver & Boyd, 1825). (Hibbert-Ware 1825) and Joseph Taylor's *Apparitions; or, The Mystery of Ghosts* (1815). (Taylor 1815) and David Brewster, *Letters on Natural Magic, addressed to Sir Walter Scott* (New York: Harper & Brothers, 1843), p. 21. (Brewster 1843).

83. John Macculloch, *A Description of the Western Isles of Scotland including the Isle of Man; comprising an account of their geological structure; with Remarks on their agriculture, scenery, and antiquities* 3 vols. (London: J. Moyes, 1819), vol. 2 p. 33. (Macculloch 1819) and Robert MacNish, *The Philosophy of Sleep* (W.R. M'Phun: Glasgow, 1838), p. 261. (MacNish 1838).

84. See Lewis Spence, *Second Sight: Its History and Origins* (London: Rider and Company, 1951). (Spence 1951).

85. Walter Scott, *Letters on Demonology and Witchcraft, addressed to J. G. Lockhart Esq.* 2 vols. (Edinburgh: Cadell) p. 389. (Scott 1830).

86. Ibid., p. 390.

87. Ibid., p. 6.

88. Terry Castle, *The Female Thermometer: Eighteenth-Century Culture and the Invention of the Uncanny* (New York and Oxford: Oxford University Press, 1995), pp. 143–144. (Castle 1995).

89. The theme of the double also appears in Walter Scott's *Redgauntlet* (1824)

90. Ian Duncan, 'The Upright Corpse: Hogg, National Literature and the Uncanny', *Studies in Hogg and His World* 5 (1994), 29–54. (Duncan 1994) and see also P.D. Garside, 'Hogg's *Confessions* and Scotland', *Studies in Hogg and His World* 12 (2001), 118–138. (Garside 2001).

91. *The Secret Commonwealth*, p. 80.

92. *Description of the Western Isles of Scotland*, p. 311.

93. Frazer, p. 45.

94. James Hogg, *The Private Memoirs and Confessions of a Justified Sinner: Written by Himself: With a Detail of Curious and Traditionary Facts and Other Evidence by the Editor* (London: Longmans, Hurst, Rees, Orme, Brown, and Green, 1824), p. 175. (Hogg 1824).

95. Karl Miller, *The Double: Studies in Literary History* (Oxford: Oxford University Press, 1985), p. 49. (Miller 1985).

96. Jenny Ford, *Coleridge on Dreaming: Romanticism, Dreams and the Medical Imagination* (Cambridge: Cambridge University Press, 1998), p. 101. (Ford 1998).

97. J. J Volkmann's *Neueste Reisen durch Schottland und Ireland* (1784) which includes an extract from Thomas Pennant's *A Tour in Scotland* (1769), a text which was translated in full in 1780, *Tagebuch einer Reise nach den Hebridischen Inseln mit Doctor Samuel Johnson. Nach der zweyten Ausgabe aus dem Englishen ubersetzt* (1787).

98. See Edward Larrissy, 'The Celtic Bard of Romanticism: Blindness and Second Sight', *Romanticism* 5 (1999) 43–57. (Larrissy 1999) and Matthew Wickman, 'Of Mourning and Machinery', in *The Ruins of Experience: Scotland's 'Romantick' Highlands and the Birth of the Modern Witness* (Philadelphia: University of Pennsylvania Press, 2007), pp. 140–170. (Wickman 2007).

99. Peter Womack, *Improvement and Romance: Constructing the Myth of the Highlands* (London: MacMillan, 1989), p. 94. (Womack 1989).

100. See Matt Ffytche, *The Foundation of the Unconscious: Schelling, Freud and the Birth of the Modern Psyche* (2012). and Henri F. Ellenberger, *The Discovery of the Unconscious: The History and Evolution of Dynamic Psychology* (1994).

101. J. Dupotet de Sennevoy, *An Introduction to the study of animal magnetism* (London: Churchill, 1838), p. 275. (De Sennevoy 1838).

102. A.J.L. Busst, 'Scottish Second Sight: The Rise and Fall of a European Myth', *European Romantic Review* 5.2 (Winter, 1995). (Busst 1995).

103. Busst, p. 164.

104. Ibid., p. 36.

105. Ibid., p. 36.

106. Ibid., p. 36.

107. Thomas Warton, *The History of English Poetry,* 3 vols. (London: J. Dodsley, Warton 1774–1781) vol. 2, pp. 462–463. (Warton 1774–1781).

108. Michel de Certeau, *The Writing of History,* trans. Tom Conley (New York: Columbia University Press, 1988), p. 101. (De Certeau 1988).

109. David Stewart, *Sketches of the Character, Manners and Present State of the Highlanders of Scotland; with Details of the Military Service of the Highland Regiments* vol. 1 (Edinburgh, 1822), p. 121. (Stewart 1822).

110. *Journey to the Western Isles,* p. 103.

References

Andrews, Malcolm, *The Search for the Picturesque: Landscape, Aesthetics and Tourism in Britain 1760–1800* (Palo Alto, CA: Stanford University Press, 1989).

Aubrey, John, *Miscellanies Upon Various Subjects* (1696) (London: John Russell Smith, 1857).

Bath, Jo, and John Newton, '"Sensible Proof of Spirits": Ghost Belief during the Later Seventeenth Century', *Folklore* 117.1 (2006), 1–14.

Beattie, James, *Essays on Poetry and Music* (Edinburgh: William Creech, 1779).

Boswell, James, *The Journal of a Tour to the Hebrides with Samuel Johnson* (1775), ed. Mary Lascelles (New Haven, CT: Yale University Press, 1971).

Boswell, James, *The Life of Samuel Johnson*, vol. 1 (1791) (London: J. Davis, 1820).

Brewer, John, *The Pleasures of the Imagination: English Culture in the Eighteenth Century* (London: Harper Collins, 1997).

Busst, A.J.L., 'Scottish Second Sight: The Rise and Fall of a European Myth', *European Romantic Review* 5.2 (Winter 1995) 149–175.

Buzard, James, *The Beaten Track: European Tourism, Literature and the Ways to 'Culture' 1800–1918* (Oxford: Clarendon Press, 1993), p. 51.

Castle, Terry, *The Female Thermometer: Eighteenth-Century Culture and the Invention of the Uncanny* (New York and Oxford: Oxford University Press, 1995).

Chapman, Malcolm, *The Celts: The Construction of a Myth* (London: Macmillan, 1992).

Clark, Stuart, *Vanities of the Eye: Vision in Early Modern European Culture* (Oxford: Oxford University Press, 2007).

Coleridge, Samuel Taylor, *Notebook* 1812 (4166), quoted in Gregory Leadbetter, *Coleridge and the Daemonic Imagination* (London: Palgrave, 2011), p. 43.

Daston, Lorraine, and Peter Galison, *Objectivity* (New York: Zone Books, 2007).

Daston, Lorraine, and Katherine Park, *Wonders and the Order of Nature, 1150–1750* (New York: Zone Press, 1998).

Davie, George E., *The Scottish Enlightenment* (London: Historical Association, 1981).

Davis, Leith, *Acts of Union: Scotland and the Literary Negotiations of the British Nation, 1707–1830* (Palo Alto, CA: Stanford University Press, 1998).

De Certeau, Michel, *The Writing of History*, trans. Tom Conley (New York: Columbia University Press, 1988).

De Sennevoy, J. Dupotet, *An Introduction to the Study of Animal Magnetism* (London: Churchill, 1838).

Defoe, Daniel, 'The Highland Visions, or The Scots New Prophecy' (1712) quoted in *Bardic Nationalisms*, p. 98.

Donnachie, Ian, and Christopher Whatley, *The Manufacture of Scottish History* (London: Palgrave Macmillan, 1992).

Duncan, Ian, 'The Upright Corpse: Hogg, National Literature and the Uncanny', *Studies in Hogg and His World* 5 (1994), 29–54.

Feibel, Juliet, 'Highland Histories: Jacobitism and Second Sight', *Clio* 30.1 (2000), 51–77.

Ferriar, John, *Essay Towards a Theory of Apparitions* (London: Cadell and Davies, 1813), p. 95.

Ferris, Ina, 'Melancholy, Memory, History' in *Scotland and the Borders of Romanticism*, ed Leith Davis, Ian Duncan and Janet Sorensen (Cambridge: Cambridge University Press, 2004), pp. 77–93.

Ford, Jenny, *Coleridge on Dreaming: Romanticism, Dreams and the Medical Imagination* (Cambridge: Cambridge University Press, 1998).

Forsythe, J.S, *Demonologia; or, Natural Knowledge Revealed, Being an Expose of Ancient and Modern Superstitions* (London: A.K. Newman and Co, 1833).

Chapman, Malcolm, *The Gaelic Vision in Scottish Culture* (London: Croom Helm, 1978).

Garside, P.D., 'Hogg's *Confessions* and Scotland', *Studies in Hogg and His World* 12 (2001), 118–38.

Glanvill, Joseph, *Saducismus Triumphatus: Or, Plain Evidence Concerning Witches and Apparitions* (London: J. Collins and S. Lownds, 1681).

Glendening, John, *The High Road: Romantic Tourism, Scotland, and Literature, 1720–1820* (New York: St. Martin's Press, 1997), p. 7.

Grenier, Katherine Haldane, *Tourism and Identity in Scotland, 1770–1914: Creating Caledonia* (Aldershot: Ashgate, 2005), p. 81.

Handley, Sasha, *Visions of an Unseen World: Ghost Beliefs and Ghost Stories in Eighteenth-Century England* (London: Pickering & Chatto, 2007).

Harris, Jason Marc, *Folklore and the Fantastic in Nineteenth-Century British Fiction* (Aldershot: Ashgate, 2008).

Hibbert-Ware, Samuel, *Sketches of a Philosophy of Apparitions; or, an Attempt to Trace Such Illusions to Their Physical Causes* (Edinburgh: Oliver & Boyd, 1825).

Hogg, James, *The Private Memoirs and Confessions of a Justified Sinner: Written by Himself: with a Detail of Curious and Traditionary Facts and Other Evidence by the Editor* (London: Longmans, Hurst, Rees, Orme, Brown, and Green, 1824).

Holder, Geoff, *The Jacobites and the Supernatural* (Gloucestershire: Amberley Publishing, 2013).

Hunter, Michael, *The Royal Society and its Fellows: The Morphology of an Early Scientific Institution* (Stanford in the Vale: British Society for the History of Science, 1994).

Hunter, Michael, *The Occult Laboratory: Magic, Science and Second Sight in Late 17th Century Scotland*, ed. Michael Hunter (Woodbridge: The Boydell Press, 2001).

Inglis, David, and Mary Holmes, 'Highland and Other Haunts: Ghosts in Scottish Tourism', *Annals of Tourism Research* 30.1 (2003), 57–61.

Insulanus, Theophilus, *Treaties on Second Sight, Dreams and Apparitions* (Edinburgh: Ruddiman, Auld and Company, 1763).

Jemielity, Thomas, 'Samuel Johnson, the Second Sight and His Sources', *Studies in English Literature, 1500–1900* (Summer 1974), 403–20.

Johnson, Samuel, *A Journey to the Western Isles of Scotland* (1775) (London: A. Strahan and T. Cadell, 1785).

Kirk, Robert, *The Secret Commonwealth, An Essay on the Nature and Actions of the Subterranean (and for the Most Part) Invisible People, Heretofore Going Under the Name of Elves, Fauns and Fairies* [1691], with comment by Andrew Lang and an introduction by R.B. Cunninghame Graham (Eneas MacKay: Stirling, 1893).

Landy, Joshua, and Michael Saler, *The Re-Enchantment of the World: Secular Magic in a Rational Age* (Palo Alto, CA: Stanford University Press, 2009).

Lang, Andrew, *The Book of Dreams and Ghosts* (London: Longman, Green & Co., 1897).

Larrissy, Edward, 'The Celtic Bard of Romanticism: Blindness and Second Sight', *Romanticism* 5 (1999), 43–57.

Macculloch, John, *A Description of the Western Isles of Scotland including the Isle of Man; Comprising an Account of their Geological Structure; with Remarks on their Agriculture, Scenery, and Antiquities*, 3 vols (London: J. Moyes, 1819), vol. 2, p. 33.

MacNish, Robert, *The Philosophy of Sleep* (Glasgow: W.R. M'Phun, 1838), p. 261.

Lang, Andrew *The Making of Religion* [1898] (Fairfield, IA: 1st World Library, 2007).

Martin, M., *A Description of the Western Isles of Scotland*, 2nd edition (London: A. Bell, 1716).

Martin, Martin, *A Late Voyage to St. Kilda, the Remotest of all the Hebrides or Western Isles of Scotland* (London: D. Brown and T. Goodwin, 1698).

Miller, Karl, *The Double: Studies in Literary History* (Oxford: Oxford University Press, 1985).

More, Henry, *An Antidote Against Atheisme* (London: Roger Daniel, 1653), p. 64.

Salber, Mark, Phillip's *Society and Sentiment: Genres of Historical Writing in Britain 1740–1840* (Princeton, NJ: Princeton University Press, 2000).

Scott, Walter, *Letters on Demonology and Witchcraft Addressed to J. G. Lockhart Esq* (London: Murray, 1830b).

Scott, Walter, *The Minstrelsy of the Scottish Border: Consisting of Historical and Romantic Ballads Collected in the Southern Counties of Scotland' with a Few of Modern Date, Founded upon Local Tradition*, 3 vols (1802–3) (Edinburgh: James Ballantyne and Co, 1810).

Scott, Walter, *Rob Roy*, 2 vols, (Edinburgh: Cadell, 1830a), vol. 2.

Scott, Walter, *Waverley; or, 'Tis Sixty Years Since* (1814), ed. Claire Lamont (Oxford: Oxford University Press, 1986), pp. 261, 372.

Shapin, Steven, *A Social History of Truth: Civility and Science in Seventeenth-Century England* (Chicago: Chicago University Press, 1994).

Sinclair, George, *Satan's Invisible World Discovered* (1685) (London: T.G. Stevenson, 1871).

Spence, Lewis, *Second Sight: Its History and Origins* (London: Rider and Company, 1951).

Stewart, David, *Sketches of the Character, Manners and Present State of the Highlanders of Scotland; with Details of the Military Service of the Highland Regiments* (Edinburgh: Archibald Constable and Co., 1822), vol. 1.

Stroh, Silki, *Uneasy Subjects: Postcolonialism and Scottish Gaelic Poetry* (Amsterdam and New York: Rodopi Press, 2011).

Taylor, Joseph, *Apparitions; or, The Mystery of Ghosts* (1815) and David Brewster, *Letters on Natural Magic, addressed to Sir Walter Scott* (New York: Harper & Brothers, 1843).

Thomas, Keith, *Religion and the Decline of Magic: Studies in Popular Beliefs in Sixteenth and Seventeenth-Century England* [1971] (London: Penguin, 1991).

Todorov, Tzvetan, 'The Origin of Genres', *New Literary History: A Journal of Theory and Interpretation* 8.1 (1976), 159–67.

Trevor-Roper, Hugh, 'The Invention of Tradition', in *The Invention of Tradition*, eds Terrance Ranger and Eric Hobsbawm [1983] (Cambridge: Cambridge University Press, 1992).

Trevor-Roper, Hugh, *The Invention of Scotland: Myth and History* (London: Yale University Press, 2008).

Walsham, Alexandra, *The Reformation of Landscape: Religion, Identity, and Memory in Early Modern Britain and Ireland* (Oxford: Oxford University Press, 2011).

Warton, Thomas, *The History of English Poetry*, 3 vols (London: J. Dodsley, 1774–1781).

Whyte, Ian D., *Landscape and History Since 1500* (London: Reaktion, 2002).

Wickman, Matthew, *The Ruins of Experience: Scotland's 'Romantick' Highlands and the Birth of the Modern Witness* (Philadelphia: University of Pennsylvania Press, 2007).

Wither, Charles, 'The Historical Creation of the Scottish Highlands', in *The Manufacture of Scottish History*, ed Ian Donnachie and Christopher Whatley (Edinburgh: Polygon, 1992), pp. 143–56.

Womack, Peter, *Improvement and Romance: Constructing the Myth of the Highlands* (London: Macmillan, 1989).

Wordsworth, Dorothy, *Recollections of a Tour Made in Scotland 1803* (London: Edmonston and Douglas, 1874).

hrenology and Supernatural History

At a dinner party held at the Edinburgh home of the publisher Robert Chambers and his wife Anne, the conversation around the table turned to a recently published work of speculative natural history and to the mystery of its unnamed author. The book in question was *Vestiges of the Natural History of Creation* (1844), an account of the origins and projected course of creation, which precipitated a volley of scientific and religious debate through the middle of the nineteenth century. Beginning with the formation of the solar system and closing with utopian imaginings of future development, the ambitious study synthesised previously distinct scientific theories into a singular philosophical vision. Running through 11 editions by 1860, *Vestiges* familiarised the reading public with the idea of species transmutation, a controversial theory that applied the developmental models favoured by astronomers and geologists to the vexed question of human evolution. Despite the text's placatory deference to a Creator, the concept of transmutation was widely interpreted as a blasphemous refutation of natural theology and the absolute limits dictated by revelation, and a flurry of denunciatory tracts followed the anonymous publication. Speculations over the authorship of this scandalous new work occupied daily newspapers, weekly journals and private correspondence alike, and before public interest waned several figures had emerged as popular candidates. These included the geologist Charles Lyell; the mathematician and daughter of Lord Byron, Ada Lovelace; the social theorist Harriet

© The Author(s) 2017
E. Richardson, *Second Sight in the Nineteenth Century*,
Palgrave Studies in Literature, Science and Medicine,
DOI 10.1057/978-1-137-51970-2_3

Martineau; the naturalist Charles Darwin; and even Prince Albert. Not surprising then, given the growing controversy, that the topic should arise and precipitate a 'brisk fire of conversation' in the home of an educated middle-class couple. What makes this incident worth retelling, however, is that as 'guesses were hazarded', the book's author and host for the evening, Robert Chambers, was busy exchanging furtive glances across the dinner table with his co-conspirators, the journalist Alexander Ireland and the phrenologist Robert Cox.[1]

More than the 'delicious' and comedic occasion that Ireland would later recall, this dinner party offers a snapshot of a particularly rich moment in the cultural history of Scotland's capital. The Chamberses and their guests embodied the political liberalism and scientific rationalism that defined the intellectual character of Edinburgh's Georgian New Town against the conservative institutions of the city's Old Town. Committed to a progressive view of human history inherited from their Enlightenment forerunners, these middle-class Whigs pursued campaigns for reforms in education, penology, medicine and psychiatry.[2] A similar set of concerns were echoed by *Chambers' Edinburgh Journal*, a weekly publication founded by Robert and William Chambers in 1832 to advocate for political economy, secular education and social improvement. In articles and in such textbooks as *The Chambers' Elementary Science Manual*, the brothers also attempted to educate the common reader in the history and basic principles of modern science. These shared democratic ideals also produced *Vestiges*, a work written with the intention of introducing a non-specialist audience to a revolutionary cosmology and refused scientific specialisation by combining insights from chemistry, geology, astronomy and natural history. What made *Vestiges* a publishing sensation, its marshalling of different forms of evidence into a single philosophical scheme, also made it deeply unpalatable to those invested in the idea of academic expertise, and it was condemned as the work of an ill-informed amateur by many within the scientific community.[3] Its pursuit of a grand developmental narrative based on evolutionary imaginings also provoked the ire of Edinburgh's religious community. Published a year after the Disruption of 1843, which saw around 450 ministers break away from the moderate Church of Scotland to form the Free Church in protest at the perceived encroachment of the State on religious matters, the book tested already strained relations among the capital's religious, educational and political institutions. Denounced from the pulpit and described as 'one of the most insidious pieces of practical atheism that has appeared in Britain during the present century', the theory of species transmutation was perceived as a blasphemous undermining of God's interventionist powers and by extension the authority of the Church.[4] Written in the spirit of reform and modernisation, *Vestiges* pursued a democratic epistemology that threatened to undermine the basis of both scientific and theological authority.

To return briefly to the dinner party, where, according to Ireland, the situation has begun to verge on the ridiculous. One guest, a 'noisy obtrusive *gobe-mouches*, with a strident voice' addresses himself across the table to a middle-aged lady novelist: "'I have a strong suspicion that my *vis-à-vis*, Mrs.—is the author of that naughty book. Is it not so? Come now, confess. You cannot deny it.'"[5] The writer in question was Catherine Crowe, a well-connected fixture of the capital's literary scene and a close friend of the household. Born Catherine Stevens, she spent the early part of her life in Kent before marrying an army officer, Major John Crowe, and giving birth to a son. The details of the first decade after her marriage remain clouded, but it is known that by 1838 she was living in Edinburgh, separated from her husband and beginning to find her way as a writer.[6] Described by *Tait's Edinburgh Magazine* in 1849 as a 'leader of literary coteries', Crowe contributed short stories to *Chambers's Edinburgh Journal* and *Household Words*, and wrote several well-received stories.[7] A popular novelist, she also published a number of plays, several stories for children and a collection of short supernatural tales called *Ghost Stories and Family Legends* (1859). In addition to this prodigious and varied literary output, she was also known for 'dabbling a little in science'; a reputation that may account for her popularity as candidate for the *Vestiges* authorship, as its critics frequently attributed its tendency toward conjecture and its refusal to properly attend to detail as betraying the constitutional laxity of the female mind.[8] More specifically, her close involvement in Edinburgh's phrenological community and her long friendship with its primary British theorist George Combe implicated her further in the scandal. In his *The Constitution of Man in Relation to External Objects* (1828), a work that expanded on the work of continental theorists like Franz Joseph Gall and Johann Gaspar Spurzheim, Combe established himself as Britain's chief proponent of the science, and under his guidance Edinburgh became a key site of activity in the field.[9] Operating on the premise that the brain is in truth an organ of mind, with localised mental functions readable through the shape of the skull, this new theory of mind promised that, once accurately mapped, the head's lumps and bumps gave over an account of individual character. Promoted as a uniquely democratic form of scientific enquiry, phrenology offered an easily graspable mental philosophy accessible to the layperson, as well as a blueprint for political and institutional form based on sound materialist principles. As is suggested by the popular attribution of *Vestiges* to Combe—who remained credited in the British Museum catalogue until 1877—nineteenth-century readers recognised the shaping influence of phrenological doctrines of mind on the theory of species transmutation.

Brought together by their shared membership of the Phrenological Society of Edinburgh, this circle of friends and acquaintances found commonality in a mutual vision of progressive social change, conceptually underpinned by natural science. The story that appears to emerge in the retelling of a 'ludicrous incident' at the Chambers's Doune Terrace house, is one of a radical theory of human development formed by the rationalist heritage of the Enlightenment, situated in opposition to the city's evangelical Presbyterianism, incubated by the middle-class liberalism of the *Chambers's Edinburgh Journal* and guided by the friendship of a like-minded social circle. Such a version of mid-nineteenth-century Edinburgh could not seem further removed from the ghostly doubles, spectral funeral shrouds and eerie predictions of the second-sight tradition of the Highlands and Islands. However, it is the work of this chapter, against this assumption, to argue for the proximity of prophetic narratives to the intellectual terrain occupied by Robert Chambers and his educated guests. Part of what the *Vestiges* controversy reveals is that how, even in a period of increasing specialisation and professionalisation, the boundaries between areas of expertise remained largely provisional, with distinctions between orthodox and unorthodox knowledge especially vulnerable to contestation.[10] By placing disputed doctrines such as astrology, mesmerism and phrenology on an equal footing with the established authority of the natural sciences, Chambers underlined the intimacies that remained between marginal and established disciplines. It was in these smudged boundaries that second sight was re-formed for an informed cosmopolitan audience, and this chapter examines how tales of dark portents and uncanny presentiments were constituted under the gaze of new concepts of body and mind circulating in mid-century culture.

Prominent among these was the theory of animal magnetism or, as it was more commonly termed in Britain, mesmerism.[11] Based on the theory of universal fluid, an ethereal substance acting inside and outside the body, the manipulation of which could serve a healing purpose, mesmerism offered not only boundless therapeutic possibilities but also a new language by which to conceptualise the human mind and its architecture.[12] In his reading of the *Vestiges* scandal, James Secord has pointed to the instances in which the extraordinary abilities revealed by mesmerism's so-called *higher phenomena*—the clairvoyant visions, miraculous curative powers and clairaudience sometimes uncovered by magnetised patients—were cited by its supporters as evidence for the book's utopian vision, as confirmation of its prediction that the 'present race might be succeeded by "a nobler type of humanity"'.[13] Discussing the remarkable cultural reach of mesmeric practices, A.J.L. Busst has argued that by the mid-nineteenth century, Highland second sight had ceased to operate as a discrete tradition. According to Busst, the rise of animal magnetism, 'with its somnambulistic prophetic vision' and its claims to academic authority, transformed instances of second sight into only a 'local manifestation of a universal phenomenon'.[14] What this assimilatory narrative elides, however, are the complex patterns of influence that connected the supernatural tropes associated with second sight—the corpse lights, fetches, death shrouds and premonitions—to the scientific claims being staked out by mesmeric practitioners. In the first place, to assert that second sight was demoted as an outmoded synonym for clairvoyance is to ignore the continued assertions of its specificity. An 1845 article published in *Blackwood's Edinburgh Journal* is typical in its attempt to draw a subtle yet essential distinction between two forms of extra-sensory vision: while the clairvoyant abilities associated with magnetic sleep represent the 'power of perception without the use of the visual organs', we learn that second sight remains the 'power of prediction'.[15] Further, to accept that the legends and lore associated with this special 'power of prediction' were simply absorbed into a new discourse is to overlook how disruptive native superstitions and local mysticism thwarted attempts by mesmerists to establish their practice as one grounded in rational, rather than supernatural, principles. What had once existed as part of the folklore of a geographically, culturally and linguistically distant people could now be observed at work in middle-class parlours, theatres, lecture halls and medical schools across the country.

Catherine Crowe is a particularly useful figure through which to consider the transformations enacted on and by second sight in this period. This is partly because her prominent role in Edinburgh literary life and wide-ranging interests open up unrecognised connections between individuals and subject areas, but it is also because of the book for which she is now best remembered. Published in 1848, *The Night Side of Nature, or Ghosts and Ghost-Seers* gives an historical account of dreams, ghostly warnings, wraiths, presentiments, apparitions and poltergeists, with the aim of instituting a new and more open-minded ghost-seeing culture. This popular study negotiates a discursive space between antiquarian miscellany and didactic argument by bringing famous hauntings from history together with personal testimony and local folklore, in order to illustrate the continued existence of the preternatural and the supernatural in the modern world. Although *The Night Side* explores a subject area that is quite distinct from the expansive narrative of species transmutation outlined by *Vestiges*, the two emerged from a similar intellectual milieu. Aligning her project with the marginal sciences pursued by her friends and contemporaries, Crowe found commonality in their pursuit of a shared enemy: unthinking materialist scepticism. Just as the odd happenings recounted in *The Night Side* were typically met with disbelief, so too do the experiences of phrenologists and mesmerists testify to the fact that 'any discovery tending to throw light on what most deeply concerns us, namely, our own being, must be prepared to encounter a storm of angry persecution'.[16] In what Shane McCorristine has described as an 'uncanny reflection of positivistic scientific practice', the author demanded that objective investigations be made of the world's vast miscellanea of unexplained phenomena.[17] More than a collection of strange stories, this compendium of unexplained phenomena was intended as a riposte to what its author condemned as the 'farcical scepticism' of the age, which denied without enquiry and gloried in its own 'ignorance'.[18] Widely disseminated in the popular press, *The Night Side* contributed to a broader debate over the limits of human sight and the nature of perception, being staked out in relation to the contested claims of ghost-seers and mesmerised clairvoyants. The value of these debates lies with what the art historian Norman Bryson has described as the collective orchestration of visual experience. Vision is socialised and thus any 'deviation from the social construction of visual reality can be measured and named, variously, as hallucination, misrecognition, or visual disturbance'.[19] Considering the heterodox sciences of mesmerism and phrenology, alongside the claims of supernatural debunkers and ghost-seers, this chapter argues that through the mid-nineteenth century second sight emerged as a key point around which new theories of perception and 'visual disturbance' coalesced.

SUPERNATURAL DEBUNKERS AND THE SPIRITUAL EYE

In 'What Was It? A Mystery', a short story by Fitz-James O'Brien, an unscrupulous landlady convinces her tenants to rent a reputedly haunted, but enticingly cheap, property in upstate New York. On their first evening in the house the conversation around the dinner table is dominated by questions of the supernatural and what terrors the night might bring with it. One of the boarders has, we are told, prepared for what lies ahead by purchasing 'Mrs. Crowe's "Night Side of Nature" for his own private delectation'. This makes him deeply unpopular with the rest of the group, who chastise him for 'not having bought twenty copies', and we learn that when he 'incautiously laid the book down for an instant and left the room, it was immediately seized up and read aloud in secret places to a select few'.[20] By the time this story appeared in *Harper's Monthly Magazine* in 1859, *The Night Side* had run through 16 editions, with select passages often reprinted in isolation by newspapers and periodicals. Contemporary reviews often described the book as a ghostly revenant, returning to puncture modern incredulity: *Chambers's Edinburgh Journal* characterised it as 'published for the purpose of rationalising the ancient, though of late exploded belief in prophetic dreams, spiritual appearances and other mysterious things', while the *Athenaeum* cited it as evidence that the 'powers which some centuries ago ruled the world, and which have never lost all their dominion, are concentrating their scattered and remembered detachments to try the chance of one great battle for the recovery of their empire'.[21] For the spooked houseguests of O'Brien's short story, *The Night Side* functions both as an informative primer for the ghost-seeing experience and the possible cause of ghost-seeing itself, as reading the book appears to provoke an 'immediate clanking of chains and a spectral form'.[22] The manner in which this story plays with self-reflexivity, bringing to bear a polemic on the reality of apparitions upon the success of a fictional depiction, blurs the distinction between veridical and imagined phenomena, calling the boundaries of the natural world into question.

By the close of 'What Was It?' the curious tenants, having battled with an invisible but physically powerful force that attacks one of their members, leave assured of the material reality of their experience and its deserved place in the 'annals of the mysteries of physical science'.[23] The story begins, however, by throwing their ability to accurately interpret such events into doubt. In addition to reading *The Night Side*, two of the guests find themselves in a 'metaphysical mood' before bed and engage in a lengthy discussion of some of the pleasurable horrors offered by modern fiction.[24] What this conversation leaves open is the possibility that the strange goings on that follow may be as accountable to a temporary delusion brought on by an overexcited imagination as they are to the machinations of malevolent outside forces. Recounted in the first person without the mediation of an omnipresent author, the story invites the reader to speculate on the interpretative faculties and mental coherence of its narrator. The cultivation of this ambiguity is indebted to, among other things, a rich tradition of supernatural debunking tracts dating back to the early decades of the nineteenth century. Common to works such as John Ferriar's *Essay Towards a Theory of Apparitions* (1813) and Samuel Hibbert-Ware's *Sketches of the Philosophy of Apparitions* (1825) was a psychopathological model of ghost-seeing that situated supernatural experience with the deluded eye of the beholder, led astray by either phantasmagorical technologies or confused visual memories.[25] One of the consequences of this developing retinal paradigm was a growing consensus over the role of individual pathology in producing uncanny experience. In his *Letters on Demonology* (1830), for instance, Walter Scott described ghost-seeing as 'entirely of a bodily character' consisting 'principally of a disease of the visual organs, which present to the patient a set of spectres or appearances, which have no actual existence'.[26] An 1841 article 'Sketches of Superstitions' in *Chambers' Edinburgh Magazine* described second sight as similarly grounded in the body. Designated as a variety of 'spectral illusion', the uncanny visionary abilities of the Scottish Highlander are accounted for in language common to anti-supernatural tracts: 'Certain mental functions becoming diseased, the sense of sight is imposed upon by the appearance of things which are purely imaginary, but nonetheless supposed to be prophetic of future events.' This particular form of delusion, moreover, enjoys support from both the mental character and external circumstances of the seer, by 'Idleness, solitude, insufficient diet and an imagination led astray'.[27] Miraculous visions of events to come are, according the sceptical author, simply the results of misreading after-images and blind spots, a perceptual error that is encouraged by the ingrained superstitions of the seer.

It is against the discursive shift toward biologically and environmentally determinist models that Crowe positioned her thesis and its call for a new investigative approach to reports of uncanny phenomena such as ghostly warnings, wraiths, presentiments, apparitions and poltergeists. Defining her project as a 'desire to awaken' her reader to the possibility that such things '*may be* so' and as such are worthy of objective consideration, she attempted to reorientate the meaning ascribed by such terms as 'natural', 'supernatural' and 'preternatural'.[28] In *The Night Side* this was achieved by shifting taxonomical boundaries, so that occurrences once designated as supernatural, beyond nature and thus open to falsification, can be absorbed into the realm of the preternatural, where they skirted the edges of the natural but were ultimately contained by that category.[29] From the book's preface, which explains that its title is derived from a German astronomical term for the side of the earth furthest from the sun, it is made clear that the phenomena being held up for scrutiny belong not to other worlds but to a 'veiled department of nature'.[30] What appears to supernatural is in fact governed by natural laws of which we are largely ignorant and that we must strive to understand.[31] In this regard, Crowe avows, the human eye is indeed limited in its powers, as we are surrounded by sub-visible matter and forces—vapours, gases, light waves, vibrations— that only become detectable through the aid of 'artificial appliances'.[32] What sceptics and debunkers fail to recognise, however, is that our imperfect retinal vision composes only one method of seeing among many other possibilities. In a refutation of the retinal paradigm established by writers such as Brewster and Scott, she argues that if 'spectral illusions are so prevalent, so complicated in their nature, and so delusive', then 'life is reduced to a mere phantasmagoria'. In what amounts to a quite complex assessment of the relation between sensory perception and the interpretation of reality, the obstinate pathologisation of ghost-seeing is accused of having precipitated an ontological collapse of the boundary between the real and the illusionary.[33] *The Night Side* extricates human vision from this materialist dead end by calling for a fuller appreciation of inner vision as both a creative resource and a force capable of shaping exterior reality.

Writing in opposition to those who would define sight in purely physiological terms, Crowe offered her readers an expansive understanding of vision that pressed the importance of interiorised and spiritual sight. More specifically, as a review in the *Athenaeum* recognised, her work can be

affiliated with a broader 'school of thought' that referred 'once supernatural appearances to natural causes' by taking up the new science of
'Mesmerism'.[34] Predicated on the concept of an unseen universal fluid or
powerful influences acting on and through the body, animal magnetism
relied upon an expanded version of the natural that welcomed the inclusion
of invisible powers and energies. Taking up the language of sympathy,
influence and transmission, *The Night Side* resituated historic and contemporary reports of strange happenings in a new mesmeric framework. Most
productive were the so-called 'higher phenomena' associated with the
practice of mesmerism that, in addition to composing key sites of magnetic
healing, also provided dreamy spaces in which to explore forms of perception 'not comprised with the function of our bodily organs'.[35] The French
word *clairvoyance* made its way into common usage in English as a way of
describing the fairly broad range of extra-sensory experiences associated
with mesmerism, and for Crowe this new terminology had the potential to
bring elements of the supernatural under the purview of scientific investigation. Discussing the similarities between second sight and clairvoyance,
she maintains that both occur in temporary magnetic states where the
'untrammelled spirit' is momentarily freed from the distractions of the
corporeal senses and is able to gain access to scenes 'transacting at a
distance' or to events to 'be acted at some future period'.[36] Where phenomena such as second sight were once dismissed as the superstitions of
the uneducated, their likeness to the kinds of powers now being uncovered
by middle-class patients and mesmerised somnambulists cast peasant lore
in a new light. In *The Night Side*, for instance, we learn of a man of business
living in Glasgow who dreamt that he saw a coffin, on which was 'inscribed
the name of a friend with the date of death', only to experience the
unhappy fulfilment of his dream some weeks later. This is a clear instance,
Crowe argues, of second sight in sleep where the 'external senses, being
placed in a negative and passive state' allow the 'universal sense of the
immortal spirit within, which sees and hears' to work unencumbered.[37]
This description transforms the relation between body and mind posited by
anti-supernatural tracts: the businessman in this example is not imagined as
having fallen prey to delusion and he is not subject to technologies of
illusion; rather, in dream he is temporarily 'released from the trammels—
the dark chamber of the flesh' and is thus able to gain access to a privileged
form of natural perception unrestrained by the limits of the physical eye.[38]
Writing against the retinal paradigm, Crowe recognised in the altered
mental conditions explored by mesmerists the means to reframe instances

of prevision and ghost-seeing in terms of evolving understandings of trance and somnambulism.

Enthused by its seemingly boundless possibilities, the author submitted a number of supportive articles on the topic of mesmerism to *Chambers' Edinburgh Journal*. One of these, published in May 1851, outlined six 'principal stages in the development of the mesmeric powers', the pinnacle of which greatly resembled those powers formerly associated with the second sighted: 'To this stage belongs the remarkable phenomenon of mental travelling by entranced persons [in which] the mind of the clairvoyant actually pays a visit to the scene in question, and can see things, or pass on to remote places, of which the fellow-traveller has no cognisance.'[39] For Crowe, extraordinary manifestations such as 'mental travelling' demonstrated the limitless scope of mesmeric action, but many other proponents of the new science sought to distance mesmerism from such marvellous applications. In contrast to their continental counterparts, British practitioners largely ignored the spiritual or non-physical questions raised by animal magnetism to instead expose the solidly physical nature and boundless medical application of the newly discovered force.[40] Through the middle decades of the nineteenth century a concerted effort was made to advance mesmerism as a viable diagnostic and therapeutic tool. This effort is perhaps best exemplified by attempts to promote its use as an analgesic during surgical procedures, made most famously by the Scottish surgeon James Esdaile in India.[41] Administered in homes, private surgeries and dedicated facilities such as the London Mesmeric Infirmary, mesmeric treatment—brought on by passes over the body and prolonged eye contact—was widely advocated as a means to alleviate bodily aliments or diseases, rather than to facilitate the kinds of temporary ekstasis envisaged by Crowe.

The most outspoken advocate of medical mesmerism, through the 1830s and 1840s, was John Elliotson. A former professor of medicine at University College London and the first president of the Royal Medical and Chirurgical Society, no figure more clearly embodied the rational pragmatism and physiological mastery to which the mainstream of British mesmerism aspired. Having resigned his position at University College Hospital in 1838 amidst a storm of controversy over his experiments with the Irish O'Key sisters, Elliotson established a quarterly journal devoted to mesmerism that promised to 'grapple with nature [and] cease speculating on the unseen'.[42] Founded in 1843, with the help of another physician, William Engledue, *The Zoist: A Journal of Cerebral Physiology and Mesmerism, and their Applications to Human Welfare* attracted a wide readership and was quickly instituted as a key platform for debates over the nature and application of magnetic power.[43] Writing in the first number, the editor characterised the influence of mesmerism as a 'mighty engine for man's regeneration, vast in its power and unlimited in its application, rivalling in morals the effects of steam in mechanics', one naturally bound to a programme of social change and improvement.[44] A typical issue of the journal featured case studies of successful mesmeric cures and testimonials from patients, alongside articles expounding the need for penal, educational and medical reform. Conceived of as a purely physical force acting upon body and mind, mesmerism offered valuable insights into the physiological workings of the brain, but of instances of supernatural premonition or visions of distant events, Elliotson concluded simply that such matters were 'too wonderful for belief'.[45] When *The Zoist* touched upon instances of the supernatural, such as in a short article where we learn that in 'the subject of second sight, the eyes are generally described as open, while in these cases [mesmerised clairvoyants] they were closed', credence was given only to questions of physical manifestation, and the content of the vision or prophecy remained undisclosed to the reader.[46] For its physician advocates, the case for mesmerism as a reforming force that was 'vast' in scope had to be made on the basis of its analgesic and curative applications, claims that could be staked out in relation to another, more established, scientific practice.

Recognising mesmerism as a natural corollary to the understandings of mind and matter hypothesised by phrenologists, Elliotson and his colleagues advocated for their amalgamation under the banner of 'phreno-mesmerism'. In an address to the London Phrenological Society in 1842, William Engledue delineated the boundaries of this new discipline: phreno-mesmerism does not concern itself with 'essences, spirits, or the immaterial mind', rather it investigates 'one portion of man's organism—brain'.[47] Phrenological principles, grounded in the solid structures of the body, could provide a materialist bulwark against the mystical readings of mesmeric phenomena circulating in Victorian culture.[48] The two already shared in a democratic epistemology, working against the perceived aristocratism of the scientific establishment, and proponents of both phrenology and mesmerism emphasised the accessibility of their methods and techniques to the plebeian experimenter.[49] As is revealed by Robert Chambers's description of phrenology as a 'system of mental philosophy for the unlearned man', lay participation in these 'less abstract' sciences of mind was framed by the language of optimistic self-help, popular progress and meritocracy.[50] In appealing to the amateur and encouraging self-experimentation, however, these marginal sciences risked being mistaken for entertainment or worse, forms of magical practice. In 1844 the writer Harriet Martineau, who was an enthusiastic advocate of mesmerism's 'mighty curative powers' and a keen follower of George Combe, warned that 'there is no doubt that the greatest of all injuries done to Mesmerism is by its itinerant advocates'.[51] Insisting upon mesmerism as a highly unsuitable subject for public display, she condemned the 'perilous rashness of making a public exhibition of the solemn wonders yet so new and impressive' and 'exhibiting for money on a stage states of mind and soul held sacred in olden times'.[52] Mesmerism is, she assures her readers, a force capable of great physical and psychological healing, but it will never be utilised to its full potential while it remains tainted by theatrical display and individual profiteering. In his discussion of the bourgeois magical imagination, Karl Bell has pointed to the way that Martineau attempted to conduct this 'debate above the heads of the working classes', first by holding it on the pages of the *Athenaeum* and then by insisting that the proper use of mesmeric power be confined to middle-class doctors.[53] This example underscores the tension between the contrary demands of popularisation and professionalisation, but it also reveals how the egalitarian promise of mesmerism generated its own unruly and potentially supernatural meanings.

Though medical mesmerism, in its dogged pursuit of academic respectability, largely evaded the metaphysical questions raised by phenomena such as clairvoyance and somnambulism, within popular culture such demarcations were harder to maintain. Writers such as Crowe undermined the legitimising efforts of physician advocates such as Elliotson by blurring the line between modern science and a shared supernatural imaginary. As an 1848 review of *The Night Side* recognised, in the text 'mesmerism and ghosts are placed in support of each other, like two slanting cards in a house of cards. Either would fall by itself—but together they support each other.'[54] A methodological codependency that ascribed meanings to the predictions and observations of the entranced mesmeric subject that were largely uncontainable by the physical paradigm upon which the practice's tenuous medical authority rested. More dangerous still was the way in which texts such as *The Night Side* brought tales and legends harvested from folklore to bear upon the theorisation of mesmerism. A contributor to *The Zoist* might promise to reveal the origins of 'witchcraft, dreams

[and] second sight' as resulting from the natural influence of 'magnetism' on 'inanimate substances' and 'living beings', but the authority of mesmerism as an explanatory paradigm was never assured.[55] As a public investigative culture, one validated through platform lectures and practical demonstrations, the practice of mesmerism could not avoid being drawn into border disputes over the nature and limits of human perception. The discourse of spectral illusions, in ascendance through the early decades of the nineteenth century, maintained a clear connection between physiological optics and ghost-seeing in order to relocate supernatural experience in the disordered senses of the beholder. This retinal model found imaginative expression in ghost stories such as Fitz-James O'Brian's 'What Was It?', whose plots rely on the cultivation of empiricist uncertainty over the truth of what has been witnessed and who feature, in Srdjan Smajic's terms, 'people who cannot *see* otherwise than with their bodily eyes, and who invoke science more often than religion when they see something unexpected, something possibly not of this world'.[56] Promoted as a new terrain of scientific knowledge, mesmeric discourse cultivated a similarly incredulous attitude to strange phenomena by reducing historical reports of apparitions, presentiments and so on to the little-understood actions of a wholly physical force. The demonstrations of mesmerists and the positivistic plots of ghost stories were alike in promoting a mode of engagement with the supernatural that was amenable to contemporary scepticism; as edification or entertainment they promised enchantment befitting an informed public well versed in the doctrines of modern rationalism. That supernatural debunkers, medical mesmerists, platform lecturers, fiction writers, phrenologists and ghost-seekers such as Crowe all made claims to scientific authority should not, however, be taken to indicate that any consensus existed over the nature and boundaries of that authority.

HIGHLAND SEERS AND LOWLAND SCIENTISTS

In December 1831 the *Derby Mercury* published an enthusiastic account of the 'double-sighted phenomenon' on display in London's Egyptian-Hall. Standing 'with his back to his visitors' and 'dressed in plaid', eight-year-old Lewis Gordon McKean demonstrated a range of extraordinary sensory abilities. In addition to describing with the 'utmost promptitude and accuracy', the appearance of objects collected from the audience, he also recounted conversations undertaken whilst he was out of the room and read messages scrawled on a slate blindfolded.[57] Located at the eastern side of Piccadilly and modelled after the Temple of Osiris, the Egyptian Hall was originally commissioned to house the extensive personal collection of the antiquarian and explorer William Bullock, but through the early decades of the nineteenth century it also played host to a range of entertainments such as phantasmagoric projections, panoramas, magic shows and scientific demonstrations.[58] McKean was billed alongside magic acts that included displays of second sight in their repertoire, demonstrations of mesmeric clairvoyance and platform lectures that derided the faculty as evidential only of the eye's hallucinatory potentials, so the meaning of his 'double sight' was subject to constant negotiation.[59] Audience members may have recently attended a show by 'The Wizard of the North' that featured his young daughter as the 'Second-Sighted Sybil', or they could be on their way to a series of lectures delivered on the broad topic of medical reform, in which a physician named Samuel Dickson would cite Samuel Johnson as 'a believer in ghosts and the second-sight' in order to demonstrate the fallibility and delusional capacity of even the most learned minds. Though by no means the first instance of a Scottish seer visiting his talents upon an English audience—the deaf-mute and healer Duncan Campbell can be cited as a well-documented forerunner—the young McKean demonstrated his prophetic abilities in a peculiarly ambiguous cultural space.[60] Recognising this equivocality, the *Derby Mercury* closed its review by wondering whether the 'double-sighted phenomenon' was a demonstration of miraculous power or 'the results of art'?[61]

On 13 March 1845 the *Morning Herald* printed a review of a performance at the Egyptian Hall, the content of which bore striking resemblance to the 'double-sighted phenomenon' reported a decade earlier. The 'Mysterious Lady [...] apparently endowed with the faculty of second-sight' turns her back upon the audience and yet remains able to 'speak of everything that takes place with the most unfailing accuracy'. Unable to detect any deception or uncover any trickery, the reviewer concludes that this 'clairvoyant personage' is able, through the application of some mysterious force, to see 'without eyes'.[62] Elsewhere, the *Brighton Guardian* praised the act as a fine example of stage magic; while both the *Norwich Courier* and the *Boston Transcript* compared the feats performed on stage to historical accounts of witchcraft; and an article printed by the *Medical Times* suggested that the 'attention of the medical world, which is engaged in discussing the merits of the higher phenomena of animal magnetism should be directed to the exhibition', where a spectacular 'feat of clairvoyance' will be witnessed.[63] What emerges from these reviews is a quite capacious model of seership, where extraordinary powers are at once entertaining and scientifically edifying, mystical and contrived, constitutional and learned. Discussing these fluctuations in meaning, Peter Lamont has pointed to the ways in which stage magic set the terms on which mesmerism entered public discourse in the early nineteenth century. For sceptics, the fact that clairvoyant feats could be produced by professional entertainers provided 'demonstrable proof that such feats were the results of trickery', while for committed mesmerists acts such as those performed by Master McKean threatened to undermine the scientific respectability of their nascent discipline.[64] Belief, then, comes down to the question of demonstrability, so that the truth or trickery of an event depends largely on how it is framed and, according to Lamont, 'those who wished to do so could frame any event as evidence for or against the reality of mesmerism'.[65] Performances of second sight, while certainly not exempted from issues of artifice and veracity, also provoked debate over national identity and its enactment in public space. When, for instance, an article in *Blackwood's Edinburgh Magazine* voiced concern over the growing popularity of such clairvoyant acts as the Mysterious Lady, it did so on the basis that such entertainments undermined the unique cultural value of established folkloric traditions. Once 'preternatural powers, long supposed to be confined to Skye, Uist and Benbecula, are demonstrated on the platform by scores of urchins picked up at random from the gutter', these cease to be a 'marvel'.[66] Now performed on the 'platform' and not by poetic mountain dwellers but by street 'urchins', second sight is in danger, the author implies, of becoming only another conjuring act among many. Absorbed into the mesmeric performances taking place in venues such as the Egyptian Hall, second sight might lose not only its geographical, cultural and linguistic peculiarity, but also its assuredly untutored quality.

It is perhaps surprising that a respected and somewhat conservative Edinburgh periodical would spring to the defence of a superstition associated with the Highland peasantry, but this article is by no means the only example of Lowland writers taking up the cause. Writing in a similar vein, *Tait's Edinburgh Magazine* boasted in 1843 that 'We have reached a stage in Scotland which may well make England envious', as while clairvoyance might now be popular in France, 'it ought to be remembered that second-sight, and second-hearing, though extinct for generations, was an exclusive attribute of the Scottish Highlanders, and chiefly of the Hebrideans; and, consequently, that modern clairvoyance is, in Scotland, but a recovered faculty'.[67] The objective 'truth' of the phenomenon is not of interest here; rather there are issues of ownership and identity at stake. The enthused reclaiming of 'modern clairvoyance' as in some way originally Scottish raises questions regarding the work that visionary or supernatural narratives might be said to perform in establishing the imagery, symbolism and history of a nation. In this instance, the claiming of second sight as a source of national pride underscored the persistence of the romantic Highlands—its sublime landscape, elegiac heroes and tragic history—in constructing a common post-Union identity. This was evident elsewhere in the country's burgeoning tourist industry, which marketed a very particular version of itself, as mountainous, rural, pre-industrial, to an expanding Victorian audience.[68] After Queen Victoria and Prince Albert established a summer residence at Balmoral Castle on the banks of the River Dee, and with the completion of the first Anglo-Scottish rail link in 1848, the Highlands were firmly established as an accessible and respectable tourist destination for English travellers. Sold as a domestic retreat from the industrial and urban pressures of the south, the region was marketed through an established iconography of tartan pageantry, ancient traditions and poetic peasants. The stories and legends associated with second sight, alongside the figure of the dreamy Gaelic seer, contributed a great deal to the creation of this sentimental and highly-marketable image.

The popularisation of a national character garnered from mythologised history and idyllic visions of rural primitivism left those engaged with the industrialisation of the country's economy and the modernisation of its institutions with a difficult representational conciliation. A short story in *Chambers's Edinburgh Journal* from 1860 that satirises the credulity and impressionability of English visitors to the Scottish Highlands gives some insight into this fraught negotiation. Titled 'The Second-Sight of Mr. John Bobells', it recounts a holiday taken by the narrator and his friend, a London stockbroker, to escape 'metropolitan' pressures and effect an improving change of 'constitution'. John Bobells takes to Highland culture with rather too much enthusiasm: donning a 'kilt', drinking whiskey with 'avidity' and learning Gaelic from a drunken piper. Most telling, however, is his conviction that he is possessed of a 'peculiar species of the second sight that never fails', and that a dream of a funeral procession forecasts his imminent demise. The story concludes not with the fulfilment of this prophecy, however, but with the reassurance that he 'did *not* die, according to expectation, but gave up whusky [*sic*], took to trousers, and has become once more a decent member of the Stock Exchange'.[69] Appearing in an Edinburgh journal politically allied to the progressive liberalism of the city's New Town and positioned along-side articles advocating self-improvement and the efficacy of rational entertainments, this humorous tale should be read as, in part, a morally improving one directed at the folly of superstitions and their ultimate incompatibility with modern life. This bumptious didacticism also coded a desire to more clearly define the cultured intellectualism of the city against the superstitious, backwards customs of rural communities. In what amounted to a discursive redrawing of the Highland line, attempts were made throughout the middle of the nineteenth century to distance the economic and academic advancements of cities such as Edinburgh from the concerns of an increasingly pauperised northern populace.[70]

Where the uneducated Gaelic speaker had once been incorporated into an Enlightenment-led narrative of progress or valorised as the poetic embodiment of a shared national heritage, in certain circles he found himself the subject of rather less favourable representations. Particularly revelatory is the stance adopted by Catherine Crowe's friend and mentor, the phrenologist George Combe. Founder of the Phrenological Society of Edinburgh (1820) and the author of a bestselling exposition of phrenological principles, *The Constitution of Man*, Combe was an influential advocate and populariser of the new anatomical science. As a method of biological divination, wherein the size of particular organs of the mind gave indications of the character and likely future course of the individual, phrenology could offer a pragmatic framework for institutional improvement. Yet because this project also depended upon fixing physiology as a reliable index of human behaviours and actions, its deterministic conclusions often worked to reify rather than reform established cultural stereotypes and social structures. This is clearly illustrated by Combe's thoughts on Scotland and its peoples. Having identified the Lowland population as a 'mixed race of Celts and Saxons' who are responsible for 'everything by which Scotland is distinguished', he goes on to attribute the socio-economic failings of the Highland population to a congenital 'narrowness in the anterior region' of the brain.[71] Most striking is the Gael's oversized 'organ of Wonder', which in his *System of Phrenology* (1825) is attributed to the tendency 'to believe in dreams, sorcery, astrology, in the mystic influence of spirits and angels, in the power of the devil'. Strange visionary experiences, such as second sight, are brought about by the confluence of this unique physical constitution with a particular topography.

'The mountains and the wild lawless habits of those who inhabited them are', Combe explains, 'peculiarly adapted to foster the growth of such impressions in imaginative minds.'[72] Though the determinist typologies underwriting phrenological discourse could be marshalled in defence of reformist and even anti-imperialist positions, they also offered a means to annex, under the guise of science, elements of the population seemingly antithetical to the values of modern Scottish society.[73]

Within Edinburgh's wider scientific community, the desire to distinguish the capital's scientific and literary endeavours from the regressive nostalgia framing the Highlands was most starkly expressed in the emerging ethnographic positions that sought to divide the two in terms of distinct racial heritage. The polygenist racial typologies of Robert Knox, an Edinburgh anatomist famously associated with the body-snatching scandals of 1828, drew clear and ideologically weighted distinctions between Lowland and Highland peoples.[74] In his *Races of Man: A Fragment* (1850), for instance, Knox asserted that the 'Caledonian Celt of Scotland appears a race as distinct from the Lowland Saxon of the same country: as Negro from American'. Identifying himself as a 'Saxon', he goes on to characterise Highlanders as lazy, irrational, feminine and beyond reform, but happily on the brink of extinction.[75] Race is realised here primarily in terms of temporality and history-making, so that while the resilient Anglo-Saxon drags civilisation onwards, the 'dreamy Celt, the seer of second sight' lives only in the past—where they are 'nature's antiquaries'.[76] By the middle of the nineteenth century, the question posed by Knox, 'how to dispose' of Britain's Celtic peoples and thus ensure the unhindered progress of the nation, had found an answer in the voracious Clearances and the large-scale emigration scheme established by the Highland Destitution Board.[77] And while the racialist thesis pursued by *Races of Man* did not constitute a consensus view, it did reflect the growing and problematic currency of taxonomic practices such as craniotomy, anthropometry and comparative anatomy in public scientific culture. In what was partly a sign of the preoccupations of the mainstream medical community and partly the result of its own presuppositions, the study of phrenology was likewise dominated by the question of race. Through the application of an endless variety of cranial measurements, including the cephalic index, the nose index and cephalo-orbital index, it appeared possible for thinkers such as Combe and other members of the Phrenological Society to not only divine the moral and intellectual character of the individual under analysis, but also through comparison and conjecture provide insight into the differences between the races.

Under this classificatory scheme second sight retained its status as an inherited trait—a feature that had been established by canonical studies such as Theophilus Insulanus's *Treaties on Second Sight, Dreams and Apparitions* (1763) and M. Martin's *A Description of the Western Isles of Scotland* (1703)—but the nature and meaning of this genealogical transmission shifted. No longer a visionary gift passed through generations of seers, it was transformed under the phrenologist's gaze into a species of imaginative delusion, to which a hereditary propensity to 'wonder' made certain subjects more prone. Recalling the case of a man 'in the west of Scotland, who is liable to spectral illusions', for example, Combe lamented that this 'peculiarity has descended to his son'.[78] Transposing psychological traits onto particular physiognomies, phrenology, in collusion with more orthodox ethnographical sciences, worked to translate cultural phenomena into coherent racial identities. Where Crowe understood second-sighted visions as presenting the investigator with certain methodological difficulties regarding the testimony of seers—those from the 'humbler classes' being rarely believed and those from the 'higher' being generally unwilling to 'make the subject a matter for conversation'—Combe's system recognised such experiences as more simply the result of an individual predisposition to the 'unexpected, the grand, the wonderful, and extraordinary'.[79] Phrenological thinking, then, produced the body as a newly legible document whose cranial map revealed, to the enlightened reader, a person's innate abilities, character traits and likely future potential. This hereditary determinism, moreover, mapped a wholly disenchanted understanding of second sight, whereby belief was reduced to a question of physiology and incredulity was reified as physical attribute.

Sciences such as phrenology and physiognomy attempted to produce the body as a stable text, but such claims were made vulnerable by the question of performance. As W.D. King writes, the 'pitfall of a system based in the empirical and the repeatable (that is, based on science) is the unique performance and every performance is initially that'.[80] In addition to illusionists and lecturers, bearded ladies and conjoined twins, nineteenth-century visitors to the Egyptian Hall could witness live 'zoological' displays. In 1822 a Laplander family and live reindeer were installed among the faux-sphinxes and sarcophagi, and three evenings a week a Mr Catlin presented a 'Tableaux Vivant Indiennes', which was mainly composed of hired Cockneys.[81] These displays, whether composed of genuine or impersonated indigenous people, functioned to simulate exotic exploration, encourage comparative ethnographic observation and offer up safely contained spectacles of racial difference. The novelist Charles Dickens, reflecting on his visit to a family of Bushmen displayed in 1847, was most impressed by 'the ugly little man' who gave 'a dramatic representation of the tracking of a beast, the shooting of it with poisoned arrows, and the creatures death'.[82] Acting out their daily tasks against a painted African backdrop, the Bushmen were presented as at once authentic examples and dramatic representations. Master McKean, recently arrived from the remote regions of North Britain, 'dressed in plaid' and bestowed with the fabled power of second sight, could be said to have enacted a comparably theatricalised version of national and racial characteristics.[83] The same audience that was captivated by displays of 'genuine' African tribespeople and exhibited Eskimos was also encouraged to indulge its taste for the exotic with a demonstration of authentic second sight by an artless and half-savage young northerner. Making use of a popular imaginary of the Highlands, the performing seer in London called upon the tropes of tartan, romance, poetry and superstition to establish a highly marketable stage act.[84]

Read against the prophetic determinism of phrenology, wherein racial traits are produced and fixed by observable organs of the mind, McKean's knowing enactment of cultural signifiers—undertaken in collusion with the audience—suggests a means to reinterpret both second sight and national identity as feints rather than embodied characteristics. Just as the act itself provoked interpretive uncertainty—the *Literary Gazette* described it as a 'very clever and unaccountable deception', while the *Theatrical Observer* advertised his ability to 'enlighten the City folks with his astonishing witchcraft'—the life story that framed the performance was also open to speculation.[85] This is evident in a mock interview with the 'Double-Sighted Youth of the Egyptian-hall' featured by *Monthly Magazine*, which skewers McKean's somewhat hackneyed Highland persona. The imagined conversation takes place 'over a bowl of whiskey', which raises the possibility that his double-sight may be the 'natural consequence of six large beakers of strong toddy', rather than a miraculous power. Worse still, the second-sighted boy arrives dressed in the 'Gordon' tartan rather than McKean—an error that leads the interviewer to avow, 'I could have wagered a trifle you were a Lowlander.' Having discovered that his first 'supernatural vision' occurred after he had run away from school to lie idle in a 'state between sleeping and waking' in the heather, the interview closes by suggesting that a form of spectral delusion might be at play in the young boy's prophecies.[86] In terms of how we choose to situate second sight in a mid-nineteenth-century context, the interpretative uncertainty that surrounded McKean's act reveals a tension between involuntary and voluntary modes of enactment. The former found precedence in the reiteration of the divinely inspired poetic seer, but also in the determinist tendencies of contemporary racialist and phrenological discourse. Against these positions, the interpretative blurring between stage magic and supernatural phenomena occasioned by performers such as the 'Double-Sighted Youth' produced visionary powers as, problematically, subject to the manipulations of the individual.

VISIONARY EXPERIMENTATION

Towards the close of the *Monthly Magazine*'s pseudo-interview with Master McKean, the young Highlander is asked to comment on another demonstration of prophetic sight being staged in a popular London venue by one of his countrymen, the 'Rev. Edward Irving'.[87] A radical millenarian preacher and a close friend of Thomas Carlyle and Samuel Taylor Coleridge, Edward Irving began his career in Edinburgh and came to national attention around the time of McKean's performances at the Egyptian Hall. In well-attended sermons and in texts such as *The Judgement to Come* (1823) and *Babylon and Infidelity Foredoomed* (1826), the clergyman outlined his vision of the approaching Second Advent. The espousal of this millenarian position led to his eventual expulsion from the ministry of the Church of Scotland, after which his followers broke away to form the Holy Catholic Apostolic Church. Having always operated on the fringes of orthodoxy, Irving fell further out of favour after one of his Regent Square sermons was disrupted by an outbreak of extraordinary manifestations of the Spirit.[88] Over the course of 1831, several female members of the congregation developed a variety of supernatural abilities, including spiritual healing, glossolia and automatic writing. The sensational nature of these manifestations, which were reported in the press alongside descriptions of his remarkable oratorical abilities, transformed the charismatic Scot into something of a celebrity. Importantly, the line drawn by *Monthly Magazine* between the 'double sighted' performances of McKean and Irving's sermons also suggests an overlap in the representation of religious prophecy and the more mundane predictions of the platform clairvoyant. It was not only that the millenarian

prophecy and the second-sighted performance engaged the same teleological process—by which the materials of reality are compelled to fulfil and
make real a version of future events—but also that these visions were
enacted in similar public spaces through comparably spectacular means.

Beyond the question of performance, the reception these Scottish seers
received in early nineteenth-century London also gives insight into
broader understandings of nationhood and identity. While the youthful
McKean, clad in tartan and offering light entertainment, presented a fairly
unthreatening version of the Highland character, Irving constituted a
rather more disquieting presence. In his chapter on the preacher, composed as Irving was just beginning to make his mark on London society,
the essayist William Hazlitt complained that through 'the grape-shot of
rhetoric, and the crossfire of his double vision' the preacher desired to
'reduce the British metropolis to a Scottish heath'.[89] Here Hazlitt takes
issue not only with Irving's characterisation of London as degenerate
metropolis and the relegation of 'religion to his native glens', but also
with his attempt to impose a peculiarly northern religious vision on an
English audience.[90] When the essayist describes Thomas Chalmers, the
leader of the Free Church of Scotland and Irving's mentor, as little more
than a 'Highland-seer with his second sight [...] training his eyeballs till
they almost start out of their sockets, in pursuit of a train of visionary
reasoning', he gives some insight into the dangers that he imagines such
manifestations of faith might pose to civilised British culture.[91] In early
nineteenth-century literary culture, Hazlitt could reasonably compare the
preaching of a respected theologian to the eerie premonitions of Gaelic
peasants, because of the perceived closeness of folk tradition and Christian
doctrine in Scottish interpretations and manifestations of faith. The impo-
sition of Irving's 'prophetic' fury on Britain's capital city threatens, in the
mind of the moderate southerner, to bring with it not only the excessive
religiosity associated with the Kirk and, more dangerously, the superstitious beliefs said to flourish under its ministry.

The scandal that erupted around the publication of the *Vestiges of the
Natural History of Creation* exposed a deep division within Edinburgh's
intellectual community, between the reformist spirit of the New Town and
the conservative evangelicalism of the Old Town. One of the most vocal
critics of the theory of species transmutation was Hugh Miller, a friend of
Thomas Chalmers and a respected geologist, who condemned the book as
'one of the most insidious pieces of practical atheism that has appeared in
Britain during the present century'.[92] The editor of the evangelical weekly

Witness and a key participant in the formation of the Free Church in 1843, Miller was a prominent fixture of Scotland's influential Presbyterian community. His autobiography, *Scenes and Legends of the North of Scotland* (1834), recounts his upbringing and early life as a stonemason in the small town of Cromarty on the north-west coast. Religious matters loom large in this memoir and Miller describes how his faith was shaped by both the teaching of the Kirk and the 'wild scenes and wild legends' of everyday Highland life.[93] Looking to his family history, the author offers a particularly striking example of the codependency of religious and folk tradition in the story of his great-grandfather, Donald Roy. Miller writes that his relative, by no means a devout believer, underwent a remarkable religious conversion following the death of several cattle, a disaster that he interpreted as an act of divine retribution for having missed church on several successive Sundays. Perhaps surprisingly, Miller also notes that his great-grandfather's sudden immersion in Christian worship did not lead him to reject old Cromarty folk beliefs as irreligious or anachronistic. Rather, his notoriety and popularity as a Presbyterian elder within the community was the result of his avowed second sight, a faculty that was said to have emerged only after his religious awakening. Bracketing the religious sibyl with the second-sighted visionary, Miller goes on to reflect that no 'prophets of the Covenant were favoured with clearer revelations than some of the Highland seers. What was deemed prophecy in the one class, was reckoned indeed merely second sight in the other.'[94] Bridging the gap between old mythologies and new evangelicalism, lay-preachers and seers such as Donald Roy imbued the teachings of the Kirk with populist mysticism.[95] It is this aspect of Scottish religious practice that Hazlitt identified with the charismatic Irving and set firmly in opposition to the judicious rationalism undergirding modern British society.

By likening the preaching of evangelicals to the 'visionary reasoning' of the second sighted, writers such as Hazlitt sought to diffuse the threat that religious prophesising posed to established understandings of authority and knowledge. Against the progressive linearity guaranteed by texts such as *Vestiges*, believers such as Miller asserted the primacy of Biblical truth in shaping the historical record, while millenarian reasoning produced historical narratives that were out of synch with agreed-upon conceptions of causality. As J.F.C. Harrison has it, it was one thing 'to study and preach on Daniel and the Revelation' but to 'act as though the last days were actually here was quite another. The former could be a mainly intellectual exercise [...] the latter reduced all questions to a few basic simplicities before the urgency of the imminent arrival of the Messiah.'[96] Instead of acquiescing to a version of historical process based on human action and natural law, preachers such as Edward Irving placed authority in super-natural gifts and strange portents as indicators of the future to come. In the early decades of the nineteenth century the Highlands and Islands played host to a number of millenarian awakenings, in which various religious sects recast the present as a prelude to the rapidly approaching judgement. Adventists, following a variety of year–day theories interpreted everything from major socio-political events such as the French Revolution to the publication of 'ungodly' works such as *Vestiges* as evidence of the coming apocalypse, and these prophecies were often accompanied by sudden outpourings of religious enthusiasm in the form of revivals. It was along the north-west coast of Scotland, in small towns such as Roseath, Row and Port Glasgow, that Irving's controversial escha-tology produced its first manifestations.[97] These centred on the figures of Mary Campbell and Margaret MacDonald, two bed-bound and deeply religious women miraculously relieved of previously untreatable ailments, who made prophetic revelations, spoke in tongues and discovered healing powers. On a visit to the area in 1830, Irving was made aware of the influence of his teachings upon the women, and after witnessing their remarkable spiritual gifts and the mass awakening they occasioned, he anticipated that soon further manifestations of the Holy Spirit would awaken ever greater numbers of Christian believers to the coming rapture.[98]

Towards the end of the following year, the National Scotch Church in Regent Square played host to its own mass awakening. 'Last Sunday evening,' the *Morning Post* reported on Wednesday 19 October 1831, 'one of the most singular occurrences took place' during Mr Irving's sermon. After finishing his oration, the preacher informed the congrega-tion that joining them that evening was a woman who 'never spoke but when the gift of prophecy was on her' and that if she chose to speak 'every person should listen to her with the most profound attention'. What followed this remarkable pronouncement, the article continued, led pious attendees to flee 'such a scene of sacrilege and profanation', while the less virtuous 'rushed forward to have a nearer view of the frantic bedlamite':

No sooner had the Reverend Divine concluded this most extraordinary announcement than the ears of the congregation were assailed with the

> most discordant yells proceeding for the prophetess, who only wanted the
> hint to be inspired with the aforesaid gift, when she roared and bellowed in
> such a manner that the whole of the congregation were thrown into a state
> of the greatest confusion.[99]

The woman responsible for this pubic affray is named at the article's close
as '—Campbell from Scotland', who is reported to be already recognised
'as a prophet in her own country'.[100] Here we find Mary Campbell, once
confined to bed in a small west coast town, commanding the rapt attention of a busy London chapel with her 'barely suppressed hysterical
cry'.[101] Respecting Diana Basham's characterisation of the 1840s as
'among other things, *the* decade of female prophecy', it is possible to
read Irving's elevation of a fairly ordinary woman to the role of oracle as
in keeping with a broader shift in the gendering of the seer in popular
culture.[102] Elsewhere evinced by the figure of Joanna Southcott, a religious visionary who believed herself to be pregnant with the new Messiah
and who commanded a substantial following after her death in 1814,
through the early decades of the nineteenth century prophetic authority
came increasingly under the purview of remarkable women.[103] With this
came censure as well as adoration: as the description of Campbell as a
'frantic bedlamite' reveals, the social discordance occasioned by visionary
proclamations, the abandonment of bodily control and the surrender of
the self to impulse and sensation these seemed to encourage, invited
condemnation from various quarters.

As the congregation of the National Scotch Church fell into fits and
convulsions, sceptical observers began to note the similarities between
signs of religious ecstasy and the kind of entranced behaviours associated
with mesmerism. Reflecting with alarm on the growing popularity of
animal magnetism, an article printed by *The Spectator* in 1845 claimed
that the 'gaping crowds' attending public exhibitions of mesmeric phenomena were demographically indistinguishable from those formerly
enticed by the 'melodramatic displays of poor Edward Irving' and 'the
gift of speaking in tongues'.[104] On the one hand, by conflating the
revivalist with the mesmerised clairvoyant it became possible to dismiss
the celestial prophecies of the former to the action of magnetic fluid or
the workings of a superior will on the nervous system of a susceptible
subject.[105] But on the other, the shared imaginary of conversion and
trance irrationality also served a highly effective way of discrediting
mesmerism's claims to medical authority. Writing in his *Human*

Physiology (1835), John Elliotson lamented that this proximity allowed sceptics to equate mesmeric influence with the 'prophecies of the Delphian priestess of Apollo' and the 'ecstasies of Dervishes and Santons, and of Shakers and Quakers, Irvingites', as comparable illustrations of how 'strongly fear or enthusiasm will work upon the brain and all the other organs'.[106] Where Christian visionaries baulked at the tricks of platform mesmerists and physician advocates such as Elliotson fretted over the taint of religious enthusiasm, others identified the magnetic sleep as a site of unique spiritual knowledge. Discussing Christian models of personality, Rhodri Hayward has suggested that 'philosophers, theologians and visionaries' were alike in celebrating 'the dream as a form of minor ascension, a moment in which the spirit escaped the constraints of the material world' and the 'ephemeral glimpses of the soul's transcendence' it appeared to offer.[107] In a mid-nineteenth-century context this model of inspired dreaming came to be strongly associated with the powers of mind revealed by mesmerism and, more specifically, with the visions of mesmerised female patients.

In a number of case studies, which included William Reid Clanny's *Faithful Record of the Miraculous Case of Mary Jobson* (1841), Robert Young's *The Entranced Female; or, The Remarkable Disclosures of a Lady, concerning another world* (1841) and Joseph Haddock's *Somnolism and Psycheism* (1851), bedbound women offered remarkable clairvoyant testimony of the dreaming soul's travels through time and space. The magnetic sleep, during which the sleeper was placed under careful observation and her utterances dutifully recorded, presented an important site of spiritual authority in nineteenth-century culture. Most famous among the somnambulistic prophets was Friederike Hauffe, a young German woman who claimed from an early age to be conscious of the presence of spirits and whose semi-conscious revelations were carefully recorded in Justinus Kerner's *Die Seherin von Prevorst* (1829). Recounting his magnetic experiments with Hauffe, Kerner described his patient as inhabiting a borderland state between life and death, sleep and dream. With the wasting of her physical body came a heightening of her 'spiritual faculties', a visionary capacity that allowed her to access images and knowledge unavailable to those 'whose inner life is overshadowed and obscured to the world-possessed brain'.[108] Confined to bed and at one stage emaciated to a nearly fatal degree, Hauffe experienced inspired dreams in which she encountered worlds beyond our own, learned of a complex cosmological ordering system and glimpsed into the afterlife.

For Kerner, who was a poet and philosopher as well as a physician, these somnambulistic journeys served to confirm the transcendental nature of mesmeric practice. Alongside works such as Johann Jung-Stilling's *Theory of Pneumatology* (1834) and Joseph Ennemoser's *History of Magic* (1854), *Seherin von Prevorst* contributed to a growing body of European literature devoted to exposing the spiritual and mystical potentials of magnetic theory.

Catherine Crowe produced the first English edition of *The Seeress of Prevorst* in 1845 and, as precursor to *The Night Side*, this translation is significant in instituting the German psycho-poetic tradition as an important influence on the author's own approach to the supernatural.[109] Kerner's magnetic treatment of Hauffe constitutes a key reference point throughout the study, one that allows the author to expound on the transcendental possibilities of trance and dream-like states. When, for instance, Crowe describes presentiments as arising from a 'vague and imperfect recollection of what we knew in sleep', she does so not with the intention of debunking the idea of uncanny foreknowledge, but in order to privilege the dream as an authoritative mode of information gathering.[110] That dreams may, under particular conditions, correspond to events occurring far beyond the dreamer's self or personal history, is a possibility explored at length in *The Night Side*, with 'second sight and clairvoyance' presented as techniques by which the subject is able to view events 'transacting at a distance, or that is to be transacted at some future period'.[111] For Crowe, as for Kerner and other magnetic practitioners, a clear divide existed between the earthly concerns of men and the higher spiritual concerns of women: so that the female 'will more frequently be a seer, instinctive and intuitive' and the man 'a doer and a worker'.[112] In line with the expectations of the period, feminine nature is coded here as passive and placed in opposition to masculine action, but it is important to note that values attributed to passivity shift in this context. Rather than implying a lack of action or willpower, to exist in a passive or 'negative' state is to be receptive to knowledge unavailable to the waking mind. Framed as an observational methodology, Crowe's insistence on the efficacy of inspired dreaming wrested perceptual authority from the bodily senses and frames 'intuitive' or 'inner' sight as more significant ocular technology.

When at a small social gathering in August 1847 Crowe inhaled ether with another female guest, it was in the hope of gaining access to clairvoyant information, to pure revelations 'unclogged' by the perceptual confusions of everyday reality.[113] The Danish author Hans Christian Andersen was also present at this strange party and recounted later in his diary: 'Dinner at Dr Simpson's, where Mrs. Crowe and yet another authoress (Mrs. Liddell) drank ether; I had the feeling of being with two mad people, they laughed with open, dead eyes. There is something uncanny about it; I find it wonderful for an operation, but not as a way of tempting God.'[114] Drawing a strict demarcation between the proper and improper use of ether, Andersen appears to have glimpsed something unsettling in the non-medical application of the chemical as a means of bringing about hallucinatory experiences. Writing in *The Night Side* a year after her experiment, Crowe reflected on the benefits of a brain excited by 'intoxication' and the 'remarkable exaltation of certain faculties' that certain chemicals can catalyse.[115] Part of what makes this self-experimentation interesting is that it was motivated by a desire to achieve the dissociative effects promised by the mesmeric trance, without subjecting oneself to the dominating influence of a mesmeric practitioner. The use of ether to bring about altered states of mind is doubly significant because of the decisive role the chemical played in discrediting mesmerism's therapeutic claims. After an American dentist, William T.G. Morton, began to publicise the anaesthetising properties of inhaled ether in 1846, medical supporters of mesmerism were forced to largely abandon what had previously been a cause célèbre. Championed by James Esdaile in India, mesmeric techniques had proved effective as a means of sedating patients ahead of surgical procedures.[116] This success had provided physicians with a persuasive argument for the continued trial of mesmerism as a medical technique, and without it they were forced back into murkier questions concerning suggestion, consciousness and the will. Worse still, by the close of the 1840s, metaphysical readings of magnetism long dismissed as the follies of European mysticism began to impact British culture. Particularly damaging was the translation and publication of Louis Alphonse Cahagnet's *The Celestial Telegraph; or, Secrets of the Life to Come* (1850), which detailed the French mesmerist's experiments with opium, belladonna and hashish. According to Cahagnet, these drugs facilitated ecstatic magnetic sessions, during which he was able to made contact and ask questions of the spirits of the dead.[117] Far from the stolidly practical applications its physician advocates envisioned for it, in Cahagnet's experiments the mesmeric trance became a direct channel to the afterlife.

In May 1853, Crowe once again joined Robert Chambers at the dining table of a middle-class Edinburgh household. On this occasion the evening's hosts were George Combe and his wife Cecilia Siddons, and instead of discussing a mysterious work of natural history the party entertained themselves by attempting to make contact with the dead. In a letter to the chemist Samuel Brown, Combe recounted that 'Robert Chambers and Mrs. Crowe took tea here the other evening, and then we had a ghostly session. Mrs. Hayden the medium being with us. While Mrs. Crowe and my wife catch the proper personality of the rappers and make them spirits, Chambers is blown like a feather not knowing what to think.'[118] Modern spiritualism arrived in Britain from upstate New York in the same year that *The Night Side* was published and echoed its call for a more open-minded approach to the supernatural. By offering proof of the soul's existence after death amenable to the empirical standards of evidence demanded by modern scepticism, the spiritualist movement promised to transfigure both religious and scientific belief.[119] As the participation of Combe and Chambers indicates, this new necromancy drew upon elements of the plebeian investigative culture that had been instituted in early nineteenth-century Britain by popular sciences such as phrenology and mesmerism.[120] Most often staged in private homes among small circles of interested parties, the spiritualist seance followed the template set by the mesmeric practice of gathering round a table and holding hands in order to intensify the magnetic force, with mediums serving as the locus of spirit communications. An early convert to this new religion, Crowe counted the aforementioned Mrs. Hayden and the spiritualist historian Sophia de la Morgan among her personal acquaintances, and went on to compose a rigorous defence of the movement in *Spiritualism and the Age We Live In* (1859), where she argued that though 'table turning and rapping may appear insignificant operations' these manifestations were capable of precipitating a revolution in the popular consciousness by 'convincing mankind that the fact of spiritual influence in human affairs is both possible and true'.[121] Spreading through after-dinner seances held in towns and cities around the country, the miraculous truth of spiritualism had the potential, like *The Night Side* before it, to awaken minds to the possibility of realms and forces beyond the material world.

Her enthusiastic and public involvement with the spiritualist movement left Crowe open to charges of credulity and worse. One year after the Combes's party, she found herself the subject of a damaging rumour circulating in Edinburgh and London literary circles. Charles Dickens, in a letter to the Reverend James White, recounted with some merriment that:

> Mrs Crowe has gone stark mad—and stark naked—on the spirit-rapping imposition. She was found the other day on the street, clothed in only her chastity, a pocket-handkerchief and a visiting card. She is now in a mad-house, and, I fear, hopelessly insane. One of the curious manifestations of her disorder is that she can bear nothing black. There is a terrific business to be done even when they are obliged to put coals on her fire.[122]

Reportedly found wandering the streets naked after the spirits with which she was in communication promised to grant her invisibility, Crowe was said to have succumbed to insanity after participating in a seance. News of this strange incident spread quickly among the author's acquaintances: Mary Ann Evans (George Eliot) wrote to George Combe to express her condolences: 'I can imagine how closely it must affect you and Mrs. Combe who have been her friends so long'; Robert Chambers gossiped with Alexander Ireland over the 'condition of mad exposure' in which his former dinner guest was found; and Dickens dismissed her in a letter to another correspondent as 'a medium, and an Ass' who was now 'under restraint'.[123] After the episode it was alleged that Crowe spent several months under the care of the alienist John Conolly, who confirmed in a letter to Combe that her mind had indeed given way to 'Spirit-rapping' and postulated that perhaps it was a sign of 'some Epidemic influence raging, affecting the brains of multitudes with vain belief, as in the Middle Ages with a propensity to perpetual dancing?'.[124] Though Crowe contested this account of events and instead attributed her absence from society to a ongoing medical condition, her naked ramble through Edinburgh was interpreted, by friends and enemies alike, as the natural result of her foolish adherence to a deluded system of belief.[125]

The salacious story of Crowe's alleged descent into seance-induced madness was most ardently pursued by *The Zoist*. Working under the title 'More Insanity from Spirit-Rapping Fancies', the publication's founder and editor, John Elliotson, cited the alleged incarceration of a prominent author in Hanwell Asylum as conclusive proof on the debilitating effect of spiritualism on the nation's 'superstitious' women.[126] Long after acquaintances had ceased gossiping and newspapers had tired of speculating, articles in *The Zoist* continued to speculate on the fine details of her humiliation. Querying the condemnatory attitude adopted by the editor, in a letter to the periodical Crowe questioned why, when 'the world has been ready enough to call you mad for your heterodox beliefs', Elliotson was so 'ready and eager to persecute others'.[127] The answer lay with the threat that the rise of spiritualist discourse posed to mesmerism's already tenuous claims to scientific orthodoxy. Having found himself, for the first time since the scandal of his mesmeric experiments at University College Hospital erupted in the press, in concurrence with mainstream medical and religious thinking, Elliotson's sustained critique of spiritualist beliefs should be read as an attempt to distinguish his own practice from the extraordinary claims of table rappers and mediums. The next chapter of this book spends time with the spiritualist movement, but here it is enough to note that this recuperative project was doomed to failure, as after the middle of the nineteenth century the practice of mesmerism was eclipsed by the more remarkable claims of modern spiritualism. One of the difficulties that mesmerists faced, was that, viewed in a certain light, spiritualism could be read as only an extension of the principles and techniques of their discipline. Emanations from the seance, one disgruntled mesmerist complained, could only really be accused of finishing the work begun by the 'ecstatic' somnambulists of an earlier tradition, whose published 'impertinences' have 'hurt the character of animal magnetism far more than any frauds that have been detected or suspected at public exhibitions'.[128] Two years after the Edinburgh scandal *The Zoist* folded, and by the time of his death in 1868 even Elliotson had become an enthusiastic convert to the spiritualist cause.[129]

The varying degrees of participation of Crowe, Combe, Chambers and eventually even Elliotson in spiritualism could be used to illustrate the easy traction between heterodox systems of thought in the mid-nineteenth century or perhaps, more simply, the willingness of open-minded practitioners to investigate other unorthodox forms of knowledge. On the face of it, the flowering of the spiritualist movement in Britain, which saw people from all walks of life conducting controlled experiments and carefully recording their ghost-seeing experiences, appeared to have answered the call made by *The Night Side* for a new and objective approach to the question of the supernatural. But the virulence with which Crowe's friends and professional acquaintances denounced her foray into spirit communication as pathological also suggests the transgression of carefully maintained boundaries. Modern spiritualism, which offered believers access to the same forms of transcendent sight and similarly accessed the unseen, threatened to reinstate the supernatural and the miraculous as sculptors of everyday reality. Recognising this, Crowe maintained in *Spiritualism and the Age We Live In* that the seemingly insignificant operations of 'table turning and rapping' had demonstrated that 'Spiritual interference in human affairs is both possible and true'.[130] And this intervention was necessary because neither orthodox religion or modern science had yet elucidated the mysteries of human consciousness, and thus 'of ourselves, as composite beings, we know absolutely nothing'.[131] The seance was, for Crowe, both a means of connecting with worlds beyond the terrestrial and, more mundanely, a route to a more expansive understanding of self.

—

In a letter to Lady Ashburton on 28 June 1848, the Scottish essayist Thomas Carlyle reported that '[Ralph Waldo] Emerson is coming here tomorrow evening and Mrs Crowe with the *eyes*'.[132] What exactly did it mean to have 'the *eyes*' in mid-nineteenth-century Edinburgh? Writing in the same year that *The Night Side* was published, Carlyle may have been alluding to her growing reputation as a ghost-seer possessed of otherworldly expertise; maybe he was referencing rumours of the author's ether-fuelled clairvoyant experiments, or perhaps his description was intended to convey the oddness of a prospective dinner guest. Most simply, it is possible that to have 'the *eyes*' was to be implicated in debates over the nature of vision and the limits of human perception that were being played out in relation to the contested claims of ghost-seers, mesmerised clairvoyants, religious visionaries and even second-sighted Highlanders. According to the history given by A.J.L. Busst, second sight did not function in these debates as a discrete tradition: having been popularised in the late eighteenth century and bound up with the visionary aesthetics of Romantic period, the 'myth' fell into decline when the power's 'resemblance to other phenomena' became too clear. For Busst, the popularisation of animal magnetism, and the subsequent fascination with states such as clairvoyance and somnambulism, meant that by the early decades of the nineteenth century this 'peculiarly Scottish manifestation' had been 'de-particularized', 'de-localized' and 'de-nationalized'.[133] What this narrative of decline overlooks, however, are the ways in which discourses such as phrenology and craniometry worked to re-entrench the tradition in a specific geographical or social locale by interpreting it as a superstition borne of the Celt's physical constitution. Considering Lorraine Datson and Katherine Park's description of secular modernity as contingent upon the expulsion of 'credulity' from public discourse, it is possible to read the reassertion of second sight as a superstition reliant upon certain racial characteristics, religious conditions or delusive conditions of mind, as an attempt to maintain this division.[134] Efforts to contain second sight in the miasma of uneducated credulity were thwarted by its slippery cultural hybridity, which saw it shift between distinct categories such as oral folklore, religious prophecy, stage magic and mesmeric phenomena.

NOTES

1. Alexander Ireland, intro. Robert Chambers, *Vestiges of the Natural History of Creation* 13th edn. (W. & R. Chambers: London and Edinburgh, 1884), p. xxi. (Chambers 1884) The publication of this edition following Chambers' death in 1871 marks the first time that the identity of the text's author was verified in public.
2. See L.S. Jacyna, *Philosophical Whigs: Medicine, Science and Citizenship in Edinburgh, 1789–1848* (London: Routledge, 1994). (Jacyna 1994).
3. For accounts of the scientific response to *Vestiges,* see Frank N. Egerton, 'Refutation and Conjecture: Darwin's Response to Sedwick's Attack on Chambers', *Studies in the History and Philosophy of Science* 1 (1870, 176–183). (Egerton 1870) and James Secord, *Victorian Sensation: The Extraordinary Publication, Reception, and Secret Authorship of the 'Vestiges of the Natural History of Creation'* (Chicago and London: University of Chicago Press, 2000). (Secord 2000).
4. Hugh Miller, 'The Physical Science Chair', *Witness* (17 Dec. 1845), 2–3. (Miller 1845).
5. Alexander Ireland, p. xxi.
6. Joanna Wilkes, 'Crowe, Catherine Ann Stevens (1803–1876)', *Oxford Dictionary of National Biography* (Oxford: Oxford University Press, 2004). (Wilkes 2004). See also G.T. Clapton, 'Baudelaire and Catherine Crowe, *Modern Language Review* 25.3 (1930), 286–305. (Clapton 1930).
7. 'Literary and Scientific Society of Edinburgh 1848–1849', *Tait's Edinburgh Magazine* (January 1849), 55. Crowe contributed short stories to *Chambers's Edinburgh Journal* with reasonable frequency in the 1840s, see: 'The Story of Gaspar Mendez' 10 January 1852, 18–22, 'The Lost Portrait' 18 September 1847, 178–183, 'Madame Louise' 5 November 1847, 289–293, 'The Brides Journey' 11 October 1845, 232–237, 'Louis Mandrin' 25 July 1846, 51–54 and 'The Tile-Burner and His Family' 14 February 1846, 99–103.
8. Ireland, p. xxi and see Adam Sedgwick, 'Natural History of Creation', *Edinburgh Review* 82 (1845), 3–4. (Sedgwick 1845) and David Brewster, 'Explanations of Vestiges of the Natural History of Creation', *North British Review* 4 (1846), 503. (Brewster 1846).

9. Steven Shapin, 'Phrenological Knowledge and the Social Structure of Early Nineteenth-Century Edinburgh', *Annals of Science* 32 (1975), 219–243. (Shapin 1975).

10. Richard Yeo, 'Science and Intellectual Authority in Mid-Nineteenth-Century Britain: Robert Chambers and *Vestiges of the Natural History of Creation*', *Victorian Studies* 28.1 (Autumn, 1984) 5–31. (Yeo 1984).

11. Adam Crabtree, *Animal Magnetism, Early Hypnotism and Psychical Research 1766–1925* (New York: Krus International Publications, 1988). (Crabtree 1988) and Alan Gauld, *A History of Hypnotism* (Cambridge: Cambridge University Press, 1992). (Gauld 1992).

12. First developed by a German physician, Franz Anton Mesmer (1774–1815), *magnétisme animal* was the subject of a French Royal Commission in 1784, which found no convincing evidence of the existence of a mysterious magnetic fluid.

13. James Secord, Victorian, *Sensation: The Extraordinary Publication, Reception, and Secret Authorship of the 'Vestiges of the Natural History of Creation'* (Chicago and London: University of Chicago Press, 2000), p. 162. (Secord 2000).

14. A.J.L. Busst, 'Scottish Second Sight: The Rise and Fall of a European Myth', *European Romantic Review* 5.2 (Winter, 1995), 149–177. (Busst 1995).

15. *Blackwood's Edinburgh Magazine* (February 1845), 220.

16. *Night Side,* vol. 1, p. 6.

17. Shane McCorristine, *Spectres of the Self: Thinking about Ghosts and Ghost-seeing in England, 1750–1920.* (Cambridge: Cambridge University Press, 2010), p. 12. (McCorristine 2010).

18. Catherine Crowe, *The Night Side of Nature, Or Ghosts and Ghost-Seers,* 2 Vols. (London: T.C. Newby, 1848), vol. 1, p. 3. (Crowe 1848).

19. Norman Bryson, 'The Gaze of the Expanded Field', in Hal Foster ed., *Vision and Visuality* (Seattle: Bay Press, 1998), p. 91. (Bryson 1998).

20. Fitz-James O'Brien, 'What Was It? A Mystery', *Harper's Monthly* (March 1869), in *Fantastic Tales of Fitz-James O'Brien*, ed. Michael Hayes (London: John Calder, 1977), pp. 55–67 (55). (O'Brien 1977).

21. 'The Night Side of Nature', *Chambers's Edinburgh Journal*, Feb 12 1848, 215 and 'The Night Side of Nature; or Ghosts and Ghost Seers' *The Athenaeum*, 22 January, 1848, 79–80 (79). ('The Night Side . . .' 1848).

22. Ibid., p. 55.

23. O'Brien, p. 55.

24. Ibid., p. 60.

25. Other texts in this tradition include Robert Buchanan's *The Origin and Nature of Ghosts, Demons and Spectral Illusions* (1840), Charles Ollier's

Fallacy of Ghosts, Dreams, and Omens (London, 1848). (Ollier 1848) and John Netten Radcliffe's *Fiends, Ghosts and Sprites* (1854). (Radcliffe 1854).

26. Walter Scott, *Letters on Demonology, addressed to J. G. Lockhart* (London: Murray, 1830, p. 27. (Scott 1830).
27. 'Sketches of Superstitions', *Chambers's Edinburgh Journal* 2 January 1841, 395–398 (395). ('Sketches of Superstitions'. . . 1841).
28. *Night Side,* vol. 1, p. 242 (original italics).
29. See Lorraine Daston, 'Marvelous Facts and Miraculous Evidence in Early Modern Europe', *Critical Inquiry* 1 (Autumn, 1991), 93–124. (Daston 1991).
30. Ibid., p. iv.
31. *Night Side,* vol. 2, pp. 349–350.
32. Ibid., p. 18.
33. *Night Side,* vol. 1, p. 24.
34. 'The Night Side of Nature; or Ghosts and Ghost Seers', *The Athenaeum* (January 1848), 79–80 (79). ('The Night Side . . . 1848).
35. *Night Side,* vol. 1, p. 20.
36. Ibid., p. 57 (my italics).
37. *The Night Side,* vol. 1, p. 61.
38. Ibid. p. 94.
39. Catherine Crowe, 'Mesmerism', *Chambers's Edinburgh Journal* 10 May 1851, 195–198 (196). (Crowe 1851).
40. There are British examples of metaphysical or spiritual readings of mesmerism. See George Bush, *Mesmer and Swedenborg; or, The Relation of the Developments of Mesmerism to the Doctrines and Disclosures of Swedenborg* (New York: John Allen, 1847). (Bush 1847) and J.C. Colquhoun's *A History of Magic, Witchcraft and Animal Magnetism* (1851). (Colquhoun 1851).
41. James Esdaile, *Mesmerism in India and its Practical Application in Surgery and Medicine* (London: Longman, Brown, Green and Longmans, 1847). (Esdaile 1847) and John Elliotson, *Numerous Cases of Surgical Operations without Pain in the Mesmeric State* (London: H. Bailliere, 1843). (Elliotson 1843).
42. 'Cerebral Physiology', *The Zoist* (April 1843), 5–25 (23). ('Cerebral Physiology'. . . 1843).
43. Jennifer Ruth, '"Gross Humbug" or "The Language of Truth"? The Case of the *Zoist*', *Victorian Periodicals Review,* 32.4 (Winter, 1999), 299–323. (Ruth 1999).
44. 'Prospectus', *The Zoist* (April 1843), 1–5 (3). ('Prospectus'. . . 1843).
45. *John Elliotson on Mesmerism,* ed. Fred Kaplan (London: Da Capo Press, 1982), p. 153 (my italics). ('*John Elliotson on* . . .' 1982).
46. Mr. J. Hands, 'Cure of a Case of Supposed Consumption', *Zoist* (January 1850), 295–297 (297). (Hands 1850).

47. William Engledue, *Cerebral Physiology and Materialism, with the result of the application of animal magnetism to the cerebral organs, An address delivered to the phrenological association of London, June 20, 1842,* (London: J Watson, 1842), p. 4. (Engledue 1842).

48. Jennifer Ruth, '"Gross Humbug" or "The Language of Truth"? The Case of the *Zoist*', *Victorian Periodicals Review,* 32.4 (Winter, 1999), 299–323. (Ruth 1999).

49. Barry Barnes and Stephen Shapin, 'Science, Nature and Control: Interpreting Mechanics' Institutes', *Social Studies of Science,* 7.1 (Feb. 1977), 31—74. (Barnes and Shapin 1977).

50. Robert Chambers quoted in Roger Cooter, *The Cultural Meaning of Popular Science: Phrenology and the Organization of Consent in Nineteenth-Century Britain* (Cambridge: Cambridge University Press, 1984), p. 174. (Cooter 1984).

51. Harriet Martineau's (1802–1876) described Combe as being 'the greatest benefactor of his generation, by giving the world his 'Constitution of Man'', 'Representative Men' (1861), p. 578. See also Martineau's portrait of Combe in *Biographical Sketches* (1852–1875).

52. Harriet Martineau, *Letters on Mesmerism* (London: Edward Moxon, 1845), p. 48 (Martineau 1848). These were originally printed a series of letters to the *Athenaeum* in 1844, which positioned the at the centre of a fractious and long-running dialogue over the nature, morality and reality of this invisible yet pervasive force.

53. Karl Bell, *The Magical Imagination: Magic and Modernity in Urban England 1780–1914* (Cambridge: Cambridge University Press, 2012), p. 151. (Bell 2012).

54. 'The Night Side of Nature', *Athenaeum* 22 January 1848, 79. ('The Night Side of…' 1848).

55. Joseph Hands, 'Mesmeric Cure of a Case', *Zoist* (January 1848), 328–343 (343). (Hands 1848).

56. Srdjan Smajic, *Ghost-Seers, Detectives and Spiritualists: Theories of Vision in Victorian Literature and Science* (Cambridge University Press, 2010), p. 47. (Smajic 2010).

57. 'The Double-Sighted Phenomenon', *Derby Mercury* 7 December 1831. ('The Double-Sighted…' 1831).

58. Richard Daniel Altick, *The Shows of London* (Cambridge M.A: Harvard University Press, 1978), pp. 250–251. (Daniel 1978).

59. Peter Lamont also discussed Master McKean at the Egyptian Hall in *Extraordinary Beliefs: A Historical Approach to a Psychological Problem* (Cambridge: Cambridge University Press, 2013). (Lamont 2013).

60. Duncan Campbell (1680–1730). He arrived in London in around 1694, where he courted the attentions of fashionable society through fortune

telling and displays of second sight. An account of his life *Secret Memoirs of the Late Mr. Duncan Campbell* appeared in 1732 and has been attributed to Daniel Defoe.

61. 'The Double-Sighted Phenomenon', *Derby Mercury* 7 December 1831. ('The Double-Sighted . . . ' 1831).
62. Egyptian Hall Advertisement, BL. Evans. 2501.
63. Ibid.
64. Peter Lamont, *Extraordinary Beliefs: A Historical Approach to a Psychological Problem* (Cambridge: Cambridge University Press, 2013), pp. 103–104. (Lamont 2013).
65. Ibid., p. 108.
66. 'Scottish Second Sight', *Blackwood's Edinburgh Magazine* (August 1840) 277. ('Scottish Second . . . ' 1840).
67. 'Magic and Mesmerism', *Tait's Edinburgh Journal* (October 1843), 179. ('Magic and Mesmerism' . . . 1843).
68. Penny Fielding, *Scotland and the Fictions of Geography: North Britain, 1760–1830* (Cambridge: Cambridge University Press, 2008), p. 187. (Fielding 2008).
69. 'The Second-Sight of Mr. John Bobells', *Chamber's Edinburgh Journal* 8 December 1860, 364–366. ('The Second-Sight of . . . ' 1860).
70. The Highland Line' refers to a geographical boundary fault running from Helensburgh in the south-west to Stonehaven in the north-east and this topographical feature also served as a metaphor for cultural, political, religious and linguistic divisions.
71. George Combe, *A System of Phrenology* (New York: William H. Colyer, 1842), pp. 37–38. (Combe 1842).
72. *System of Phrenology,* pp. 321–322.
73. Colin Kidd 'Race, Empire, and the Limits of Scottish Nationhood', *The Historical Journal* 46.4 (Dec. 2003), 873–892 (883). (Kidd 2003).
74. Knox's polygenist position on race—a theory that sees the human race as having descended from different lineages—was undertaken against the grain of the monogenist thinking—which, in line with orthodox Christianity, posits a common descent for all peoples—as supported by The Ethnological Society of London and espoused by figures like the historian Thomas Hodgkin and the ethnologist James Cowles Prichard.
75. Robert Knox, *The Races of Man: A Fragment* (London: Henry Renshaw, 1850), p. 379 and 378. (Knox 1850).
76. Ibid., p. 216.
77. Ibid., p. 378 and Krisztina Fenyo, *Contempt, Sympathy and Romance: Lowland Perceptions of the Highlands and the Clearances During the Famine Years, 1845–1855* (Edinburgh: Tuckwell Press, 2006). (Fenyo 2006).

78. *System of Phrenology*, pp. 320–321.
79. *The Night Side*, vol. 2, p. 328 and George Combe, *The Constitution of Man, Considered in Relation to External Objects* (Boston: Marsh, Caen, Lyon and Webb, 1841), p. 54. (Combe 1841).
80. W. D. King, '"Shadow of a Mesmeriser": The Female Body on the "Dark" Stage', *Theatre Journal* 49.2 (May, 1997), 189–206 (193). (King 1997).
81. Altick, p. 276.
82. Charles Dickens quoted in Barbara Kirshenblatt-Gimblett, *Destination Culture: Tourism, Museums, and Heritage* (Berkley, CA: University of California Press, 1998), pp. 45–47. (Kirshenblatt-Gimblett 1998).
83. The Double-Sighted Phenomenon', *Derby Mercury,* 7 December 1831. (The Double-Sighted . . .' 1831).
84. Master McKean appears as the defendant in an assault case two years later. As is reported by the 'London Police' correspondent to *The Belfast News-Letter* 9 April 1833, the boy, now named as 'Thomas', under charge at the 'Bow Street Office' was induced to perform a feat of second sight for a Mr. Halls.
85. 'Sights of London', *The Literary Gazette* (July 1832) 446. ('Sights of London' . . . 1832), 'Fashionable Lounges', *The Theatrical Observer* (June 1832), 1–2 (2). ('Fashionable Lounges' . . . 1832).
86. Mark O'Gorman, 'A Conversation with the Double-Sighted Youth of the Egyptian Hall', *Monthly Magazine* (May 1832), 577–583 (577). (O'Gorman 1832).
87. Ibid., 582.
88. Stuart J. Brown, 'Irving, Edward (1793–1834)' *Oxford Dictionary of National Biography* (Oxford: Oxford University Press, 2004). (Brown 2004).
89. William Hazlitt, *The Spirit of the Age, or Contemporary Portraits* (London: Henry Colburn, 1825), p. 83. (Hazlitt 1825).
90. Ibid., p. 87.
91. Ibid., p. 93.
92. Hugh Miller, 'The Physical Science Chair', *Witness* (17 Dec. 1845), 2–3. See also Miller's riposte to *Vestiges,* his *The Footprints of the Creator* (1849) which argued that as the fossil record revealed the co-existence of simple and complex forms, the theory of transmutation was intrinsically flawed. Instead, Miller argued that the progress of man and all other species reveals the direct intervention of a benevolent creator.
93. Hugh Miller, *Scenes and Legends of the North of Scotland; or, The Traditional History of Cromarty* (London: Johnson and Hunter, 1834), p. 458. (Miller 1834).
94. Miller, *Scenes and Legends,* p. 160.
95. See Patrick Bayne, *The Life and Letters of Hugh Miller* (London: Stahan & Co, 1971). (Bayne 1971).

96. J. F. C. Harrison, *The Second Coming: Popular Millenarism 1780–1850* (London: Taylor and Francis, 1979), p. 208. (Harrison 1979).

97. David Bebbington, *Religious Revivals: Culture and Piety in Local and Global Contexts* (Oxford and London: Oxford University Press, 2012), pp. 4–5. (Bebbington 2012).

98. Margaret Oliphant, *The Life of Edward Irving* 2 vols. (London: Hurst and Blackett, 1862). (Oliphant 1862).

99. 'Extraordinary Scene in the Scotch Church', *The Morning Post,* 19 October 1831. ('Extraordinary Scene . . .' 1831).

100. Ibid.

101. The Rev, Edward Irving and the Un-Known Tongue', *The Standard* 25 October 1831.

102. Diana Basham, *The Trial of Woman: Feminism and the Occult Sciences in Victorian Literature and Society* (London: MacMillan, 1992), p. 419 (original italics). (Basham 1992).

103. See Barbara Taylor, *Eve and the New Jerusalem: Socialism and Feminism in the Nineteenth Century* (London: Virago, 1983). (Taylor 1983).

104. 'Mesmerism', *The Spectator,* 10 June 1843 ('Mesmerism' 1843).

105. Ann Taves, *Fits, Trances and Visions: Experiencing Religion and Explaining Experience from Wesley to James* (Princeton NJ: Princeton University Press, 1999). (Taves 1999).

106. John Elliotson, *Human Physiology* (London: Longmans, 1835) pp. 663–664. (Elliotson 1835).

107. Rhodri Hayward, 'Policing Dreams: History and the Moral Uses of the Unconscious', *History Workshop Journal,* 29 (2000), 143–160 (145, 146). (Hayward 2000).

108. Justinus Kerner, *The Seeress of Prevorst being revelations concerning the inner-life of man, and the inter-diffusion of a world of spirits in the one we inhabit* communicated by Justinus Kerner and translated from the German by Catherine Crowe (London: J. C. Moore, 1845), p. 57. (Kerner 1845).

109. Crowe provides the first English translation in 1845, but there is evidence that the text was read and reviewed in Britain before this date. In 1836 for example, a review describes it as the ideal book for those of a 'nervous and ghostly turn of mind like ourselves; a tendency which we attribute to an early course of Miss. Radcliffe's romances', 'The Devils Doings, or Warm Work in Wittenberg', *Blackwood's Edinburgh Magazine* (1836).

110. *Night Side of Nature,* vol. 2, p. 334.

111. Ibid., p. 53.

112. *Night Side of Nature,* vol. 1, p. 34.

113. *Night Side of Nature,* vol. 1, p. 60.

114. 17 August 1847, Hans Christian Andersen, *Dagbøger 1845–1850* (Copenhagen: G.E.C. Gads Forlag, 1974). (Andersen 1974).

115. *Night Side of Nature,* vol. 1, p. 54.

116. Richard Liston, Elliotson's former colleague gloated: "Rejoice! Mesmerism, and its professors, have met with a heavy blow and great discouragement. An American dentist has used ether (inhalation of it) to destroy sensation in his operations, and the plan has succeeded ...' *Zoist,* (July 1848), 210–211.

117. The full title illuminates this, it reads: *The Celestial Telegraph; or, Secrets of the Life to Come, revealed through Magnetism; wherein the existence, the form, and the occupations of the soul after its separation from the body are proved by many years' experiments, by the means of Eight Ecstatic Somnambulists, who had eighty perceptions of thirty-six deceased persons of various conditions: a description of them, their conversation, etc., with proofs of their existence in the spiritual world* (London: Arno Press, 1850).

118. Samuel Brown to Robert Chambers, 22 May 1853, Geoffrey Larken Collection, University of Kent UKC-CROWEBIO.F191889.

119. Mrs. Hayden or Maria Hayden was one of the first American spirit mediums to arrive in Britain See Katherine H. Porter, *Though a Glass Darkly: Spiritualism in the Browning Circle* (Kansas: University of Kansas Press, 1958). (Porter 1958) for a discussion of Maria Hayden's impact on British literary society and in particular, her influence upon the poet Elizabeth Barrett Browning.

120. Logie Barrow, *Independent Spirits: Spiritualism and English Plebeians, 1850–1910* (London: Routledge, 1986). (Barrow 1986).

121. Catherine Crowe, *Spiritualism and the Age We Live In* (London: T.C. Newby, 1859), p. 136. (Crowe 1859).

122. Graham Storey (Oxford: Oxford University Press, 1993), pp. 285–286. (Storey 1993).

123. Marion Evans to George Combe 9 March 1854, UKC-CROWEBIO. F191889 Geoffrey Larken Collection, University of Kent, Robert Chambers to Alexander Ireland, 4 March 1854, W&R Chambers Papers NLS Dep/341/112/115–116 and Charles Dickens to Emile de la Rue 9 March 1854, *The Letters of Charles Dickens: 1853–1855,* ed. Graham Storey (Oxford: Oxford University Press, 1993), pp. 285–286.

124. Dr. John Conolly to George Combe 2 April 1854, UKC-CROWEBIO. F191889 Geoffrey Larken Collection, University of Kent.

125. For an account of Dr. Conolly see Andrew Scull, *The Most Solitary of Afflictions: Madness and Society in Britain, 1700–1900* (New Haven: Yale University Press, 1993). (Scull 1993).

126. John Elliotson, 'More Insanity from Spirit-Rapping Fancies', *Zoist* (July 1854), 175. (Elliotson 1854).

127. Catherine Crowe to John Elliotson, *Zoist* (July 1854), 177.

128. Dr. R. R. Madden, *Mesmerism and Clairvoyance,* Wellcome Trust Library MS/75831.

129. Lewis Spence, 'Elliotson, John (1791–1868)', *Encyclopedia of Occultism and Parapsychology* (Montana, Kessinger, 2003). (Spence 2003).
130. *Spiritualism and the Age We Live In*, p. 119.
131. Ibid., p. 7.
132. Thomas Carlyle to Lady Ashburton 28 June (1848), *The Carlyle Letters Online* [*CLO*], ed. Brent E. Kinser, Duke University Press, 14 September 2007, accessed 18 September 2013 (original italics).
133. A.J.L. Busst, 'Scottish Second Sight: The Rise and Fall of a European Myth', *European Romantic Review* 5.2 (1995), 149–175 (167–168, 169). (Busst 1995).
134. Lorraine Datson and Katherine Park, *Wonders and the Order of Nature, 1150–1750* (New York: Zone Press, 1998). (Datson and Park 1998).

REFERENCES

Altick, Richard Daniel, *The Shows of London* (Cambridge, MA: Harvard University Press, 1978), pp. 250–1.

Andersen, Hans Christian, *Dagbøger 1845–1850* (Copenhagen: G.E.C. Gads Forlag, 1974).

Barnes, Barry, and Stephen Shapin, 'Science, Nature and Control: Interpreting Mechanics' Institutes', *Social Studies of Science*, 7.1 (February 1977), 31–74.

Barrow, Logie, *Independent Spirits: Spiritualism and English Plebeians, 1850–1910* (London: Routledge, 1986).

Basham, Diana, 'The Trial of Woman: Feminism and the Occult Sciences', in *Victorian Literature and Society* (London: Macmillan, 1992).

Bayne, Patrick, *The Life and Letters of Hugh Miller* (London: Stahan & Co., 1971).

Bebbington, David, *Religious Revivals: Culture and Piety in Local and Global Contexts* (Oxford and London: Oxford University Press, 2012).

Bell, Karl, *The Magical Imagination: Magic and Modernity in Urban England 1780–1914* (Cambridge: Cambridge University Press, 2012).

Brewster, David, 'Explanations of Vestiges of the Natural History of Creation', *North British Review* 4 (1846), 503.

Brown, Stuart J., 'Irving, Edward (1793–1834)', in *Oxford Dictionary of National Biography* (Oxford: Oxford University Press, 2004).

Bryson, Norman, 'The Gaze of the Expanded Field', in *Vision and Visuality*, ed. Hal Foster (Seattle, WA: Bay Press, 1998), p. 91.

Bush, George, *Mesmer and Swedenborg; or, The Relation of the Developments of Mesmerism to the Doctrines and Disclosures of Swedenborg* (New York: John Allen, 1847).

Busst, A.J.L., 'Scottish Second Sight: The Rise and Fall of a European Myth', *European Romantic Review* 5.2 (Winter 1995), 149–77 (167–8, 169).

'Catherine Crowe to John Elliotson', *Zoist* (July 1854), 177.

'Cerebral Physiology', *The Zoist* (April 1843), 5–25 (23).

Clapton, G.T., 'Baudelaire and Catherine Crowe', *Modern Language Review* 25.3 (1930), 286–305.

Colquhoun, J.C., *A History of Magic, Witchcraft and Animal Magnetism* (London: Longman, Brown and Green, 1851).

Combe, George, *The Constitution of Man, Considered in Relation to External Objects* (Boston: Marsh, Caen, Lyon and Webb, 1841).

Combe, George, *A System of Phrenology* (New York: William H. Colyer, 1842).

Crabtree, Adam, *Animal Magnetism, Early Hypnotism and Psychical Research 1766–1925* (New York: Krus International Publications, 1988).

Crowe, Catherine, 'Mesmerism', *Chambers's Edinburgh Journal* (10 May 1851), 195–8.

Crowe, Catherine, *The Night Side of Nature, Or Ghosts and Ghost-Seers*, 2 vols (London: T.C. Newby, 1848), vol. 1, p. 3.

Crowe, Catherine, *Spiritualism and the Age We Live In* (London: T.C. Newby, 1859), p. 136.

Daston, Lorraine, 'Marvelous Facts and Miraculous Evidence in Early Modern Europe', *Critical Inquiry* 1 (Autumn 1991), 93–124.

Datson, Lorraine, and Katherine Park, *Wonders and the Order of Nature, 1150–1750* (New York: Zone Press, 1998).

'The Double-Sighted Phenomenon', *Derby Mercury* (7 December 1831).

Egerton, Frank N., 'Refutation and Conjecture: Darwin's Response to Sedgwick's Attack on Chambers', *Studies in the History and Philosophy of Science* 1 (1870), 176–83.

Elliotson, John, *Human Physiology* (London: Longmans, 1835), pp. 663–4.

Elliotson, John, *John Elliotson on Mesmerism*, ed. Fred Kaplan (London: Da Capo Press, 1982).

Elliotson, John, 'More Insanity from Spirit-Rapping Fancies', *The Zoist* (July 1854), 175.

Elliotson, John, *Numerous Cases of Surgical Operations without Pain in the Mesmeric State* (London: H. Bailliere, 1843).

Engledue, William, *Cerebral Physiology and Materialism, with the Result of the Application of Animal Magnetism to the Cerebral Organs, An Address Delivered to the Phrenological Association of London, June 20, 1842* (London: J. Watson, 1842), p. 4.

Esdaile, James, *Mesmerism in India and its Practical Application in Surgery and Medicine* (London: Longman, Brown, Green and Longmans, 1847).

'Extraordinary Scene in the Scotch Church', *The Morning Post* (19 October 1831).

'Fashionable Lounges', *The Theatrical Observer* (June 1832), 1–2 (2).

Fenyo, Krisztina, *Contempt, Sympathy and Romance: Lowland Perceptions of the Highlands and the Clearances During the Famine Years, 1845–1855* (Edinburgh: Tuckwell Press, 2006).

Fielding, Penny, *Scotland and the Fictions of Geography: North Britain, 1760–1830* (Cambridge: Cambridge University Press, 2008).

Gauld, Alan, *A History of Hypnotism* (Cambridge: Cambridge University Press, 1992).

Hands, Joseph, 'Mesmeric Cure of a Case', *The Zoist* (January 1848), 328–43.

Hands, Mr. J., 'Cure of a Case of Supposed Consumption', *The Zoist* (January 1850), 295–7.

Harrison, J.F.C., *The Second Coming: Popular Millenarism 1780–1850* (London: Taylor and Francis, 1979).

Hayward, Rhodri, 'Policing Dreams: History and the Moral Uses of the Unconscious', *History Workshop Journal* 29 (2000), 143–60.

Hazlitt, William, *The Spirit of the Age, or Contemporary Portraits* (London: Henry Colburn, 1825).

Ireland, Alexander, and Robert Chambers, *Vestiges of the Natural History of Creation*, 13th edn (London and Edinburgh: W. & R. Chambers, 1884), p. xxi.

Jacyna, L.S., *Philosophical Whigs: Medicine, Science and Citizenship in Edinburgh, 1789–1848* (London: Routledge, 1994).

Kerner, Justinus, *The Seeress of Prevorst Being Revelations Concerning the Inner-life of Man, and the Inter-diffusion of a World of Spirits in the One we Inhabit* communicated by Justinus Kerner and translated from the German by Catherine Crowe (London: J.C. Moore, 1845).

Kidd, Colin, 'Race, Empire, and the Limits of Scottish Nationhood', *The Historical Journal* 46.4 (December 2003), 873–92.

King, W.D., '"Shadow of a Mesmeriser": The Female Body on the "Dark" Stage', *Theatre Journal* 49.2 (May 1997), 189–206 (193).

Kirshenblatt-Gimblett, Barbara, *Destination Culture: Tourism, Museums, and Heritage* (Berkeley: University of California Press, 1998), pp. 45–7.

Knox, Robert, *The Races of Man: A Fragment* (London: Henry Renshaw, 1850).

Lamont, Peter, *Extraordinary Beliefs: A Historical Approach to a Psychological Problem* (Cambridge: Cambridge University Press, 2013).

'Magic and Mesmerism', *Tait's Edinburgh Journal* (October 1843).

Martineau, Harriet, *Letters on Mesmerism* (London: Edward Moxon, 1845).

McCorristine, Shane, *Spectres of the Self: Thinking about Ghosts and Ghost-Seeing in England, 1750–1920* (Cambridge: Cambridge University Press, 2010).

'Mesmerism', *The Spectator* (10 June 1843).

Miller, Hugh, 'The Physical Science Chair', *Witness* (17 December 1845), 2–3.

Miller, Hugh, *Scenes and Legends of the North of Scotland; or, The Traditional History of Cromarty* (London: Johnson and Hunter, 1834).

'The Night Side of Nature', *Chambers's Edinburgh Journal* (12 February 1848), 215.

'The Night Side of Nature; or Ghosts and Ghost Seers', *The Athenaeum* (January 1848), 79–80.

O'Brien, Fitz-James, 'What Was It? A Mystery', *Harper's Monthly* (March 1869), in *Fantastic Tales of Fitz-James O'Brien*, ed. Michael Hayes (London: John Calder, 1977), pp. 55–67.

O'Gorman, Mark, 'A Conversation with the Double-Sighted Youth of the Egyptian Hall', *Monthly Magazine* (May 1832), 577–83.

Oliphant, Margaret, *The Life of Edward Irving*, 2 vols (London: Hurst and Blackett, 1862).

Ollier, Charles, *Fallacy of Ghosts, Dreams, and Omens* (London: Charles Ollier, 1848).

Porter, Katherine H., *Through a Glass Darkly: Spiritualism in the Browning Circle* (Kansas: University of Kansas Press, 1958).

'Prospectus', *The Zoist* (April 1843), 1–5.

Radcliffe, John Netten, *Fiends, Ghosts and Sprites* (1854).

'The Rev Edward Irving and the Un-Known Tongue', *The Standard* (25 October 1831).

Roger Cooter, *The Cultural Meaning of Popular Science: Phrenology and the Organization of Consent in Nineteenth-Century Britain* (Cambridge: Cambridge University Press, 1984).

Ruth, Jennifer, '"Gross Humbug" or "The Language of Truth"? The Case of the *Zoist*', *Victorian Periodicals Review* 32.4 (Winter 1999), 299–323.

Scott, Walter, *Letters on Demonology, addressed to J. G. Lockhart* (London: Murray, 1830).

'Scottish Second Sight', *Blackwood's Edinburgh Magazine* (August 1840), 277.

Scull, Andrew, *The Most Solitary of Afflictions: Madness and Society in Britain, 1700–1900* (New Haven, CT: Yale University Press, 1993).

'*The Second-Sight of Mr. John Bobells*', *Chamber's Edinburgh Journal* (8 December 1860), 364–6.

Secord, James, *Victorian Sensation: The Extraordinary Publication, Reception, and Secret Authorship of the 'Vestiges of the Natural History of Creation'* (Chicago and London: University of Chicago Press, 2000).

Sedgwick, Adam, 'Natural History of Creation', *Edinburgh Review* 82 (1845), 3–4.

Shapin, Steven, 'Phrenological Knowledge and the Social Structure of Early Nineteenth-Century Edinburgh', *Annals of Science* 32 (1975), 219–43.

'Sights of London', *The Literary Gazette* (July 1832), 446.

'Sketches of Superstitions', *Chambers's Edinburgh Journal* (2 January 1841), 395–8.

Smajic, Srdjan, *Ghost-Seers, Detectives and Spiritualists: Theories of Vision in Victorian Literature and Science* (Cambridge: Cambridge University Press, 2010).

Spence, Lewis, *Encyclopedia of Occultism and Parapsychology* (Whitefish, MT: Kessinger, 2003).

Storey, Graham ed., *The Letters of Charles Dickens: 1853–1855* (Oxford: Oxford University Press, 1993).

Taves, Ann, *Fits, Trances and Visions: Experiencing Religion and Explaining Experience from Wesley to James* (Princeton, NJ: Princeton University Press, 1999).

Taylor, Barbara, *Eve and the New Jerusalem: Socialism and Feminism in the Nineteenth Century* (London: Virago, 1983).

Thomas Carlyle to Lady Ashburton, 28 June 1848, *The Carlyle Letters Online* [*CLO*], ed. Brent E. Kinser and Duke University Press (14 September 2007), accessed 18 September 2013.

Wilkes, Joanna, 'Crowe, Catherine Ann Stevens (1803–1876)', in *Oxford Dictionary of National Biography* (Oxford: Oxford University Press, 2004).

Yeo, Richard, 'Science and Intellectual Authority in Mid-Nineteenth-Century Britain: Robert Chambers and *Vestiges of the Natural History of Creation*', *Victorian Studies* 28.1 (Autumn 1984), 5–31.

CHAPTER 4

Primitive Spiritualism and Origin Stories

During the long sea voyage from England to Australia in 1852, William Howitt dreamed of the house towards which he was slowly journeying, an attractive property surrounded by a 'wood of dusky-foliaged trees'. Arriving in Melbourne weeks later, he was stunned to find the minutest details of the dream realised: the house 'stands exactly as I saw it, only looking newer; over the wall of the garden, is the wood, precisely as I saw it'.[1] In a letter to the *Spiritual Magazine* in October 1871, Howitt recalled how this prevision, in addition to revealing his brother's home to him for the first time, also conveyed practical information regarding the specifics of the unemployment problem they would encounter on disembarking far more accurate than 'news received before leaving England'.[2] Precise knowledge of the labour market—conveyed by dream or via more orthodox methods—was of particular value to Howitt, whose lengthy journey had been necessitated by pecuniary troubles at home. The expedition was prompted by a failed publishing venture, *Howitt's Journal of Literature and Popular Progress*, which had survived for barely a year and left the family in a precarious financial position. Aimed at a working-class demographic, with fiction by writers such as Elizabeth Gaskell printed alongside articles espousing political reform, this short-lived journal reflected the varied interests of one of the nineteenth century's most prolific literary couples.[3] Hailing from Quaker families and married in 1821, William and Mary Howitt published works of poetry, travel guides,

© The Author(s) 2017
E. Richardson, *Second Sight in the Nineteenth Century*,
Palgrave Studies in Literature, Science and Medicine,
DOI 10.1057/978-1-137-51970-2_4

histories and translations, as well as making regular contributions to *Household Words* and *Tait's Edinburgh Magazine*.[4] In 1848, following a dispute with a former business partner and the collapse of their journal, the Howitt family were forced to declare bankruptcy and take lodgings in a less salubrious area of St John's Wood. Now £4000 in debt and all too aware of the unreliability of writing work, Howitt and two of his sons, Alfred and Charlton, set out to seek the family's fortune in the goldfields of South East Australia.

In 1854 the family returned to England with very little in the way of gold, but many stories and observations. From notes and letters written during the trip, Howitt published two comprehensive accounts of public life in Britain's furthest colony: *Land, Labour and Gold; or, Two Years in Victoria* (1855) and *The History of Discovery in Australia, Tasmania and New Zealand* (1865). These works imparted engaging accounts of colonial life, detailing the dangers one might encounter, the beauty of the landscape, the difficulties presented by the harsh climate, the demography of the settlements and their troubled engagement with native peoples. Novels inspired by the expedition, *A Boy's Adventure in the Wilds of Australia* (1854) and *Tallangetta, the Squatter's Home, a Story of Australian Life* (1857), were rich in minute local detail, promising insights into isolated regions where neither 'white man nor the black had ever come'.[5] As fact and fiction, these works spoke to the conditions of an expanding imperial mission that saw the British Empire push into Australia, New Zealand and Oceania. The family's courageous fortune-seeking, documented in ethnographic surveys and robust adventure fictions, could be knitted easily into a triumphalist narrative of colonial expansion. William Howitt was, however, far from an unthinking champion of the Empire. A zealous reformer who took up campaigns against alcohol, vivisection, game and poor laws, he was also a passionate anti-imperialist who warned against the corrupting sins of imperialism. Prior to the gold trail adventure, he published *Colonisation and Christianity* (1838), which examined the 'treatment of natives by the Europeans' and sought to expose centuries of 'crimes and marvellous impolicy' toward the 'unlettered nations'.[6] Further, though his Australian writings traded imaginatively in wild spaces and tropes of masculine self-discovery, they also lit upon matters not usually documented as part of the colonial experience. As his sea-bound prophecy indicates to some extent, his account of overseas exploration also trafficked in the unexplained and the seemingly supernatural.

In the preface to *Tallangetta*, a realist novel set in a makeshift community of gold miners, Howitt was forced to defend the presence of two seemingly incongruous characters: Dr Woolstan, a recent spiritualist convert, and Mr Flavel, a seer with the gift of second sight. Their inclusion was, the author explained, a reflection of his own experiences in the outback, where he was first introduced to the miraculous phenomenon of modern spiritualism. This movement had since instituted a remarkable network of cultural exchange, exemplified by an 'Australian spiritualist in London' who is now 'astonishing daily circles of the most intelligent and unsuperstitious classes'.[7] Published three years after the family had returned from their failed fortune-seeking trip, *Tallangetta* reflects upon the geographical and temporal dimensions of its author's own spiritualist awakening. Arriving home to London, Howitt had found the capital absorbed by the strange goings on of the seance: furniture levitated, musical instruments played untouched, entranced women spoke with the tongues of famous dead men and clairvoyants described journeys to far-off realms. Originating in upstate New York and popularised in Britain by American mediums such as Mrs Hayden, the movement grew through the transatlantic exchange of individuals, texts and transcribed visions of the 'Summerland'.[8] Initially taking the form of slowly rotating tables and unexplained rappings, spirit communications were later realised by slate writing, trance mediumship and, eventually, full-form materialisation.[9] Though international in its scope, spiritualist practice was constituted primarily through experimentation undertaken in private residences, where believers uncovered talented mediums in the midst of their own familial and social groups. This non-hierarchical structure, under which any member of the circle could become the locus of spirit communications, appealed to the self-improving and politically radical working classes from which a significant percentage of membership was drawn. Intersecting with strains of secularism, Christian Socialism, Owenism, Millennialism, temperance and the remnants of Chartism, the doctrine of 'Universal Love' preached by the movement promised religion without the elitism of the Church and the means to connect progressive social action to spiritual development.

Having left the Society of Friends in 1847, William and Mary Howitt lent the reformist zeal of their former Quakerism to furthering the cause of modern spiritualism in Britain. This conversion story resonates in *Tallangetta* when Dr Woolstan, the camp's stolidly rational physician, finds himself in possession of remarkable mediumistic gifts. For the doctor the revelation that he is able to contact the spirits of the dead precipitates something of an intellectual crisis, but he is helped toward an understanding of this ability by another prospector, Mr Flavel. The doctor's confidant has visionary powers of his own, divinatory skills that are described as a kind of 'inheritance'. He comes from a family in which 'there runs a peculiarity which, ever and anon, in the course of ages, shows itself in a species of second-sight'.[10] In the Dunellens, the 'ancient barony' from which Flavel hails, the second sighted perceive not only 'phantasmal pictures of coming events', but they are also 'aware of the spirits of the dead and hold communication with them, as with their living friends'.[11] Through *Tallangetta* the power of second sight is written into a kind of spiritualist *Bildungsroman*, where it functions as an established precursor to the nascent methods of extraterrestrial communication being uncovered by modern mediums. The uncanny lineage Howitt traced here between the concerns of spiritualism and the legacies of second sight produced, among other things, an altered relationship with the dead. While there had long existed a spectrum of ghosts associated with the possession of second sight—ranging from a *tannasg*, the apparition of one already dead, to a *tamhasg*, a spectre of the living, a *taslach*, whose presence is only aurally perceptible, and a *tartan*, the ghost of an unbaptised child—these were commonly interpreted as harbingers of death or enforcers of metaphysical justice. The assumption that such spectres might be open to friendly interaction developed only with the rise of spiritualism; or as Owen Davies comments, before this 'the main reason for wishing to encounter the dead was in order to banish them rather than seek their spiritual guidance'.[12] From the mid-nineteenth century, the second-sight tradition was taken up and transformed by the discursive power of this new ghost-seeing culture.

The line of transmission pursued in *Tallangetta* sees Mr Flavel travel from the old world to the new, carrying with him an ancient power that makes itself felt on the very edge of empire, while Dr Woolstan's awakening in the wilds of Australia posits an affinity between colonial and spiritualist adventure. In the book's preface Howitt reflects on the early days of the spiritualist movement and marvels that practice had become so entrenched in the humdrum of everyday life that within many families 'daily conversation with the spirits of their departed friends' go on as 'regularly with those still incarnate'.[13] The metaphorical resonance of what is literalised here—the possibility of direct contact with the spirits of the dead—is also put to work in describing the exchange between

Britain and her colonies.[14] Using Victoria as an example of what we are assured is a universal truth, we are reminded that the remote colony has a population composed of the 'overflowings of England' and that these 'overflowings have carried with them every possible theory and practice, every idea, feeling, passion, speculation, pursuit and imagination which are fermenting in the old countries'.[15] This paralleling of domestic and colonial concerns, elsewhere reflected in Howitt's premonitory dream, evoked the sympathetic ties forged between individuals as a grid system of affective transmission, linking the traditions of home with foreign concerns. As historians such as Pamela Thurshwell and Richard J. Noakes have commented, this imagined network drew on intersecting occult and technological modes of contact; while the British public, Noakes writes, 'grappled with mysterious spiritual communications', the new 'telegraph companies told them it was possible to use electricity to contact friends on earth'.[16] The reappearance of the fabled second sight in the wilds of the Australian outback, however, speaks to possibilities beyond the technological, to forms of communication more closely tied to ideas of embodiment, heredity and race.

Much critical attention has already been paid to Victorian spiritualism: it has been read as a site of working-class protest, as a vehicle for radical gender politics, an alternative to narratives of secularisation or disenchantment and a form of proto-modernist aesthetics.[17] Less has been said, however, of the movement's interaction with popular theories of evolution and scientific disciplines such as anthropology. Important exceptions to this include Janet Oppenheim's *The Other World: Spiritualism and Psychical Research in England, 1850–1914* (1985) and, more recently, Christine Ferguson's work on the shared ideological spaces of spiritualism and early eugenics. Building on these readings, this chapter will attend to the ways in which spiritualism, along with other iterations of popular Darwinism, approached the power of prevision as a signifier of both advancement and regression, civilisation and savagery, race and nationhood. In common with Ferguson, this line of argument presses the connections between discourses of racial and spiritual health partly as a means to challenge the 'wishful critical thinking' that has seen spiritualists praised by modern historians as evincing 'morality far in advance of their age', where in fact the seance tended to reproduce established hierarchies more often than it transgressed them.[18] This chapter plots the 'golden age of spiritualism' alongside the institutional and popular beginnings of modern anthropology, an intellectual tradition that transformed tales of exotic tribes and customs, superstitions, ghosts and myth into schematic visions of human development.[19] Cultivated in new institutional contexts like the Anthropological Institute and the Folklore Society, and explicated by texts such as Charles Darwin's *The Descent of Man* (1871) and John Lubbock's *The Origin of Civilisation* (1870), the theory of evolutionary gradualism and natural causation transformed the intellectual landscape of the period. Transacted outside biology, the metaphoric expansiveness of this theory gave over an account of social development that plotted the world's cultures and their peoples, past and present, along a scale from primitive to civilised. Spiritualist belief, like second sight and other superstitions, was frequently conceived of as akin to the primitive religion and magic practised by peoples at the imperial margin, a rebuke that located the credulous both temporally and geographically elsewhere to the privileged cultural space occupied by their home nation. Yet the habitual cross-articulation of spiritualist and anthropological concepts, during a period of rapid professionalisation and popularisation, suggests a more complicated picture.

The description, given by the naturalist Alfred Russel Wallace in a letter to Thomas H. Huxley, of spiritualism as a 'new branch of Anthropology' best captures the ambiguities informing this analysis. Building on the ambivalence of Wallace's phrasing, where it is unclear whether spiritualism is being promoted as a subject for anthropologists or as a new method of anthropological investigation, it is possible to make legible the proximity shared by occult and scientific epistemologies.[20] Rather than reject the theoretical basis of cultural evolutionism, spiritualists appropriated its language to produce alternative readings that divorced ideas of human progress from materialist goals. Victorian proponents of spirit communication sought not only to establish the afterlife as a material and quantifiable reality, but they also drew from biological models of species development and cultural evolution to describe its scientific significance. As one believer termed it, spiritualism is a form of 'transcendental anthropology' that extends the study of evolution beyond the death of the body.[21] In dedicated journals, newspapers and books, believers took up the lexicon of evolutionism to debate the progression of the spirit after death and the developmental significance of the extraordinary powers of perception being unearthed by the seance. These discussions took place in publications such as *Human Nature: A Monthly Journal of Zoistic Science, Intelligence and Popular Anthropology* and *Light: A Journal Devoted to the Highest*

Interests of Humanity Both Here and Hereafter, journals that featured articles such as 'Evolution, Agnosticism, and Spiritualism', 'Hereditary Genius' and 'Origin of the First Man'. Evolutionary thinking appeared in many guises, under a range of disciplinary headings, and remained open to multiple, conflicting interpretations; and the application of this theory by spiritualist believers should not be read as simply a distortion of scientific knowledge to occult ends. Rather, anthropology was constituted in remarkably close contiguity to the ghostly emanations of the seance; this was observable at the level of both the individual, who might work in opposition to or in collusion with spiritualist thinking, and beyond to the practices, techniques and theoretical structures undergirding their disciplinary formations.

This chapter thinks about how the second-sight tradition began to be pressed, by evolutionist thinking in various guises, as a type of inheritance: whether written into the biographies of famous mediums, as an example of where civilisation has progressed from and might journey to, or as a part of a living archaeology uncovered in the remote regions of Britain and the Empire. This argument is made through separate but informing lines of enquiry. One details how second sight came to be written into both anthropological treatises and supernatural histories; another assesses the impact of popular evolutionism, as expressed in scientific and spiritualist accounts, on the concept of an indigenous tradition; and finally, attention is paid to the positioning of second sight in the teleological account of heredity produced by evolutionary thinking. What emerges from these interactions is the possibility of a cross-cultural model of seership, one that underlined the persistence of domestic supernaturalism and threatened to undermine the image of the British nation as a rational and improving force in the world. Bolstered by the activities of folklorists, the Scottish Highlands were constructed as a unique repository of superstitious belief in an otherwise civilised country. Understood in evolutionary terms, this placed its inhabitants elsewhere in time and place, stalled at an earlier stage and alike to other non-domestic savages, like the 'aboriginal race' Howitt encountered on his Australian adventure.[22] Thinking broadly about the biographical function the tradition was asked to play in spiritualist writing, second sight offers a means of accessing the ancestries negotiated by the movement and the modality of the primitive in its ideology. Read through the complex geographical and temporal plotting of the second-sight tradition, these discourses reveal common etiological and genealogical preoccupations.

GHOSTLY METHODS

An image captioned 'Spirit Photograph of William Howitt (in the flesh) and granddaughter (in the spirit)' joins photographs of 'Mr. John Jones, & a spirit supposed to be deceased relative', 'The Three Fox Sisters of Rochester' and a *carte de visite* of the medium Daniel Dunglas Home that are glued into the pages of a notebook now held by the Pitt Rivers Museum in Oxford (Fig. 4.1).[23] In the photograph an elderly Howitt is pictured with a woman—perhaps his wife Mary—and what appears to be a child garbed in layers of white fabric. Composed through the same stiff, held-too-long poses that characterised Victorian studio portraiture, the faded document purports to be the image of a much-desired family reunion. Spirit photographs rendered the afterlife dramatically visible as departed spirits, prompted by the presence and prayers of loved ones, imprinted themselves on the negative plates. The Howitt photograph speaks of personal loss, and the amelioration of that loss through hetero-dox religious belief and ancestral bonds that transcend the destruction of the body. But it is not certain which members of the family are represented here and which familial ties are being maintained. In *Chronicles of the Photographs of Spiritual Beings and Phenomena Invisible to the Material Eye* (1882) the image is reproduced, but a living daughter and dead son are identified; here the photo is accompanied by an account from Howitt of an 1872 visit to the spirit photographer Frederick Augustus Hudson, where he obtained several images of 'sons of mine, who passed into the spirit-world years ago'. In this letter we also learn that on viewing the photograph a reliable 'lady-medium' identified the figure of a spirit-sister who had 'died in infancy'.[24] What appears like the post-mortem recom-position of a family seems, on closer inspection, more akin to the recrea-tion of an ancestral record.

Read *in situ*, in the archive of the cultural anthropologist Edward Burnett Tylor, the strange connections and displaced ancestries invoked by this spectral image take on new dimensions. The photograph forms part of a small notebook dedicated to the subject of spiritualism, in which Tylor recorded details of the seances he attended in November 1872. His notebook provides a fascinating account of the spiritualist scene in London during this period: in it he corresponds with the chemist and spiritualist investigator William Crookes, attends a seance organised by the automatic writer William Stainton Moses, spends evenings in dedicated venues such as the Burns Progressive Library

Fig. 4.1   Pitt-Rivers Museum Photo Collections 2009. 148.3

and witnesses the exploits of a famous levitation medium.[25] The anthropologist's trips from Somerset to the capital were undertaken at the height of the movement's popularity in Britain, as table rapping gave way to trance mediumship and spectacular feats of materialisation began to dominate the public debate. These new claims were met by formal investigations by the Anthropological Society in 1868 and the London Dialectical Society in 1871, as well as by the formation of dedicated organisations such as the Ghost Club in 1862 and the Society for Psychical Research in 1882.[26] The contested and increasingly sensational phenomena of the seance elicited responses from a broad range of disciplines, including physics, psychiatry, neurology, biology and, as is illustrated by this notebook, the nascent science of comparative anthropology.

While in London Tylor paid a visit to the Howitt family in Notting Hill and consulted with Anna Mary, an accomplished painter who would go on to write a biography of her father, on how to best further his enquiries into the subject.[27] By the early 1870s, William and Mary Howitt had established themselves as key figures in the British spiritualist movement. Discussing his contributions, the psychical researcher Frank Podmore went as far to claim that 'But for William Howitt, it is doubtful whether the movement would have secured either so early or so favourable a hearing in this country.'[28] Alongside the mathematician Augustus De Morgan, the first British translator of Swedenborg J.J. Garth Wilkinson and Royal Physician Dr John Ashburner, the Howitts formed a key component of the educated middle-class response to spiritualism. Distancing themselves from the freethinking radicalism of its American exponents, these initial propagators drew on a combination of phrenological, mesmeric and Swedenborgian teachings to form a new Christian eschatology capable of meeting the needs of a changing intellectual culture. As their personal commitment to the cause deepened, several members of the Howitt family also uncovered mediumistic abilities. Both William and Mary discovered a talent for automatic writing, while Anna Mary displayed remarkable clairvoyant gifts and produced watercolour paintings under trance.[29] Though his wife eventually renounced spiritualism in favour of Roman Catholicism in 1880, William remained a fervent believer until his death in 1879, and over the course of articles published by the *British Spiritual Telegraph, Spiritual Magazine* and *Christian Spiritualist* he produced an encyclopaedic and hugely influential account of the movement.[30]

The informal investigation to which the Howitts were asked to contribute commenced a year after the publication of *Primitive Culture* (1871), a work that had established Tylor as a key practitioner of the still heterodox theory of cultural evolution. Spurred by observations made during travel in the Americas, from which he also produced *Anahuac: or Mexico and the Mexicans, Ancient and Modern* (1861), Tylor pioneered a comparative approach to the 'condition of culture among the various societies of mankind', one that sought out universal concepts and common practices as evidence of humanity's shared evolutionary development.[31] Despite being barred from further study on grounds of his Quakerism, Tylor became a central figure in the British scientific establishment. Elected as a fellow of the Royal Society in 1871 and named Keeper at the Oxford University Museum of Natural History, he was eventually appointed the university's first Professor of Anthropology in 1895.[32] Foundational to the intellectual vision on which this remarkable academic career was built was the doctrine of 'survivals': the proposition that while human society is characterised by its steady progress towards civilisation, in its movement from one stage to the next it often carries with it the remnants of the 'older condition of culture' from which it has evolved.[33] Examples of these 'relics of primitive barbarianism' include children's games, popular sayings, strange customs and superstitions. According to Tylor, the table rapping and necromantic communications being hosted by respectable homes across the country represented a particularly potent example of the 'survival and revival of savage thought'.[34] The success of this paradigm, elsewhere notable in the work of the biologist Herbert Spencer and the ethnologist John F. McLennan, was that it provided a means of rationalising the reappearance of irrationality in modern Britain that maintained the assurance of an ever-progressing civilisation.[35] So that while the 'alleged visions, and rappings and writings' of the seance clearly stemmed from the 'philosophy of savages', the movement itself represented only a temporary resurrection of primitive thinking.[36]

The remarkable clarity of the survival trope also authorised a detailed taxonomy by which it became possible to mark the distribution of superstitions across time and space. In published essays, lectures and private diaries, Tylor used this comparative method to diffuse the extraordinary claims of modern spiritualism. While believers insisted on the revolutionary nature of spirit communication, the anthropologist classified these as part of the same animistic theory of apparitions peddled by colonial subjects, for example the 'Red Indian medicine-man' and the 'Tatar necromancer'. Profitable analogies could also be drawn closer to home, and he finds much to connect the 'Boston medium' with the second-sighted Highlander.[37] Correcting an earlier supposition made by a Dr Macculloch that second sight had 'undergone the fate of witchcraft; ceasing to be believed, it has ceased to exist', he insists that with the advent of table rapping the belief in supernatural premonition was now 'reinstated in a far larger range of society, and under far better circumstances of learning and material prosperity'. Not only, he continued, had the powers of the Gaelic 'ghost-seer' been buoyed by this new movement, they themselves could be cited as a corroborating factor in the 'spiritualistic renaissance' sweeping Britain.[38] Drawing a genealogy between second sight and modern table-rapping phenomena served to discredit the scientific claims of the latter by associating its practices with the persistent peasant traditions of 'North Britain' and their atavistic 'doctrine of wraiths'; this equivalency assigned spiritualist manifestations their proper taxonomical weighting, not as worthy objects of empirical observation, but as superstitions akin to many others around the world.

Near the beginning of the notebook, Tylor recalls the details of a seance he attended years earlier with the materialisation medium Mrs Samuel Guppy, hosted at the London home of Alfred Russel Wallace, a leading evolutionary thinker who spent the latter portion of his career urging his fellow scientists to consider objectively the possibility of communication with the dead. Spirit manifestation provoked a revision of Wallace's thinking on the question of evolution: where once the principle of natural selection, developed in parallel with Charles Darwin, had been sufficient to account for the origins of life, the phenomena of the seance led him to reconsider this position in relation to man.[39] His defence of spiritualism, articulated in private letters and in publications such as *Miracles and Modern Spiritualism* (1875), built upon data gathered under test conditions with controls and multiple witnesses, and he pressed the need for a systematic and unbiased examination of such material. Writing five years after their shared experience of the seance, Tylor was forced to acknowledge that he had not yet heeded his host's calls for an empiricist approach to spiritualism, having instead traced its 'ethnology' and exposed its absurdities by 'examining the published evidence'.[40] Regarded through the materials of the 'armchair anthropologist'—the library of travel literature, colonial biography, missionary reports and antiquarian miscellanea that formed the basis of *Primitive Culture*—Tylor could dismiss reports of ghostly appearances in middle-class drawing rooms as simply the last gasp of a savage and anachronistic cosmology.[41]

Clearly this assessment did not accord with how believers viewed themselves, many of whom considered the advent of ghostly communications as a great advancement in human history, but rather than reject the theoretical basis of cultural evolutionism some spiritualists appropriated its language to produce alternative readings. This rhetorical strategy was most thoroughly worked through in the movement's intellectual histories. Wide-ranging and erudite surveys such as Sophia De Morgan's *Light in the Valley* (1863) and Emma Hardinge Britten's *The Facts and Frauds of Religious History* (1879) sought to demonstrate the universality and continuity of spiritualist belief across time. Though keen to demonstrate the superiority of modern spiritualist theology, these histories situated the practice within a wider preternatural schema. William Howitt's two-volume *History of the Supernatural* (1863) is an early example of the genre that sees the author transform traditions such as second sight along with those associated with medieval mystics, Protestant dissenters, Shaker visionaries and Swedenborgian teachings, into an historical counter-narrative in which the development of human society can be mapped in terms of spiritual, not scientific, advancement. Charting progress in opposition to the model of advancement staked out by cultural evolutionism, the *History of the Supernatural* also privileges genealogies denigrated by rationalist discourse. So instead of denying the connection between 'spiritualistic theory' and the 'fanciful symbolic omens' associated with second sight, this lineage becomes a way of accessing important historical testimony as to the veracity of seance phenomena.[42]

In dedicated periodicals and newspapers, tales from ancient myth, accounts of the witchcraft trials of the seventeenth century, famous British hauntings, divinatory practices and folk beliefs were reframed through the explanatory paradigm of spirit communication. Traditions and stories associated with second sight provided particularly rich material for this revisionary work: the 16 June 1883 edition of *Light* gives a spiritualistic reading of visions associated with the Battle of Culloden; the August edition of the same paper corrects Walter Scott's incredulous dismissal of wraiths; a later issue recognises the prophecies of a famous seventeenth-century seer as remarkably attuned to the precepts of spiritualist theology; and in an article entitled 'Remarkable Instances of Second Sight', Howitt retells the story of Lord Talbot's vision of invading troops.[43] In *History of the Supernatural*, the author gives over a chapter to the subject of second sight with the express intention of forging a link between the ancient peasant tradition and the burgeoning spiritualist movement. Attributing previsions of 'battles, wrecks and murders' as down to the mysterious workings of 'magnetic influence', he proposes that the faculty of 'second-sight is, in truth, clairvoyance produced by the conditions of the mountains and the Isles'.[44] Expanding on this, he goes on to note that an eighteenth-century student of the phenomenon, Theophilus Insulanus, arrived at the 'same conclusion as the spiritualists of the present day, that the seers do not see the objects observed with the outer, but with the inner eye'.[45] This genealogical understanding of spirit possession elided temporal distance to guarantee a sense of precedence, by recasting the extraordinary claims of modern spiritualists as the expression of some essential truth that was observable in the remarkable visions of the second sighted, a truth as 'old as the hills, and as ubiquitous as the ocean'.[46] In a comparable fashion to Catherine Crowe's *The Night Side of Nature* (1848), Howitt's comparative study made legible a mass of unexplained and disparate phenomena from around the world through the identification of an underlying universal principle.

In a letter to Wallace in 1886, Tylor endeavoured to draw an absolute distinction between his own work and the ill-conceived drivel produced by scholars such as Howitt; where the trained anthropologist records strange customs and beliefs from around the world, believers credulously endorse the 'opinions of half-civilised and savage races'.[47] What this anxious protestation reveals, however, is the extent to which spiritualist histories utilised the same taxonomic and stylistic gestures as comparative anthropology. Despite their insistence on the valuable sensory proofs offered up by the seance, believers relied heavily on print media—books, dedicated journals and newspaper articles—for the dissemination of their message. In the necessary conciliation of the immaterial with the material, or experiential with discursive substantiation, spiritualist writers embedded the time space of the seance with resonances exterior to that specific temporal and spatial reality; so that traditions of religious prophecy or folkloric prevision became synecdochal of the spiritual knowledge being rendered empirically verifiable. As Wallace proposed in an article for *Light*, the empirical potential of the seance could eventually transform 'local folklore and superstitions' into a 'living interest' based upon phenomena now being produced 'under proper conditions'.[48] The powers of mind suggested by the premonitory narratives of the second sighted, once subject to the romantic musings of travel writers or substantiated only by the scholarship of antiquarians, might now be tested and authenticated in a controlled environment.

Considering once more the family photograph that illustrates Tylor's notebook, it is possible to interpret the multiple temporalities captured within this single image as usefully analogous to the complex positioning of modern spiritualism. On the one hand, the genealogy of the spirit photograph, which dissolved distance and time between family members, undermined the idea of linear progress by insisting on the active and ongoing influence of the dead upon the living. But on the other, there was something in the physical encounter with an ancestral past, as staged in the Howitt family image, that chimed with the evolutionary thinking. In *History of the Supernatural*, second sight is described as akin to the 'geni and peri of the East' and the 'lares, lemures, and penates of Greece', a power bound to the Highlands of Scotland by the force of genealogy; despite being geographically specific, the tradition resonates with modern spiritualism because in the seance 'ancestral spirits are always coming forward to notice'.[49] This statement reveals something of the complex evidentiary value second sight held for spiritualist believers. It was not only that recorded tales of uncanny foresight could be used to demonstrate the universality of supernatural experience, but also that modern mediums might access similar capabilities through the mysterious workings of 'ancestral spirits'. In other words, second sight was not only written into spiritualist annuals, it could also be experienced as a kind of living and embodied history, accessed through heredity lines.

SURVIVALS AND HISTORY MAKING

Reporting on the recent history of 'Table Turning and Spirit Rapping', an 1860 article for *Bentley's Miscellany* drew attention to the role played by indigenous magical traditions in providing the groundwork for new outbreaks of superstitious belief, with Scotland singled out as the porous site of the first invasion of American spiritualism. The spirits, we are told, 'landed first in Scotland, the country of second sight' and following a sympathetic welcome there 'were soon seen in England'.[50] Written from the perspective of a bemused sceptic, this account establishes a native framework of beliefs—in second sight, faeries, brownies and wraiths— uniquely amenable to spiritualist precepts, and grounds these firmly in northern soil. While it is hardly surprising, the article continues, that this 'latest hallucination' should find support among the notoriously superstitious Scots, it is disappointing that it originated in the 'New World' from which 'we had a right to expect great things toward the emancipation and enlightenment of the human mind, and yet from which we have got as yet only table turning, spirit rapping and Mormonism'.[51] Balanced against the historical inevitability of inbred credulity, America is chastised for having squandered the fresh start afforded by emigration and resettlement. Defining the potential of the new against the outmoded beliefs of the old, Scotland not only signifies the latter, but it also threatens the material progress of Britain as a whole. Considering what new connotes in this context and from whom the author expects 'enlightenment' and 'emancipation' raises questions regarding what exactly was at stake in the relationship between race, nationhood and revivals of the supernatural.

Modern spiritualism developed through the transatlantic exchange of ideas and individuals, aided by a theological framework that synthesised religious, occult and magical beliefs from around the world. It was in another 'New World', after all, that William Howitt first encountered spirit rapping in 1852 and the lines of influence he traced—running from the Australian medium to the parlours of London, and between a fictional Celtic seer and the wilds of the outback—privileged exactly the kind of dialogue denigrated in *Bentley's Miscellany*. One could read the *History of the Supernatural*, for instance, as an extension of many of the arguments made in his anti-imperial treatise *Colonisation and Christianity*. Where this earlier work condemned the violence of the colonial project as antithetical to Christian values, his cross-cultural study of the supernatural went further to argue for the superior 'moral qualities' possessed by natives of India, Egypt, Africa and the Americas. We learn that supernaturalism amongst the 'aborigines of the New World' gives them a spiritual advantage over 'their so-called Christian oppressors'; that the native Australian's close proximity to the 'spirit world' demonstrates his uncorrupted nature; and that where the light of spiritualism is only just dawning on 'educated' Europeans, colonised Indians have been 'ghost-seers' and 'table-rappers' for generations.[52] Not all believers adopted an anti-imperialist position, but many did take an interest in the supernatural beliefs and practices of non-Western peoples. In popular publications such as *Light, Medium and Daybreak* and the *Spiritualist Newspaper*, readers could expect to see reports of savage rituals and strange phenomena from around the world printed alongside accounts of recent seances and updates on the movement's progress in Britain. Within the seance, colonial subjects were often invoked as spirit guides, with Arab children and

Native American chiefs acting as emissaries to the dead, while Indian coolies and Persian princes conducted mediums on extra-terrestrial journeys. What is more, lavish accounts of other-worldly travel recounted by entranced mediums tended to echo the stylistic conventions of the adventure narrative, so that the celestial and the exotic often came to resemble one another. These intellectual and affective encounters were driven by a complex set of desires—the allure of exotic, the pull of the East as a fount of ancient wisdom, the imagined purity of primitive religious worship—all of which worked to place the project of empire at the heart of spiritualist experience.

For the sceptic writing in *Bentley's Miscellany*, supernaturalism is not a foreign import; rather, credulity is nourished and catalysed by superstitions that lurk on the peripheries of civilised Britain, in rural backwaters and remote corners, among the poor and the unlettered. A number of historians have observed that most spiritualists attempted to distinguish their beliefs from those of the 'uneducated and ignorant whose belief in supernatural beings and events was untouched by the rationalism of educated opinion'.[53] Though this assessment captures something of the scientific aspirations of the movement, it also occludes the ways in which its theories and practices engaged with an established network of native traditions, a project that brought believers into even closer proximity to questions of colonisation and appropriation. Home-grown magical beliefs were framed by 'domestic and colonial spheres of otherness', a shared imperial imaginary translated across geographical and cultural borders.[54] These overlapping 'spheres' had material consequences, with marginalised groups in Britain subjected to the kinds of cultural erasures, state sanctioned violence and enforced migration enacted overseas. In their appropriation of peasant beliefs and folk customs, spiritualist writers often reproduced this dynamic in discursive terms. This is legible in Alfred Russel Wallace's *Defence of Modern Spiritualism* (1874), when he attributes the visions of the second sighted to the fact that 'mediumistic power is more frequent and more energetic in mountainous countries', before stressing that because such wild landscapes are 'generally inhabited by the less civilised' the phenomenon is consequently often wrongly 'imputed to coincident ignorance'.[55] Though he writes in support of a belief typically dismissed as irrational, he does so in this instance within an ideological framework that reinscribes the Highlander as primitive, so that the visionary power is understood as a valid subject for examination, but the testimony of the seer is reiterated as unenlightened and untrustworthy.

Just as the racialist theories of the mid-century had explained and justified the socio-economic divide between Lowland and Highland, social evolutionism offered a new set of discursive tools to delineate and cement the distinction between colonial subject and object.[56] The strength of the survival paradigm, for instance, depended upon its application not only to anomalous traits or brief revivals of 'savage' philosophy, but also to entire societies. So where spiritualism represented the vestige of an earlier stage puncturing the Anglo-American present, elsewhere whole cultures remained stalled at a prior phase.[57] Part of what sustained this hierarchy was the model of historical process that was bound to what the anthropological theorist Johannes Fabian has termed the 'temporal slope' of evolutionary thought, in which civilised Europeans occupy the present in relation to the delayed primitive. Through a 'denial of coevalness', Fabian argues, anthropology represents the observed culture as inhabiting a time previous to the temporal space shared by the reader and ethnographer alike.[58] This understanding of time, though most rigorously applied in the study of non-white peoples, also informed the representation of marginal communities in Britain. Writing in regard to the disparity between the advanced industrialisation of nineteenth-century England and the recent 'tribal' history of the Highlands, the Scottish ethnologist John F. McLennan proposed that in a 'progressive community all the sections do not advance *pari passu*, so that we many see in the lower some phases through which the more advanced have passed'—an assertion that connected the northern populace with modes of existence removed in both time and space from the country's hegemonic centres.[59] In addition to providing an explanation and justification for the industrial, economic and educational lag of the Highlands relative to their Lowland neighbours, the 'temporal slope' could also help to account for the persistence of superstitious and irrational thinking in those communities.

With the establishment of the Folklore Society (FLS) in 1878 and the publication of its official mouthpiece *The Folk-Lore Record*, the study of local beliefs, superstitions and popular traditions was elevated from the realms of amateur antiquarianism to the world of institutionalised scientific practice. Prompted by a suggestion made in *Notes and Queries*, this newly formed society bridged the gap between the encyclopaedic traditions long associated with the collecting and cataloguing of folk beliefs and the observational strategies being developed within the Anthropological Institute. Made clear by the description given by Alfred Nutt, a specialist in Celtic history and a founding member of the FLS, of folklore as 'anthropology dealing with primitive man', the discipline was one formed by conceptual and institutional crossovers.[60] The Highlands provided a geographically accessible proving ground for the methods of this kind of comparative anthropology, and the early years of the FLS mark a significant period in the history of second sight, during which collectors working largely from fieldwork toured the northern reaches of the country and employed Gaelic-speaking locals to record the last vestiges of a dying oral culture. In works such as John Francis Campbell's *Popular Tales of the West Highlands, Orally Collected* (1860–2) and James Napier's *Folklore: or Superstitious Beliefs in the West of Scotland* (1879), Scotland's remote regions were hailed repositories of pre-Christian beliefs. Investigations were undertaken on the assurance that the thought of early man might be observed in the Highlands and Islands, where the traditional music, folk ballads, ghost stories, customs and beliefs of this developmentally stalled people provided a glimpse into our common evolutionary past.[61]

The problematic at the centre of this freshly institutionalised discipline, as identified by the historian Malcolm Chapman, was that in defining folklore as the 'retreat from the rational' its practitioners were motivated by the fear that their 'field of study would soon disappear'.[62] Underpinned by an evolutionary discourse that equated rationalism with improvement, this materialist trajectory ultimately threatened to obliterate the materials of the discipline itself. Thus an article in *The Folk-Lore Record* complained that in the cities of England where civilisation has reached its pinnacle, the 'genuine popular tale' was all but extinct.[63] It was not only that the components of traditional cultures—ballads, stories and customs transmitted across the generations—were under threat, but also that the loss of this customary knowledge signalled the inevitable decline of the race itself. Western Europe's Celtic constituencies, located in Scotland, Wales, Ireland, Cornwall, Belgium and Brittany, were especially vulnerable to decline. Over the course of the nineteenth century a romanticised version of the Celt became synonymous with the idea of folk culture, set firmly in opposition to the values of a scientifically managed society and doomed to extinction.[64] The elegiac lament for the waning of an ancient people was taken up most famously in four lectures delivered by the poet and critic Matthew Arnold at the University of Oxford in 1866. Eventually published as 'On the Study of Celtic Literature', these lectures valorised the 'undisciplined, anarchical' qualities of the Celt as a necessary balance to excessive rationalism of the Anglo-Saxon political centre.[65] Defining his interest in the Celtic race in terms of 'what it has been, what it has done',

Arnold discounted the lived experience of the people in favour of ancient lore and peasant tradition.[66] Recalling Fabian's 'denial of coevalness', the newly institutionalised science of folklore made its subject by attempting to establish it as a subject for academic study, located, or soon to become so, in the past.

This sense of impending cultural erasure did not arrive with the founding of the FLS. From the claim made in 1716 that second sight was 'much more common twenty years ago that at present; for one in ten do not see it now, that saw it then', to James Boswell's lament in 1773 that he had come 'too late' to experience the wild country and 'antiquated' way of life documented by explorers, traditional Highland society was habitually forecast for annihilation.[67] What is unique to this context, however, is the way that phenomena such as second sight begin to be viewed through a particular colonial relation: one that fixes the seer in an earlier temporal space, while simultaneously guaranteeing its authority as the proper producer and arbiter of historical truth. This chronological mapping of culture, whereby superstitious or irrational beliefs were explained as survivals from an earlier developmental stage, also helped to author a new understanding of mind. Evolutionary psychology, a discipline in ascendancy through the latter half of the nineteenth century, placed emphasis on the connection between advanced mental life and the imbrication of linear time, so that the unbroken continuity of past experience and present identity became a key structuring of individual psychology.[68] In the first volume of Herbert Spencer's *Principles of Psychology* (1876–96), for example, 'mental evolution' was measured by the 'degree of remoteness from primitive reflex action'; so that those people who pass from a 'single passion into the conduct it prompts' remained inferior to the self-governing and will-driven Englishman.[69] Here stadial history found its mirror image in a privileged emotional regime characterised by the 'hesitating passage of compound emotions into kinds of conduct determined by the joint instigation of their compounds'.[70] In other words, the psychology of the race is determined by how it interprets and records historical process, and thus the failure of savage peoples to adequately imbibe the patterns of evolutionary time serves to confirm their inferiority.

In *Primitive Culture* Tylor cautioned against misrecognising the stories of the second sighted as 'actual evidence'. Worse than their content—tall tales of 'apparitions' and 'phantoms'—are their jumbled causal structures; the histories produced by visionary peasants begin not with the past but with hazy forecasts of the future. With the aid of 'fanciful symbolic omens', seers predict deaths according to the position- ing of a 'phantom shroud' or forecast the loss of children from a 'spiritual vision of a spark of fire' landing on the arm of the soon-to-be bereaved parent.[71] The anthropologist's intention is, of course, to discredit the stories of the second sighted by attributing them to an animistic misread- ing of causation, but his injunction against mistaking such prophecies for 'actual evidence' also hints at their potency. Along similar lines, the folklorist Alfred Nutt argued that because the Celt was largely disenfran- chised from print culture and appeared to place no importance on 'the chronicle, the record, the document', the race existed only in the present and again, this dismissal of oral culture betrays certain assumptions regarding what constitutes history.[72] Britain's rural peripheries did not exist outside time; instead their folk metaphysics presented alternative temporal patterns, woven by prophecy, second sight and divination, that made other ways of imagining the individual in history possible. What is more, the disruptive historiography of the second-sighted vision, which ascertains the effect before the cause and privileges inner visionary experi- ence over external observation, found prominent expression in the tem- poral negotiations of modern spiritualism.

Spiritualist practice, founded on the belief that the dead can materi- alise and communicate with the living, also produced a version of the historical record counter to the linear causality posited by evolutionary thinkers. Spirit photographs, for instance, captured not only deceased family members, but also the spectral imprint on the present of history's famous dead, so that the murky visage of John the Baptist or Abraham Lincoln might appear in the developed image. Returning in the form of ghostly revenants to amend or rewrite the record, these temporary res- urrections threatened to call into question the assumed importance of history itself, reflecting instead upon ideals of mystical synchronicity and repetition, as well as prophetic, millenarian or second-sighted rupture or disjuncture. These newly vocal historical actors did not often behave in ways that cohered with their terrestrial activities, published opinions or biographical data. *The Future Life: as Described and Portrayed by Spirits* (1878), for instance, recorded the American medium Elizabeth Sweet's communications with a number of famous figures including Joan of Arc and the more recently deceased Margaret Fuller, both of whom returned to confirm the truths of spiritualist theology from the other side. Over the course of her career, Sweet was also placed in communication with the spirit of Voltaire, who in addition to recounting the glory of the 'spirit land' also renounced his former atheistic convictions.[73]

The distance between the ghostly emanations of the seance and the teleological work of evolutionism was not, however, as vast as it might first appear. In an article mocking Wallace's recent conversion to the spiritualist cause, the *Anthropological Review* wondered in 1867 if the views held by him on the 'past and coming unity of mankind' were 'communicated to him by some kind departed spirit, perhaps that of the "first man"'.[74] Though obviously not intended as a serious consideration of anthropological practice, this proposed methodology does reflect upon some of the unexpected resonances between the timelessness of the seance and the trans-historical negotiations of evolutionism. Is Tylor's assertion, made in a paper on the use of stone tools among the Tasmanian people, that the 'condition of modern savages illustrates the condition of ancient Stone Age peoples', so different from the folly of which Wallace is accused?[75] Viewed in a certain light, anthropology's 'super vision', to adopt a phrase from the historian Peter Pels, promotes the same intimacy with history and historical actors as that promised by spirit communication.[76] Evolutionary thinking engages in acts of divination; in seeking to forecast probable progressions and developments it produces a scientific theory imbided with futurity. Conversely, though the phenomena of the seance and the spirit photograph made possible new ways of accessing the past—through the automatic writing, trance speech and full-form materialisations—the stories spiritualism told about itself were often scripted along strictly progressivist lines.[77] Though undertaken with the intention of demonstrating the ascendancy of spiritual rather than rationalist principles, studies such as the *History of the Supernatural* replicated the discursive gestures of cultural evolutionism by setting recent manifestations of spiritual agency in a developmental narrative stretching backwards to the ancient world and forward to utopian imaginings of an enlightened future state. Thus the overarching structure of the text remains orientated toward the production of a reliably linear account, one that posits the advent of modern spiritualism as a step forward in the spiritual evolution of humanity.[78]

Utopian visions of mystical other worlds or the life to come were similarly mapped along clear evolutionary lines. The theory of natural selection and the common animal origins it implied have been typically read as threatening rather than bolstering assumptions of man's spiritual nature, as contributing factors to the decline of religious belief and the subsequent disenchantment of the Western world. But evolutionary science could also serve as a blueprint for the 'development of man's spiritual being'.[79] Addressing the London Spiritualist Alliance, the Reverend John Page Hopps proposed that the theory of evolution demonstrated that: 'Man did not begin perfect and end in a "fall"; he began imperfect, and is steadily going on in the onward and upward path, out of the animal's darkness into the angel's marvellous light. He is not a fallen but a rising creature.'[80] The notion of spiritual progress, the extension of individual development and racial improvement into the afterlife, was a key tenet for many believers. In Andrew Jackson Davis's *Stellar Key to the Summerland* (1867), for example, the American seer describes a higher sphere of existence towards which humanity, in its painstaking spiritual progress, is slowly ascending. Influenced by the writings of the Swedish mystic Emanuel Swedenborg, Davis outlined a highly detailed and intricately imagined 'inhabitable sphere or zone among the suns and planets of space', aimed at providing a 'solid, rational, philosophical foundation on which to rest [...] hopes of a substantial existence after death'.[81] For Davis, the question of how to ensure the continued spiritual development of humanity was fundamental: could steady upwards progress be relied upon or were more direct interventions necessary? Was the faculty of second sight a vestige of spiritualism's past or a part of its future? And did the practices of spiritualism belong to the old world or the new?

SCOTTISH ANCESTORS AND SPIRITUALIST FUTURES

The International Health Exhibition opened in 1884 to showcase a range of exhibits encompassing food, sanitation, clothing and domestic management. Alongside promotional displays of Pears Soap, model sanitation systems, hydrotherapeutic clinics and a fully operational vegetarian restaurant, visitors to the South Kensington site were encouraged to try out the world's first Anthropometric Laboratory. Having been introduced to new methods of measuring and tabulating their physical characteristics, members of the public were encouraged to submit information such as arm span, visual acuity and head size to the growing bank of data.[82] The temporary laboratory was the work by Francis Galton, a psychologist and psychometrician, who pioneered the application of statistical methods to the study of human development and difference. Hugely popular with the thousands that frequented the exhibition, the pop-up test centre employed techniques that had been developed over the course of a large-scale comparative study of the nation's physical features, undertaken by the British Association for the Advancement of Science (BAAS) between 1875 and 1883.[83] As part of this project, an Anthropometric Committee, which boasted the medical statistician William Farr and the anthropologist Augustus Lane Fox among its members, examined variations in physiological development across the country and established parametric techniques to calibrate divergences. Data gathered by the BAAS found practical application in eugenics, a science developed by Galton that identified and propagated traits deemed useful to the further evolution of the species; because man's abilities are derived from his inheritance, each generation has 'enormous power over the natural gifts of those that follow'.[84] From the beginning, the practice of eugenics relied heavily on lay participation, cultivated through population surveys, data collection, self-reporting and the occasional public laboratory.[85]

For eugenicists the category of race served as a key structural and conceptual device around which genealogical characteristics could orbit. Perhaps unsurprisingly, the systems developed by scientists such as Galton to measure intelligence in a given population tended to systematise racialist perceptions of non-Western cultures. *Hereditary Genius* (1870), for one, featured a 15-point scale along which to plot the 'worth' of different races that placed the Anglo-Saxon above the 'Negro' and the Australian Aboriginal several grades below, according to their perceived receptivity to the 'civilising' process.[86] Conditions of racial fitness were, however, by no means wholly contingent upon the division of non-white from white, or colonised from coloniser. While it was certainly possible to observe the highest cultivation among some members of the British Isles, others, such as London's 'draggled, drudged' urban poor, exemplified exactly the kind of hereditary weakness to which science should urgently apply itself.[87] One of the most extreme positions adopted in relation to variances in the domestic population was maintained by John Beddoe, a founding member of the Ethnographical Society and Chair of the Anthropometric Committee. In his best-known work, *The Races of Britain* (1885), Beddoe utilised data on hair and eye colour, head size and bone structure to effectively dismantle the Union. He argued that where the English and Lowland Scots are clearly descended from the Anglo-Saxons, the Celts—Scottish, Welsh and Irish—are more alike to the 'Africanoid' races.[88] Working from fieldwork in the Highlands undertaken during his medical training at Edinburgh University, Beddoe examined the northern population through an 'index of nigrescence' and identified the inhabitants of the Western Isles and the Outer Hebrides as those furthest alike from the superior Teutonic type.[89] Though we should avoid reading Beddoe's description of the Celt as retaining the traits of 'Cro-Magnon' man as typical of scientific thinking in this period, the biological determinism underpinning this assessment speaks to an understanding of the interdependency of individual fate and racial heritage that was sustained across a number of fields.[90]

One field that was particularly receptive to emerging understandings of inheritance was spiritualism, with many of its proponents applying the language of hereditary transmission to man's after-death experience. After all, evolutionary biology and spiritualist philosophy shared in a vision of human behaviour as directed by unseen forces: for eugenicists this force was heredity, while for believers it was the 'spirits of the dead who worked through the living to improve the species and enable biological perfection'.[91] Informed by older theories of mind and character such as phrenology, spiritualist writers attempted to tackle the question of race improvement and considered what direct interventions might be made into that process. Where the genealogical stories told by scientists such as Galton ended with the death of the body, spiritualist writers extended humanity's development into the hereafter. In response to the futurism of evolutionary theory, for instance, an author writing in *Light* complained that it requires us to accept a lesser form of post-mortem survival in which the death of the individual is ameliorated only by the continuity of their genetic material: 'We are told that the aspiration after immortality in the individual must be satisfied by the result of his life on the race.'[92] What rankled was the notion that 'Perfected Humanity' was the only ideal towards which mankind could aspire; a proposition that not only denied the existence of an afterlife, but also the possibility that the individual may be further 'perfected' in the next world.[93] Thus the metaphoric promise of evolutionary theory—that genealogical traits compose a form of immortality mapped along hereditary lines—was literalised by spiritualist theology. For evolutionary biologists such as Alfred Russel Wallace, who risked his professional reputation by endorsing the claims of the movement, communication with the dead provided proof of the 'ultimate aim and outcome of all organised existence—intellectual, ever advancing, spiritual man'.[94] Plotted onto man's post-mortem existence, evolutionism demonstrated humanity's slow movement towards an increasingly enlightened state.

The enthusiasm with which spiritualism engaged with determinist models of development—both earthy and heavenly—exposes a contradiction in the story the movement told about itself. Despite being sold on the basis that anyone with belief and devotion could communicate with the dead, mediums consistently described their gift as inherited and innate. In published autobiographies and in the personal memoirs that regularly featured in periodicals such as *Medium and Daybreak*, the ability to channel the dead was framed in the language of evolutionary predestination and ancestral progression. It was on these grounds that second sight was taken up in the personal mythology of famous and not so famous mediums. A letter sent to the editor of *Light* on 5 March 1881, for example, tells of a robbery at a family's counting house and of the uncanny 'prescience' of that event shared by father and son. Recounting this remarkable experience, the younger of the two finds he can only begin to account for it through the family's history: 'we are members of an old Highland family for ages located in Skye [from which] we seem to have inherited the faculty of "second sight"'. Prior to sudden activation of this legacy, the correspondent admits that he would have 'denounced Spiritualism as devilish if true, but probably mere illusion', but now he has been 'compelled to alter' his opinion.[95] Woven into a redemptive narrative of personal enlightenment, the prophecy activates, simultaneously, an ancestral past and a spiritualist future. By choosing to characterise second sight as a form of racial inheritance, spiritualists built upon studies such as Robert Kirk's *The Secret Commonwealth* (1690) and Martin Martin's *Description of the Western Isles* (1716), foundational accounts that had established the power as contingent upon the conditions of the Highlands and Islands. Though early collectors did not necessarily agree as to the specifics of transmission, with some citing the machinations of faeries and others the natural magic of the seventh son, the subject of inheritance had long dominated discussions of second sight. What is legible in this particular context is a shift in the imaginary of this uncanny inheritance, precipitated by the prominence of evolutionary biology and eugenics in public discourse. When 'Mrs Blevin' wrote to *The Spiritual Magazine* in 1867 to tell them that her powers as a medium almost certainly originated in her family history, where 'second sight' was 'hereditary', she did so under the influence of a lay conception of genealogical transmission.[96] Alike to Herbert Spencer's imagined psychical evolution, given in his *Principles of Psychology* (1855), wherein 'the countless connections among the fibres of the cerebral masses, answers to some permanent connection in the experiences of the race', the affinities mapped out by believers posited a direct line of descent between ancient peasant traditions and the new environs of the urban seance.[97]

Such connections were commonly forged along transatlantic lines, and the personal histories of several American mediums alluded to the possibility of second-sighted Highlanders somewhere down the family line. Prominently, Daniel Dunglas Home, one of the most celebrated mediums of the age who stunned onlookers with his remarkable feats of levitation, was born in Scotland and claimed to belong to a family of seers.[98] As an account given by the *Scots Observer* detailed: 'He was born near Edinburgh in 1833, but while still a child was taken to America. At the age of thirteen his first experience began with an instance of what is usually termed second sight. A vision of a school friend appeared to him and shortly afterwards he heard of his death.'[99] In his memoir, *Incidents in My Life* (1863), Home placed great importance on the many 'instances of second sight' he experienced as a child; formative visionary events that laid the ground for his later communications with the dead. We learn that from a very young age he was subject to sudden and involuntary premonitions, in which 'distant events, such as the death of friends and relatives' would appear before his eyes, and that these visions were common on both sides of his family.[100] One particularly poignant example concerns the death of his mother, a Scottish woman of aristocratic stock 'gifted with the second sight' who foresaw her own death. This 'incredible prophecy' was communicated to her by a daughter, long passed away, through a symbolic dream imparting details of the time and the place.[101] In *Incidents in My Life* Home recalls being understandably unwilling to credit this prediction, only to have it confirmed when he too experienced a second-sighted vision of his mother, miles away from him, at the moment of her death. Handed down through generations, second sight appears to have outlasted the upheaval of emigration to mark a point of cultural and genealogical continuity.

Further examples of this transatlantic traffic can be found in the autobiography of Andrew Jackson Davis, an American medium known as the 'Poughkeepsie Seer', in which instances of clairvoyance in childhood are grouped under the chapter heading 'Signs of Second Sight'; or in William Howitt's claim that the Fox sister's grandmother had been 'possessed of the second-sight, and saw frequently funerals, whilst living in Long Island, before they really took place'; or in a report on 'Spiritualism in America' given by a London periodical which detailed the arrival of 'Mrs. French', a 'trance-speaking medium and medical clairvoyant' who possessed the 'power of second sight at a very early age'.[102] Recalling Howitt's description of Australia's population as one composed of Britain's 'overflowings', who have carried with them 'every possible theory and practice, every idea, feeling, passion, speculation, pursuit and imagination which are fermenting in the old countries', it is possible to situate claims to Scottish ancestry within a similar affective network.[103] Specifically, the biographical function performed by second sight suggests a retracing of the lines of mass emigration from the Highlands to the New World and the reclaiming of the fabled visionary power as a component of a denigrated ancestral heritage. Early accounts of the faculty mapped similar patterns of migration, but these typically forecast the inevitable decline of second sight outside its natural environs. In 1699, for instance, Lord Reay reported to Samuel Pepys that 'several who did see the Second Sight when in the Highlands or Isles, yet, when transported to other countries, especially America, quite lose this quality'.[104] It is taken up in spiritualist biographies partly as a way to signify the afterglow of exile and estrangement on the home life of the medium. But in these accounts second sight, instead of simply vanishing when forced from its original locality, goes on to shape the history of its new home by providing a familial and cultural framework for the advent of spirit manifestations. Suspended in the racial ancestry of Scottish emigrants, it is empowered to return to British soil in a far more potent cultural form.

The enthusiastic incorporation of second sight into spiritualist genealogies is attributable, at least partly, to imageries of the Gaelic world in broader circulation. The figure described in an article for the *Celtic Magazine* in 1876 is typical of the Celt produced by popular Victorian culture: anarchical, ungovernable and more imaginative than their 'Anglo-Saxon brethren', members of this ancient race are also privy to a special kind of inspiration or 'second-sight of nature comparable to prophecy, which gives their highest poetic utterance a rapt enthusiasm'.[105] It was at this intersection between the poetic seer and the primitive subject, delineated by evolutionary folklore, that modern spiritualism fashioned a Highland ancestry for itself. The qualities attributed to the visionary Scot were, moreover, largely homologous with those ascribed to another venerated figure—the 'Red Indian' spirit guide favoured by many Anglo-American mediums. In *Modern American Spiritualism* (1870), Emma Hardinge Britten reflected on the prevalence of such guides, finally concluding that because of their faith in 'ancestral spirits as guardians to mortals' it was quite natural that the 'redmen' should devote themselves to 'guarding and protecting the toiling mediums through whom the truths of Spiritualism are mediated'.[106] Not only did the ancient beliefs of Native Americans authenticate those espoused by the modern movement, the spirits of their dead appeared remarkably amenable to its tenants; as Brian Inglis comments, it 'was as if the Red Indians, passionate believers in the existence of spirits have thereby acquired a standing in the spirit world'.[107] Just as the power of second sight was idealised as the product of 'simple habits, quiet peaceful pursuits, lives passed chiefly amid the grand and simple beauties of nature', so too was the success of Red Indian 'operators' attributable to the 'nomadic and simply natural life which these poor children of the forest lived on the earth'.[108] At one with the landscape, untouched by civilisation and innately spiritual, the northern seer and ingenious tribesperson were made legible through the same representational motifs.[109]

In his notebook on spiritualism, Tylor observed the frequent appearance of Native American ghosts at the seances he visited. On 4 November, for instance, he attended a session with a 'stout pasty-faced half-educated American' named Mrs Jeannie Holmes, who became 'possessed by a little Indian girl-spirit named Rosie' who 'talked what she called Ojibwa Indian and I call gibberish', and the next evening, during a seance which was also attended by members of the Crookes family, a medium named Mrs Olive was 'first possessed by Indian child-spirit' named 'Sunshine'.[110] Commenting on the frequency with which 'Indians' adopted the role of tutelary spirits, the anthropologist conjectured that 'the origin of the movement being in America is clearly betokened by the same set of Indian and negro spirits going through the whole posse of mediums, who are possessed very much after a set pattern developed no doubt by the American practitioners'.[111] What he detected in the seance, then, was not the miraculous channelling of native spirits, but the hackneyed performance of stock cultural signifiers. And though native guides came to form an integral part of the seance repertoire, some within the movement also expressed reservations regarding the value of cross-racial masquerade. In a letter sent to Daniel Dunglas Home, for instance, one female believer worried that the 'Pioneers of Spiritualism' were being pushed to one side in favour of 'Indian gibberish' and 'Punch and Judy' shows, while others condemned the adoption of savage instructors as evidence of the theatrical immorality of a new generation of materialisation mediums.[112] Where Tylor interpreted the mawkish amateurism of the spirit controls he observed as evidence of their performed nature, spiritualist believers were forced to negotiate a more nuanced position. Though keen to absorb the magical beliefs of colonised people into their own system, they were also aware of the need to distinguish spiritualist practice as ultimately superior. Thus Britten, having praised Native Americans as ideal hosts in the great beyond, can go on to warn of a darker side to 'Indian spiritualism' involving 'rites and phenomena of strange, occult and repulsive character' that modern believers have rightly thrown off.[113] Resistance to 'Indian gibberish' and to the more 'repulsive' aspects of primitive religions coded an ambivalence over the currency held by certain voices within the seance and revealed doubts over the value of supernatural testimony gathered from non-white spirits.

As the spiritualist movement gathered pace in mid-century Britain, the public imagination was gripped by a set of events that brought the question of how to interpret and evaluate the reports of native witnesses to the fore. At the close of 1854 the Admiralty made public a report concerning an expedition led by Sir John Franklin to map the Northwest Passage from Europe to Asia, which had departed with two ships, enough food for five years and a crew of over 100 men in May 1845. Much to the government's dismay the well-funded voyagers disappeared soon afterwards and their fate remained a mystery for nearly ten years. This was until the Scottish explorer John Rae, travelling through the Arctic regions, encountered a group of Inuit people who reported having communicated, some winters before, with a group of 'Kabloonas' (white men) who had decided to trek south after their boat had become stuck in the ice. Returning the following spring to hunt for seals, the Inuit came across the bodies of upwards of 30 men who, judging by the badly mutilated appearance of some of the corpses and the gruesome contents of their kettles, had resorted to cannibalism. When Rae's report on the fate of the Franklin expedition was made public, several prominent figures, including Lady Franklin and Charles Dickens, denounced it on the grounds that not only did Englishmen not eat each other, but that the 'Esquimaux' did not qualify as reliable witnesses. In a number of vitriolic articles published in his weekly periodical *Household Words*, Dickens questioned the content and form of the Inuit reports. Not only was Rae mistaken in endorsing the word of savages known to be 'covetous, treacherous and cruel', he was also foolish to accept oral testimony as viable evidence in the first place.[114] In the backlash that followed the report, Sarah Moss has argued that 'the idea of cannibalism and the idea of Inuit testimony' merged; it was 'unspeakable that the British Navy should have resorted to eating each other', but it was worse still that illiterate primitives should 'be the ones to tell the *Times* about it'.[115] Multiple well-funded search parties had failed to learn the fate of the lost men, and once the British were forced to rely on evidence supplied by native witnesses, it appeared to many that they had ceded their natural authority.

One way to restore the proper colonial hierarchy was to win back control of the narrative, to retell the story of the doomed expedition in terms that affirmed the superior spirit and heroic forbearance of the English explorers. The question of how to reposition this traumatic event in the national imaginary was answered by a play, *The Frozen Deep* (1856), co-written by Dickens and the novelist Wilkie Collins. Initially produced as an amateur theatrical but later given as a series of public performances, the play recounts the search for the Northwest Passage through a gripping tale of true love, adventure and bitter revenge. The central plot details the engagement of Clara Burnham to Frank Aldersely on the night before the departure of the expedition and her rejection of another suitor, Richard Wardour, who in despair joins the party of explorers and sets sail for the Arctic. Years later, with their ships stuck and supplies running low, Wardour finds himself alone on the ice with his injured love rival and considers leaving him to die. Meanwhile, back in England and with no news of the expedition's progress, Clara's childhood nurse—who hails from the Highlands and claims to possess the power of second sight—has a disturbing vision of far-away events: 'Doos the Sight show me Frank? Aye! and anither beside Frank. I see the lamb i' the grasp o' the lion.'[116] This premonition terrifies Clara, but the audience knows, having seen Nurse Esther eavesdropping on an earlier conversation, that her word is not to be trusted. In the end her doomy prediction does not come to pass and the play closes with the lovers reunited by an act of courageous self sacrifice, when Wardour saves the life of Aldersely and loses his own in the process. If we read this redemptive conclusion as an attempt to soften the serious blow dealt to Britain's self-image by the failure of the Franklin expedition and the charges of cannibalism levelled at its members, it is significant that the only Scottish character featured in the play is excluded from this unifying national narrative. Instead Nurse Esther embodies the idea of an unreliable primitive witness: in place of the deceitful Inuit who attempts to describe events that cannot have taken place, the audience was presented with a thickly accented working-class Scot making dangerous claims to knowledge that she does not possess. By switching one northern savage for another, *The Frozen Deep* attempted to discredit the testimony of Orkney-born Rae by pressing the image of Scotland and its people as backward and uncivilised.

This substitution spoke of a connection between the 'Esquimaux' and the Highlander, established in works of fiction, history and ethnography, and typically formulated on the basis of their shared latitude and developmental equivalence.[117] Writing in his *History of Dreams* (1850), for instance, the French psychiatrist Alexandre Brierre de Boismont uncovered a common folklore in the persistence of 'ecstatic visions of cold countries' and noted how closely accounts of second sight mirrored stories told by the 'Laplanders, Samoiédes, Ostiaks, and Kamtschatdales'.[118] As a work of propagandist theatre, *The Frozen Deep* exploited and amplified these equivalences, but this was not the only way the story was told. Written by Wilkie Collins and serialised for *The Temple Bar* in 1874, the short story adaptation retained most of the play's original plot, except that it dispensed with the deceitful nurse and had Clara predict the course of the doomed expedition instead. In the opening chapter we learn that the young woman has been educated at a school in the Highlands, where her impressionable mind was 'filled with the superstitions which are still respected as truths in the wild North'. Before Frank sails out in search of the Northwest Passage, Clara is haunted by foreboding dreams and becomes convinced that the expedition will end in tragedy.[119] While theatre audiences were encouraged to dismiss Nurse Esther's prediction as a calculated ploy, readers of *Temple Bar* were presented with a far more ambiguous take on the question of supernatural foresight. On the one hand, the happy conclusion of the story would appear to invalidate any premonition to the contrary; but on the other hand, because Clara's visions drive the action of the story, their meaning cannot be entirely discounted. What is more, those who might be tempted to dismiss second sight as the preserve of a remote and superstitious people are reminded that even the most 'enlightened' now believe in 'dancing tables' and 'messages sent from the other world'.[120] Where the play demarcated the nurse as resolutely savage and untrustworthy, Collins's reinterpretation made space for the supernatural as an active force in civilised culture by locating the power of prevision with Clara, a reassuringly English, middle-class heroine, whom the reader first encounters dancing the quadrille at a society ball.

In *The Frozen Deep* the incongruous appearance of primitive superstition in an English drawing room is profoundly unsettling, but for many spiritualists such revenants formed an important political and practical resource. Discussing the imperial encounters that took place with the seance, Marlene Tromp proposes that the 'fluidity implied in the identity of the colonised and the coloniser in these acts of materialisation undermined the English sense of superiority and Orientalist inferiority'.[121] More fully realised in the occult interests of the Theosophical Society, which relocated its headquarters to India in 1879 and participated in that country's campaign for independence, nineteenth-century thinkers habitually located other-worldly and religious authority in the mystical practices and beliefs of indigenous cultures.[122] In doing so it became possible to imagine colonial relations outside a hierarchal framework by, as Gauri Viswanathan has argued, loosening the boundaries between closed social networks.[123] Such a reading fits well with an established image of spiritualism as a movement supportive of the anti-slavery cause and closely allied to other nineteenth-century radicalisms such as socialism, vegetarianism, woman's suffrage and anti-vivisection. By claiming second-sighted ancestry or affinity with the 'redman', spiritualist discourse retraced lines of domestic expulsion and colonial expansion in order to privilege systems of knowledge antithetical to modern Western European society. What is more, the elevation of Native Americans within the seance sometimes translated to direct political action, such as when spiritualists called for the protection of land or supported campaigns for tribal self governance.[124] However, though native spirits might have impressed seancegoers with their simple natural wisdom and even inspired some well-meaning reformers to press for political change in the terrestrial world, such spirits were still framed by language of colonisation and subject to the same power relations.

The ancient and uncorrupted rituals of indigenous peoples, though venerated to a degree, were ultimately written into the movement's own evolutionary timeline, where they remained representative of an earlier or lower iteration of the spiritualist message. Where in *Primitive Culture* Tylor flattened out the differences between the 'Red Indian medicine-man, the Tatar necromancer, the Highland ghost-seer, and the Boston medium', spiritualist writing produced a hierarchy that acknowledged the practices of the primitive tribesperson and the second-sighted crofter as necessary stages in an evolutionary process, the pinnacle of which was currently being realised in the spirit communications being held in the comfortable parlours of Britain and North America. Writing in the *History of the Supernatural*, William Howitt argued that though we can observe the same 'eternal law' that guides spiritualist practice in the 'very lowest manifestations, as in the Australians and Negroes', it does so in these cases 'under mountains of encumbrance'.[125] Modern spiritualism had, its proponents argued, wrested sacred knowledge from the crude rituals of the world's savage peoples and reformed it under the enlightened gaze of science, technology and print culture. Considering the biographical function served by second sight in this project, it is significant that the faculty featured far more prominently in the early life of mediums; just as the primitive islander presents, in evolutionary terms, the childhood of the race, so too are his visionary traditions designated as prior. Written into the spiritualist *Bildungsroman*, the second sight of the Highlander was subject to generational erasure, dismissed as an early iteration of a visionary faculty whose potential could only be fully realised in the form of spirit mediumship.

———

In a paper delivered to the International Folklore Congress in 1891, Edward Tylor described for his audience some of the charms and amulets held by the Pitt Rivers Museum. Of particular interest was a 'large *corp cre* [...] made only two years ago in a parish in the far north of Scotland', that had been found with pins and needles pressed into its roughly hewn form. Concluding his thoughts on the object, the anthropologist mused that it composed 'curious evidence for the conservatism of magic—the most conservative of human arts—that our civilised country still furnishes specimens which Australia or Egypt cannot rival'.[126] According to Tylor, attempts to contact the dead being made in drawing rooms around the country were, like the dark arts still practised in remoter regions, evidence not of progress but of the deeply 'conservative' nature of irrational beliefs. Spiritualist thinkers recognised the same connections, between 'our civilised country' and the primitive peoples of the world, but framed these in oppositional terms. The continuities mapped out by evolutionary anthropologists demonstrated, to believers such as William Howitt, not the anachronistic folly of spiritualism but rather the universality of its principles. Spiritualism was but the 'last blossom on a very ancient tree' as 'old as the hills and as ubiquitous as the ocean'.[127] Peculiar affinities existed between the discourses of anthropology and spiritualism. For one, they shared in the same alchemical impulse to transform disparate tales of exotic tribes and customs, superstitions, ghosts and myths into coherent narratives; schematic visions of human and spiritual development that drew 'our civilised country' into closer proximity with the 'unlettered nations' of the world. Such nations were, of course, the unwilling subjects of colonial rule. Like ethnographic studies and anthropometric surveys, spirit-rapping affirmed, for believers at least, Britain's sense of itself as an enlightened society; Tylor may have dismissed it as a survival of savage thought, but for many the advent of other-worldly communications represented the absolute pinnacle of spiritual advancement.

The teleological work of evolutionist thinking, whether performed as anthropological orthodoxy or spiritualist heterodoxy, cemented the distinction between colonial subject and object. Importantly, this demarcation was not wholly contingent on the elevation of white over non-white, as domestic populations were also marked out as primitive. In the 'far north of Scotland', where crofters still practised magic with ominous clay figures, it was possible to catch a glimpse of the savage past lurking in the outer regions of 'our civilised country'; supernatural beliefs persisted in the rural peripheries because these communities remained stalled at an earlier phase, from which the rest of Britain had long progressed. Transposed from culture to biology, evolutionism recast the individual as an entity composed by a series of ancestral adaptations and progressions. Under this model, folk traditions and local customs took on the status of hereditary remnants, the enduring fragments of a genealogical past. The power of second sight was, as we have seen, pressed by spiritualist thinkers as a living and embodied history, accessed through hereditary lines. Written into biographical narratives, the prophetic tradition made it possible for mediums to situate their powers within a history of involuntary and inherited gifts. Written into a spiritualist *Bildungsroman*, second sight functioned as a precursor to the superior and more-evolved methods of extraterrestrial communication being uncovered by modern mediums.

NOTES

1. William Howitt quoted by his daughter Anna Marie Howitt in her *Pioneers of the Spiritual Reformation: Biographical Sketches* (Cambridge University Press: Cambridge, 2010), pp. 235–236. (Howitt 2010)
2. *Pioneers of the Spiritual Reformation*, pp. 235–236
3. 'Howitt's Journal of Literature and Popular Progress (1847–1848)', in *Dictionary of Nineteenth-Century Journalism in Great Britain and Ireland*, eds. Laurel Brake and Marysa Demoor (Gent and London: Academia Press and British Library, 2009), pp. 293–294. ('Howitt's Journal of...' 2009).

4. Peter Mandler, 'Howitt, William (1792–1879)' and Susan Drain 'Howitt, Mary (1799–1888)', *Oxford Dictionary of National Biography* (Oxford: Oxford University Press, 2004). (Mandler 2004)

5. Howitt, *A Boy's Adventure in the Wilds of Australia; or, Herbert's Notebook* (Boston: Ticknor and Fields, 1855), p. 157. (Howitt 1855).

6. Howitt, *Colonisation and Christianity: A Popular History of the Treatment of Natives by Europeans in all Their Colonies* (London: Longman, 1838), p. 508. (Howitt 1838).

7. Howitt, *Tallangetta, the Squatter's Home: A Story of Australian Life* 2 Vols. (London: Longman, Brown, Green & Roberts, 1857), vol. 1 p. iv. (Howitt 1857).

8. 'Summerland' being the afterlife, or rather, as was popularised by Andrew Jackson Davis's *The Great Harmonia* (1850–1861) and *A Stellar Key to the Summerland* (1868) a realm that represents the pinnacle of human spiritual achievement.

9. Ruth Brandon's *The Spiritualists: The Passion for the Occult in the Nineteenth and Twentieth Centuries* (London: Weidenfeld and Nicholson, 1983). (Brandon 1983) and Roland Pearsall's *The Table-Rappers: The Victorians and the Occult* (Stroud: Michael Joseph, 1972). (Pearsall 1972) provide detailed overviews of the movement's Victorian history.

10. *Tallangetta*, vol. 2, p. 26

11. Ibid., p. 27

12. Owen Davies, *The Haunted: A Social History of Ghosts* (Basingstoke: Palgrave Macmillan, 2007), p. 71. (Davies 2007).

13. *Tallangetta*, vol. 1, pp. v–iv

14. Ibid., pp. v–iv

15. Ibid., p. iii

16. Richard J. Noakes, 'Telegraphy Is an Occult Art: Cromwell Fleetwood Varley and the Diffusion of Electricity to the Other World', *The British Journal for the History of Science* 32.4 (Dec. 1999), 421–459 (422). (Noakes 1999). See also Pamela Thurschwell, *Literature, Technology, and Magical Thinking, 1880–1920.* (Cambridge: Cambridge University Press, 2001). (Thurschwell 2001).

17. See Daniel Cotton's *Abyss of Reason: Cultural Movements, Revelations and Betrayals* (Oxford: Oxford University Press, 1991). (Cotton 1991) and Logie Barrow's *Independent Spirits: Spiritualism and English Plebeians, 1850–1910* (London: Routledge, 1986). (Barrow 1986).

18. Christine Ferguson, 'Eugenics and the Afterlife: Lombroso, Doyle, and the Spiritualist Purification of the Race', *Journal of Victorian Culture* 12.1 (Spring, 2007) 68–85. (Ferguson 2007) and *Determined Spirits: Eugenics, Heredity and Racial Regeneration in Anglo-American Spiritualist Writing,*

1848–1930 (Edinburgh: Edinburgh University Press, 2012). ('*Determined Spirits: Eugenics...*' 2012)

19. Alex Owen, *The Darkened Room: Women, Power and Spiritualism in Late Victorian England* (Chicago: University of Chicago Press, 1989), p. 70. (Owen 1989).

20. Alfred Russel Wallace to Thomas Huxley, November 1866 quoted in Malcolm Jay Kittler, 'Alfred Russel Wallace, the Origin of Man, and Spiritualism', *Isis* 65.2 (June, 1974) 144–192 (169). (Kittler 1974).

21. *Light: A Journal devoted to Highest Interests of Humanity, both Here and Hereafter* 29 July 1881, 354.

22. William Howitt, *The History of Discovery in Australia, Tasmania and New Zealand* 2 Vols. (London: Longman, Green and Roberts, 1865), vol. 2 p. 202. (Howitt 1865).

23. Edward Burnett Tylor, 'Notes on "Spiritualism"', *Tylor Papers Pitt Rivers*, 3/12 2009.148.1 (Tylor 2009).

24. Georgiana Houghton, *Chronicles of the Photographs of Spiritual Beings and Phenomena Invisible to the Material Eye: Interblended with Personal Narratives* (London: E.W. Allen, 1882), pp. 39–40. (Houghton 1882).

25. George W. Stocking Jr., 'Animism in Theory and Practice: E.B. Tylor's Unpublished Notes on "Spiritualism"', *Man* 6. 1 (Mar. 1971), 88–104. (Stocking 1971) and *Victorian Anthropology* (London: Macmillan, 1987), pp. 191–192.

26. 'Report on Spiritualism, of the Committee of the London Dialectical Society', (London: Longmans, Green, Reader and Dyer, 1871). ('Report on Spiritualism...' 1871)

27. Pam Hirsch, 'Howitt [Watts], Anna Mary (1824–1884)', *Oxford Dictionary of National Biography* (Oxford: Oxford University Press, 2004). (Hirsch 2004).

28. Frank Podmore, *Modern Spiritualism: A History and Criticism,* vol. 2 (London: Methuen and Co., 1902), p. 163. (Podmore 1902).

29. Rachel Oberter provides an account of her life and her mediumistic abilities in 'The Sublimation of Matter into Spirit: Anna Mary Howitt's Automatic Drawings', *Ashgate Research Companion to 19th Century Spiritualism and the Occult,* eds. Tatiana Kontou and Sarah A. Wilburn (Surrey and Burlington VT: Ashgate, 2012). (Oberter 2012).

30. See Alison Twells, 'The Innate Yearnings of Our Souls': Subjectivity, Religiosity and Outward Testimony in Mary Howitt's *Autobiography* (1889)', *Journal of Victorian Culture* 17.3 (2012), 309–328. (Twells 2012).

31. Edward Burnett Tylor, *Primitive Culture: Researches into the Development of Mythology, Philosophy, Religion, Art and Custom* 2 Vols. (London: John Murray, 1871), vol. 1 p. 1. (Tylor 1871).

32. C. Holdsworth, 'Tylor, Edward Burnett' (1832–1917), Anthropologist', *Oxford Dictionary of National Biography* (Holdsworth 2004).
33. *Primitive Culture*, vol. 1, p. 15
34. Edward Burnett Tylor, On the Survival of Savage Thought in Modern Civilisation', *Proceedings of the Royal Institute* 5 (1869), 522–535 (528). (Tylor 1869).
35. J.W. Burrow, *Evolution and Society: A Study in Victorian Social Theory* (Cambridge: Cambridge University Press, 1966) pp. 240–241. (Burrow 1966).
36. Tylor, 'The Religion of Savages', *Fortnightly Review* 15.8 (1866), 71–86 (83). (Tylor 1866).
37. *Primitive Culture*, v. 1 p. 141
38. Ibid., p. 130
39. Malcolm Jay Kittler, 'Alfred Russel Wallace, the Origin of Man, and Spiritualism', *Isis* 65.2 (Jun. 1974), 144–192. (Kittler 1974).
40. Ibid. 93
41. For a discussion of the Victorian 'armchair' anthropologist see Henrika Kuklick, 'After Ishmael: The Fieldwork Tradition and its Future', in *Anthropological Locations: Boundaries and Grounds of a Field Site* (Berkeley CA: University of California Press, 1997), pp. 47–65. (Kuklick 1997)
42. *Primitive Culture*, vol. 1, p. 405
43. 'Visions in Connection with the Rebellion of 1745, and the Battlefield of Culloden', *Light* 16 June 1884, 277, 'Excessive Lamentation for the Dead painful for the Departed', *Light* 23 August 1883, 382–383 (383), *Light* 11 October 1884, 415–416 and Howitt's 'Remarkable Instances of Second Sight', *Light* January 1881 published posthumously
44. *History of the Supernatural*, vol. 2, p. 442. See Chapter 1 for a discussion of Theophilus Insulanus,*Treaties on Second Sight, Dreams and Apparitions* (Edinburgh: Ruddiman, Auld and Company, 1763) (Insulanus 1763).
45. Ibid., p. 443
46. *History of the Supernatural*, vol. 1, p. 18
47. Edward B. Tylor to Alfred R. Wallace 26 November 1886, BL Tylor Papers, Adel 46339 ff. 6
48. Alfred Russel Wallace, 'Are the Phenomena of Spiritualism in Harmony with Science?', *Light* 30 May 30 1885, 1. (Wallace 1885).
49. *The History of the Supernatural*, p. 442
50. 'Table Turning and Spirit Rapping', *Bentley's Miscellany* 48 (July 1860), 568–578 (572).
51. Ibid., 573
52. *History of the Supernatural*, vol. 2, pp. 395, 390, 402

53. Nicola Bown, Carolyn Burdett and Pamela Thurshwell, *The Victorian Supernatural* (Cambridge: Cambridge University Press, 2004) p. 8. (Bown et al. 2004).
54. George W. Stocking, *Victorian Anthropology* (New York and London: Macmillan Press, 1987), p. 192. (Stocking 1987).
55. Alfred Russel Wallace, *Defence of Modern Spiritualism* (Boston: Colby and Rich, 1874), p. 53. (Wallace 1874).
56. See Krisztina Fenyo, *Contempt, Sympathy and Romance: Lowland Perceptions of the Highlands and the Clearances During the Famine Years, 1845–1855* (Edinburgh: Tuckwell Press, 2000). (Fenyo 2000).
57. *Primitive Culture*, p. 2
58. Johannes Fabien, *Time and the Other: How Anthropology Makes its Object* (Chicago: Columbia University Press, 1983), 11–12. (Fabien 1983).
59. John Ferguson McLennan, *Studies in Ancient History: Comprising an Inquiry into the Origin of Exogamy*, ed. Arthur Platt (London: Macmillan and Co., 1896), p. 14. (McLennan 1896).
60. Alfred Nutt, 'Folk-Lore Terminology', *The Folk-Lore Journal* 2.10 (1884), 311. (Nutt 1884).
61. Richard Dodson, *The British Folklorists: A History* (Chicago: University of Chicago Press, 1968), pp. 392–393. (Dodson 1968).
62. Malcolm Chapman, *The Gaelic Vision in Scottish Culture* (London: Croon Helm, 1978), p. 123. (Chapman 1978).
63. W. R. S. Ralston, 'Notes on Folk-Tales', *The Folk-Lore Record* 1 (1878), 71–98 (72). (Ralston 1878).
64. Malcolm Chapman, *The Celts: The Construction of a Myth* (London: MacMillan, 1992), p. 117. (Chapman 1992).
65. Matthew Arnold, *On the Study of Celtic Literature* (London: Smith, Elder & Co., 1867), p. 40. (Arnold 1867).
66. *On the Study of Celtic Literature,* p. 15
67. M. Martin, *A Description of the Western Isles of Scotland,* 2nd edition (London: A. Bell, 1716), p. 312. (Martin 1716), James Boswell, *The Journal of a Tour to the Hebrides with Samuel Johnson* (1775) ed. Mary Lascelles (New Haven: Yale University Press, 1971), p. 103. (Boswell 1775) and Tylor, On the Survival of Savage Thought in Modern Civilisation', 524
68. Roger Smith provides a useful account of the development of willpower as an emotional ideal from the Enlightenment onwards, *Inhibition: History and Meaning in the Sciences of Mind and Brain* (California: University of California Press, 1992). (Smith 1992).
69. Herbert Spencer, 'Emotions in Primitive Man', *Popular Science Monthly* 6 (January 1875) 331–339 (332). (Spencer 1875).
70. Ibid.

71. Ibid., p. 406
72. Alfred Nutt, 'The Critical Study of Gaelic Literature Indispensable for the History of the Gaelic Race', *The Celtic Review* 1 (1904), 49. (Nutt 1904), this is echoed by Arnold who insists that the Celtic culture expressed 'What it has been, what it has done, let is ask to attend to that, as a matter of science and history; not what it will be, or will do, as a matter of modern politics', *On the Study of Celtic Literature,* p. 22–23
73. Mrs. Elizabeth Sweet, *The Future Life: as Described and Portrayed by Spirits through Mrs. Elizabeth Sweet* with intro. Judge J.W. Edmonds, 6th edn. (Boston: Colby & Rich, 1878), p. 359. (Sweet 18787).
74. 'Science and Spiritualism', *The Anthropological Review* 5 (1867) 242–243 (242). ('Science and Spiritualism'... 1867).
75. Tylor, 'On the Tasmanians as Representatives of Palaeolithic Man', *The Journal of the Anthropological Institute of Great Britain and Ireland,* 23 (1894) 141–152 (152). (Tylor 1894).
76. Peter Pels, 'Alfred Wallace, Edward Tylor, and the Visual Politics of Fact' in *Magic and Modernity: Interfaces of Revelation and Concealment* eds. Peter Pels and Birgit Meyer (California: Stanford University Press, 2003), pp. 241–271. (Pels 2003).
77. Sarah Wilburn, *Possessed Victorians: Extra Spheres in Nineteenth-Century Mystical Writings* (Aldershot and Burlington VT: Ashgate, 2006), p. 131. (Wilburn 2006).
78. *History of the Supernatural,* vol. 1, p. 444
79. Ibid., p. 12
80. John Page Hopps, *The Future Life* (London: Simpkin and Marshall, 1884), p. 12. (Hopps 1884).
81. Andrew Jackson Davis, *A Stellar Key to the Summerland* Vol. I (Boston: William White & Co., 1867), p. 1. (Davis 1867).
82. Francis Galton, *The Anthropometric Laboratory* (London: William Clowes and Sons, 1884). (Galton 1884).
83. See James Urry, 'Englishmen, Celts and Iberians: The Ethnographic Survey of the United Kingdom, 1892–1899', in *Functionalism Historicized: Essays on British Social Anthropology* ed. George Stocking (Wisconsin: University of Wisconsin Press, 1984) 83–105. (Urry 1984).
84. Francis Galton, *Hereditary Genius* (New York: D. Appleton and Co., 1870), pp. 1–4. (Galton 1870).
85. Ibid., pp. 1–4
86. Ibid., pp. 336–350
87. Ibid., p. 340
88. Douglas Lorimer, 'Theoretical Racism in Late-Victorian Anthropology 1870–1900', *Victorian Studies,* 31, 1988, 405–432. (Lorimer 1988).

89. John Beddoe, *The Races of Britain: A Contribution to the Anthropology of Western Europe* (London: Trubner and Co., 1885), pp. 9–11. (Beddoe 1885).

90. Beddoe represents an extreme, but similar sentiments were expressed else-where. Thomas Huxley, for instance, despite adhering to a monogenist view of descent, still divided Anglo-Saxon from Celt (Xanthochroi from Melanchroi) in 'On the Geographical Distributions of the Chief Modifications of Man', *Journal of the Ethnographical Society* 2 (1869–1870). (Huxley 1869–1870)

91. *Determined Spirits*, p. 10

92. 'The Problem of Individual Life', *Light* 27 May 1882, 248–249 (248).

93. Ibid., p. 248

94. Alfred Russell Wallace, *Contributions to the Theory of Natural Selection* (London, 1870), p. 351. (Wallace 1870).

95. 'An Hours Communion with the Dead', *Light* 5 March 1881, 71

96. *The Spiritual Magazine* (December 1867), 545

97. Herbert Spencer, *The Principles of Psychology* (London: Longman, Brown, Green and Longmans, 1885), p. 581. (Spencer 1885).

98. See Peter Lamont, *The First Psychic: The Peculiar Mystery of a Notorious Victorian Wizard* (Preston: Abacus Press, 2005). (Lamont 2005).

99. 'Defence of Spiritualism' *Scots Observer* 5 January 1889, 194–195 (194)

100. Daniel Dunglas Home, *Incidents in My Life*, intro. Judge Edmonds (New York: A.J. Davis & Co., 1864), pp. 107–108. (Home 1864).

101. *Incidents in My Life*, pp. 20–22

102. Andrew Jackson Davis, *The Magic Staff: An Autobiography of Andrew Jackson Davis* (1857). (Davis 1857), Howitt *History of the Supernatural* Vol. II, p. 189, Benjamin Coleman, 'Spiritualism in America—IV', *Spiritual Magazine* (October 1861) 433–439 (Coleman 1861).

103. William Howitt, *Tallangetta, the Squatter's Home*, vol. 1, pp. iii

104. Lord Reay to Pepys, 24 October 1699, quoted in Michael Hunter, *The Occult Laboratory: Magic, Science and Second Sight in Late 17th Century Scotland* (Boydell Press: Woodbridge, 2001) pp. 161–165 (163). (Hunter 2001).

105. P. Hately Waddell, 'The State of the Ossianic Controversy', *The Celtic Magazine* 3 (January 1, 1876) 67–71 (67). (Waddell 1876).

106. *Modern American Spiritualism*, p. 482

107. Brian Inglis, *Natural and Supernatural: A History of the Paranormal for the Earliest Times to 1914* (London: Hodder and Stoughton, 1977), p. 207. (Inglis 1977).

108. Thomas Brevoir, 'Mysteries of Nature and of Spirit Prevision', *Spiritual Magazine* (December, 1865) 566–571 (570). (Brevoir 1865) and Emma

Hardinge Britten, *Modern American Spiritualism: A Twenty Years' Record of the Communication Between Earth and the World of Spirits* (New York: Banner of Light, 1870), p. 482. (Britten 1870).

109. See Rene L. Bergland, *The National Uncanny: Indian Ghosts and American Subjects* (Hanover and London: Dartmouth, 2000). (Bergland 2000).

110. Stocking, 'Animism in Theory and Practice', 97

111. Ibid., p. 94

112. Margaret S. Cooper to Daniel Dunglas Home 24 Monday 1876, SPR.MS 28/7 (ii), Cambridge MS

113. *History of the Supernatural,* vol. 1 p. 56 and *Modern American Spiritualism,* p. 482

114. Charles Dickens, 'The Lost Arctic Voyagers', *Household Words* 10 (2 December 1854) 361–365 (362). (Dickens 1854).

115. Sarah Moss, *Scott's Last Biscuit: The Literature of Polar Travel* (Oxford: Oxford University Press, 2005), p. 143. (Moss 2005)

116. Charles Dickens and Wilkie Collins, *The Frozen Deep* (1856), quoted in Heather Davis-Fisch, *Loss and Cultural Remains in Performance: The Ghosts of the Franklin Expedition (London: Palgrave Macmillan, 2012) p. 54*

117. Lillian Nayder, *Unequal Partners: Charles Dickens, Wilkie Collins and Victorian Authorship* (Ithaca and London: Cornell University Press, 2002), p. 70. (Nayder 2002).

118. Alexandre Brierre de Boismont, *History of Dreams, Visions, Apparitions, Magnetism and Somnambulism* (Philadelphia: Lindsay and Blakiston, 1855), p. 243. (De Boismont 1855). The author proposes that these similarities may be explained by 'the effect of cold' in bringing about certain 'nervous states' and thus ecstatic visions' (26)

119. Wilkie Collins, *The Frozen Deep* (London: Richard Bentley, 1874), p. 10. (Collins 1874).

120. Collins, p. 12

121. Marlene Tromp, *Altered States: Sex, Nation, Drugs and Self-Transformation in Victorian Spiritualism* (Albany: State University of New York Press, 2006), p. 81. (Tromp 2006).

122. Jeffrey D. Lavoie, *The Theosophical Society: The History of a Spiritualist Movement* (Florida: BrownWalker Press, 2012). (Lavoie 2012).

123. Gauri Viswanathan, 'The Ordinary Business of Occultism', *Critical Inquiry,* 27.1 (Autumn, 2000) 1–20. (Viswanathan 2000).

124. See Molly McGarry, *Ghosts of Futures Past: Spiritualism and the Cultural Politics of Nineteenth Century* (California: University of California Press, 2008). (McGarry 2008).

125. *The History of the Supernatural,* vol. 1, p. 56 and *Modern American Spiritualism,* p. 482

126. Edward B. Tylor, *Exhibition of Charms and Amulets'*, *Transactions of the International Folk-Lore Congress 1891* (London: D. Nutt, 1892) Tylor Papers Pitt Rivers, Box 4 4/12 387–394 (390). (Tylor 1892).
127. *History of the Supernatural*, vol. 1, p. 18

REFERENCES

Arnold, Matthew, *On the Study of Celtic Literature* (London: Smith, Elder & Co., 1867).

Barrow, Logie, *Independent Spirits: Spiritualism and English Plebeians, 1850–1910* (London: Routledge, 1986).

Beddoe, John, *The Races of Britain: A Contribution to the Anthropology of Western Europe* (London: Trubner and Co., 1885).

Bergland, Renée L., *The National Uncanny: Indian Ghosts and American Subjects* (Hanover, NH and London: Dartmouth, 2000).

Boswell, James, *The Journal of a Tour to the Hebrides with Samuel Johnson* (1775), ed. Mary Lascelles (New Haven, CT: Yale University Press, 1971).

Bown, Nicola, Carolyn Burdett and Pamela Thurshwelleds eds., *The Victorian Supernatural* (Cambridge: Cambridge University Press, 2004).

Brandon, Ruth, *The Spiritualists: The Passion for the Occult in the Nineteenth and Twentieth Centuries* (London: Weidenfeld and Nicholson, 1983).

Brevoir, Thomas, 'Mysteries of Nature and of Spirit Prevision', *Spiritual Magazine* (December 1865), 566–71.

Britten, Emma Hardinge, *Modern American Spiritualism: A Twenty Years' Record of the Communication Between Earth and the World of Spirits* (New York: Banner of Light, 1870).

Burrow, J.W., *Evolution and Society: A Study in Victorian Social Theory* (Cambridge: Cambridge University Press, 1966).

Chapman, Malcolm, *The Celts: The Construction of a Myth* (London: Macmillan, 1992).

Chapman, Malcolm, *The Gaelic Vision in Scottish Culture* (London: Croom Helm, 1978).

Coleman, Benjamin, 'Spiritualism in America—IV', *Spiritual Magazine* (October 1861).

Collins, Wilkie, *The Frozen Deep* (London: Richard Bentley, 1874).

Cotton, Daniel, *Abyss of Reason: Cultural Movements, Revelations and Betrayals* (Oxford: Oxford University Press, 1991).

Davies, Owen, *The Haunted: A Social History of Ghosts* (Basingstoke: Palgrave Macmillan, 2007).

Davis, Andrew Jackson, *The Magic Staff: An Autobiography of Andrew Jackson Davis* (New York: J.S. Brown, 1857).

Davis, Andrew Jackson, *A Stellar Key to the Summerland* (Boston, MA: William White & Co, 1867), vol. 1.

De Boismont, Alexandre Brierre, *History of Dreams A History of Dreams, Visions, Apparitions, Magnetism and Somnambulism* (Philadelphia, PA: Lindsay and Blakiston, 1855).

Dickens, Charles, 'The Lost Arctic Voyagers', *Household Words* 10 (2 December 1854), 361–5.

Dodson, Richard, *The British Folklorists: A History* (Chicago: University of Chicago Press, 1968).

Fabien, Johannes, *Time and the Other: How Anthropology Makes its Object* (Chicago: Columbia University Press, 1983).

Fenyo, Krisztina, *Contempt, Sympathy and Romance: Lowland Perceptions of the Highlands and the Clearances During the Famine Years, 1845–1855* (Edinburgh: Tuckwell Press, 2000).

Ferguson, Christine, *Determined Spirits: Eugenics, Heredity and Racial Regeneration in Anglo-American Spiritualist Writing, 1848–1930* (Edinburgh: Edinburgh University Press, 2012).

Ferguson, Christine, 'Eugenics and the Afterlife: Lombroso, Doyle, and the Spiritualist Purification of the Race', *Journal of Victorian Culture* 12.1 (Spring 2007), 68–85.

Galton, Francis, *The Anthropometric Laboratory* (London: William Clowes and Sons, 1884).

Galton, Francis, *Hereditary Genius* (New York: D. Appleton and Co., 1870).

Hately Waddell, P., 'The State of the Ossianic Controversy', *The Celtic Magazine* 3 (1 January 1876), 67–71 (67).

Hirsch, Pam, 'Howitt [Watts], Anna Mary (1824–1884)', in *Oxford Dictionary of National Biography* (Oxford: Oxford University Press, 2004).

Holdsworth, C., '"Tylor, Edward Burnett" (1832–1917), Anthropologist', in *Oxford Dictionary of National Biography* (Oxford: Oxford University Press, 2004).

Home, Daniel Dunglas, *Incidents in My Life*, intro. Judge Edmonds (New York: A.J. Davis & Co., 1864).

Hopps, John Page, *The Future Life* (London: Simpkin and Marshall, 1884).

Houghton, Georgiana, *Chronicles of the Photographs of Spiritual Beings and Phenomena Invisible to the Material Eye: Interblended with Personal Narratives* (London: E.W. Allen, 1882).

Howitt, Anne Mary, *Pioneers of the Spiritual Reformation: Biographical Sketches* [1883] (Cambridge: Cambridge University Press, 2010).

Howitt, William, *A Boy's Adventure in the Wilds of Australia; or, Herbert's Notebook* (Boston, MA: Ticknor and Fields, 1855).

Howitt, William, *Colonisation and Christianity: A Popular History of the Treatment of Natives by Europeans in all Their Colonies* (London: Longman, 1838).

Howitt, William, *Tallangetta, the Squatter's Home: A Story of Australian Life*, 2 vols (London: Longman, Brown, Green & Roberts, 1857), vol. 1.

Howitt, William, *The History of Discovery in Australia, Tasmania and New Zealand*, 2 vols (London: Longman, Green and Roberts, 1865), vol. 2.

Hunt, James, 'Science and Spiritualism', *The Anthropological Review* 5 (1867), 242–3.

Hunter, Michael, *The Occult Laboratory: Magic, Science and Second Sight in Late 17th Century Scotland* (Woodbridge: Boydell Press, 2001), 161–5.

Huxley, Thomas, 'On the Geographical Distributions of the Chief Modifications of Man', *Journal of the Ethnographical Society* 2 (1869–70) 404–412.

Inglis, Brian, *Natural and Supernatural: A History of the Paranormal for the Earliest Times to 1914* (London: Hodder and Stoughton, 1977).

Insulanus, Theophilus, *Treaties on Second Sight, Dreams and Apparitions* (Edinburgh: Ruddiman, Auld and Company, 1763).

Kittler, Malcolm Jay, 'Alfred Russel Wallace, the Origin of Man, and Spiritualism', *Isis* 65.2 (June 1974), 144–92.

Kuklick, Henrika, 'After Ishmael: The Fieldwork Tradition and its Future', in *Anthropological Locations: Boundaries and Grounds of a Field Site* eds. Akhil Gupta and James Ferguson (Berkeley: University of California Press, 1997), pp. 47–65.

Lamont, Peter, *The First Psychic: The Peculiar Mystery of a Notorious Victorian Wizard* (Preston: Abacus Press, 2005).

Lavoie, Jeffrey D., *The Theosophical Society: The History of a Spiritualist Movement* (Boca Raton, FL: BrownWalker Press, 2012).

Lorimer, Douglas, 'Theoretical Racism in Late-Victorian Anthropology 1870–1900', *Victorian Studies* 31 (1988), 405–32.

Maidment, Brian, 'Howitt's Journal of Literature and Popular Progress (1847–1848)' in *Dictionary of Nineteenth-Century Journalism in Great Britain and Ireland*, ed. Laurel Brake and Marysa Demoor (Gent and London: Academia Press and British Library, 2009), pp. 293–4.

Mandler, Peter, 'Howitt, William (1792–1879)' and Susan Drain 'Howitt, Mary (1799–1888), *Oxford Dictionary of National Biography* (Oxford: Oxford University Press, 2004).

Martin, M., *A Description of the Western Isles of Scotland*, 2nd edition (London: A. Bell, 1716), p. 312.

McGarry, Molly, *Ghosts of Futures Past: Spiritualism and the Cultural Politics of the Nineteenth Century* (California: University of California Press, 2008).

McLennan, John Ferguson, *Studies in Ancient History: Comprising an Inquiry into the Origin of Exogamy*, ed. Arthur Platt (London: Macmillan and Co., 1896).

Moss, Sarah, *Scott's Last Biscuit: The Literature of Polar Travel* (Oxford: Oxford University Press, 2005).

Nayder, Lillian, *Unequal Partners: Charles Dickens, Wilkie Collins and Victorian Authorship* (Ithaca, NY and London: Cornell University Press, 2002).

Noakes, Richard J., 'Telegraphy Is an Occult Art: Cromwell Fleetwood Varley and the Diffusion of Electricity to the Other World', *The British Journal for the History of Science* 32.4 (December 1999), 421–59.

Nutt, Alfred, 'The Critical Study of Gaelic Literature Indispensable for the History of the Gaelic Race', *The Celtic Review* 1 (1904), 49.

Nutt, Alfred, 'Folk-Lore Terminology', *The Folk-Lore Journal* 2.10 (1884), 311.

Oberter, Rachel, 'The Sublimation of Matter into Spirit: Anna Mary Howitt's Automatic Drawings', in *Ashgate Research Companion to 19th Century Spiritualism and the Occult*, ed Tatiana Kontou and Sarah A. Wilburn (Aldershot and Burlington, VT: Ashgate, 2012).

Owen, Alex, *The Darkened Room: Women, Power and Spiritualism in Late Victorian England* (Chicago: University of Chicago Press, 1989).

Pearsall, Ronald, *The Table-Rappers: The Victorians and the Occult* (London: Michael Joseph, 1972).

Pels, Peter, 'Alfred Wallace, Edward Tylor, and the Visual Politics of Fact', in *Magic and Modernity: Interfaces of Revelation and Concealment*, ed Peter Pels and Birgit Meyer (Palo Alto, CA: Stanford University Press, 2003), pp. 241–71.

Podmore, Frank, *Modern Spiritualism: A History and Criticism* (London: Methuen and Co., 1902), vol. 2, p. 163.

Ralston, W. R. S., 'Notes on Folk-Tales', *The Folk-Lore Record* 1 (1878), 71–98.

Report on Spiritualism, of the Committee of the London Dialectical Society (London: Longmans, Green, Reader and Dyer, 1871).

Smith, Roger, *Inhibition: History and Meaning in the Sciences of Mind and Brain* (Berkeley, CA: University of California Press, 1992).

Spencer, Herbert, 'Emotions in Primitive Man', *Popular Science Monthly* 6 (January 1875), 331–9.

Spencer, Herbert, *The Principles of Psychology* (London: Longman, Brown, Green and Longmans, 1885).

Stocking, George W., 'Animism in Theory and Practice: E.B. Tylor's Unpublished Notes on "Spiritualism"', *Man* 6.1 (March 1971), 88–104.

Stocking, George W., *Victorian Anthropology* (New York and London: Macmillan, 1987).

Sweet, Elizabeth, *The Future Life: as Described and Portrayed by Spirits through Mrs. Elizabeth Sweet* with intro. by Judge J.W. Edmonds, 6th edn (Boston: Colby & Rich, 1878).

Thurschwell, Pamela, *Literature, Technology, and Magical Thinking, 1880–1920* (Cambridge: Cambridge University Press, 2001).

Tromp, Marlene, *Altered States: Sex, Nation, Drugs and Self-Transformation in Victorian Spiritualism* (Albany: State University of New York Press, 2006).

Twells, Alison, 'The Innate Yearnings of Our Souls': Subjectivity, Religiosity and Outward Testimony in Mary Howitt's *Autobiography* (1889)', *Journal of Victorian Culture* 17.3 (2012), 309–28.

Tylor, Edward B., 'Notes on "Spiritualism"', *Tylor Papers Pitt Rivers* 3.12 (2009), 148.1.

Tylor, Edward B., *Exhibition of Charms and Amulets'*, *Transactions of the International Folk-Lore Congress 1891* (London: D. Nutt, 1892).

Tylor, Edward B., 'On the Survival of Savage Thought in Modern Civilisation', *Proceedings of the Royal Institute* 5 (1869), 522–35.

Tylor, Edward B., 'On the Tasmanians as Representatives of Palaeolithic Man', *The Journal of the Anthropological Institute of Great Britain and Ireland* 23 (1894), 141–52.

Tylor, Edward B., *Primitive Culture: Researches into the Development of Mythology, Philosophy, Religion, Art and Custom*, 2 vols (London: John Murray, 1871), vol. 1.

Tylor, Edward B., 'The Religion of Savages', *Fortnightly Review* 15.8 (1866), 71–86.

Urry, James, 'Englishmen, Celts and Iberians: The Ethnographic Survey of the United Kingdom, 1892–1899', in *Functionalism Historicized: Essays on British Social Anthropology*, ed. George Stocking (Madison: University of Wisconsin Press, 1984), pp. 83–105.

Viswanathan, Gauri, 'The Ordinary Business of Occultism', *Critical Inquiry* 27.1 (Autumn 2000), 1–20.

Wallace, Alfred Russel, 'Are the Phenomena of Spiritualism in Harmony with Science?', *Light* 30 (30 May 1885), 1.

Wallace, Alfred Russel, *Contributions to the Theory of Natural Selection* (London: Macmillan and Co., 1870).

Wallace, Alfred Russel, *Defence of Modern Spiritualism* (Boston: Colby and Rich, 1874).

Wilburn, Sarah, *Possessed Victorians: Extra Spheres in Nineteenth-Century Mystical Writings* (Aldershot and Burlington, VT: Ashgate, 2006).

CHAPTER 5

Psychical Research, Folklore and Romance

In 1893 the literary critic and belletrist Andrew Lang contributed to a revised edition of a seventeenth-century tract on second sight, *The Secret Commonwealth of Elves, Fauns and Fairies* (1691). Existing only in manuscript form until it was published by Walter Scott in 1815, this discourse on fairyland was the work of a Church of Scotland Minister and Gaelic scholar from Aberfoyle in the Trossachs, the Reverend Robert Kirk. Working with stories and lore collected from his parishioners, Kirk compiled a treatise on the metaphysics and social structure of an other world, existing in parallel to our own but peopled by airy creatures with 'Chamaeleon-like' bodies. Uniting Celtic tradition with Christian faith and elements of Neo-Platonist philosophy, this strange ethnography details the 'nature and actions of the subterranean (and for the most part) invisible people', who occasionally cause mischief in the human world by curdling milk or raiding larders at night.[1] Most remarkable is the codependent relationship that is said to exist between fairies and the second sighted: having inherited or acquired this special power of vision, seers alone can perceive the flitting of formless bodies through the air or sense the shadows of the '*coimimeadh*', the invisible fairy co-walkers who ape the movements of men. Those in possession of the second sight must also act as emissaries to the veiled fairy kingdom and inveigh on behalf of the human world, an onerous duty that most interpret as a curse. After Kirk passed away in 1692, rumours began to circulate that what appeared

© The Author(s) 2017   151
E. Richardson, *Second Sight in the Nineteenth Century*,
Palgrave Studies in Literature, Science and Medicine,
DOI 10.1057/978-1-137-51970-2_5

as sudden death was in fact part of a magical plot to imprison the author in a local fairy hill, so as to prevent him from publishing the treatise and exposing the hidden subterranean world. For over a century the fairies succeeded in their bowdlerising and the book remained in manuscript form. It was not until the beginning of the nineteenth century, after Scott chanced upon an incomplete and handwritten document in the Advocates Library in Edinburgh, that the *Secret Commonwealth* entered circulation. Seventy years on, Lang used this transcription as the basis for a new imprint, but despite their common source material the two editions pursued distinct editorial agendas.[2] Where Scott praised the treatise as a melancholy and poetic relic of the 'ancient traditions and high spirit of a people' long faded into history, Lang chose to validate the study as an early example of the successful application of the scientific method to the observation of supernatural phenomena.[3] A proper consideration of the *Secret Commonwealth* must, he argued, 'have a double aspect'. On the one hand it must be an essay on 'folk-lore, on popular beliefs, their relation to similar beliefs in other parts of the world', but on the other 'as mental phenomena are in question—such things as premonitions, hallucinations, abnormal or unusual experiences generally—a criticism of Mr Kirk should verge on "Psychical Research"'.[4] The unusual fairy metaphysic was not, Lang insisted, merely an antiquarian remnant; rather, Kirk's attempts to reposition the anomalous experiences of his parishioners within the realms of the natural presented the modern reader with a coherent and replicable methodology.

In his lengthy introduction to the 1893 edition of the *Secret Commonwealth*, Lang brought an encyclopaedic knowledge of folklore, religion, tribal customs, myth and not least the history of second sight, to bear upon the treatise. Indeed, no history of the prophetic tradition would be complete without reference to the writer, who returned frequently to the subject over the 30-year course of his career. In addition to republishing Kirk and editing another dedicated study, Alexander Mackenzie's *The Prophecies of the Brahan Seer* (1899), Lang recounts tales of premonitions among the Highlanders and speculations as to their nature throughout his expansive body of work on subjects as various as comparative anthropology, folklore, psychical research, Scottish history and literary criticism. Born in Selkirk in the Scottish Borders, Lang attended St Andrews University, enrolled in Balliol College, Oxford, on a scholarship and went on to spend most of his working life in England.[5] He began a career in journalism as a reviewer for *The Academy*, wrote regularly for the *Daily*

News and *The Morning Post* and published columns in *Fraser's Magazine, Cornhill Magazine, Blackwood's Edinburgh Magazine, Saturday Review, The Critic* and *Contemporary Review*. A prolific writer and hugely versatile thinker, his interests romped through fairy tale, traditional ballads, mythography, religion, literary criticism, poetry, biography, classical scholarship and golf, and his ideas helped to shape developing fields of knowledge such as ethnography and psychology. In the editorials that followed his death in 1912 the remarkable breadth of Lang's scholarly pursuits, though praised as evidence of an 'insatiable curiosity', was also condemned as evidence of an intellectual engagement that 'was wide' but 'not deep'.[6] For the *Athenaeum* he had 'outlived his age, for he was almost the last writer of the causerie on scholarly subjects', while an article printed in the *Academy* proposed that his 'very versatility became his undoing'.[7] By his own admission no 'specialist' who chose instead to 'dabble in a good many topics', Lang was dismissed by many of his contemporaries as a dilettante, lacking in expertise and unable to speak with sufficient authority on any one subject. Working in the boundary areas between disciplines and continually diverted by marginal and contested areas of knowledge such as second sight, for many he lacked the bearing of a serious scholar.

Modern historians have not, by and large, deviated far from this assessment of Lang's career, and he is usually to be found haunting footnotes or noted as the correspondent of a more prominent, easier to place, figure.[8] This is particularly true of his relationship with the Society for Psychical Research (SPR). Established in 1882, the SPR expanded on the investigative imperatives of earlier organisations such as the Ghost Club (1863) and the Oxford Phasmatological Society (1879–85) to present an 'organised and systematic attempt to investigate the large group of debatable phenomena designated by such terms as mesmeric, psychical and Spiritualistic'.[9] While older groups had operated along the lines of an informal club, whose members were encouraged to share an 'original Ghost Story' or 'some psychological experience of interest' with the similarly inclined, the SPR assumed the characteristics of a scientific body by instituting a system of peer review, publishing its findings and, pertinently, distancing its research from the language of the supernatural, the occult and the ghostly.[10] From its inception, Lang contributed his considerable public platform to the dissemination and popularisation of psychical topics. In addition to publishing articles in the *Proceedings of the Society for Psychical Research* (*PSPR*), from the late 1880s onwards he also gave over a sizeable portion of his weekly column in *Longman's Magazine* to discussion of the Society's work, before eventually taking up presidency of the organisation in 1911. Psychical questions also formed the basis of studies such as *The Book of Dreams and Ghosts* (1897) and *Magic and Religion* (1901), and informed his rereading of historical texts such as the *Secret Commonwealth*. Despite these substantial contributions, Lang has remained a minor figure in histories of the Society, one whose diverse academic interests and lack of experimental contributions have made it hard to claim him as a truly dedicated psychical researcher.[11] He cannot be credited with the careful working through of any one particular hypothesis, for example Frederic W.H. Myers's 'telepathy' or Edmund Gurney's 'phantasm', and as such it has proved difficult to quantify his influence on the intellectual or organisational development of the SPR.

To dismiss the Scot as an amateur among experts is, however, to misunderstand the intellectual climate of the period and his unique contribution to it.[12] Though now largely confined to the margins of history, for most of his career Lang occupied a remarkably prominent position in British public life. Such was his influence that even persistent detractors, such as the celebrity novelist and religious polemicist Marie Corelli, were forced to concede the power of his writing on the public imaginary. Reflecting on the multifarious evils of the modern world in an article for *Belgravia* in 1890, Corelli summoned the image of 'Mr. Andrew Lang' sat 'on his little bibliographic dust-heap' wondering 'Was Jehovah a stone Fetish?', before bemoaning the age as 'one of Prose and Positivism' where 'we take Deity for an Ape, and Andrew Lang as its Prophet!'.[13] Identified as a harbinger of the irreligious evolutionism spreading like cancer through the social body, this scathing assessment of the critic acknowledges his immense popular authority in the same moment that it reviles his use of it. For Corelli, the 'Scotchman' is a particularly formidable adversary because, rather than restrict his influence to one sphere, he has a 'finger in every pie' and insists on proclaiming on not only literature, but also on science, evolutionary biology and ethnology.[14] That one individual might be said to have had an impact upon so many different fields and amassed such a diverse 'bibliographic dust-heap' reveals something of how spheres of knowledge were constituted and demarcated in a late nineteenth-century context. When, in the introduction to *Secret Commonwealth*, the author calls on the methods of folklore, comparative anthropology and psychical research, his easy movement between these subjects is symptomatic not of his dilettantism, but rather of the status of these disciplines in the academy. These nascent fields of study lacked prestige, tradition or clearly defined objects of study and, as such, their research findings were exposed to shifting interpretations, popular interventions and new configurations. Recognising the precariousness of their position, such organisations as the Folklore Society and the Anthropological Institute geared their activities toward specialisation and professionalisation in order to more clearly define the scope of their authority. As was made stark by a speech delivered to the International Folklore Congress of 1891, in which he claimed to be unable to distinguish between anthropology and folklore, Lang's roving, multi-disciplinary approach was largely incompatible with and sometimes antagonistic to these imperatives.[15] Instead, the voracious inclusivity of his interests cut pathways between subjects, forcing literary criticism to reflect on the customs of colonised races or demanding that ethnology attend more closely to the questions raised by the mysteries of artistic creativity. This boundary-hopping also set the terms for his treatment of second sight. His prolonged engagement with the question of uncanny foreknowledge transacted the subject through folkloric, anthropological, literary and historical studies, so that it took on new meanings and resonances, but remained unbound by any single interpretive frame

In his introduction to the *Secret Commonwealth* Lang draws the reader's attention to yet another possible reading of second sight. Following his insistence that we recognise Kirk as 'an early student in folk-lore and psychical research' concerned with strictly 'mental phenomena', the reader is presented with a dedicatory verse, given in Scots, to the novelist Robert Louis Stevenson. In the ode Stevenson is characterised as a modern descendant of the seventeenth-century minister and the writer now charged with keeping the strangeness and imaginative potentials of Scottish supernaturalism alive for modern readers:

> O Louis! you that like them maist,
> Ye're far frae kelpie, wraith, and ghaist
> And fairy dames, no unco chaste,
> And haunted cell
> Among a heathen clan ye're placed
> That kens na hell!'.[16]

In the same moment that Lang asserts the value of second sight as a phenomenon grounded in reality and best approached through the scientific methodologies of psychical research, he also claims it as the proper subject for literature and fantasy. Specifically, as his use of Scots over English makes clear, the petition pertains to the needs of an overtly national imaginary. Despite residing in London for most of his working life, the Oxford-educated *litterateur* retained a strong sense of Scottish identity, one born of a rich vernacular culture and sustained across borders by a common literary heritage. Reflecting on the position he shares with his friend Stevenson, this dedicatory verse bemoans the sad fate of the exiled writer who is forced to live in an 'awfu' place' with 'nae heather, peat, nor birks', where he must try to hold tight to the uncanny lore and supernatural tales of his homeland, despite the sneering indifference of his southern compatriots.[17] Greatly influenced by the Calvinist supernaturalism of James Hogg and an unfailing champion of writers such as Stevenson, Kenneth Grahame and James M. Barrie, Lang identified in the writing of his fellow countrymen a shared desire to preserve and enliven their country's history, myths and traditions. Tales of second sight, gathered from poetic fishermen and visionary crofters, are elevated in this honorific poem and elsewhere as essential contributors to the literary culture and character of the Scottish people.

The imaginative life, both of individuals and of nations, was a subject of enduring fascination, and as a literary critic Lang participated in debates concerning its nature and appetites. Through the closing decades of the nineteenth century, he contributed to a romance revival that saw the genre championed as the home of adventure, creative freedom and wholesome masculinity. The renascent romance—key examples of which include H. Rider Haggard's *She: A History of Adventure* (1887) and Stevenson's *Treasure Island* (1883)—was configured as part of a transatlantic debate over the proper form and function of modern literature. In 'Realism and Romance', published in the *Contemporary Review* in 1887, Lang took up the cause of the latter by arguing that, unlike the excessive and debilitating interiority of the realist novel, adventure narratives performed a distinct moral function. Where a critically sanctioned realist aesthetic could only reflect contemporary manners and mores, the wild creative flights of romance permitted one to glimpse the timeless, essential truths of human experience. According to Lang, nature has left us 'all savages under our white skins' so that we might appreciate the 'joy of adventurous living'.[18] Ostensibly about questions of literary form, this dispute drew upon conflicting evolutionary narratives: one that pressed realism as a key contributor to the psychological advancement of readers and another that understood romance as petitioning a more authentic, primitive self. The discovery of a savage consciousness, uncovered in colonial encounter and dramatised by imperial exploration, brought investigative practices such as archaeology, ethnography and comparative mythology to bear upon the daring plots of late nineteenth-century romance novelists. A respected folklorist and mythologist as well as a literary critic, Lang used his weekly column in *Longman's Magazine* to champion adventure fiction and anthropological discovery as largely codependent and interconnected subject areas. Praising the romance as an appeal to the 'ancestral barbarism of our natures', he recognised in the novels of writers such as Haggard, Hall Caine and Rudyard Kipling the narrative hallmarks of myth, epic and oral folklore, recuperated in new forms for the benefit of modern readers.[19]

Importantly for the exiled devotee of Walter Scott, romance existed not only in the world's remote and unchartered regions, but it could also be found in a richly embellished version of Scotland, one culled from childhood memories and early vivid impressions of 'fairy tales and chapbooks about Robert Burns, William Wallace and Rob Roy'.[20] Tales of supernatural foresight in wild Highland regions formed an important part of this imaginary, and this chapter attends to the complex and often contradictory reading of second sight that this inspired. Over multiple sites and sometimes simultaneously, Lang made the case for second sight as a piece of local folklore, a primitive curiosity, a psychical reality, a product of the romance genre and finally as a unique creative faculty. Respecting the suggestion made by Robert Louis Stevenson in his 1884 essay 'A Humble Remonstrance', that the fantastic in literature 'appeals to certain sensual and quite illogical tendencies in man', this chapter asks what kind of visionary modes second sight made possible and what contributions it might be said to have made to evolving understandings of the imagination.[21] Part of what characterises Lang's extended discussion of second sight is a tension, similar to the one voiced in broader discussions of the imagination, between the desire for explanation and the insistence that some essential mystery be preserved. His treatment of Robert Kirk's 'metaphysic of the Fairy world', for instance, established psychical research as the best scientific model for understanding strange visionary experiences, only to assert that ultimately phenomena such as second sight are unexplainable. The SPR might claim that 'second sight is now called telepathy', but this denomination does not 'essentially advance our knowledge of the subject', as the faculty connotes a 'belief and system' that ultimately precedes and exceeds the boundaries of that categorisation.[22]

This friction exposes the disjuncture—between the universalising impera-tives of the various scientific discourses to which he held allegiance and the historical, geographic and literary peculiarities of the second-sight tradi-tion in Scotland—to which this chapter attends.

ANDREW LANG AND 'PSYCHO-FOLKLORE'

Writing to Edward Burnett Tylor in March 1894, Andrew Lang reported that he had just arrived home from a holiday in the Highlands where, in addition to hill walking and grouse shooting, he had spent time with 'a set of second sighted Celts'.[23] In another letter, this one undated, he recounted that 'I am only just returned from Glencoe, where you should go if you want to see "Primitive Culture". The Second Sight man is a regular institu-tion. I interviewed him through an interpreter.'[24] Playing to the interests of his correspondent, whose foundational *Primitive Culture* (1871) had framed peasant customs as the cultural analogies of prehistoric relics, Lang concludes his letter by describing the strange powers of the Gaelic peasant as constituting a kind of 'modern palaeolithiscism'.[25] The correspondents had first encountered each other at Oxford University in the early 1870s, where the younger of the two attended Balliol College and was eventually elected as a Fellow to Merton College.[26] Already familiar with the work of ethnol-ogists such as John Lubbock and John F. McLennan, during his time at Oxford Lang immersed himself in the burgeoning field of cultural evolu-tionism and became particularly well acquainted with Tylor's research. Having been greatly influenced by the work of the elder anthropologist during these foundational years, his own anthropological studies—works such as *Custom and Myth* (1884) and *Myth, Ritual and Religion* (1887)—were undertaken along strictly Tylorian lines. These early studies expanded on the theory that archetypal stories, shared customs and universal myths provide a glimpse into not only the culture of modern savages, but also the evolutionary past of more advanced nations. Along with the Glaswegian mythologist James George Frazer, the young Scot joined a cohort of anthropological thinkers coming to prominence at the close of the nine-teenth century, whose formative training was dominated by the diachronic theory of civilisation pursued by *Primitive Culture*.

In 1873 his enthusiasm for the comparative method prompted Lang to mount a scathing critique of the mythological theories of the German philol-ogist, Friedrich Max Müller. A well-respected Sanskrit scholar and a pioneering Orientalist, Müller was best known for his theory of 'degeneration' which interpreted peasant customs and fantastic tales as the detritus of solar myths, descended from ancient India, now tainted and made vulgar by language.[27] Against this narrative of decline and in keeping with the progressivism of evolutionary orthodoxy, Lang argued in an article on 'Mythology and Fairy Tales' that the 'supernatural element in these tales is more easily explained as a survival of animal worship, and of magic, than as a degraded shape of myths of the elements'.[28] In other words, myths were not simply handed down to and sullied by pre-modern culture, because such narratives composed the creative heritage of early society.[29] This insight set the terms of his involvement with the Folklore Society (FLS), cofounded in 1878 by Laurence Gomme, Alfred Nutt, Edward Clodd and William A. Clouston, in which he quickly established himself as a vocal advocate for the application of the evolutionary model to the study of ritual, myth and religion. However, his critique of Müller, printed in the widely read and non-specialist *Fortnightly Review*, had an impact far beyond any one institutional context. Indeed, Lang's most valuable contribution to Tylorian anthropology was, arguably, his dissemination of its key principles and insights through the mainstream press. His monthly 'At the Sign of the Ship' column for *Longman's Magazine* gave significant time to charting the folkloric parallels and borrowings between savage rituals and European customs, so as to introduce a broadly composed audience to the revolutionary theory of cultural development. Depicting himself as an accomplished amateur rather than a professional insider, his journalistic writing promoted anthropology as simply a way of observing and engaging with the world, that was accessible to non-specialist readers.

By the date of his letter detailing 'modern palaeolithiscism' in the Highlands of Scotland, however, Lang's thinking on the subject of folk customs and superstitions such as second sight had moved away from the progressivist position maintained by his Oxford mentor. The publication of *The Making of Religion* in 1898 marked a definitive break from anthropological orthodoxy, by undermining the assumption that as society progressed towards the apex of scientific development, spiritual belief was necessarily relegated to the status of myth. Originally given as the Gifford Lectures at the University of St Andrews, this text dismantled the theory of 'animism' by refusing to dismiss belief in spirits as only ever attributable to the faulted logic or primitive reasoning of savages. This position was unsustainable, Lang claimed, in the face of the countless 'supernormal experiences' recounted by 'civilised people'. Or as the historian Richard Dorson has observed, the 'original evolutionary thesis tended to fade before the realization that ghost stories seemed more congenial to Englishmen than to savages'.[30] Using the 'cavalier' dismissal of second sight in *Primitive Culture* as a key example, Lang argued that if one were to consider properly the merits of these stories 'they may, if well attested, raise a presumption that the savage's theory has a better foundation than Mr Tylor supposes'.[31] In other words, what if animism was more than an archaic and flawed method of deduction and was instead a perfectly reasonable response to as yet unexplained phenomena? Elsewhere, in an article for the *Contemporary Review* the author complained that 'Mr Tylor', having provided his reader with 'abundant accounts of veridical hallucinations', considers that his 'duty is done' and fails to ask 'Are these tales true, and, if so, what do they mean?'.[32] Thus where orthodox evolutionism mapped superstitions and marked these out as 'survivals' of savage thought, Lang was increasingly occupied by the question of evidence in relation to the supernatural.

Seeking a favourable institutional context for the 'new branch of the Science of Man, the Comparative Study of Ghost Stories', Lang turned from the Anthropological Institute to the SPR.[33] Founded at the University of Cambridge by, among others, the physicist Professor W.F. Barrett, the psychologist Edmund Gurney and the classicist Frederic W.H. Myers, the Society was to adopt a 'spirit of exact and unimpassioned enquiry' in relation to the questions raised by anomalous phenomena.[34] Membership to the SPR spanned nineteenth-century society, drawing in affiliates from the aristocracy, the academic elite and the medical profession. Despite conducting their investigations on the periphery of the scientific establishment, the Society exercised a cultural influence that far exceeded the conceivable reach of a fringe organisation, with its findings reproduced widely in mainstream newspapers and arguments over their veracity conducted through the periodical press. Though dismissed by some as little more than a club for 'ghost-seers and ghost-seekers' and conflated by others with the credulous excesses of the spiritualist movement, under the leadership of the philosopher Henry Sidgwick its members observed a consciously agnostic stance. Extraordinary extra-sensory abilities, spirit possessions, instances of prophetic foresight, death wraiths and so on were to be subjected to rigorous scientific scrutiny from a position of scepticism rather than unquestioning belief.[35] For Lang, the methodological principles and nomenclatural categories of this emerging discipline opened up fresh perspectives on questions raised by anthropological and folkloric data, by contributing a scientifically orientated

language to address the common underpinnings of culturally and historically dispersed folk tales, customs and myths.[36]

This methodological approach proved especially applicable to the second-
sight tradition. In his introduction to Alexander Mackenzie's *The
Prophecies of the Brahan Seer (Coinneach Odhar Fiosaiche)* (1899), the
errant evolutionist discussed the possibility of finding scientific evidence
to support the experiential dynamics of folk myth. First published in
1877, the text claimed to be a transcription of the predictions of a
seventeenth-century seer given as oral accounts in Gaelic and translated
into written English.[37] According to Mackenzie's account, 'Sallow
Kenneth' was born in Uig on the Isle of Lewis and became renowned
for premonitory powers harnessed through the use of a divining stone.
Eventually entering into the employ of Kenneth of Kintail, chief of the
Clan Mackenzie, the seer incurred the displeasure of the earl's wife and
was imprisoned in the Chanory of Ross at Fortrose on the Black Isle.
Eventually found guilty of witchcraft, he was executed in a barrel full of
burning tar, but not before he prophesised the eventual downfall of his
tormentors.[38] In his opening to the 1899 edition, Lang alludes to the
difficulties presented by the Brahan Seer legend. Though stories of
Coinneach Odhar and his role in the demise of the Clan Mackenzie
were said to have circulated in the Highlands for generations, the book
was the only written source on the topic and no primary materials could
be cited in support of its claims.[39] Reflecting on these complications,
Lang admits to a preference for 'modern cases, at first hand, and corro-
borated' over the 'rumours of the Brahan Seer', which are impossible to
verify because there is no 'evidence that the prophecies were recorded
before the event'.[40] Modern researchers can avoid repeating past errors
by ensuring that the 'statements of second-sight men (they are common
enough, to my personal knowledge, in Sutherland, Lochaber, and
Glencoe)' are taken down 'before fulfilment'.[41] His insistence on the
need to apply more rigorous evidential standards to the study of the
phenomenon, with the aim of evaluating the '*modus* of second sight,
"how it is done"', marks a shift away from simply cataloguing folk beliefs
and towards an engagement predicated on the assumption that some
quantifiable truth might be at stake. Such measures must be taken, the
author concluded, 'in the interests of Folk Lore' and 'Psychology', as the
two were equally invested in the method and meaning of second sight.[42]

Reflecting on the necessary reconciliation of folklore with the new
investigative paradigms being instituted by psychical research, Lang

proposed a new disciplinary formation. He termed this 'psycho-folklorism', a hybrid practice that would bring collected myths, customs and peasant beliefs to bear upon a vastly expanded understanding of the human mind and its capacities. This call for an interdisciplinary alliance, made in a number of speeches, journal articles and newspaper columns, was not particularly well received by the FLS and a series of bad-tempered exchanges followed in its wake. Edward Clodd, a self-identified rationalist, keen evolutionist and persistent critic of the SPR, was especially critical of the proposed union. In reply to a particularly acerbic speech, in which Clodd dismissed an instance of apparent crystal vision as more likely the result of a disordered liver, Lang protested that while his fellow folklorists seemed happy to discuss supernaturalism as part of 'savage, mediaeval, or classical belief', as soon as well-attested modern examples were at stake they suddenly dropped the subject.[43] According to Clodd, it was necessary to maintain a clear distinction between the 'psychical researcher [who] represents a state of feeling' and 'the folklorist [who] represents an order of thought', and thus to try to negotiate an intellectual space for the study of 'psychic lore' would be to overstep an important disciplinary boundary.[44] Having only established an institutional basis in 1878, the study of folklore was itself a young and marginal science, and at least part of the reluctance to credit the proposed partnership stemmed from the perceived need to protect folklore's already tenuous claim to orthodoxy from the taint of this new 'bastard supernaturalism'.[45] The disavowal of psychical theories as subjective and illegitimate constitutes a form of 'boundary-work', what the sociologist Thomas Gieryn has defined as the attempt to demarcate scientific from non-scientific knowledge in the public realm, in order to 'enlarge the material and symbolic resources' of such institutions as the FLS.[46] Reflecting on these strategies of self-preservation in the *Making of Religion*, Lang adopts a suitably folkloric analogy to complain that 'Anthropology adopts the airs of her elder sisters among the sciences, and is as severe as they to the Cinderella of the family, Psychical Research.'[47]

Where for Clodd modern hauntings and the alleged phenomena of the seance evinced only the tenacity of animistic belief and the excessive gullibility of the British public, for the psycho-folklorist these presented opportunities to apply scientific principles to anomalous experience. The appeal of psychical research was that it allowed him to bring the universalism guiding his treatment of folklore, in which 'similar conditions of mind produce similar practices', to bear upon the 'obscure corners' of human consciousness.[48] Put simply, if one can observe resemblances between the stories and beliefs of disparate communities of people, might it also be possible to conceive of a shared psychology? The visionary practices of different world cultures—scrying, crystal gazing, religious ecstasy, trance—offered particularly valuable parallels for this kind of analysis. Equivalences could draw the power of second sight into communication with the remarkable feats of perception exercised by modern somnambulant, which were in turn similar to the kinds of clairvoyance experienced by the Lapps and comparable to the belief in distant seeing held among the Zulus. Despite their cultural specificities these coincident phenomena were said to be underpinned by the common psychical structures. Writing to the Catholic historian Lord Acton, Frederic W.H. Myers—a founding member of the SPR and one of its most prominent thinkers—described psycho-folklore as representing a 'kind of "believing back" [...] a kind of future of the past'; a description that captures something of the temporal and geographic synthesis that was made possible by the portmanteau.[49] In the broad sweep of this 'believing back', powers of prophecy long associated with the Scottish Highlander could be unmoored from any specific geographic or cultural context. Disentangling second sight from questions of national identity and local environment, Lang described the fabled power as really 'only a Scotch name which covers many cases called telepathy and clairvoyance by psychical students, and casual or morbid hallucinations, by other people'.[50] Reclassifying the sight of the Gael as a kind of mental capacity transformed strange tales of ominous winding sheets and phantom funeral processions into data that might provide insight into our 'universal' psychology.[51]

From the late 1880s onwards, the phenomenon of second sight was subsumed by a larger epistemological project invested in marking out new psychical territories; what Shane McCorristine has termed the 'contemporary grid-system of thought-transference and telepathy'.[52] Most fully explicated in *Phantasms of the Living* (1886), a two-volume work that analysed over 700 reports of what were termed 'crisis apparitions', the telepathic theory of ghost-seeing developed by the SPR posited a non-pathological and largely physiological scenario: a mode of transmission or rapport established between an 'agent' and 'precipitant', in which changes in brain activity affected the nerve centres of another person and, in turn, produced visual and non-visual hallucinations. The explication of this telepathic hypothesis precipitated a significant narratological evolution in the study of prophetic or previsionary phenomena.[53] The Literary Committee, which was charged with collecting historical and current evidence of the supernormal, invited 'exactly recorded and fully attested' testimony concerning not only the public's experience of 'apparitions', but also their 'premonitory, symbolic' dreams and 'instances of so-called second sight'.[54] A correspondence, printed in the *Journal of the Society for Psychical Research* (*JSPR*) and promising a 'remarkable story of the faculty of second sight', is typical of the kind of material gathered by the committee. It details the accurate prognostication of a 'Miss Jessie Wilson's' early arrival into Bangalore to join her missionary fiancé, as predicted by the 'Rev. John Drake, of Arbroath' some weeks before. The story is verified by four separate accounts, comprising dated letters and signed documents, which are supported by newspaper reports independent of the unfolding prophecy.[55] The strange premonition experienced by the Reverend John Drake is best understood, according to Myers's assessment, as a clear example of 'telepathic clairvoyance': a point or centre 'towards which many lines of recorded phenomena converge', including 'second-sight in the Highlands'.[56] The mundane prophecy of 'Miss Jessie Wilson's' speedy sea journey, authenticated by a dossier of written documentation and situated within a telepathic framework, is indicative of a new approach to the question of prophetic sight. Developed in the thousands of cases submitted to the society every year, in the epistolary data processed by the Literary Committee and in dedicated investigations such as Eleanor Sidgwick's survey of premonitions in 1887, an innovative analytic emerged that recast the second-sighted vision in psychical terms.

Essential to the alchemy of psychical research, which transformed tales of the supernatural into serviceable scientific data, was the wary negotiation of narrative register. The opening pages of Eleanor Sidgwick's report 'On the Evidence for Premonitions' typifies the carefully measured tone struck by Society members. Having defined her subject as 'predictions or foreshadowings or warnings of coming events', the author avows that though 'some cases are certainly very striking', she has encountered few cases of a high evidential standard, a situation that may be attributed to the phenomenon's 'remoteness from the analogy of our established sciences' and which can only be partially remedied by excluding any account not given 'first-hand'.[57] In prescribing and managing these veridical conditions, the SPR established a new descriptive criterion for supernatural experience. On the one hand, by privileging epistolary accounts, mining their own personal and professional networks for testimony and setting membership fees, the Society effectively restricted their evidence base to middle- and upper-class correspondents.[58] Needless to say, the Gaelic-speaking Highlander interviewed 'through an interpreter', did not constitute the archetype of a reliable psychical witness.[59] This is not to suggest that the phenomenon does not appear in the pages of the *JSPR*, but rather that it did so only under carefully managed and class-dependent conditions: a tale of 'second sight' is recounted by a 'Mr. Pierce of Chelmsford' for instance, and a classic case of the 'Highland' phenomena is given by the respected 'Colonel Campbell' with the supporting testimony of honourable 'Captain Macneal'.[60] This exclusivity extended, moreover, to the narrative form of that gathered testimony. Beyond the requirement that personal accounts submitted for consideration be supported by multiple witnesses or verified by their correlation with an external reality, such as a dated letter or newspaper report, respondents were also encouraged to strike a tone of detachment; a quality that would help to distinguish accurate statements of fact from the tales and superstitions of the credulous. Reports of poltergeists, hauntings and strange premonitions were presented in the *PSPR* in the 'narrator's simplest phraseology, quite unspiced for the literary palette'.[61] By expunging certain voices and modes of storytelling from their records, namely those not affiliated with a dominant literate culture, the SPR distanced itself from the oral, the folkloric and the popular.

It was in this strained interaction between the beliefs and lore of the uneducated and the scientific ghosts created by an elite intellectual community that Lang's sympathies with the project of psychical research came under strain. Implicit in psycho-folklorism was a critique of not only the unwillingness of folklorists to properly attend to the evidence for faculties such as second sight, but also of the SPR's refusal to countenance either 'old accounts of the phenomena which it investigates at present' or testimony gathered from witnesses at the margin.[62] The supernatural tale, situated at an intersection between several different strands of intellectual allegiance, signified something more for the author than the procedural accounts collected in the *JSPR* could account for. Writing in *Cock Lane and Common Sense* (1894), Lang complained that the methodical exactitude with which the SPR approached the study of anomalous phenomena had exercised a pernicious influence on the modern ghost story. Compared to the 'positively garrulous' apparitions uncovered by seventeenth-century writers such as Joseph Glanvill, the ghost haunting the pages of the *PSPR* was a rather 'purposeless creature. He appears nobody knows why; he has no message to deliver, no secret crime to reveal, no appointment to keep, no treasure to discover, no commissions to be executed, and, as an almost invariable rule, he does not speak, even when you speak to him.'[63] Worse still, this narrative incompatibility was mutually contaminative: in an article for the *Contemporary Review* Lang complained that, from the perspective of psychical research, 'Good evidence is becoming more difficult to attain', as the reading public are now schooled in the 'genuine symptoms of telepathy' by fictions written 'along psychical lines'.[64] In other words, popular fictions that adhere too closely to the precepts of psychical research provide their readers with a form of narrative training that ultimately undermines the authenticity of accounts submitted to the SPR. Underlying the jocular tone of these statements was a serious concern with what violence may be enacted by the expansion of a positivist regime into the territory traditionally occupied by poetry and fantasy, the 'free space' untouched by science where author hoped 'Romance may still try an unimpeded flight'.[65] Calling science and the imagination into too close a communion with one another might ultimately undermine the discrete strengths and qualities of both.

For their part, some members of the SPR took issue with what they perceived as the clouding influence of a romantic temperament detectable in their fellow researcher's habitual criticisms. In his review of the *Making of Religion*, Frank Podmore—a prominent society member who co-wrote *Phantasms of the Living* with Gurney and Myers—complained that the text composed only 'restored', aesthetically pleasing 'psychical bric-a-brac'.[66] Writing in relation to Lang's dismissal of Leonora Piper, a trance medium who was the subject of an investigation headed by the Australian-born researcher Richard Hodgson, Podmore attributed the psycho-folklorist's 'curiously inadequate appreciation' of the evidence associated with this inquiry to the form in which the seance transcripts were published: because the 'trance utterances are presented in their original crudity, with repetitions, incoherencies, loose tags' in place, they present too stark a contrast 'to the smooth and finished narratives with which Mr. Lang has so often delighted himself and us'.[67] In its unadulterated form data gathered from the seance lacked linearity or poetic nicety, stylistic shortcomings that provoked the literary critic to dismiss Mrs Piper without attending to the evidence. Here Lang is accused of having failed to adequately embody or perform the conditions of objective scientific research, having instead privileged the subjective pleasures of literary form. But the methodological inexactitude that Podmore perceived as the psycho-folklorist's weakness could also be interpreted as an expression of his reluctance to submit fully to either the naturalist paradigm informing the work of the society or, more generally, to the performative strictures of this particular observational regime. Refusing the statistician Karl Pearson's assertion that 'the scientific man has above all things to strive at self-elimination in his judgements', Lang did little to disguise the spectre of the critic, the romancer and the novelist haunting his psychical work.[68]

Balancing his repeated calls for science to direct its attention to the objective study of unexplained human faculties—what Lang described as the 'X region of our nature'—was a growing anxiety with what the encroachment of the empiricist project might mean for the imagination itself.[69] Marjorie Wheeler-Barclay has captured this dichotomy, where on 'the one hand, he seemed to be asking that science account for such occurrences, while at the same time he implied that any explanation it was likely to give would be futile, no more than an explaining away'.[70] His occasional frustration with the SPR should be understood as, at least partly, symptomatic of this duality. While the Society's investigative rigour served to validate supernatural phenomena as a worthy area of academic study, the application of scientifically orientated language to the realms of the mysterious and the supernormal threatened to undermine the intrinsic value of those sites. Where it suited his purpose Lang was willing to concede to a purely 'psychical' reading, as when he described second sight as a 'state between telepathy and clairvoyance', but such concessions were usually undercut by the reiteration of a value system that far exceeded the scope of those categories. For Lang, the cultural form that most articulated these possibilities was adventure fiction. Citing the close articulation of literary and scientific themes in his column for *Longman's Magazine*, George Stocking has usefully proposed that these rip-roaring tales of hearty masculinity ultimately functioned as a 'kind of sublimated anthropology' for the author.[71] But the reverse is equally true. Ethnological activities such as data collection and tabulation were undertaken not only with the creative needs of the romantic novelist in mind, but also with the assurance that the romance novelist's treatment of this material might better reflect its irrational or primal underpinnings. Dismissed by many of his colleagues in the FLS and the SPR for taking seriously the superstitions of the credulous, the eclectic Scot's reading of traditions such as second sight transgressed disciplinary boundaries to gesture toward some ineffable aspect of supernatural experience.

ROMANTIC SCOTLAND

For 20 years, between October 1885 and October 1905, Andrew Lang published a regular column in *Longman's Magazine* titled 'At the Sign of the Ship'. These short articles, which roamed through history, sport, politics, literature, anthropology, European folklore and savage customs, showcased the diversity and remarkable scope of his interests.[72] Given the range of topics covered by the column, the prominence of supernatural themes is notable, with considerable space given to tales of poltergeists, vengeful revenants, brownies, witches, fairies and magic. More striking still was the frequency with which accounts of strange goings-on and inexplicable experiences seemed to originate in Scotland. From mermaid lore in Orkney and a haunted tower crumbling on the far north-east coast, to a Gaelic-speaking ghost and mischievous bogies spotted in the Borders, the author's homeland persisted as a site of abundant uncanny testimony.[73] It is not only that Scottish ghosts, siths and poltergeists appeared with more frequency in this monthly causerie, but also that these tended to be privileged as simultaneously universally coincident and culturally distinct. Reports of fairies spotted by farmers on Skye, for instance, might well invite comparison with the beliefs of African tribes or the Inuit of Greenland, but they could also provoke reminiscences of a childhood spent in the Border countryside and ruminations on the peculiarities of the national character. A series of letters written to the St Andrews lexicographer William A. Craigie in 1912 expose the mechanisms of this paradox. The correspondence took place in the weeks leading up to the publication of an article in *Blackwood's Magazine* detailing the folk history of the Norwegian *vardögr*, a phantom double said to precede a person by arriving in locations or partaking in activities before its owner does.[74] Offering feedback on an early draft of the research, Lang took issue with the geographical and cultural specificity ascribed to the *vardögr* by Craigie: though willing to concede that it may seem 'more common in Norway', he was at pains to remind his colleague that 'for Mr. Kirk, in his *Secret Commonwealth* (about 1690), the thing had a name, the Co-walker', before urging him to consider the interesting first-hand cases recently brought to light by the 'Rev Mr. Mac Innes, Glencoe'.[75] He also advised the lexicographer of testimony submitted to the SPR that bore a close resemblance to the phenomenon he described, before confessing that he had lately been informed that even his own 'father had a V. [*vardögr*]'.[76] The complex response that story of the *vardögr* elicited, with Lang straining to arbitrate between the need to maintain scholarly distance and the desire to assert national pride and even personal ownership, speaks to a broader pattern in his collection and analysis of folklore.

In biographical terms, the author appears to have possessed a keen sense of a national distinctiveness, a feeling sharpened by years of living and working south of the border. This is evident in the large body of work he dedicated to his homeland, which included a four-volume *History of Scotland* (1900–7), a series of fictionalised biographies of famous Scottish figures such as John Knox, Mary Stuart and Bonnie Prince Charlie, several edited collections of poetry and a number of books dedicated to his Border compatriot, Walter Scott. What united this diverse body of work, beyond the nostalgic longing for home common to the exile, was an investment in the continuity of Scotland as a separate nation with a distinct history and vernacular that had resisted the assimilative force of the Acts of Union.[77] The borders between Britain's constituent parts could be redrawn, according to Lang, on the basis of not only economic, religious and political peculiarities, but also in terms of folk culture. Writing in the *Folk Lore Record*, the author claimed that while it was the 'characteristic misfortune of the English people' to have lost the fairy tales, customs and oral history of their ancestors, it was the 'characteristic good fortune of the Scottish people' to have kept them.[78] Down south, industrialisation and modernisation have led the people to abandon their old 'poetical beliefs', but north of the border these continue to shape collective experience.[79] This 'foray into national tradition' runs counter, as Richard Dorson has remarked, to the anthropologist's 'damnable iteration of the universal traits in folklore'.[80] By positing an ineffable northern *Geist* and setting it firmly in opposition to the values of dominant anglicised culture, the author's treatment of Scottish lore arguably placed strain on the comparative thesis pursued in studies such as *Myth, Ritual and Religion* (1887) and *Custom and Myth*, which stated that similar 'conditions of mind produce similar practices'.[81] After all, his contention was not only that Scotland has preserved its customary knowledge where England has frittered it away, but also that these unspoiled poetical beliefs had contributed to the formation of a unique national character.

In his lengthy extrapolations on the history and nature of national identity, Lang diverged from many of his contemporaries by dismissing race as an inadequate taxonomy. The races of the world, he argued, have 'long been mixed' and, as such, racial categories are 'too profoundly obscure' to be of any real significance.[82] This ambivalence toward the

utility of race as a classificatory framework sheds some light on his seemingly contradictory approach to Scottish traditions like second sight.
Working from a theory of universality, where 'similar conditions of mind
produce similar practices', his anthropological practice was founded on the
evolutionist assumption that certain aspects of the human mind are constant across time and space. It would thus be misguided to claim second
sight as a uniquely Scottish ability, because one 'might as well call epilepsy
a Celtic gift. Every savage—the Maori, the Red Indian, the Zulu—is as full
of the second sight as any man of Moidart.'[83] Unlike the spiritualist
biographers examined in the previous chapter, who drew from early
eugenic theories to reproduce second sight as a form of biological inheritance, Lang largely refuted the idea of such faculties as innate in heredity
terms. It was far more profitable for the comparative theorist to consider
the influence of environment, cultural experience and shared history in
generating visionary abilities. In the Highlands and Islands, second sight
might exist as a distinct 'belief and system', but this has resulted from the
situation of the Gaelic peasant, his 'isolated life in lonely forests or hills',
rather than the incomprehensible vagaries of racial heritage.[84] Likewise,
national character is determined not by inheritable biological traits, but by
the entwining influences of history and folklore, legends and biography,
ancient ballads and modern literature.

Having been absent from the country of his birth for many years, Lang's
relationship to Scotland was mediated by books; by a personal imaginary
constructed from the impressions of other writers and consolidated in the
substantial body of work that he devoted to exploring it. In line with the
strain of romantic conservatism that guided much of his thinking, he
tended to look to the nation's past as a site of superior virtue and higher
ideals. One period loomed particularly large in his writing: in biographies
and historical studies, he returned frequently to the aftermath of the Acts of
Union and the Jacobite rebellions, a tumultuous era characterised by
violence, political deception and conspiracy. Several chapters of *Historical
Mysteries* (1904), a book that revisits unsolved crimes and intrigues from
the past, concern the risings of 1715 and 1745. One details the history of a
Jacobite deserter implicated in the murder of Colin Roy Campbell, the
king's factor, who was tried in absentia after he evaded capture. The
mystery of Allan Breck's disappearance and doubts over the nature of his
involvement in the killing of the 'Red Fox' remained unresolved, and in
Historical Mysteries Lang invests it with the status of a modern myth: a myth
replayed and reshaped by fiction, first by Walter Scott's *Rob Roy* (1817),

which begins with a retelling of the Appin murder, and then by Robert Louis Stevenson's *Kidnapped* (1886), which features Allan Breck as a key character. Like *Waverley* (1814) before it, *Kidnapped* charts the journey of a protagonist (in *Kidnapped*'s case David Balfour) from his home in the civilised, anglicised Lowlands, to the tribal warring north, where after a chance meeting he becomes embroiled in a web of Jacobite intrigue. The Highlands are terra incognita, foreign lands from which the Presbyterian, English-speaking Balfour finds himself religiously, politically and linguistically estranged. The mystery has been preserved long into the nineteenth century because, according to *Historical Mysteries*, in spite of the incursions of the railway and the 'daily steamers bringing the newspapers', the communities around Glencoe remain largely unchanged. Here the 'Gaelic is still spoken, second sight is nearly as common as short sight, you may really hear the fairy music if you bend your ear, on a still day, to the grass of the fairy knowe'.[85] In the mountains and on the islands, the possession of second sight, like the ability to speak Gaelic, helps to demarcate insider from outsider, privileged from universal knowledge.[86]

   This snapshot of an elusive society resilient against the ever-imposing modern world and protective of its old ways, captures something of the immense creative appeal that the country held for Lang. Gleaned from childhood memories and embellished with fragments of poetry, Scotland was placed apart from and outside industrial Britain. Describing a fishing expedition through the Borders, for instance, the author reflected on the powerful draw of a landscape whose waters are 'haunted by old legends, musical with old songs', where the days are so 'lovely that they sometimes in the end begat a superstitious eeriness', an enchanted world in which 'one might see the two white fairy deer flit by, [which] brings to us as to Thomas the Rhymer, the tidings that we must back to Fairyland'.[87] The idea of Scotland as itself a kind of 'Fairyland' recurs throughout the author's work, most notably in his reflections on childhood. In her recent analysis of the coloured fairy books, 12 immensely popular collections of traditional tales for children that Lang gathered from sources around the world, Sara M. Hines has proposed that not only did the author conceive of his homeland as 'distinct and separate from England', but that he also 'incorporated two Scotlands within the same landscape: the real and the fairy'.[88] Such a division echoes the vision of Robert Kirk's *Secret Commonwealth*, where the subterranean fairy realm and the world of humans exist in parallel with one another. Taking inspiration from the folktales surrounding Kirk's death in 1692, Lang's poem 'The Fairy Minster' pictures the author wandering 'along his valley still/And heard your mystic voices calling/From fairy know and haunted hill', where he is eventually captured in 'the haunted dell' and spirited away to the other realm to take up his position as 'chaplain to the Fairy Queen'.[89] Mapped onto a broader understanding of Scottish culture and history, the poem produces the country itself as a border space between wild and civilised locales, an ostensibly enlightened society shot through with magical forces and irrational agencies. Remote, uncanny and peripheral, it is endorsed as a space amenable to the imagination, where the prophecies of second-sighted Highlanders, along with tales of faeries, brownies and wraiths, might be marshalled in support of an imaginative realm, one increasingly threatened with rational capture.

It is this fantastical and fey Scotland, one beyond the reach of 'cocksure' science and the 'measured, mapped, tested, weighed' world, that was brought to bear on one of the great literary arguments of the nineteenth century.[90] Precipitated by a lecture delivered by Walter Besant to the Royal Institution in April 1884 and carried on by, among others, Henry James, Thomas Hardy and Edmund Gosse, the controversy concerned the aesthetic nature and practice of the novel as an artistic form. Though they do not fully encompass the discussion's scope, the critical relations between realist fiction and its romantic antithesis composed a significant theme, with questions of narrative, thematic treatment and creative function frequently answered with recourse to this division. Enacted in the shadow of a rapidly evolving literary market, this schism reflected anxieties concerning the impact of commercialisation and mass literacy on the artistic value of the book. In articles for the *Pall Mall Gazette, Contemporary Review* and *Longman's Magazine*, Lang weighed in firmly on the side of what he described as the 'King Romance'.[91] Staged on a variously imagined colonial frontier and dramatising muscular encounters with primitive peoples, fictions by writers such as Rider Haggard and Rudyard Kipling were praised by their supporters as offering a robustly healthful alternative to both the introspective morbidity of the modern naturalist school and the tedious everyday minutiae explored by the realist novel. What is more, this new breed of romance was formed in close proximity with disciplines such as archaeology, folklore, ethnography and comparative mythology, and trafficked in the same juxtapositions of savagery and civilisation, coloniser and colonised. The relation between literary genre and emergent investigative practices was a dynamic one: the two shared the pages of such periodicals as the *Academy* and *Cornhill Magazine;* romancers such as Grant Allen made contributions to both evolutionary science and imperial fiction; folklorists such as Lang co-wrote adventure novels, namely *The World's Desire* (1890) and *Montezuma's Daughter* (1893), and readers of the 'King Romance' could be expected to have some familiarity with ethnographic language and basic anthropological principles.

Though most visibly associated with the adventures of English men in foreign lands, Scotland's remote corners also furnished ample material for the modern writer of adventurous fiction. Judging the country's influence on the renascent romance, the historian Penny Fielding has identified two recurrent sites of enquiry: the conception of a 'traditional hero' who is 'warlike, and out of doors' and the return to folklore as evidential of a 'primitive racial inheritance'.[92] By locating colonial exploration in the wilder regions of Britain, romance novelists regrounded the connection, long central to cultural evolutionism, between foreign and domestic configurations of savagery. In common with intellectual traditions stretching back to the Scottish Enlightenment, adventure fictions such as Stevenson's *Kidnapped* and *The Master of Ballantrae* (1889) configured the north as an extraterritorial region, distinct from the prosperous Lowlands, where anachronistic beliefs and ancient ways of life might still be observed. Elsewhere, in ethnographic studies of his travels around the eastern and central Pacific, Stevenson observed commonalities between life in crofting communities and the tribal societies he encountered. We learn that several 'points of similarity between a South Sea people' and the Highlander can be observed, likenesses that are especially stark in terms of shared 'traits of barbarism'. Where the Polynesian holds fast to his superstitions, the Highlander too keeps up belief in 'second-sight' and the 'water kelpie'.[93] Importantly, the authorial position Stevenson negotiates in his encounter with Marquesan society at once confirms and negates his own 'primitive' racial inheritance: he begins by describing the stories of his 'fathers' and his 'own folk' as comparable to those of the South Seas islander, but goes on to complicate this seemingly straightforward identification by picturing himself as only a visitor to the Highlands, entertained by local tales in dwellings that, like the rudimentary huts inhabited by the islanders, are mere 'sluttish mounds of turf and stone'.[94] For the Edinburgh-born novelist, then, it seemed possible to access the north and its traditional ways of life as simultaneously familiar and foreign, as understood and untranslatable. In this cross-cultural celebration of oral tales and local customs, the power of representation remains bound to the privilege of the literate, the educated, the English-speaking.

Oscillating expressions of affiliation and detachment are equally present in Lang's writings on Scotland and especially notable in his treatment of peasant lore. Writing in *Magic and Religion*, he boasted that while most outsiders find themselves 'unable to extract legends of fairies, ghosts and second-sight from Gaelic Highlanders' they are 'kind enough to communicate to me plenty of their folktales'.[95] Mediating between interior and exterior positions, he appears as both an honorary bearer of local knowledge and an informed researcher capable of tabulating that information as data. Elsewhere, in a story recounted in 'At the Sign of a Ship', Lang described how, on a fishing trip near Inverness, he had encountered an old gillie in possession of the second sight. Together they witness a crofting family being evicted from their home, a sad scene that infuriates the seer and prompts the author to muse that while an 'Englishman would have perhaps though it well to leave a farm that he could not make profitable' the 'Celtic tenant simply declined to leave', a variance in behaviour that he attributes to the mysterious workings of the 'Titanic Celtic temper'. Observing smoke from the burning croft rising through the hills, he goes on to reflect on the gulf between his experience and that of the 'Celtic peoples', concluding that in their material advancement Lowland Scots had sacrificed the 'old poetical beliefs, the *Taishtaragh* and the rest of it'.[96] This tale of the evicted crofters has some affinity with Matthew Arnold's notorious characterisation of the Celts as a people always ready to 'react against the despotism of fact', as politically impotent and economically dispossessed, sustained only by myth and poetry.[97] But what distinguished Lang's nostalgia for 'old poetical beliefs' from the Arnoldian stereotype was the faith he placed in these primitive traditions as a potentially regenerative force in modern culture. Scotland offers more than a setting for wild adventure novels; rather its customs and superstitions provide a way back to a more primal, instinctive consciousness.

SECOND SIGHT AND THE ROMANTIC IMAGINATION

In his short account of evicted crofters and second-sighted predictions, Andrew Lang managed to disparage both the plight of a dispossessed family and the visionary proclamations of his guide. When the gillie attributes the bucking of his pony to its possessing the gift of *Taishtaragh*, the author remarks derisively that a simpler explanation might lie with the 'big sheep which had bounced up under its nose'. Still, where he remains incredulous as to the prophetic capacity of the 'quadruped', there is little doubt as to the 'poetical' gifts of the horse's owner. No 'English beater', he asserts, 'could have talked as that old gillie talked', as despite being 'unschooled', 'history was tradition to him, a living oral legend'.[98] Drawing equivalencies between the gillie's second sight and his remarkable capacity for storytelling, Lang broadened the category of the visionary to encompass minstrelsy alongside moments of supernatural revelation: questions of the supernatural and the folkloric should not be disentangled from those raised by creativity and artistic production, because they share a common point of origin in the 'X region' of human personality. This anthropological concept made it possible for Lang to toggle between theories of individual psychology and broader cultural configurations; the 'X region' is both a universal feature of human nature and the source of all myth, miracle and prophecy. In late nineteenth-century Britain, this region was under attack from the forces of rationalism, materialism and an increasingly dictatorial brand of empiricism that, for Lang, threatened to undermine the important work performed by the irrational, the fantastic, the inexplicable. Having evaded the menace of industrialisation and modernisation, the Highlands and Islands remained a world 'still rich in legends of every sort' where Gaelic myths and customary tales continued to thrive in a lively oral culture.[99] His emphasis on the primacy of the spoken word and the vitality of active verbal language over the inertia of the fixed written text reflected a growing interest in preliterate societies current in both the Anthropological Society and the FLS. On the scale of human development instituted by evolutionism, a key indicator of progress lay with the shift from oral to written culture. Following this teleological model, folklorists interpreted old stories passed down and retold through the generations as the relics of a more primitive past. As a student of the comparative method in anthropology, Lang also recognised 'living oral legends' as survivals of a more archaic form of life, but he diverged from many of his contemporaries by conflating orality with the mysterious workings of the 'X region', where oral traditions were more than remnants of the past and instead communicated some essential, elemental aspect of human experience.

In late nineteenth-century Britain, the artistic form that came closest to fulfilling the psychological function of oral culture was the revived masculine romance. Lang's preference for adventurous fictions was based upon an understanding of the imagination as an irrational, primitive, essential aspect of the self. Formulated in reaction to an essay by William Dean Howells that praised Henry James's character studies for refusing to cater to the 'childish' demand for incident and for recognising instead that in 'one manner or other the stories were all told long ago', Lang's defence of the romance was founded upon a fundamental belief in 'stories told for stories sake'.[100] Intersecting at key points with a broader cultural critique, his advocacy of plot-driven adventure fictions pitted simple tales told by old gillies against the morbid complexities of the realist novel. The 'Battle of the Books' took place among the ideologically weighted literary categories of high and low, middle-brow and modern, feminine and masculine that had come to define the intellectual landscape of the period. Following the institution of the 1870 Elementary Education Act, which established schooling for all children between the ages of 5 and 13, literacy levels in Britain increased steadily and a growing cohort of readers began to access the literary marketplace for the first time. Capitalising on this new customer base, periodicals such as *Longman's Magazine* directed themselves to fulfilling the needs of the self-improving working classes, while cheap newspapers such as *Tit-Bits* attached a wide-readership with a mixture of current affairs, gossip and serialised fiction.[101] The vast expansion of the literary market also provoked anxiety, especially for those who believed themselves to be witnessing the irreversible commodification and monetisation of the book. Underwriting concerns for the fate of artistry of fiction was the assumption that the regiment of new readers produced by the Education Act could possess only a rudimentary understanding of literature and that writers would soon be forced to cater to their undeveloped tastes. Such concerns were often framed in explicitly evolutionary terms: as Christine Ferguson notes, the analytic powers of working-class readers were frequently 'aligned with that of primitive humans', while understandings of 'mass literacy drew on theories of human development, allying the formal aspects of certain types of literary production to different stages of mental development'.[102] Romance novels, with their emphasis on dramatic incident and intrigue over the subtleties of character development, were viewed as encouraging and exploiting the base sentimentalities of these evolutionarily stalled readers.

Rather than refute this understanding of mass literacy, advocates for the romance flattened the hierarchal relations on which it was based, those between childhood and adulthood, savagery and civilisation, oral and written. Adventurous fictions do indeed speak to the archaic and the barbaric underside of modern civilisation, but they do so in order to revitalise that culture, and the new reading public were charged, alongside old second-sighted gillies and other poetic rustics, with enacting this transformation. It is the 'natural people, the folk', Lang claimed in *Adventures Among Books* (1905), that 'has supplied to us, in its uncon-scious way, with the stuff of all our poetry'.[103] Having found in local customs and folktales similarities and parallels that transcended geogra-phical and temporal distances, he endorsed the popular romance as a modern flowering of the same archetypal narrative desires and patterns. To return to the legends and stories of the 'folk', then, was to gain access to a more elemental kind of creative expression. Unlike the 'majority of Culture's modern disciples', who are 'guided only by a feverish desire to admire the newest thing, to follow the latest artistic fashion', the common reader can be relied upon to express only 'natural taste or impulse'.[104] Conservative by nature, Lang's habitual eulogising of the 'people' never translated into calls for political reform, being bound instead to a love of tradition and an amorphous nostalgia for old ways. Indeed, there is some-thing patronising in his acclamation of the average reader and romantici-sation of oral culture, given his prominence in the world of academia, literature and publishing. The author's populist views were, as Margaret Beetham reminds us, 'articulated with all the resources of the scholar whose education had been anything but popular'.[105] Without contradict-ing this measured assessment of Lang as an elite establishment figure, it is possible to interpret his use of the term 'unconscious' in relation to the 'folk' as denoting not only an unknowing or unaware form of engagement with the world, but also of a particular model of inspiration and artistic production, allied to the 'X region' of our being.

Amid the intellectual currents of the *fin de siècle*, the reading of crea-tivity as something instinctual and irrational gained some traction in the developing field of evolutionary psychology. The work of theorists such as Herbert Spencer and James Sully rendered the mind in developmental terms, so that it became possible to observe the history of the race persisting in the make-up or 'organic memory' of the individual.[106] For proponents of this nascent discipline, unconscious processes such as dream and imagination revealed the persistence of the ancient past operating in the present. But where evolutionary theorists remained largely wedded to an idea of progress, by which the human mind moved beyond ancestral animism towards higher, more refined forms of cognition, writers such as Lang celebrated the endurance of precivilised states of consciousness and cited the romance as a means of recapturing this lost heritage.[107]Under the gaze of evolutionary psychology, literary preference became more than a matter of individual taste and began to speak of the customary and inherited knowledge that every reader brings with them to a text. When Lang, writing to Stevenson on the publication of *Kidnapped*, remarked that the story was 'rather too good for the British public which is not Scotch, and is confoundedly stupid', he did so with reference to the idea of an embodied heritage made visible in oral history, bardic traditions and old tales, one that made certain nations peculiarly receptive to the simple pleasures of the adventure novel.[108] The power of second sight constituted another element of the Scot's savage heritage, being the 'product of an earlier day and earlier mental condition than ours' and alike to a form of 'temporary atavism'.[109] Brought to bear on the author's associated literary and anthropological enterprises, traditions such as second sight offered insight into the shared life of the nation. The stubborn persistence of magical beliefs and uncanny lore among the Scottish people was, for Lang, indicative of the deep connection that they had managed to sustain with an earlier developmental stage; a connection that had inured the national imagination against the corrosive effects of mechanised modernity and sterile over-civilisation.[110]

Discussing the history of the late Victorian romance, Linda Dryden echoes many of its nineteenth-century adversaries when she argues that these 'represented simple escapism' whose 'appeal lay in their ability to transport readers away from everyday concerns'.[111] What is erased in the dismissal of 'uncomplicated exotic' novels is the absolute seriousness with which authors and supporters of the 'restored Romance' advocated for the genre's important psychological qualities.[112] Where realism promised 'characters most admirably studied from life', the wild imaginative flights and persistent supernaturalism of the romance offered insight into the more mysterious spaces of the psyche; or, as Gillian Beer has put it, where the realist novel is 'preoccupied with representing and interpreting the known world', the romance strives to make 'apparent the dreams of the world'.[113] In his introduction to the 1888 edition of *Waverley*, Lang attributes the enduring appeal of Walter Scott's historical novels to the important social function they continued to perform: in 'contradiction of real life', his books often end like a 'fairy tale' and such fantasies 'make life bearable'.[114] Though he has typically been characterised as an unthinking defender of 'second-rate romances', during the Art of Fiction debate Lang actually mounted a fairly balanced argument that acknowledged the artistic skill of the realist novel and its value to the literary canon.[115] But where

'Literature (with a capital L)' can only ever reflect the surface of human experience, its present manners and customs, the revived romance offered access to a deeper, more elemental reality.[116] Romance commanded the critic's attention not because he loathed realism, but because in its most fantastic and unrestrained moments the genre spoke to the same animistic or myth-making impulse that he had observed in the customs of African tribes and the stories of Gaelic Highlanders. Where evolutionary anthropologists such as Tylor interpreted myth as a kind of primitive reasoning to be surpassed by more advanced discursive modes, for Lang it was possible to observe the operations of what he termed the 'mytho-poeic faculty' in all stages of culture.[117] Having delineated the 'mythical tendencies' of ghost stories and fairy tales, he argued that there 'are necessary forms of the imagination which in widely separated peoples must produce identical results'. Bringing evidence about those residing on the imperial margin to bear upon the experiences of his British readers, this comparative method collapsed temporal and geographical boundaries to posit the existence a 'common species of hallucination' found in 'all lands and all ages'.[118]

Working under the rubric of psycho-folklore, Lang's analysis trans-formed myth-making from a hermeneutical activity associated with the exterior conditions of a particular stage in the development of human culture into a universal facet of the mind. He was joined in this effort by psychologists like James Sully, who used an evolutionary model of mind to explore affinities between dreaming, myth-making and literary inspira-tion, as well as by his colleagues at the SPR, who looked to the myster-ious regions of the subliminal as a possible source of human creativity. As we have seen, Lang was critical of the way psychical research had reduced the modern ghost story to a 'scientific exercise', but this view was not shared by all.[119] In reply to a query from a reader regarding the defining themes of British fiction, the journalist William T. Stead postulated in 1897 that 'the Psychic problem is already submerging Mudie's and the circulating libraries [and] the immense field which the psychic opens up to the modern novelist is at last beginning to be appreciated'; and going further, the literary critic Rolf A. Scott-James observed 'how nearly akin' psychical research is to 'Romance'.[120] Recognising a border between the 'visible, sensible world' and the realm occupied by fiction, 'that vague sphere whence and whither all our imaginings, ideals and dreams of perfectibility seem to pass', Scott-James noted that this boundary had now 'been given a technical meaning by psychologists, who wish to distinguish between different kinds of consciousness which have been found to exist in the human personality'.[121] Where Lang worried at the encroachment of psychological methods into the sacred realm of the imagination, others perceived clear affinities between the two.

To dismiss the SPR as the positivist enemy of fantasy and reverie would be to ignore the fact that so much of the research carried out by the Society was informed by questions of creativity and inspiration. This was especially true of the work of Frederic Myers. A literary and classical scholar first, who published several collections of poetry, a monograph on William Wordsworth (1888) and a two-volume work of literary criticism entitled *Essays, Classical and Modern* (1883), Myers took up the psychical as a bridge between the psychological and the literary. His theorisation of the subliminal, undertaken in articles for the *PSPR* and in the posthumously published *Human Personality and its Survival of Bodily Death* (1903), was grounded in the idea of a continuum wherein the waking consciousness, the 'supraliminal' self that is our social identity, constitutes only an everyday disguise for a deeper functional level, the one typically revealed in trance, dream, possession and ecstasy. What is more, he extolled the 'dream world' that lies beneath normal cognisance as offering a 'truer representation than the waking world of the real fractionation or multiplicity existing beneath that delusive simplicity which the glare of consciousness imposes on the mental field of view'.[122] This 'margin undiscovered' is the wellspring of all creative fantasies and the seat of what Myers described as our 'mythopoetic' capacity.[123] Identified as a 'superior function' of the subliminal self—as opposed to the 'inferior functions' exercised in dissociative states—within the subliminal schema, the drive to produce unrealities was extolled as one of the mind's higher capacities.

In a similar fashion to Lang's 'X region', the mythopoetic transacted meaning between the fantasy-producing capacities of the subliminal self and the types of work fantasy might perform in human culture. In the essay 'Tennyson as Prophet', Myers defined the true artist or 'sage' as one who is able to speak convincingly from the mythopoeic, to produce poetry or prose that draws from this deeper self. Where lesser writers concern themselves with 'representing and idealising' objective truth, more essential are those artists who speak of 'undiscoverable things which can never be wholly ignored or forgotten'.[124] The 'inspiration of genius' that it is possible to perceive in great works of literature is the result of a 'subliminal up-rush' of ideas shaped in the 'profounder regions' of the mind.[125] So the great William

Wordsworth experienced 'flashes' of inspiration and unique moments of spiritual insight, and the poetry of William Blake revealed the 'subliminal self flashing for moments into unity, then smouldering again in a lurid and scattering glow'.[126] In spite of his quarrels with the SPR, Lang's conceptualisation of creativity also drew on the idea of the subliminally inspired writer.[127] As is made clear by his praise of Walter Scott for having 'reeled' off his novels in a 'white heat', he placed emphasis on certain forms of creative production as particularly conducive to the pursuit of deeper meaning.[128] In his editor's introduction to *Waverley*, he commented approvingly that about 'Shakespeare it was said that he never "blotted a line". The observation is almost literally true about Sir Walter. The pages of his manuscript novels show scarcely a retouch or an erasure.' This constitutes proof of his 'greatness' as the 'heart which beats in his works, the knowledge of human nature, the dramatic vigour of his character, the nobility of his whole being win the day against the looseness of his manner'.[129] Vital storytelling was not to be found in the careful editing of 'Flaubert or Mr. Ruskin' but in the 'white heat' of an almost automatic process; like clairvoyance or telepathy creativity transacts information from the deeper realms of the self to up to the level of consciousness.[130] Under this scheme, visionary traditions such as second sight occupied a dual position, being both the folkloric inspiration for romance and a psychical state alike to artistic inspiration itself. Working in the space between disciplines, Lang interpreted second sight as simultaneously myth and mythopoetic technique; literary inspiration and anthropological object; fairy tale and psychological phenomenon.

On a warm evening in 1845, Colonel Campbell was walking past the ruins of an old castle in Skipness in the Highlands when he spotted two local fishermen and exchanged a passing greeting. Later that night a storm blew in and the next morning the bodies of two fishermen were washed up on the beach. When the colonel saw the pair standing by the ruined castle, they had to have been far out at sea; having dismissed stories of second sight and death wraiths as superstitions, he found himself at a loss to explain what he had seen. Still perplexed by these strange events, 40 years later his daughter submitted an account to the SPR for consideration. Reproduced in *Phantasms of the Living*, the incident is attributed to the workings of telepathy, with its 'prophetic character' dismissed as probably the result of 'assumption'. In the days when there was 'no distinct conception of psychical transference', events such as this were typically interpreted as 'supernatural'.[131] As we have seen, the evolution marked out here, from superstitious misrecognition to psychical enlightenment, presented Lang with a problem.

Though willing to concede 'telepathy' or 'phantasms' some ground in describing phenomena, second sight always contradicted or exceeded these explanatory frames. Rather than simply an expression of his tendency towards disciplinary dilettantism, his reluctance to fully settle the question reveals its significance. The prophetic narratives of the Highlander could not be fully assimilated by the scientific paradigms posited by the SPR because these remained wedded, for this 'Son of the Borders', to imagination and to romance. In an essay on 'The Supernatural in Fiction' Lang wrote, 'Perhaps it may die out in a positive age—this power of learning to shudder. To us it descends from very long ago, from the far-off forefathers who dreaded the dark, and who, half starved and all untaught, saw spirits everywhere, and scarce discerned waking experience from dreaming.' Second sight preserved a connection to these primitive 'forefathers' and defended against the dreariness of a 'positive age'.[132]

NOTES

1. Robert Kirk, *The Secret Commonwealth, An Essay on the Nature and Actions of the Subterranean (and for the Most Part) Invisible People, Heretofore Going Under the Name of Elves, Fauns and Fairies* [1691], with comment by Andrew Lang and an introduction by R.B. Cunninghame Graham (Enemas MacKay: Stirling, 1893). (Kirk 1893a).
2. See *The Secret Commonwealth of Elves, Fauns and Fairies: A Study in Folklore and Psychical Research* (1691) ed. Andrew Lang (London: David Nutt, 1893). Another edition of the treatise was published in 1933 by Enemas MacKay of Stirling, which featured a new introduction by the Scottish politician Robert Bontine Cunningham Green alongside a reprinting of Lang's opening remarks.
3. Walter Scott, *Letters on Demonology and Witchcraft addressed to J. G. Lockhart Esq.* (London: Murray, 1830), p. 14. (Scott 1830).
4. Kirk, p. 24.
5. There are a couple of full-length studies: Eleanor de Selms Langstaff, *Andrew Lang* (Boston: Twayne, 1978). (Eleanor de Selms Langstaff 1978) and Roger Lancelyn Green *Andrew Lang: A Critical Biography with a Short-Title Bibliography of the Works of Andrew Lang* (London: Edmund Ward, 1946). (Lancelyn Green 1946).
6. Robert Steele, 'Andrew Lang and His Work', *The Academy* (July 27, 1912), 117–118 (118). (Steele 1912).
7. 'Andrew Lang', *The Athenaeum* (July 27, 1912) 92–93 (92) and *The Academy* (May 17, 1913), 628–629 (628).

8. Lang to Donald Hay Fleming, April 11 1912, St. Andrews ms. dept. 113-22-26d-26d.

9. 'Objects of the Society', *PSPR* 1 (1882–1883), 3.

10. Janet Oppenheim, *The Other World: Spiritualism and Psychical Research in England, 1850–1914* (Cambridge: Cambridge University Press, 1998), p. 77. (Oppenheim 1998).

11. Exceptions to this include Roger Luckhurst, *The Invention of Telepathy, 1870–1901* (2002) and Alan Gauld, *Andrew Lang as Psychical Researcher* (London: Society for Psychical Research, 1983). (Gauld 1983).

12. This has shifted with the publication of *The Selected Works of Andrew Lang* eds. Andrew Teverson, Alexandra Warwick and Leigh Wilson (Edinburgh: Edinburgh University Press, 2015). (*'The Selected Works of…'* 2015).

13. Marie Corelli, 'A Word about "Ouida"', *Belgravia: A London Magazine,* April 1890, 362–371 (367). (Corelli 1890).

14. Marie Corelli, *The Sorrows of Satan* (Philadelphia: Lippincott, 1896), p. 94. (Corelli 1896). In this moral fable set in the London literary scene, Lang makes an appearance as 'David McWhig' an unscrupulous and powerful critic.

15. *International Folk-Lore Congress, 1891, Papers and Transactions* ed. Joseph Jacobs and Alfred Nutt (London 1892), p. 3. (*'International Folk-Lore…'* 1892).

16. Lang, 'Introduction' *The Secret Commonwealth,* pp. 23–24.

17. Ibid., p. 23.

18. Lang, 'Realism and Romance', *Contemporary Review* 49 (1886), 689. (Lang 1886). See also 'Romance and the Reverse', *St. James Gazette* (7 November 1888) 3–4, ('Romance and the…' 1888) 'The Reading Public', *Cornhill Magazine* 11.66 (December 1902) ('The Reading Public'…1902) and 'The Evolution of Literary Decency', *Blackwood's Edinburgh Magazine* (March 1900) 363–370. ('The Evolution of…' 1900).

19. Lang, *Realism and Romance,* 688.

20. Lang, *Adventures Among Books* (London: Longmans, Green and Co., 1905), p. 5. (Lang 1905).

21. Robert Louis Stevenson, 'A Humble Remonstrance', *Longman's Magazine* 5 (1884), 139–147. (Louis Stevenson 1884).

22. 'Superstition and Fact', *The Contemporary Review* (Dec. 1893), 882–892. and Robert Kirk, *The Secret Commonwealth of Elves, Fauns and Fairies* with comment by Andrew Lang and an introduction by R.B. Cunninghame Graham (Eneas MacKay: Stirling, 1893), p. 55. (Kirk 1893b).

23. Lang to Edward B. Tylor, 23 March 1894., Tylor Collection Pitt Rivers, Lang II.

24. Lang to Tylor, 6 October n.d., Tylor Collection Pitt Rivers, Lang II.

25. Lang to Tylor, 18 March 1897, Tylor Collection Pitt Rivers, Lang II.
26. Lang 'Edward Burnett Tylor', *Anthropological Essays Presented to Edward Burnett Tylor in Honour of his 75th Birthday* ed. Northcote Whitridge Thomas (Oxford: Clarendon Press, 1907) pp. 1–16 (1). (Lang 1907).
27. For a detailed account of the argument between Müller and Lang, see Marjorie Wheeler-Barclay, *The Science of Religion in Britain, 1860–1915* (Virginia: University of Virginia Press, 2010), pp. 115–118. (Wheeler-Barclay 2010).
28. Lang, 'Mythology and Fairy Tales', *Fortnightly Review* (May 1873) 618–631 (622). (Lang 1873). The folklorist William A. Clouston provides another contemporary critique of solar mythology in *Popular Tales and Fictions: their Migrations and Transformations* (1887).
29. Richard M. Dorson, *The British Folklorists: A History* (Chicago: Chicago University Press, 1968) pp. 180–220. (Dorson 1968).
30. Lang, *The Making of Religion* [1898] (Fairfield, IA: 1st World Library, 2007), p. 30 (Lang 1898) and *The British Folklorists: A History*, p. 216.
31. Ibid., p. 101.
32. Lang, 'Superstition and Fact', *Contemporary Review* (December 1893), 882–892 (884). (Lang 1893d).
33. Lang, 'The Comparative Study of Ghost Stories', *The Nineteenth Century* 17 (1885), 623–632 (624). (Lang 1885).
34. 'Objects of the Society', *Proceedings of the Society for Psychical Research* 1 (1882–1883), 3 ('Objects of the Society' 1882–1883).
35. Henry Maudsley, *Natural Causes and Supernatural Seemings,* 3rd edn. (London: Kegan Paul, 1897), p. 73. (Maudsley 1897).
36. On the establishing of the SPR see, Alan Gauld, *The Founders of Psychical Research* (London: Routledge and Kegan Paul, 1968). (Gauld 1968) and Reneé Haynes, *The Society for Psychical Research 1882–1982: A History* (London: MacDonald & Co., 1982) (Haynes 1982) and Adam Crabtree *Animal Magnetism, Early Hypnotism and Psychical Research 1766–1925* (New York: Krus International Publications, 1988). (Crabtree 1988).
37. Elizabeth Sutherland provides a useful account of the legend in *Ravens and Black Rain: The Story of Highland Second Sight* (1985).
38. See Alex Sutherland's *The Brahan Seer: The Making of a Legend* (Bern: International Academic Publishers, 2009). (Sutherland 2009).
39. I could find on one pre-MacKenzie account of the Brahan Seer: Sir Bernard Burke, 'The Fate of Seaforth', *Vicissitudes of Families* Vol. III (London 1863), pp. 266–228. (Burke 1863).
40. Lang, 'The Brahan Seer and Second Sight' in Alexander Mackenzie, *The Prophecies of the Brahan Seer (Coinneach Odhar Fiosaiche)*, (Stirling: Cook & Wylie, 1899), p. x. (Lang 1899).

41. Ibid., viii.
42. Ibid., vi.
43. 'Protest of a Psycho-Folklorist', *Folk Lore* 6 (Sept.1895), 236–248 (247)..
44. Edward Clodd, 'A Reply to the Foregoing 'Protest'', *Folk-Lore* (October 1895), 248–258 (258). (Clodd 1895).
45. Edward Clodd, 'Presidential Address', *Folk Lore* 6 (Sept. 1895) 80. (Clodd 1895).
46. Thomas F. Gieryn, 'Boundary-Work and the Demarcation of Science from Non-Science: Strains and Interests in Profession Ideologies of Scientists', *American Sociological Review* 48.6 (December, 1983) 781–795 (782). (Gieryn 1983).
47. *The Making of Religion,* p. 75.
48. Lang, *Custom and Myth,* p. 22 and 'Protest of a Folklorist', 243.
49. Frederic Myers to Lord Acton, n.d. in Alan Gauld, 'Appendix C' *Founders of Psychical Research* (London: Keagan Paul, 1968) pp. 364–367. (Frederic Myers to Lord Acton 1968).
50. Lang, *Cock Lane and Common Sense* (London: Longman & Green, 1894), p. 224. (Lang 1894).
51. Ibid.
52. Shane McCorristine. *Spectres of the Self: Thinking about Ghosts and Ghost-seeing in England, 1750–1920* (Cambridge: Cambridge University Press, 2010), p. 106. (McCorristine 2010).
53. Frederic Myers is credited with having coined the term from the Greek 'tele' (distant) and 'patheia' (feeling), 'First Report of the Literary Committee', *PSPR* 1 (1882–1883), 105.
54. 'Circular No. 1', *PSPR* 1 (1884), 272–273.
55. *JSPR* 1 (July 1885), 496–498.
56. *JSPR* 1 (September 1884), 151–152.
57. Eleanor Sidgwick, 'On Evidence for Premonitions', *PSPR* 5 (1887), 288–354 (288–289). (Sidgwick 1887).
58. Luckhurst, *The Invention of Telepathy,* p. 56.
59. Lang to Tylor, 6 October n.d., Tylor Collection Pitt Rivers, Lang II.
60. *JSPR* 2 (June, 1886), 334–335 and *JSPR* 2 (September, 1885), 43–45.
61. William F. Barrett, A. P. Perceval Keep, C. C. Massey *et al.,* 'First Report of the Committee on Haunted Houses', *PSPR* 1 (1882–1883), 118. (Barrett 1882–1883).
62. Lang, 'Comparative Psychical Research', *Contemporary Review* (September 1893) (Lang 1893a).
63. *Cock Lane and Common Sense,* p. 94. This complaint is repeated in *The Book of Dreams and Ghosts* (London: Longmans, Green and Co., 1897), in which Lang contrasts the purposeless modern ghost to older ghosts who 'knew what they wanted, asked for it, and saw they got it' (110).

64. Lang, 'Superstition and Fact', *Contemporary Review* (December 1893) 882–892 (886). (Lang 1893d).

65. Lang, 'Ghosts up to Date', *Blackwood's Magazine,* 155 (January 1894), 47–58 (56–57). (Lang 1894).

66. Frank Podmore, 'Review of *The Making of Religion*', *PSPR* 14 (1898), 128–139 (131). (Podmore 1898).

67. Critiqued here is Lang's avowed lack of interest in Richard Hodgson's 'A Further Record of Observations of Certain Phenomena of Trance', *PSPR* 13 (1897–1898), in which Hodgson had admitted himself to be 'fully convinced that there has been such actual communication through Mrs. Piper's trance' (357).

68. Karl Pearson, *The Grammar of Science* (London: Walter Scott, 1892), pp. 7–8. (Pearson 1892).

69. *The Making of Religion*, p. 30.

70. Marjorie Wheeler-Barclay, *The Science of Religion in Britain, 1860–1915* (Virginia: University of Virginia Press, 2010), p. 127. (Wheeler-Barclay 2010).

71. George Stocking, *After Tylor: British Social Anthropology 1888–1951* (London: Athlone Press, 1995), p. 52. (Stocking 1995).

72. Richard Dorson counts 136 out of a possible 241 devoted to folkloric subjects, and at my count roughly 40 of these pertain specifically to Scottish instances, 'Andrew Lang's Folklore Interests as Revealed in 'At the Sign of a Ship', *Western Folklore* 11.1 (January, 1952) pp. 1–19 (16–19). (Lang 1952).

73. Lang, 'At the Sign of a Ship', *Longmans* June 1893, April 1894, August 1890 and December 1897.

74. William A. Craigie, 'The Norwegian 'Vardögr', *Blackwood's Magazine* (March 1912) 304–315 (304). (Craigie 1912).

75. Lang to William Craigie, 4 March 1912, Andrew Lang Collection St. Andrews MS 6912.

76. Lang to Craigie, 29 February 1912 MS 36911 and 8 March 1912 ms36914 Andrew Lang Collection St. Andrews MS36914.

77. Lang, *John Knox and the Reformation* (1905), *The Portrait and Jewels of Mary Stuart* (1906), *Pickle and the Spy; or, the Incognito of Prince Charles* (1897), *The Poems and Songs of Robert Burns* (1896), *Sir Walter Scott and the Border Mintrelsy* (London: Longmans, Green and Co., 1910) (Lang 1910) and *The Life of Sire Walter Scott* (London: Longmans Green and Co., 1906). (Lang 1906).

78. Lang, 'Cinderella and the Diffusion of Tales', *Folklore* 4 (1893). (Lang 1893c).

79. 'At the Sign of the Ship', *Longman's Magazine* (November 1886) 109.

80. *The British Folklorists*, p. 219.

81. Lang, *Custom and Myth* (London: Longmans, Green and Co, 1884), p. 22. (Lang 1884).
82. Lang, 'The Celtic Renascence', *Blackwood's Edinburgh Magazine* (February 1897), 181–191 (187). (Lang 1897).
83. 'The Celtic Renascence', 188.
84. Lang, *History of Scotland published in 4 vol. 1900–1909,* p. 130.
85. Lang, *Historical Mysteries* (1904), (London: Smith, Elder & Co., 1905), pp. 75–98. (Lang 1904).
86. *Historical Mysteries,* p. 80.
87. Lang quoted in Green, *Andrew Lang: A Critical Biography*, p. 7.
88. Sara M. Hines, 'Narrating Scotland: Andrew Lang's Coloured Fairy Book Collection, *The Gold of Fairnilee,* and 'A Creefull of Celtic Stories' in *Folklore and Nationalism During the Long Nineteenth Century* eds. Timothy Baycroft and David Hopkin (Leiden, Netherlands: IDC Publishers, 2012) pp. 207–226 (209). (Hines 2012).
89. Lang, 'The Fairy Minster' in *The Poetical Works of Andrew Lang* Vol. III (Longmans, Green and Co.: London, 1923), pp. 95–96. (Lang 1923).
90. Lang, *Adventures Among Books* (London: Longmans, Green and Co., 1905), p. 116. (Lang 1905).
91. Lang, 'At the Sign of the Ship', *Longman's Magazine* (March 1887a), 554. (Lang, 1887a)
92. Penny Fielding, *Writing and Orality: Nationality, Culture, and Nineteenth-Century Scottish Fiction* (Oxford: Clarendon Press, 1996), p. 142–143. (Fielding 1996).
93. Robert Louis Stevenson, 'Anaho, Marquesas' in *Robert Louis Stevenson: His Best Pacific Writings* ed. Robert Robertson (Australia: University of Queensland Press, 2004) 23–27 (25). (Louis Stevenson 2004).
94. 'Anaho, Marquesas', p. 26.
95. Lang, *Magic and Religion* (London: Longmans, Green and Co., 1901) p. 58. (Lang 1901).
96. Lang, 'At the Sign of a Ship', *Longman's Magazine* (Nov. 1886), 105–112 (107–108).
97. Matthew Arnold, *On the Study of Celtic Literature* (London: Smith, Elder & Co., 1867), p. 154, 155, vii, viii. (Arnold 1867).
98. 'At the Sign of a Ship', (Nov. 1886), 108 (Lang 1986b).
99. Lang, 'At the Sign of a Ship', *Longman's Magazine* 16 (1890) 234–240 (236).
100. 'Realism and Romance', *Contemporary Review* 49 (1886), 689.
101. See Patrick Brantlinger, *The Reading Lesson: The Threat of Mass Literacy in Nineteenth-Century British Fiction* (Bloomington: Indiana University Press, 1998) (Brantlinger 1998) and Norman Feltes, *Literary Capital and the Late Victorian Novel* (Madison: University of Wisconsin Press, 1993) (Feltes 1993).

102. Christine Ferguson, *Language, Science and Popular Fiction in the Victorian Fin-de-Siecle: The Brutal Tongue* (Aldershot: Ashgate, 2006), p. 51. (Ferguson 2006).

103. Lang, *Adventures Among Books* (London: Longmans, 1905) p. 37.

104. Lang, 'The Art of Mark Twain', *Illustrated London News* 14 February 1891. (Lang 1891).

105. Margaret Beetham, 'The Agony Aunt, the Romancing Uncle and the Family of Empire: Defining the Sixpenny Reading Public in the 1890s' in *Nineteenth-Century Media and the Construction of Identities*, ed. Laurel Brake, Bill Bell and David Finkelstein (Basingstoke: Palgrave, 2002) p. 263 (Beetham 2002)and Julia Reid, ''King Romance' in *Longman's Magazine*: Andrew Lang and Literary Populism', *Victorian Periodicals Review* 44.4 (Winter, 2011) 354–376. (Reid 2011).

106. See Herbert Spencer, *The Principles of Psychology* (1855) (Spencer 1855) and James Sully, 'The Undefinable in Art', *Cornhill Magazine* 38 (1878) 559–572 (Sully 1878) and 'Poetic Imagination and Primitive Conception', *Cornhill Magazine* 34 (1876) 2940–2306. ('Poetic Imagination . . .' 1876).

107. See Julia Reid, *Robert Louis Stevenson, Science, and the Fin de Siécle* (Basingstoke: Palgrave Macmillan, 2006). (Reid 2006).

108. Andrew Lang to Robert Louis Stevenson 10 July 1886, in *Dear Stevenson: Letters from Andrew Lang to Robert Louis Stevenson* ed. Marysa Demoor (Ustgevorst: Peeters, 1990). (Andrew Lang to Robert Louis Stevenson 1990).

109. *Making of Religion*, p.

110. *Primitive Culture* vol. 1, p. 27. See also Julia Reid, 'King Romance in *Longman's Magazine*: Andrew Lang and Literary Populism', *Victorian Periodicals Review* 44.4 (Winter 2011) 354–376. (Reid 2011).

111. Linda Dryden, *Joseph Conrad and the Imperial Romance* (London: Macmillan, 2000), p. 2. (Dryden 2000).

112. *Realism and Romance*, 688.

113. Walter Besant, *The Art of Fiction* (Boston: Cupples and Hurd, 1884), p. 42 (Besant 1884) and Gillian Beer, *The Romance* (London: Methuen, 1970), p. 54. (Beer 1970).

114. Lang's Introduction to Walter Scott, *Waverley or 'tis Sixty Years Since* (London: Macmillan, 1910), p. cii.

115. Harold Orel, *Victorian Literary Critics: George Henry Lewes, Walter Bagehot, Richard Holt Hutton, Leslie Stephen, Andrew Lang, George Saintsbury and Edmund Gosse* (London: Macmillan, 1984), p. 137. (Orel 1984).

116. Lang, 'At the Sign of a Ship', *Longman's Magazine* (October, 1887), 659. (Lang 1887b).

117. Lang, 'The Comparative Study of Ghost Stories', *Nineteenth Century* 17 (1885), 623–632 (624). (Lang 1885).
118. *Cock Lane and Commonsense*, p. 34. See also his discussion of the 'uniformity of belief [in phantasms and apparitions] in such widely-separated peoples and ages' in 'At the Sign of a Ship', *Longman's Magazine* (January 1887), 330.
119. Lang, 'Ghosts up to Date', *Blackwood's Edinburgh Magazine* 155 (1894) 47. (Lang 1894a).
120. *Borderland: A Quarterly Review and Index of Psychic Phenomena*, 4 (January 1897), 117. (Stead 1897)
121. Rolfe Arnold Scott-James, *Modernism and Romance* (London: John Lane, 1908), pp. 237–238. (Scott-James 1908).
122. Myers, *Human Personality*, p. 58–59.
123. Henri F. Ellenberger notes that the 'mythopoetic' is the most disappointingly underdeveloped aspect of the Myersian schema, see *The Discovery of the Unconscious: The History and Evolution of Dynamic Psychiatry* (London: Fontana Press, 1970) (Ellenberger 1970).
124. Frederic Myers, *Science and a Future Life: With Other Essays* (London: MacMillan, 1893), p. 129. (Myers 1893).
125. Ibid.
126. Myers, *William Wordsworth* (London: Macmillan, 1881), p. 31 and *Human Personality*, p. 65. (Myers 1881).
127. *The Making of Religion*, p. 30.
128. 'Realism and Romance', 689.
129. Lang introduction to Walter Scott, *Waverley or 'tis Sixty Years Since* (London: Macmillan, 1910), p. xxiii. (Lang 1910).
130. Myers, 'The Subliminal Consciousness', *PSPR* 7 (1891–1892), p. 306. (Myers 1891).
131. *Phantasms of the Living*, pp. 534–535.
132. Lang, 'The Supernatural in Fiction' in *Adventures Among Books*, pp. 271–280 (279).

REFERENCES

Acton, Lord, 'Appendix C', in Alan Gauld, *Founders of Psychical Research* (London: Kegan Paul, 1968 [n.d.]), 364–7.
Andrew Lang to Robert Louis Stevenson, 10 July 1886, in *Dear Stevenson: Letters from Andrew Lang to Robert Louis Stevenson*, ed. Marysa Demoor (Ustgevorst: Peeters, 1990).
Arnold, Matthew, *On the Study of Celtic Literature* (London: Smith, Elder & Co., 1867).

Barrett, William F., A.P. Perceval Keep, C.C. Massey et al., 'First Report of the Committee on Haunted Houses', *PSPR* 1 (1882–3), 118.

Beer, Gillian, *The Romance* (London: Methuen, 1970).

Beetham, Margaret, 'The Agony Aunt, the Romancing Uncle and the Family of Empire: Defining the Sixpenny Reading Public in the 1890s', in *Nineteenth-Century Media and the Construction of Identities*, ed. Laurel Brake, Bill Bell and David Finkelstein (Basingstoke: Palgrave, 2002), p. 263.

Besant, Walter, *The Art of Fiction* (Boston: Cupples and Hurd, 1884), p. 42.

Brantlinger, Patrick, *The Reading Lesson: The Threat of Mass Literacy in Nineteenth-Century British Fiction* (Bloomington: Indiana University Press, 1998).

Burke, Sir Bernard, 'The Fate of Seaforth', *Vicissitudes of Families* (London, 1863), vol. 3, pp. 266–80.

Clodd, Edward, 'A Reply to the Foregoing "Protest"', *Folk-Lore* (October 1895), 248–58 (258).

Clouston, William A., *Popular Tales and Fictions: their Migrations and Transformations* (Edinburgh: William Blackwood and Sons, 1887).

Corelli, Marie, 'A Word about "Ouida"', *Belgravia: A London Magazine* (April 1890), 362–71 (367).

Corelli, Marie, *The Sorrows of Satan* (Philadelphia, PA: Lippincott, 1896).

Crabtree, Adam, *Animal Magnetism, Early Hypnotism and Psychical Research 1766–1925* (New York: Krus International Publications, 1988).

Craigie, William A., 'The Norwegian "Vardögr"', *Blackwood's Magazine* (March 1912), 304–15 (304).

Dorson, Richard M., *The British Folklorists: A History* (Chicago: Chicago University Press, 1968).

Dryden, Linda, *Joseph Conrad and the Imperial Romance* (London: Macmillan, 2000).

Eleanor de Selms Langstaff, *Andrew Lang* (Boston, MA: Twayne, 1978).

Ellenberger, Henri F., *The Discovery of the Unconscious: The History and Evolution of Dynamic Psychiatry* (London: Fontana Press, 1970).

'The Evolution of Literary Decency', *Blackwood's Edinburgh Magazine* (March 1900), 363–70.

Feltes, Norman, *Literary Capital and the Late Victorian Novel* (Madison: University of Wisconsin Press, 1993).

Ferguson, Christine, *Language, Science and Popular Fiction in the Victorian Fin-de-Siecle: The Brutal Tongue* (Aldershot: Ashgate, 2006).

Fielding, Penny, *Writing and Orality: Nationality, Culture, and Nineteenth-Century Scottish Fiction* (Oxford: Clarendon Press, 1996).

Gauld, Alan, *Andrew Lang as Psychical Researcher* (London: Society for Psychical Research, 1983).

Gauld, Alan, *The Founders of Psychical Research* (London: Routledge and Kegan Paul, 1968).

Gieryn, Thomas F., 'Boundary-Work and the Demarcation of Science from Non-Science: Strains and Interests in Profession Ideologies of Scientists', *American Sociological Review* 48.6 (December 1983), 781–95.

Green, Roger Lancelyn, *Andrew Lang: A Critical Biography with a Short-Title Bibliography of the Works of Andrew Lang* (London: Edmund Ward, 1946).

Haynes, Reneé, *The Society for Psychical Research 1882–1982: A History* (London: MacDonald & Co., 1982).

Hines, Sara M., 'Narrating Scotland: Andrew Lang's Coloured Fairy Book Collection, *The Gold of Fairnilee*, and "A Creefull of Celtic Stories"', in *Folklore and Nationalism During the Long Nineteenth Century*, ed Timothy Baycroft and David Hopkin (Leiden: IDC Publishers, 2012), pp. 207–26.

International Folk-Lore Congress, 1891, Papers and Transactions, ed. Joseph Jacobs and Alfred Nutt (London: David Nutt, 1892).

Kirk, Robert, *The Secret Commonwealth, An Essay on the Nature and Actions of the Subterranean (and for the Most Part) Invisible People, Heretofore Going Under the Name of Elves, Fauns and Fairies* [1691], Andrew Lang and an introduction by R.B. Cunninghame Graham (Eneas MacKay: Stirling, 1893a).

Kirk, Robert, *The Secret Commonwealth of Elves, Fauns and Fairies* Andrew Lang and an introduction by. R.B. Cunninghame Graham (Stirling: Eneas MacKay, 1893b).

Lang, Andrew, *Adventures Among Books* (London: Longmans, 1905).

Lang, Andrew, 'The Art of Mark Twain', *Illustrated London News* (14 February 1891).

Lang, Andrew, 'At the Sign of a Ship', *Longman's Magazine* (November 1886b), 105–12.

Lang, Andrew, 'At the Sign of the Ship', *Longman's Magazine* (March 1887a), 554.

Lang, Andrew, 'At the Sign of a Ship', *Longman's Magazine* (October 1887b), 659.

Lang, Andrew, 'At the Sign of a Ship', *Longman's Magazine* 16 (1890), 234–40.

Lang, Andrew, 'At the Sign of a Ship', *Western Folklore*, 11.1 (January 1952), 1–19.

Lang, Andrew, *The Book of Dreams and Ghosts* (London: Longmans, Green and Co., 1897).

Lang, Andrew, 'The Brahan Seer and Second Sight' in *The Prophecies of the Brahan Seer (Coinneach Odhar Fiosaiche)*, ed. Alexander Mackenzie (Stirling: Cook & Wylie, 1899), p. x.

Lang, Andrew, 'The Celtic Renascence', *Blackwood's Edinburgh Magazine* (February 1897), 181–91.

Lang, Andrew, 'Cinderella and the Diffusion of Tales', *Folklore* 4 (1893c), 413–433.

Lang, Andrew, 'The Comparative Study of Ghost Stories', *Nineteenth Century* 17 (1885), 623–32 (624).

Lang, Andrew, *Custom and Myth* (London: Longmans, Green and Co., 1884).

Lang, Andrew. 'Edward Burnett Tylor,' in *Anthropological Essays Presented to Edward Burnett Tylor in Honour of his 75th Birthday*, ed. Northcote Whitridge Thomas (Oxford: Clarendon Press, 1907), 1–16.

Lang, Andrew, 'The Fairy Minster', in *The Poetical Works of Andrew Lang* (London: Longmans, Green and Co., 1923), vol. 3, pp. 95–6.

Lang, Andrew, 'Ghosts up to Date', *Blackwood's Magazine* 155 (January 1894), 47–58.

Lang, Andrew, *Historical Mysteries* [1904] (London: Smith, Elder & Co., 1905).

Lang, Andrew, *The Life of Sir Walter Scott* (London: Longmans, Green and Co., 1906).

Lang, Andrew, *Magic and Religion* (London: Longmans, Green and Co., 1901).

Lang, Andrew, *The Making of Religion* [1898] (Fairfield, IA: 1st World Library, 2007).

Lang, Andrew, 'Mythology and Fairy Tales', *Fortnightly Review* (May 1873) 618–31.

Lang, Andrew, 'Realism and Romance', *Contemporary Review* 49 (1886a), 689.

Lang, Andrew, 'The Reading Public', *Cornhill Magazine* 11.66 (December 1902).

Lang, Andrew, *Sir Walter Scott and the Border Minstrelsy* (London: Longmans, Green and Co., 1910).

Lang, Andrew, 'Superstition and Fact', *Contemporary Review* (December 1893d), 882–92 (884).

Luckhurst, Roger, *The Invention of Telepathy, 1870–1901* (Oxford: Oxford University Press, 2002).

Maudsley, Henry, *Natural Causes and Supernatural Seemings*, 3rd edn. (London: Kegan Paul, 1897).

McCorristine, Shane, *Spectres of the Self: Thinking about Ghosts and Ghost-Seeing in England, 1750–1920* (Cambridge: Cambridge University Press, 2010).

Myers, Frederic, *Science and a Future Life: With Other Essays* (London: Macmillan, 1893).

Myers, Frederic, 'The Subliminal Consciousness', *PSPR*, 7 (1891–2), 306.

Myers, Frederic, *William Wordsworth* (London: Macmillan, 1881).

'Objects of the Society', *Proceedings of the Society for Psychical Research,* 1 (1882–3).

Oppenheim, Janet, *The Other World: Spiritualism and Psychical Research in England, 1850–1914* (Cambridge: Cambridge University Press, 1998).

Orel, Harold, *Victorian Literary Critics: George Henry Lewes, Walter Bagehot, Richard Holt Hutton, Leslie Stephen, Andrew Lang, George Saintsbury and Edmund Gosse* (London: Macmillan, 1984).

Pearson, Karl, *The Grammar of Science* (London: Walter Scott, 1892).

Podmore, Frank, 'Review of *The Making of Religion*', *PSPR* 14 (1898), 128–39 (131).

Sully, James, 'Poetic Imagination and Primitive Conception', *Cornhill Magazine* 34 (1876), 2940–3306.

Reid, Julia, '"King Romance" in *Longman's Magazine*: Andrew Lang and Literary Populism', *Victorian Periodicals', Review* 44.4 (Winter 2011), 354–76.

Reid, Julia, *Robert Louis Stevenson, Science, and the Fin de Siècle* (Basingstoke: Palgrave Macmillan, 2006).

'Romance and the Reverse', *St. James Gazette* (7 November 1888), 3–4.

Scott, Walter, *Letters on Demonology and Witchcraft addressed to J. G. Lockhart Esq* (London: Murray, 1830).

Scott, Walter, *Waverley or'tis Sixty Years Since* (London: Macmillan, 1910).

Scott-James, Rolfe Arnold, *Modernism and Romance* (London: John Lane, 1908).

The Selected Works of Andrew Lang eds. Andrew Teverson and Alexandra Warwick Wilson, Leigh (Edinburgh: Edinburgh University Press, 2015).

Sidgwick, Eleanor, 'On Evidence for Premonitions', *PSPR* 5 (1887), 288–354 (288–89).

Stead, William T., *Borderland: A Quarterly Review and Index of Psychic Phenomena*, 4 (January 1897), 117.

Steele, Robert, 'Andrew Lang and His Work', *The Academy*(27 July 1912), 117–18

Stevenson, Robert Louis, 'Anaho, Marquesas', in *Robert Louis Stevenson: His Best Pacific Writings*, ed. Robert Robertson (Australia: University of Queensland Press, 2004), pp. 23–7 (25).

Stevenson, Robert Louis, 'A Humble Remonstrance', *Longman's Magazine,* 5 (1884), 139–47.

Stocking, George, *After Tylor: British Social Anthropology 1888–1951* (London: Athlone Press, 1995).

Sully, James, 'The Undefinable in Art', *Cornhill Magazine*, 38 (1878), 559–72.

Sutherland, Alex, *The Brahan Seer: The Making of a legend* (Bern: International Academic Publishers, 2009).

Wheeler-Barclay, Marjorie, *The Science of Religion in Britain, 1860–1915* (Charlottesville, VA: University of Virginia Press, 2010).

CHAPTER 6

Research in the Field: Ada Goodrich Freer and Fiona Macleod

In September 1896 the *Glasgow Evening News* ran an article titled 'Ghost Hunting in the Highlands'. It reported with some bemusement that 'Miss GoodrichFreer of the Psychical Research Society was last week seen tiptoeing round the Hebrides in a careful and gallant attempt to surprise real Highland ghosts at work; capture a possessor of second sight, or collect any other evidence on the occult phenomena of the Outer Isles.'[1] Four years previously, the Society for Psychical Research (SPR) had launched an investigation, the Enquiry into Second Sight in the Highlands. Headed by Frederic W.H. Myers and financed by the influential Scottish nationalist Lord Bute, the inquiry aimed to delineate the characteristics of the second-sighted vision, establish its incidence and determine its supernormal qualities.[2] Before dispatching a researcher to go 'tiptoeing round', a designated sub-committee drafted a schedule of questions, dispatched to sympathetic parties in request of information regarding instances of prophetic sight in their local community.[3] Respondents were asked to reflect on four questions:

1. Is 'Second Sight' believed in by the people of your neighbourhood?
2. Have you yourself seen or heard of any cases which appear to imply such a gift? If so will you send me the facts?
3. Can you refer me to anyone who has had personal experience, and who would be disposed to make a statement to me on the subject?

© The Author(s) 2017
E. Richardson, *Second Sight in the Nineteenth Century*,
Palgrave Studies in Literature, Science and Medicine,
DOI 10.1057/978-1-137-51970-2_6

4. Do you know of any persons who feel an interest, and would be disposed to help, in this enquiry?[4]

The epistolary approach was not new to the SPR. It had proven hugely successful in the ongoing Census of Hallucinations, a large-scale statistical analysis of hallucinatory experiences reported among the general public, to which collated accounts of second sight were intended to contribute.[5] In the end, however, the Highland survey produced almost no serviceable data, and of nearly 2000 questionnaires sent out only 64 were returned with useable information. Reflecting on these disappointing results in a early report to the Society, the researcher charged with carrying out the investigation hazarded that the circulars had been neglected 'not from indifference', but because many potential respondents felt that a tradition so 'reverently received from their ancestors was [...] too sacred for discussion with strangers'.[6] It was with the intention of establishing proximity with these reticent Highlanders that, from early 1894, Ada Goodrich Freer, in partnership with two local folklorists, Father Allan Macdonald and the Reverend Peter Dewar, toured through remote fishing villages and rural crofting communities in search of the elusive second sight.[7]

The Enquiry into Second Sight was carried out between 1893 and 1896, and it marked a point of methodological departure from other examinations of the subject. Where previous studies had relied largely upon a recirculated corpus of texts and testimony, in this instance the SPR instituted a survey based primarily upon work in the field, involving the direct observation of subjects and the collection of materials from local sources. The decision to dispatch an emissary to the Highlands was an unusual one for the organisation, which, according to Andrew Lang, generally had no use for witnesses that could not 'be cross-examined at 20 Hanover Square'.[8] If the structure of the investigation was somewhat anomalous, then the figure chosen to lead it was even more so, as Ada Goodrich Freer occupied a unique position in London's psychical community. Originally known to the SPR as Miss X, she produced scholarly research on topics such as hypnotism and crystal vision for the *Proceedings of the Society for Psychical Research* (*PSPR*), but she was also a self-defined clairvoyant, sometimes spiritualist medium, automatic writer and the co-editor of William T. Stead's broadly spiritualist periodical *Borderland: A Quarterly Review and Index of Psychical Phenomena*. This chameleon-like quality allowed her to occupy simultaneously the roles of scientific witness and supernormal subject, elite investigator and populist disseminator, sceptic and open-minded mystic. Freer was an unusual figure in the psychical research community, whose members were predominantly male, university educated and not usually affiliated with spiritualist groups, and the investigation she was charged with managing was distinct from any previous undertaking. The atypical nature of the survey, along with the fact that the project was disbanded with no coherent account of its findings ever published, might go some way to explaining its position in modern histories of the SPR, which have largely ignored the inquiry into second sight and sidelined Freer's unique contribution to the history of the organisation.[9]

One exception is John L. Campbell and Trevor T. Hall's *Strange Things: The Story of Fr. Allan McDonald, Ada Goodrich Freer and the Society for Psychical Research* (1968), which ably reconstructs the investigation using newspaper coverage, letters, published and archival materials. The study is composed of two separate texts, but these are linked by a shared desire to rewrite a perceived historical injustice that has allegedly seen Freer take credit for the work of the Gaelic folklorist, Father Allan Macdonald. Specifically, she is charged with having used the contents of a notebook titled 'Strange Things' in her reports without sufficient public acknowledge-ment of the original source material. Making their case, Campbell and Hall raise important issues concerning ownership, authenticity and the violence of cultural appropriation, but in their exploration of these themes they consistently ignore instances in which Freer did properly credit her sources to focus instead on sensationalising her personal life.[10] Characterised as a manipulative liar who faked her way into a position of relative power, aided by the fact that the men around her found her sexually attractive, her status in the Society is accounted for by 'personal attractions which seem to have been almost hypnotic in their effect' and by a well-calculated sexual dalliance with Myers.[11] Reflecting on these unsubstantiated accusations, Hilary Grimes accurately observes that the extreme hostility with which these writers approach their subject makes it appear 'as if they want to exorcise her from both the history of the society and their own text'.[12] What damns Freer above all else, for Campbell and Hall, are her spurious claims to aristocratic Scottish ancestry, a deception intended to mask her rather more ordinary beginnings in the English Midlands, which her accusers choose to interpret as evidence of a shameless attempt to manipulate the patriotic sympathies of a potential benefactor, the nationalist Lord Bute.[13] Though there may be some truth in this charge, it is also the case that in their determination to unmask and expose, these authors are blind to what motivating factors, other than greed and pure malice, might be at stake in the fabrication of a new heritage.[14]

In a speech delivered to the Gaelic Society of Inverness in 1896, Freer spoke warmly of her Highland forebears and of her abiding love of the wild region, before outlining the aims and rationale of the ongoing second sight investigation to the assembled audience.[15] Part of what the careful weighting of this public address reveals, is the degree to which her forged northern lineage was bound up with the unique conditions of the inquiry itself. The decision to dispatch one of its members to complete research in the field—unusual for an organisation that typically gathered testimony of notable psychical experiences via newspaper advertisements and private letters—speaks not only to the nature of the phenomenon, but also to the conditions of the particular historical moment. Though the SPR began looking into second sight with the intention of exposing the universal psychical components of the visionary experience, by funding an expedition north they also affirmed its geographic, linguistic and religious exceptionalness. Instigated and bankrolled by John-Crichton-Stuart the 3rd Marquess of Bute, a Catholic aristocrat who would go on to play a prominent role in the Scottish Home Rule Association, the inquiry was shaped by a broader turn toward folk culture legible in a number of fields by the turn of the century. The distinct nationalisms that emerged across Europe at the *fin de siècle* shared in a desire to resurrect and privilege the languages, customs and histories of peripheral communities. This found clear expression in the activities of the Celtic Revival, a heterogeneous movement that sought to challenge the political, linguistic and economic marginalisation of non-Saxon peoples. Looking to myth, pre-Christian history and folklore, revivalists sought to articulate a discrete and valuable Celtic identity.[16] A shared principle that drove the formation of dedicated publications such as *The Celtic Magazine* and *The Gaelic Journal* led to the establishment of organisations such as the Gaelic League in 1893 and encouraged the recovery and celebration of traditional songs, tales and lore. Within Scotland, the revivalist project challenged and colluded in the popular image of an ethnically divided nation composed of Highland Celts and Lowland Saxons by pressing the need for a coherent national identity whilst maintaining the uniqueness of Gaelic culture. Though the SPR did not contribute directly to these debates, their investigation into second sight was prompted, framed and informed by this resurgence of Celticism.

The *Glasgow Evening News*, in its report on the progress of the survey, recognised and exploited this association. Convinced that 'Miss Goodrich-Freer' will find much to capture with her 'snap-shot camera' and many a Hebridean willing to convey a 'lot of mythology in one sitting', the article finishes by comparing her to another mystically inclined writer, similarly interested in 'stories of ghosts, fairies, supernatural cantrips'.[17] The author in question was Fiona Macleod, an 'apostle' of the 'Anglo-Celtic' movement who had secured some renown in turn-of-the-century literary circles for the weighty symbolism of such works as the *Mountain Lovers* (1895) and *The Divine Adventure* (1900). In keeping with the rather hazy mysticism of her prose, Macleod was featured in the popular press as a reticent artist, removed from society and living in the remote Western Isles; or as one newspaper had it, she is a 'Celt of the Celts' who hails from an old Scottish family.[18] For the *Glasgow Evening News* there was something unreal in this Highland prophetess, a whiff of inauthenticity heightened by her misuse and misspelling of common Gaelic words, her mispronunciation of the name of a mythical 'water horse' being enough to 'bring a blush to the cheek of Celtic modesty'.[19] The equivalency drawn here, between the telling linguistic inadequacies of a 'Celtic novelist' and the pretensions of the 'lady interviewer' who seeks to record the ineffable mysteries of second sight with a 'Kodak', establishes each as counterfeit. The article concludes that despite their best efforts neither visitor has the 'eye of faith' or the 'hereditary nose' required to comprehend the uncanny gifts they seem so keen to unearth among the local population.[20]

From Fiona Macleod's first publication, rumours concerning the true identity of the elusive author circulated through both public and private networks. Proposals included William Butler Yeats, the poet Nora J. Hopper and the Irish nationalist Maude Gonne, with some eventually concluding that she was 'simply a syndicate of young Celtic authors who write under that name'.[21] Writing to Gonne in January 1907, Yeats revealed that he now knew a 'great deal more about the Fiona Macleod mystery', having spoken with the wife of his recently deceased friend, the writer William Sharp.[22] A published poet, author of critical studies and editor of such writers as Matthew Arnold and Walter Scott, Sharp was also an active participant in the Scots Renascence and a contributor to its mouthpiece, the Edinburgh-based journal *Evergreen*. Following his early death, it emerged that Sharp had sustained two writing careers, one carried out under his own name and another forged under the pseudonym 'Fiona Macleod'. Maintained in both published works and private correspondence—with his sister providing handwritten letters—Sharp's creation consistently surpassed him in terms of sales, celebrity and credibility. The limited critical response to this remarkable project of self-disguise has so far made much of the transvestism at play in its execution. Terry L. Myers reads the author's 'trans-gendering' as representative of 'the playing out of the psychological strains that are clear in his biography', while others have pointed to his extra-marital attachment to another woman, the writer Edith Wingate Rinder, as the probable impetus for the pseudonym.[23] Such readings encourage us to reflect upon the strict binaries of gender and sexual morality in the nineteenth century, but they fail to account for what this doubling might reveal of the complexities of national identity. After all, perhaps what is immediately evident is not the gender play involved in this literary persona, but the transformation of a Lowland-born English speaker into a Gaelic Highlander.

The authorial guises negotiated by Freer and Sharp, though distinct, reveal a common fascination with the figure of the Celt; and in their appropriation of Highland personas both made demands of the second-sight tradition. During her data-collecting trips, the psychical researcher attempted to ingratiate herself with the local populace by claiming to hail from a Scottish family who 'counted seers for many generations', while the mysterious novelist attributed the production of her numinous prose to a species of magic creativity and spiritual insight peculiar to the Gael.[24] Where Freer, a self-defined clairvoyant and automatic writer, appreciated seership in terms familiar to the SPR, Sharp accessed a quite different understanding of the visionary. Initiated into London's Isis Urania Temple, the author was participant in the elite hermetic practices and ceremonial magic of the highly secretive Hermetic Order of the Golden Dawn. Established in 1888 and drawing its membership from the urban middle classes, the Order synthesised a number of occult traditions to produce a unique system of magical training for its initiated adepts.[25] Members were schooled in the methods of astral travel, incantation and scrying in order to gain access to their own divine beings, and the creation of the Fiona Macleod myth should be read in light of her creator's participation in these exploratory practices. Specifically, this mystical other self was the product of a shift within the Order toward the study of Celtic mythology and symbolism, a developing magical trajectory that overlapped at various points with the public goals of revivalists.

Formed at the intersection of the esoteric and exoteric, Macleod was both an expression of a deep self unearthed in secret rituals and a ventriloquised public voice capable of articulating an authentic Highland experience, to which her creator had no claim. Helpful here is Alison Butler's reading of the Golden Dawn as reliant upon 'invented tradition' or 'a set of practices of a ritual or symbolic nature governed by rules that seek to establish certain values and standards of behaviour through repetition of these practices'.[26] Considered in relation to one of its original critical iterations—in Hugh Trevor-Roper's acerbic assessment of the solidification of Scottish national identity around readings of a romanticised and depoliticised version of Highland history—the invented traditions of nineteenth-century occultism offer a way of thinking back to earlier configurations of second-sight's imageries and narratives. In divergence with Butler, who insists that the folklore movement 'does not appear to have had as much influence on the esoterically inclined with its emphasis upon nature-based religious rituals and folk custom and belief', this chapter argues that Sharp's mystical authorship and rise of Celtic symbolism within the Order suggests that the institutionalised study of folk beliefs contributed greatly to the production of practical magic.[27] Finding in the ballads, ceremonies and tales of the modern Celt the fragmented remains of an ancient system of belief, occultism blurred the boundary between ethnography and spirituality. This ethno-occultism engaged a reading of folklore that emphasised both the reality and reproducibility of its preternatural structures; so that accounts of second sight became not only evidence of unique psychical abilities, but also, more importantly, instructive guides to the cultivation of visionary techniques. Distinguished from the passive mediumship encouraged by spiritualism, the system of magic pursued by members of the Golden Dawn relied upon the development of scholarly knowledge and the refining of skills such as incantation and astral projection. In this context, the second-sighted vision ceased to be an involuntary forecast of future events and became an active and shaping power, capable of moulding reality.

This chapter seeks to understand the movement from passive ability to occult technique in terms of the distinct and interlocking narratives offered by psychical research and revivalism at the turn of the century. The SPR's inquiry into second sight cannot be read outside a broader resurgence of interest in Celtic themes and nor can it be placed apart from the occultism gathering pace in popular culture. Not only did the SPR share members with the Golden Dawn, its expedition into the Highlands took place in the same moment as the elite magical society was attempting to excavate the remains of an ancient system of belief from the ballads, ceremonies and tales of the modern Celt. Though distinctions must be drawn between their discrete methods and motivations, occultists, revivalists and psychical researchers all sought to represent the lives and beliefs of marginal people to a cosmopolitan public. The rediscovery of the Celt at the turn of the century was a project undertaken by educated, English-speaking, city-dwelling elites who, in Deborah Fleming's terms, 'sought to speak for people other than themselves, to "represent" them to the world, and to use them in order to establish a new national culture, and an audience for themselves'.[28] This exchange was, however, never exclusively defined by the overweening desires of dominant culture and its violent acts of appropriation. Instead, as Joshua Landy and Michael Saler contend, 'seemingly "universal" distinctions championed by the Western metropole between modernity and tradition, or secularism and superstition' do not hold up 'when viewed from the periphery'.[29] Folklore constitutes a non-official, non-institutional and potentially disruptive discourse. In previous chapters we have observed the attempts made by historians, anthropologists and psychologists to assimilate marginal forms of knowledge, but the central characters in this discussion open up different perspectives on this vexed relation. Both Ada Goodrich Freer and William Sharp attempted to cultivate authorial personas that would allow them to speak convincingly from, rather than to, the periphery.[30] Viewing second sight through these performances of cultural and linguistic proximity, this chapter considers its various discursive and etymological transformations at the *fin de siècle*.

THE IDEAL FIELDWORKER

In a series of essays published in 1899 under the heading *Psychical Research*, Ada Goodrich Freer included a history of Saint Columba and his sixth-century evangelising mission on the small Scottish island of Iona. One of the 12 Apostles of Ireland, Columba established several churches in the Hebrides and made a number of prophetic revelations regarding the fate of Christianity in Britain, eventually collected in the eighth-century *Vita Columba*. In her discussion of these predictions, Freer described the saint as the 'Father of Second Sight', before positing a clear line of succession from his religious prophecies to the special visionary capacities still observed among the island's nineteenth-century inhabitants. She saw the fate of this remarkable lineage in the modern world as far from secure. Reflecting on her own data-gathering trips through the Highlands, the author complained that because seers were forced to live in proximity with a critical public, their formerly 'careful and accurate' narration had become tainted by contemporary scepticism.[31] Worse still was the damage wrought by the increasing numbers of 'Cockney' and 'Yankee' day-trippers to Iona, who by their gullibility, encouraged the islanders to exaggerate simple stories, overly embellish customs and 'ask extortionate prices for the smallest service'. Recognising that, as an English-speaker and a visitor to the island she risked being lumped in with the much-derided tourist, Freer called upon professional expertise and local knowledge to set her apart from the gawping sightseer. On the one hand, her observations enjoyed the institutional validation of organisations such as the Folklore Society and the Royal Geographic Society, to which she belonged. On the other hand, her closeness to the indigenous island community is established through a critique of exactly the kind of detached scientific witnessing demanded by such institutions, or of those 'for whom a story is of no value unless attested by two independent witnesses'.[32] It was in the pull between these seemingly incommensurate allegiances that Freer made the case for herself as the ideal fieldworker, one versed in the expectations of empiricist method and yet also attuned to the narrative rhythms of the folk tale and thus capable of negotiating different terrains of knowledge.[33]

At Westminster Town Hall on 7 December 1894 Freer, or Miss X as she was known to the SPR, delivered her first statement on the progress of the Enquiry into Second Sight. In this address she outlined several promising lines of investigation, including the possible influence of 'Thought Transference', the role of 'memory or unconscious observation' in producing prophetic visions and the use of divinatory techniques by the second sighted.[34] Despite these encouraging leads, she was also at pains to emphasise the difficulties involved in attempting to study a phenomenon so embedded in local history and tradition. Recalling the poor results obtained from the distributed circular, which asked respondents to report on the incidence of prophetic sight in their neighbourhood and to provide well-attested examples, Freer argued that the Society's initial strategy had laid bare a profound misunderstanding of how second sight operated within small communities in remote corners.[35] It was not only the 'native reticence' of the Highlander, she explained, but also the 'secret reverence and awe' in which the power was held that made the collection of serviceable data on the subject such a challenging task. As the subjects were unwilling to discuss sacred matters with strangers, evidence of the prophetic vision could 'be obtained only by living among the people and cultivating personal relations with them', and it was this methodological demand for proximity came to define the conditions of the investigation.[36] Between 1894 and 1896 Freer made three extended visits to Scotland, sometimes accompanied by a companion, Miss Moore, during which she travelled through the Hebrides and the 'more retired glens of the mainland', searching out the knowledge of local doctors, clergy and folklorists in an attempt to succeed where the original survey had failed.[37]

The decision to dispatch one of its members to complete extended periods of research in the field was an unusual one for the SPR. Its intention to conduct 'investigations as far as possible though private channels' was written into the foundational 'Objects of the Society', which from the beginning operated as an exclusionary practice geared toward securing information from the right kind of correspondent.[38] Contributions collected through 'private channels' came largely from middle- and upper-class sources: from subscribers to the specialist *PSPR* who were drawn from the personal networks of psychical researchers, who were themselves predominantly male, highly educated and English. The Enquiry into Second Sight began along familiar lines, with questionnaires distributed only to the professional middle classes, to 'Sheriffs', 'Schoolmasters' and 'Police', while well-connected Society members made personal appeals to the local gentry. The resounding failure of this strategy, which produced almost no serviceable data, necessitated a radical change in direction. Confirming the fear, voiced by Frederic Myers, that the 'second sight evidence may be found too largely amongst fishermen and other uneducated persons', their venture into the Highlands brought researchers into contact with witnesses at significant remove from the typical psychical observer.[39] Evidence associated with second sight was problematic in several respects, being not only sourced from witnesses not usually deemed as trustworthy, but also embedded within a culture from which SPR members were largely excluded. As chief researcher, Freer was tasked not only with gaining entry into this closed world and procuring local knowledge, but also with transforming testimony usually dismissed as unreliable into serviceable psychical data.

Having deemed it necessary to conduct interviews with 'uneducated persons', those assigned to the undertaking encountered a population either unwilling to speak openly about the seers in their community or likely to regale their listener with stories that were ill suited to scientific analysis.[40] Personal accounts submitted to the SPR were usually required to be supported by the testimony of multiple witnesses and supported by external details, such as a dated letter or newspaper report. These conditions served to extricate psychical testimony from the muddled superstitions and exaggerated tales of the credulous. This model of verifiability, established in collusion with the observatory virtues of the educated middle and upper classes, proved largely untenable in regard to second sight. It was not only the reticent character of Highlanders that had to be overcome, but also his apparent 'indifference to method and system', which required careful negotiation.[41] To extract evidence from a people, Freer complained, 'apparently destitute of a sense of time, and having few events from which to date occurrences, dates more exact than "thereafter" or "heretofore" is a labour demanding all possible tact and patience'.[42] A short account titled 'The Woman and the Shroud' is typical of the kind of material collected over the course of the inquiry, and gives some indication of the difficulties encountered. It consists of an interview with a local doctor who details the 'case of a woman [. . .] who had gone to the dressmakers to be fitted for a new gown'. After the customer departs a companion of the dressmaker, known to be gifted with the sight, advises that 'Te need na hurry wi' the frock. Did ye no see she had her shroud on her?' And, as predicted, before the gown is finished the woman has died.[43] Though certainly not without interest, the account arrives undated, third hand and without corroboration from other witnesses. Where correspondents to the *PSPR* imbibed the values of psychical research and usually volunteered narratives structured around those principles, the evidence associated with second sight required multiple translations. Not only was it necessary to translate Gaelic into English, the investigation had also to transform narratives held for generations by a shared oral culture into written knowledge legible to a new audience.

That no formal report on the conclusions of the inquiry was ever published might indicate that doubts over the veracity and value of the gathered testimony could not be overcome. However, that the SPR ultimately refused to publish such seemingly insufficient material did not prevent these findings from securing a public platform in the spiritualist journal *Borderland*. Established in 1893 by the pioneering investigative journalist William T. Stead, this short-lived periodical ran articles on topics such as spiritualism, theosophy, Eastern magic, palmistry and fortune telling, alongside reports on the most recent discoveries of psychical research and experimental psychology.[44] In addition to lead articles, each issue also featured character sketches, news on recent developments in the study of the supernatural, letters to the editor and a directory of psychics.[45] Working under the name Miss X, Freer sub-edited *Borderland* for a number of years. Having been introduced by Myers in September 1891, she went on to form an extraordinary working partnership with Stead, in which editorial meetings were conducted at a distance using techniques such as telepathic communication and automatic writing. In a letter to the physicist and psychical researcher Oliver Lodge, Stead boasted of their success in 'telepathic handwriting', but acknowledged that the system was marred by an 'indifference to time' that made it impossible to know whether the events reported telepathically had 'actually happened' or were simply forecast to occur in the near future.[46] He also took a keen interest in the Highland journeying of his gifted employee and published several lengthy reports on the advance of the second-sight survey.

Having contributed articles on crystal gazing, premonitions and hypnotic phenomena to *Borderland*, Miss X gained especial notoriety after apparently receiving messages from the recently deceased explorer Sir Richard Burton that accurately predicted the day of his wife's death in 1896.[47] The journal printed the story, but on what conclusions should be drawn from this remarkable happening editor and sub-editor diverged. Stead remained convinced that spirit communication had a part to play, while Miss X interpreted the experience as more likely the result of 'externalisations of sub-conscious information'.[48] Their disagreement exposed a broader disconnect between the epistemological aims of psychical research and the journalistic coverage offered by the spiritualist periodical. Writing in the first number, Stead made explicit the populist sentiment at the heart of his new project: the journal was to be 'a medium of communication' between the 'scientific expert' and the 'great mass of ordinary people'.[49] By democratising the 'study of the spook', the journal would do for the great public what the SPR had done 'for the select few': it would facilitate the kinds of plebeian experimentation associated with phrenology, mesmerism and spiritualism.[50] Relations between the journalist and the organisation whose work he was so intent on disseminating were, however, often less than civil. While he accused the SPR of adopting a Brahman-like air of exclusivity, for many within the Society the enthusiastic inclusivity pursued by the popular editor threatened to strip psychical research of its hard-won respectability by conflating its scientific work with a broad church occultism.[51] As both a contributor to the *PSPR* and the sub-editor of *Borderland*, Freer was required to steer a path between warring factions. Her measured assessment of the Burton messages as being certainly remarkable but most likely the result of 'super-normal' rather than 'supernatural' forces should be read as a careful attempt to balance two often antagonistic positions.[52]

Tensions emerged during the Enquiry into Second Sight regarding the split affiliation of its lead researcher. Nowhere was this more evident than in the significant disparities in the tone and content between the reports printed by the *Journal for the Society of Psychical Research* and those written up specifically for *Borderland*. Where the SPR's house journal typically sidelined the narrative content of second-sighted predictions to focus instead on the investigation's methodological difficulties and taxonomic possibilities, in its public form the opposite was true, with space given over to fascinating and dramatic accounts of fulfilled prophecies, deathly omens and foretold disasters. Stories printed by the spiritualist periodical included that of a minister called to the bed of a dying woman by the wraith of her husband and a prophecy of English invasion fulfilled during the Crofters' 'agitation' of 1889, printed alongside numerous accounts of winding sheets foretelling deaths, ghostly funeral processions observed along lonely country roads and the flashes of fish scales appearing on the skin of a soon to be drowned man.[53] Respecting the founding principle of Stead's journal, that while there may be few capable of 'judging and analysing' psychical phenomena, the collection of evidence must 'necessarily be entrusted to a multitude of witnesses', it is clear that this participatory rhetoric made space for evidence and testimony deemed 'unfit' for the epistemological purposes of scientific research.[54] Under the title 'A Vision by a Child and a Cat', for example, Miss X recounts how a minister's daughter was woken early one morning by the frantic mewing of a cat and 'looking toward the window was terrified to see a man standing as if on the windowsill'. Though the figure, dressed distinctively in 'blue cloth with large bone buttons', disappeared when her nurse was called, the child no longer wished to sleep in the room and it lay empty for several months. One night the nurse's brother came to visit and was given the unoccupied room. Having walked for miles in heavy rain to reach the house, the man suffered an inflammation of the lungs and died in the room after a short illness. 'He was dressed', the author concludes, 'exactly like the figure the girl had seen out the window.'[55] Despite being prefaced by a short preamble endorsing 'Thought-Transference' as the likely explanation for instances of apparent second sight, much greater emphasis is placed here on the narrative detail and appealing strangeness of the premonition itself.

Details of Miss X's sojourn to the Hebrides were printed by *Borderland* under the heading 'psychical research' and thus, though the SPR may not have found the evidence for second sight compelling enough for publication, they remained publicly affiliated with it nonetheless. Through the closing decades of the nineteenth century, the unregulated programme of popularisation pursued by Stead threatened to undermine the authority of the SPR. Psychical research imbibed the forms of public presentation and legitimising signifiers common to a mainstream scientific institution, by working to develop a new technical language to describe experimental phenomena, instituting a system of peer review and publishing a journal of its findings. By pressing for the resignation of prominent spiritualist members such as Edward Dawson Rodgers and William Stainton Moses, the Society also sought to define more clearly its role as a trained observer of spiritualist phenomena, rather than participant or believer. It is perhaps surprising, then, given her experiments with crystal vision and spirit communication that Miss X was chosen to lead the Scottish expedition. According to G.W. Lambert, her close involvement with *Borderland* and her practice of clairvoyance made her more a suitable 'subject for investigation' than 'an investigator'.[56] This division was, moreover, overtly gendered, with men making up the vast majority of Society members and women appearing more frequently as the observed medium or ghost-seer. Despite this, in her frequent contributions to the *PSPR* Freer distinguished herself by cultivating a reputation as a sceptical and clear-eyed examiner of her own supernormal experience. Papers such as 'On the Apparent Sources of Subliminal Messages' and 'Recent Experiments in Crystal Vision' presented the 'point of view of the Subject' over the more familiar position of the 'spectator'.[57] In these lengthy reports, she demonstrated not only an extensive knowledge of the historical and anthropological context of her own remarkable visionary talents, but also a keen grasp of appropriate psychical concepts and terminology. Where Stead's enthusiastic amateurism embarrassed the SPR, his sub-editor's careful analysis and measured conclusions were largely in tune with the demands of a nascent scientific discipline. As is indicated by the praise offered to Miss X by Henry Sidgwick, a utilitarian philosopher and prominent member of the SPR, as being one who combined the 'power of self-observation and analysis' with the 'capacity for supernormal perception', visionary capacity did not always preclude the exercise of scientific authority.[58]

There was a detectable change in this open-minded position, however, in the aftermath of the controversial Ballechin House investigation. From

February to April 1897, Freer took up residence at a reputedly haunted Perthshire home and, in collaboration with Lord Bute, published an account of the experience, *The Alleged Haunting of B—House* (1899). Though the investigation was instigated by the SPR with the enthusiastic support of several members, when a public debate over Ballechin flared up in *The Times* in June 1897 the Society was quick to distance itself from the affair.[59] Sparked by an article titled 'On the Trail of a Ghost', in which an unnamed guest at the house claimed that the 'whole thing had been fudged up in London' with fraudulent results produced by their 'charming hostess', the controversy raged through the 'Letters to the Editor' until November that year.[60] Writing to *The Times* on 10 June 1897, Myers attempted to down play his involvement by claiming to have decided on first visiting the house that 'there was no evidence as could justify us in giving the results of the inquiry a place in our *Proceedings*'.[61] This disavowal placed distance between the SPR and Freer, a split that culminated in a scathing review of *The Alleged Haunting of B—House* written by Frank Podmore and printed in the *PSPR* in 1899. While Podmore allowed that other factors might have contributed to the poor evidential grounding of the investigation, he attributed primary blame to Miss X's observational abilities: her 'testimony to ghostly sights and sounds fails to impress because she is liable, in a quite unusual degree, to hallucinatory experience'. Though she is not 'responsible for this mental idiosyncrasy', Podmore continued, it nonetheless 'seriously impairs the value of her testimony to experiences which owe their interest [...] solely on the presumption that they may not be of a purely hallucinatory order'.[62] Under particular conditions, her 'supernormal perception' might be an extraordinary aid to scientific enquiry, but in others this sensitivity constituted an almost pathological debilitation that prevented her from witnessing phenomena objectively.

The Ballechin affair and the ease with which Myers withdrew his support underscore the precarious quality of the authority secured by Miss X in relation to the SPR. Even when she was charged with leading an investigation, her position within the organisation remained that of an outsider. Unsure of her status, Freer's management of the Enquiry into Second Sight was shaped by the inherent insecurities of her role as both psychical subject and object. An early report sees the author working from a carefully annotated Ordnance Survey map and attempting to realise the phenomenon in topographical terms; emphasising her movement through both physical and temporal space, we learn that she has travelled to increasingly 'unfrequented districts', where everything is 'unfamiliar—the language, the customs, the system of commerce by barter, the intensely primitive construction of the houses—even the natural features of the island'.[63] These descriptions reiterate the familiar generic hallmarks of the travel narrative, where an educated English speaker explores a north-ern landscape that is wild and barren before encountering its uncouth and superstitious people. Back in London to deliver her preliminary findings to the SPR, Freer took on the role of translator and set about converting the supernatural stories of these marginal societies into scientific data. For instance, having heard from one of her interviewees that Highlanders typically distinguish between three different types of second sight, the author recalibrated this information through a psychical filter: so that 'second sight (proper)' becomes 'visualised clairvoyance or premonition', while 'sight by wish' is reclassified as 'experimental clairvoyance' and 'sight by vision' is renamed 'symbolic vision'.[64] These findings weaved second sight into a broader epistemological narrative, so that what once resembled prophecies to the untrained observer could now be more accurately recognised as the work of 'memory and unconscious observa-tion'.[65] Assured of a common conceptual language, Freer fulfilled the expectations of the SPR by reordering the second-sight phenomenon on their terms.

Complicating this seeming deference to psychical science was the author's complex negotiation of proximity in relation to the second sighted. Rather than distance herself from the remote and seemingly primitive world mapped out in her reports, Freer laid claim to shared genealogy. In addition to citing Scottish ancestry and a childhood spent 'far away in the North', she also declared an affinity with the poetic Highlander based on common visionary powers.[66] Not only did the author's clairvoyant abilities provoke a 'feeling of awe' in her interviewees and a 'recognition of power as adepts in their own line', they also resolved some of the methodological difficulties presented by the investigation.[67] So that while it may be of 'no use marching into the house of a reputed Seer armed with a pencil and notebook and submitting him to a searching cross-examination', one possessed of similar gifts cannot be 'palmed off' with stories reserved for the 'amateur who likes a little folklore'.[68] Imagining herself as the ideal field worker, Freer attempted to navigate local constellations of knowledge through the embodiment of a particular racial, cultural and psychical inheritance. During a discussion at Westminster Town Hall on 5 December 1895, a prominent member of the society, the spiritualist and evolutionist Alfred Russel Wallace, reported that having conducted his own tour of Iona and enquired into the topic, he was informed by a local that the investigation was likely to succeed, as 'they were as good liars in that island as in any other'.[69] The reply proffered by Miss X is telling. Rather than simply refute the implication that her evidence base might be unsound, she adroitly shifted the focus of the accusation and avowed that 'owing to their contamination by English and Lowland tourists, they were probably better [liars] than in any other!'.[70] If the naturally moral, honest and 'uncontaminated' Highlander has fallen into such habits then this is absolutely the result, she assured her audience, of corrupting outside influences. In a study of Hebridean folklore published after her break with the SPR she went further, comparing the damage wrought by 'English visitors' on the traditions of these remote isles as akin to those enacted upon the 'decaying races of North American' and the 'gin sodden-tribes of Western Africa'.[71] Despite hailing from the Midlands and residing in London, she clearly did not count herself among these 'English visitors' and instead sought propinquity with 'colonised' peoples.

This project was at heart one of cultural appropriation, entailing both specific acts of plagiarism in relation to the work of Father Allan Macdonald and, more widely, the instrumentalisation of a fabricated 'Highland' heritage. But while historians such as Trevor Hall and John Campbell have treated the case of Miss X as a singular abhorrence, her acts of self-fashioning can be situated within a broader turn to Celtic themes in late nineteenth-century culture. In a damning assessment of the Enquiry into Second Sight, Malcolm Chapman has proposed that it played to 'Victorian taste for supernatural titillation' that 'did not extend to more than a vague sympathy with the distant Celt, and fond imaginings of "racial memory" in London bosoms'.[72] Though Chapman is right to point out that the inquiry reproduced an essentialist version of Gaelic identity amenable to the desires of a metropolitan audience, the kinds of identification this invoked in writers, artists and readers went far beyond 'vague sympathy'. In the first instance, the SPR's decision to send a researcher to the Highlands might be cited as an example of what Roger Luckhurst has described as a 'shift in the authority of the worker in the field', by which knowledge became secured 'by immersion in native cultures' rather than comparative analysis.[73] Though by no means typical of the fieldwork that would come to characterise twentieth-century anthropology, Freer's negotiation of detachment and identification in regard to the Highland seer does express something of the complexities of participant observation. What is more, in reiterating the inadequacy of psychical research as a framework for understanding second sight—in one newspaper article, for instance, she confidently asserted that 'modern machinery by which the supernormal is in these days reduced to the normal are powerless to transform *our* Highland second-sight to the common-place of science'—the researcher aligned her work with the broader institutional critique being undertaken by members of the Celtic Revival, who, at the turn of the century, worked to problematise the nomenclatural imperatives of folklore, anthropology and psychical research, and began to make quite demands on traditions such as second sight.[74]

Remaking of the Celt

Writing in the *Fortnightly Review* in 1900, Fiona Macleod joined Ada Goodrich Freer in celebrating the second-sighted visions of St Columba and the dramatic windswept landscape of Iona. But where the psychical researcher examined the experiences of its modern-day inhabitants, the novelist looked backwards to the island's 'pre-Columban' history.[75] Second sight looms large in both accounts, with Freer attending to questions of narrative, testimony and evidentiary standards, and Macleod crediting it, rather more obliquely, as a form of 'quickened inward vision' intimately connected to 'spiritual law'.[76] In this account, the tradition offeres more than just a snapshot of the psychical makeup of an isolated community; it also illuminates a rich and centuries-long pagan heritage. Opening with a description of Iona as the 'Mecca of the Gael', the article describes the prophetic power as a kind of 'serene perspicuity', a visionary custom that has woven itself through the history of its inhabitants and contoured the geography of the island.[77] According to Macleod, the failure of organisations such as the Folklore Society (FLS) and the SPR to recognise the true significance of second sight ought to be attributed to interrelated ideological and methodological weaknesses. Recorded third hand and almost always in English, the folk tales gathered by these institutions lacked the 'unique accent of the Gaelic original', while the gulf between the modern ways of the scholarly collector and experiences of illiterate subjects living in isolated communities meant that much was lost in translation.[78] As such English-speaking folklorists were often little more than 'tale-collectors', labouring under a kind of taxonomical monomania that drives them to amass stories without appreciating their substance.[79]

Outsiders who go 'from isle to isle' in search of second sight are unlikely to find what they seek because, Macleod insists, the kind of tales worth capturing inevitably evade those unversed in the vivid linguistic and cultural life of the Gael.[80]

Written at the turn of the century, these sentiments aligned with the efforts being made by groups such as the Gaelic League and An Comunn Gaidhealach (the Highland Association) to promote the language and encourage its use in literature, as well as with the attempts made by Gaelic-speaking folklorists such as the Reverend John Gregorson Campbell, the Reverend James McDougall and Father Allan MacDonald to collect descriptions of non-Christian beliefs, incantations, charms, spells and hymns, transcribed from oral sources.[81] Studies such as Alexander Carmichael's six-volume *Carmina Gadelica* (1900–71) chronicled legends and myths deemed to be fundamental to the Gaelic imagination, while the posthumous publication of collections like Campbell's *Superstitions of the Highlands and Islands of Scotland* (1900) drew attention to rich folk traditions thriving in northern regions. Such works made a significant impact on the Scottish Celtic Revival taking place in artistic and political circles at the *fin de siècle*. Led by prominent men of letters such as Patrick Geddes and John Stuart Blackie and bolstered by the founding of a Celtic Chair at Edinburgh University, the Scots Renascence recast indigenous folk culture as a vital political and creative resource.[82] Resurrecting a native literature grounded in fables, ceremonies and pre-Christian beliefs, writers affiliated with the movement looked to ancient tales and local customs to inspire modern poetry, prose and drama. William Sharp, a Paisley-born poet and critic, was an influential figure in the renascence. In addition to managing Patrick Geddes & Colleagues, a publishing house dedicated to printing revivalist works, he also contributed to the movement's mouthpiece, the literary magazine *Evergreen: A Northern Seasonal*. His impact on the revival was eclipsed, however, by the celebrity enjoyed by his authorial alter ego, Fiona Macleod. Praised by the *Irish Independent* as the 'one and only Highland novelist', Macleod was widely credited, along with writers such as Arthur Symons and George Meredith, for having introduced English speakers to the beauty and solemnity of traditional Gaelic stories.[83] As Sharp boasted in a letter to the American poet Edmund Clarence Stedman in 1895, where William Butler Yeats was acknowledged as the leader of the "Irish-Celtic' revival, she was admitted to be the head of the Scots-Celtic movement'.[84] Identified as a native Highlander of noble birth, for nearly 12 years this reticent author flitted through private correspondence and published interviews, forever travelling to or journeying back from some remote spot, writing from stone cottages perched on hillsides and composing poetry on element-battered peninsulas.

Elizabeth Sharp, who published a biography of her husband after his death, described his Fiona Macleod novels as 'tales and myths of old Celtic days, recaptured in dreams', published with the intention of drawing a wider audience to the neglected 'tongue' and maligned literatures of the Gael.[85] Short story collections such as *The Sin-Eater* (1895) and *The Gypsy Christ* (1895) and novels such as *The Mountain Lovers* (1895) and *Green Fire* (1896) indulged their readers with a vision of Highland life radically out of time with the modernising imperatives of the metropolis. Set in communities along Scotland's dramatic western coastline or on small islands such as South Uist, Skye and Barra, these fictional realms exist almost entirely without temporal indicators, unorientated in history and unanchored from the present. In these insular worlds, folklore signifies more than shared stories and traditions; it operates as an organising principle that binds myth, history and landscape in the creation of reality governed by non-rational forces. Interweaving elements of Gaelic mythology with reworked supernatural lore, the reader's attention is drawn repeatedly to moments of narrative tension where Christian faith rubs up against older systems of knowledge. Reviewing her early work, Yeats praised Macleod for having resisted the urge to transform the 'peasant legends' of the Hebrides into the symbols of 'some personal fantasy', by immersing herself fully in the 'emotions' of the people.[86] Rather than simply observe the beliefs of the rural Highlander, her writing sought patterns of identification and exemplified all that the revival might achieve with regard to the rehabilitation of an authentic Celtic voice.

Tales of second sight circulate in these fictions as a means of signalling the persistence, across time and space, of a shared pagan past. Writing to Grant Allen in 1895, Macleod described this common heritage as lying far below the 'fugitive drift of Civilisation and Christianity' and being like the 'deep sea beneath the coming and going of the tides'; a submerged and ancient knowledge now only glimpsed in folk tales and customs.[87] In *The Washer of the Ford* (1895), a collection of short stories set in the sixth century when St Columba was spreading Christian teachings through the west of Scotland, second sight is exalted as a kind of trans-temporal vision that allows the possessor to see through the 'foam and spray of the present' to the enduring presence of the old 'barbaric emotions'.[88] It is a power that bridges the present day and the distant past, that precedes the arrival of Christianity and yet remains knitted into the fabric of everyday life. How long second sight can continue to play this role is far from certain, however, as Macleod also foresees its extinction in a disenchanted world where such beliefs are 'smiled at by the gentle and mocked by the vulgar'.[89] With the passing of old ways comes the passing of the race itself, a rupture in the collective memory that defines a people. In 'The Sight', a short story collected in *The Dominion of Dreams* (1910), the fatal prophecy of a female seer maps onto the fate that threatens a whole community. It tells of an Iona woman, who has been unable to conceive a child, and her only nephew, Luthais, who has emigrated to Nova Scotia in search of a better life. One December she has a disturbing vision of her young relative drowning in a cold, black sea and during Easter the following year she receives word that he had indeed drowned that 'Christmas-tide'. This personal loss is made all the more acute by the fact that the dead man was the 'last of his mother's race' and without him the family line will not continue.[90] Second sight, then, exists as part of an ancestral memory, one described by the author as alike to a 'memory within a memory as layers of skin underlie the epidermis', the continuity of which is threatened by the social fragmentation occasioned by forced clearances, famine and mass emigration.[91]

One way to insure against dissolution is to preserve the imaginative life; the race can be revitalised through creative work. This restorative project guided the literary aspirations of the revival, prompting volumes such as Yeats's *The Celtic Twilight* (1893), informing the output of publishing houses such as Patrick Geddes & Colleagues and inspiring collections such as *Lyra Celtica: An Anthology of Representative Celtic Poetry* (1896), a volume edited by Sharp that gathered together the native literature of Scottish, Welsh, Irish, Cornish, Manx and Breton peoples.[92] The assumption underpinning these endeavours, that it is possible to identify a 'distinct racial genius, temper, colour and candour' in a work of art, was a point of contention in turn-of-the-century literary culture.[93] Reviewing Macleod's *Green Fire: A Romance* (1896), Andrew Lang characterised the 'windy, wailing indistinct' romance as perniciously 'bent on being "Ossianic"'.[94] The charge levelled here, that the novel is derivative of an eighteenth-century poem that was itself masquerading as ancient epic, aligns it with the inauthentic and mawkishly sentimental.[95] For Lang, the wistful nostalgia of works such as *Green Fire* was underwritten by a dangerous and misguided biological essentialism: observing the spectre of 'that unlovely enchantress, Popular Science', he characterised the 'Neo-Celtic' movement as little more than an attempt to 'claim all that is best and rarest in English literature as due to the Celtic element' under the guise of questionable race theory.[96] Making the case for a recognisably Scottish or Irish genius meant engaging with what Murray Pittock has described as the 'Celtic Darwinism' that posited the poetic sensibility of the Celt as the cause, justification and consolation for his political submission to the rationally minded and able-bodied Anglo Saxon.[97] As a number of historians have argued, in recapitulating the division of the feminine 'sentimental, weak, passive' Scot from the masculine, strong-willed, judicious Englander, the misty Celticism of the renascence could be accused of having bolstered the justificatory logic of internal colonisation.[98]

Accounts of the Celtic Revival were often drawn between the politicised nationalism of the Irish Literary Revival and the 'Ossianic' nostalgia of the Scots renascence. According to its critics, where the revival in Ireland maintained strong ties to a Home Rule movement advocating national autonomy, in Scotland writers such as Macleod simply rehearsed 'clichéd' 'Arnoldian' traits in the service of cultural unionism.[99] However, while it is true that revivalism in Scotland did not closely align itself with the nationalist cause as was the case in Ireland, it does not necessarily follow that the writers and artists featured in magazines such as *Evergreen* allied themselves with the British State. Instead revivalism in Scotland pursued an internationalist agenda that recognised the existence of a pan-Celticism, forged in opposition to Anglo-Saxon dominance. Disentangled from any discreet national identity, in the literature of the renascence the designation 'Celt' came to resemble something closer to an essential *Geist*. Writing to the American journalist Horace Scudder on the proposed publication of *Lyra Celtica*, for instance, Sharp explained that his enthusiasm for the anthology lay not with 'what is written in Scottish Gaelic or Irish Gaelic' but with uncovering the presence of a definable 'Celtic spirit'.[100] Though it is true that the author identified this 'spirit' as a decidedly lyrical, mystical, feminine one, these characteristics were not intended to complement English culture; rather they were set in direct opposition to its values. While Arnold had recommended the 'wisely directed' absorption of the Celt into British civilisation, a new generation of revivalist writers envisioned the complete transformation of that culture.[101] The first issue of *Evergreen* begins with a manifesto for national rejuvenation: 'Such is our Scottish, our Celtic Renascence—sadly set betwixt the Keening, the watching over our fathers dead, and the second-sight shroud rising about each other. Yet this is the

Resurrection and the Life, when to faithful love and memory their dead arise.'[102] Interweaving folk tradition, in the winding sheet that foretells ill fate and is seen only by the second sighted, with allusions to Christian doctrine, this accumulative rhetoric of rebirth, renaissance and resurrection, trades in the image of a newly empowered Celt, one drawn from folklore and myth, yet capable of enacting change in the present.

Accounts of pre-Christian beliefs, incantations, spells, hymns and super-stitions were essential to this regenerative project and the second-sight tradi-tion took on a particularly prominent role. In line with a broad pan-Celtic consensus, the prophetic capacity came to serve increasingly as signifier of Celtic rather than strictly Scottish genealogy. One of Lady Gregory's West Ireland informants divulged that it was only 'them that are born at midnight that has the second sight'; while the Welsh folklorist Marie Trevelyan claimed that second sight was a trait typical among the peasants of South Wales; and Yeats's maternal uncle, the occultist George Pollexfen, claimed that his own housekeeper possessed the gift.[103] Though the assertion of second sight as an exclusively Highland tradition had long been subject to contestation, under the revivalist gaze this narrative took on deeper metaphoric resonance. No longer a discrete tradition, it was rather a quality of mind born of what Macleod termed the Celt's 'close communion with the secret powers of the world'.[104] Tales of deaths and futures foretold revealed more than a surviving folkloric custom, they also suggested an ancient mode of perception lost to the modern world. So that the island fisherman and the remote crofter provided a direct link backwards to primitive ways of being: as Yeats com-mented, 'Men who lived in a world where anything might flow and change, and become any other thing [...] had not our thoughts of weight and measure.'[105] Part of the project of the Celtic Revival involved not only a recuperation of oral strategies of cultural transmission, but also an attempt to rediscover the cognitive spaces opened up by orality, ways of thinking and visualising that were shut off to the literate. This insight underpinned an ethnographic study of supernatural belief in Ireland, Wales, Scotland and Cornwall undertaken by the American Walter Yeeling Evans-Wentz and published in 1911. Citing Yeats and Lady Gregory as his sources, Evans-Wentz used *The Fairy-Faith in the Celtic Countries* to argue for a different approach to folklore, one that he termed 'anthropo-psychological'. The strength of this new method was that it acknowledged that testimony regard-ing folklore such as second sight might be found in the 'recent and con-temporary psychical experiences' as 'vouched for by many "seers"'.[106] Discussing the persistence of fairy lore in remote regions, the anthropologist drew a distinction between the 'natural mind of the uncorrupted Celt' that is 'ever open to unusual psychical impressions' and the mind of the urban dweller that 'tends to be obsessed with business affairs both during his waking and during his dream states'.[107] Detached from the materialist preoccupations of the metropolis, the remote Gael not only lives but *thinks* differently from his urban-dwelling neighbours.

The publication of the *Fairy Faith in the Celtic Countries* and its author's call for a new psychological approach to the study of customary knowledge chimed with a broader critique of the methods and motives of institutionalised folk studies, undertaken by writers, artists and scholars associated with the Celtic Revival. In the introduction to his *Fairy and Folk Tales of the Irish Peasantry* (1890), Yeats characterised the scientific pretensions of the FLS as amounting to little more than a desire for tales 'in the form of grocers' bills— item fairy king, item the queen'.[108] Setting his own studies in opposition to institutional folklore, the author explained his antagonism as arising from the shallow understanding of the subject encouraged by the discipline: what lover of Celtic lore, he asks 'has not been filled up with a sacred rage when he comes upon exquisite story, dear to his childhood, written out in newspaper English and called science?'.[109] Engaging issues of ownership, national identity and cultural appropriation, this critique resisted a misreading of folk tales that placed them, falsely, within the realm of the quantifiable or describable. Psychical research, for those sympathetic to such a critique, was guilty of the same error, as to attribute all supernatural phenomena to telepathic exchange or the power of the imagination over another was to explain away more expansive potentials. More than ethnographic or psychical curiosities, fairy tales and supernatural lore of peripheral cultures represented routes to magical and transformative self-knowledge. 'I cannot get it out of my mind', Yeats confessed in an 1899 essay, 'that this age of criticism is about to pass, and an age of imagination, of emotion, of moods of revelation about to come in its place, for certainly belief in the supersensual world is at hand again.'[110] The agent of this renewal, primed to carry European culture into a new century and a new age, was the visionary imagination of its marginal and disenfranchised people.

THE OCCULT CELT

On 3 May 1898 William Butler Yeats wrote to William Sharp from Paris to tell him of a strange incident that had occurred the previous evening, and to request that he pass on a sealed letter to Fiona Macleod as soon as possible. Whilst undertaking magical rites with Samuel Liddell MacGregor Mathers and Moina Mathers, he had encountered the 'astral form' of a man dressed in a number of clan tartans who appeared to be in a state of 'intense emotional crisis'. Suspecting that Macleod might have some connection to this spectral visitor, Yeats asked her if she had found herself 'either last night or Sunday night [...] passing through some state of tragic feeling?'.[111] Writing again two days later, he warned Sharp not to undertake any 'magical work with Miss Macleod until we meet' as 'you are both the channells [sic] of some very powerful beings and some mistake has been made'.[112] The magical work the letter refers to comprised a series of exploratory rites into the Celtic mythos that were intended to contribute to the formation of a dedicated group within the Hermetic Order of the Golden Dawn. Having been initiated into the Neophyte grade of London's Isis Urania Temple, from 1897 Sharp contributed to efforts to synthesise folk stories and sagas with the esoteric precepts of practical magic, being undertaken with the aim of establishing a new sect, the Celtic Order of Mysteries. The members of this order within an order met in a ruined castle at Lough Key in Roscommon in Ireland where, aided by the hallucinatory properties of mescaline, they used talisman and tarot to uncover the shared 'ancestral memory'.[113] Founding adepts included Maude Gonne, the actress Florence Farr and George W. Russell, who wrote under the moniker 'AE'. For Yeats, it was essential that Macleod contribute, and in private letters he encouraged her to explore the rituals and godforms of the proposed order. Believing evocations more effective when undertaken by a man and woman, he also pressed her to work in partnership with Sharp. On the evening of the unsettling psychic experiment the pair had in fact been invited to Paris to join in the 'opening ceremonials of the Celtic mysteries', but the arrangement was cancelled at the last minute owing to a 'serious and sudden collapse' in the health of 'Miss M'.[114]

Responding to his friend's worried letter, Sharp sent missives under his own name and as Macleod. Carefully balanced, these letters endorse and modify one another: so, for instance, in one she admits to having endured an 'intense emotional crisis' at the time of magical experiment, a fact that is then confirmed as a 'wave of intense tragic emotion' in a hasty postscript signed by her male author.[115] Given the care with which these two personas are maintained, it would not be unreasonable to presume that Yeats wrote under the assumption that his correspondents were discrete individuals. There are indications, however, that he was aware of their shared identity and yet continued to treat the pair as a collaborative partnership. After Sharp's death, what had been alluded to became public. In a letter to Gonne, Yeats characterised this remarkable authorial doubling as representing a 'semi-allegorical description of the adventures of [Sharp's] own secondary personality and its relation with the primary self', before opining that the 'secondary personality' wrote in a 'more impassioned way'.[116] Macleod, he recognised, was not simply a literary persona, but rather a kind of anima personality uncovered through the techniques of advanced ritual magic; and among the Golden Dawn members, Sharp was far from unique in this pursuit of a doubled or compound selfhood. Not only were the group's magical practices largely contingent on the cultivation of secondary psychic personalities, the daemon selves that worked on astral planes or the willed embodiment of multiple consciousness, as part of their initiation members of the secret organisation were also given new titles and several incorporated these into more fully realised identities.

Specifically, the creation of 'Fiona Macleod' resonated with other performances of Scottish identity enacted within the magical society. Recalling his stay with Mathers in Paris, Yeats described how in the evenings his host would wear 'Highland dress and dance the sword dance' while 'his mind brooded upon the ramifications of clans and tartans'.[117] Detecting something ersatz in this ostentatious display of nomenclature, he hazarded that in truth his friend may not have 'seen the Highlands' or even 'Scotland itself'.[118] Born in Hackney, North London, to a working-class family, Mathers helped to found the Order along with William Wynn Westcott and William Robert Woodman, assuming leadership in 1891 and eventually establishing a Parisian offshoot, Alpha et Omega.[119] As Yeats intuited, his oft-cited Scottish ancestry was indeed formed 'under the touch of the Celtic Movement', and over the years his persona took on increasingly theatrical proportions.[120] Adopting the titles Chevalier MacGregor and Comte de Glenstrae, a fabricated aristocratic heritage that he dated to the Jacobite rebellion of 1745, he became a keen supporter of Scottish nationalism and often bicycled through Paris dressed in a kilt.[121] In the final years of the nineteenth century, several members of the Isis-Urania and Amen-Ra temples began to voice concerns over Mathers's increasingly despotic rule. Of particular concern was his enthusiastic patronage of another supposedly ancestral Scot, the notorious Aleister Crowley.[122] In 1903 tensions came to a head when, having been denied initiation into the more advanced

Adeptus Minor grade, Crowley applied directly to Mathers, who overrode the group decision and conducted the ceremony in secret. On discovering that moves were being made to expel him from the Golden Dawn in light of this betrayal, Mathers dispatched his new initiate to steal papers from the London temple; a duty that Crowley undertook bedecked in full tartan regalia. Pausing on the somewhat absurd image of a kilted robber roaming the streets of Hammersmith, it is possible to observe how certain tropes— clan tartans, Jacobitism and Catholicism—circulated in this occult groups, and to ask what these appropriations reveal of the influence of the romantic Highlands on the creation of a new magical imaginary.

What is perhaps most striking about the magical personages adopted by members of the Order is how often these were furnished with an upper-class lineage. Both Mathers and Crowley claimed to be descended from nobility, and even Macleod was rumoured to be married to a rich and secretive laird. Rather than align themselves with the average crofter or fisherman, they affiliated themselves with the nation's titled elites. More than fantasies of aristocratic heritage, these fabricated histories mirrored the elitist nature of the Golden Dawn itself. Structured around three grades, through which adepts pursued a curriculum of magical training that granted ever deeper access into the mysteries of the unseen world, the Order was strictly hierarchal and purposefully exclusive. Its activities were underpinned by a number of magical texts supposedly passed down by a Masonic scholar and decoded by William Wynn Westcott. The true source of the cipher manuscripts become a matter of controversy in about 1900, after Mathers confessed to forging letters from the German adept charging with translating the material.[123] Yet in spite of their dubious origins, these texts were key in determining a philosophy for the Golden Dawn, based on a peculiar blend of Renaissance magic, Neo-Platonism and Rosicrucianism, enacted through tarot, astrology and alchemy. The ciphers, written through a cryptogram and including Hebrew, French and Latin words, also established the written word as the basis for occult activity; at the core of the ceremonies performed by the group was the belief that revelations concerning the potentials of the unconscious, non-human realms and alternative realities could be obtained through the careful study of mysterious symbols and grimoires. The scholarly nature of their magical practice, along with their restricted membership and secret meetings, set the Order apart from more democratic forms of enchantment. According to Alison Butler this included the complete exclusion of the 'folk

custom and belief' of the illiterate in favour of elite scholastic traditions.[124] But the formation of the Order of Celtic Mysteries, as well as
the idealised Highland personas negotiated by several prominent adepts,
suggests a more complicated picture.

Though their esoteric explorations were undertaken in secret, initiates brought to the study of ancient texts and ciphers a broad range of
contemporary political, cultural and artistic imperatives, which
included a shared fascination in the magical potential of native peasant
customs, folk tales and supernatural lore. Offering an esoteric mirror to
the more public activities of the Celtic Twilight, the Order of Celtic
Mysteries was established with the intention of exploring a philosophy
that found its 'manuals of devotion in all imaginative literature'.[125] In
other words, its founders sought to synthesise folklore, ancient saga
and myth with the precepts of practical magic, forging a connection
between the literary experiments of the Celtic Revival with the occult
explorations of the Golden Dawn. Second sight, as folklore, fiction and
psychical trait, came to form a key link between these sites, and this
connection was often forged in terms of the symbolic. In a 1902 essay,
Macleod praised Yeats as the 'priest of the symbolic', who 'lives with
symbols' as others live with 'facts', so that with him the 'imagination is
in truth the second-sight of the mind'.[126] Written into symbolist
poetics, second sight became exemplary of the tendency of the Celt
to see 'the thing beyond the thing' or to understand the everyday
world as a façade.[127] The practices of the Golden Dawn were, at their
core, an espousal of exactly this principle: imagination is both the
'Formative Power' that generates the universe and the 'Creative
Faculty' that manipulates it.[128] Reflecting on this philosophy of the
imagination, Sinéad G. Matter has argued for a greater critical engagement with the way in which Yeats wrestled the concept of animism
from the grips of a 'post-Enlightenment, anthropocentric insistence'
on the primary 'materialism of the cosmos' and forced it instead to
reflect upon an 'indigenous ontology of animating spirits'.[129] In *The
Winged Destiny: Studies in the Spiritual History of the Gael* (1904),
Macleod defined second sight in precisely these terms. The vision of
the seer, the author wrote, represents the 'symbolic imagination at
work' and an 'effort of the soul to create in symbolic vision a concept
of spiritual insight such as the mind cannot adequately realise'.[130]
Under the gaze of *fin-de-siècle* occultists, second sight was recast as
an active and anthropomorphic force capable of moulding reality.

This animistic universe, where imagination is reality and creation is shaped by correspondences, bound the creative aims of revivalists to the magical goals of occultists, and provided the impetus to recover and preserve the folkloric traditions on the basis that these were rooted in a symbolic reality accessible to the open-minded observer. Rigid empiricism and the pomp of objectivity were antithetical to this deeper, more primitive, truth. Reflecting on his folklore-collecting trips through Ireland with Lady Gregory, Yeats wrote that having 'noticed many analogies in modern spirits' he began attending seances, but that he 'did not go there for evidence of the kind the Society for Psychical Research would value' and instead sought to 'make Holloway interpret Aran'.[131] In other words, his interest in the seance, like his fascination with the peasant cultures of remote corners, was not predicated on the possibility of uncovering evidence for the survival of the soul; rather he sought a 'philosophy' based on marginalised forms of knowledge.[132] Significant differences divided the aims of occultists from those of psychical researchers. Where the SPR pursued the status of a scientific institution, opening itself up to paid members and publishing its findings in the public realm, the Golden Dawn remained a highly secretive and closed organisation; where psychical researchers sought objective proof of the existence of unseen forces, initiates into the Order generally distanced themselves from such grubby empirical concerns. Despite these disparities, the two groups not only shared members—the spiritualist investigator William Crookes was, for example, affiliated with both, as was Yeats—their activities were also geared toward answering the same set of basic questions. There were crossovers in the models of self being elaborated: Frederic Myers's theorisation of the subliminal self as a region of the self capable of embracing a 'far wider range both of physiological and of psychical activity than is open to our supraliminal consciousness, to our supraliminal memory' concurred closely with the transcendentally expansive vision of the unconscious pursued by the Golden Dawn's adepts, and further comparisons can be drawn over the importance of the imagination, mythmaking and dreaming to both parties.[133] Similarly invested in exploring the boundary regions of human consciousness, occultism and psychical research shared expansive self-knowledge as a common goal.

Where the two diverged most significantly was around the issue of technique. Psychical research investigated 'spontaneous' crisis apparitions, 'up-rushes' from subliminal to supraliminal levels of consciousness and moments of unwitting telepathic communication, while the Golden Dawn instituted a rigorous system of magical training, based on the conviction that it was possible to bend such experiences to the will of the individual. Firmly distinguishing their magical work from the passive mediumship encouraged within spiritualist circles, occultist practice was predicated on the active control of attention, thought processes and imagination. Their emphasis on the cultivation of active agency in relation to phenomena such as clairvoyance and thought transference set their secretive operations apart from the published findings of the SPR. Though psychical research-ers also pursued a 'non-reductionist account of mental processes', they did not share, in Alex Owen's terms, the 'reappraisal of the role of the intellect and understanding of the term knowledge that occult practice implied'.[134] The idea of the subliminal self, worked through in research articles and in the posthumously published *Human Personality and its Survival of Bodily Death* (1903), explained extraordinary phenomena such as ghost-seeing, ecstasy and trance as part of the functioning of deeper regions of the consciousness; so that, as Rhodri Hayward writes, 'mediumistic operations which had once taken place outside the person, beyond the boundary of death, could now be seen as internal phenomena'.[135] In line with this, over the course of the Enquiry into Second Sight Ada Goodrich Freer worked to reground the prophecies of the second sighted within the bounds of an agreed-upon psychical epistemology. The power, she found, was best understood as a 'sort of extension or exaltation of the normal faculties' and the premonitions associated with it were most likely due 'to memory or unconscious observation'; and because no 'empirical method' seemed to be involved in the visions, the collected data pointed toward wholly 'spontaneous phenomena'.[136] What appears to be a vision of events to come is, in fact, a case of 'information subconsciously acquired', in which the seer is the unwitting recipient of knowledge dredged up from the deeper levels of the self, rather than being an active participant in the creation of magical knowledge about the world.[137]

Formulated in the language of the subliminal, this interpretation of second sight drew upon a reading of the prophecies as unsought and usually unwanted, long established by the work of antiquarians, demonol-ogists and travel writers. With a few notable exceptions, such as the famous Coinneach Odhar who was said to have used an adder stone to divine the future, the power of second sight was conventionally classified in terms of its spontaneous and uncontrived nature. Its reinscription as an intra-psychic event was, in a sense, quite consistent with older historical repre-sentations. Questions of agency and volition were, however, never wholly absent from the experiments of psychical researchers. This was particularly true of Miss X, whose work for the SPR walked a fine line between detached observation and experimental participation. One of her most significant contributions to psychical research, outside her leadership of the Highland expedition, was a paper titled 'Recent Experiments in Crystal-Vision' for the *PSPR*. This 1889 essay, later cited approvingly by both the American psychologist William James and the French physiologist Charles Richet, begins by detailing the history of scrying, lighting upon recorded instances in ancient cultures, its prominence in Indian folklore and the visionary powers of John Dee, before going on to delineate the extensive parallels and echoes she has unearthed in her own trials with crystal gazing.[138] In one example, Miss X recounts how she stared fixedly at the surface of a crystal and observed a printed announcement of her friend's death suspended there. After the sad news is confirmed she does not wonder at her burgeoning prophetic powers, but rather recalls having recently held up a copy of *The Times* to shield her face from the parlour fire, and conjectures that the image in the crystal must consist of a revival of information subconsciously imbued from the paper. Understood as a form of self-hypnosis, the crystal or luminous surface upon which the eye is fixed becomes, according to physicist and society member William F. Barrett, a kind of 'autoscope' that brings 'forgotten memories of events or scenes' and 'latent mental impressions' to the surface of consciousness.[139]

Envisioned as a technology for exploring the regions of the subliminal, the practice of crystal gazing developed as a visionary technique realised in psychical terms. This method of self-discovery was democratic in nature and articles on the subject often encouraged the reader to conduct their own experiments. For instance, 'The Art of Crystal Gazing' published by *Borderland* provided detailed instructions on 'how to begin' practising this form of divination and offered guidance on how to interpret scenes in the crystal.[140] In the SPR, one of the most enthusiastic popularisers of crystal vision was Andrew Lang, who carried out a series of experiments with friends and acquaintances through the closing years of the nineteenth century. Having purchased a 'glass ball' in St Andrews, he found that people of 'both sexes' and of 'many social experiences' were able to perceive images on its 'milky' surface: from 'my cook of that day [...] to golfers, men of business, men of letters, a physician [...] friends, kinsfolk and chance acquaintances of my own'.[141] Theorised as 'after-images' or 'objectivations of ideas or images consciously or unconsciously present in the mind', crystal gazing provided a means to explore half-forgotten memories and unconsciously imbibed information.[142] Elsewhere, in an article for the *Monthly Review*, Lang offered simple instructions for the 'neophyte' gazer, but cautioned that the practice was grounded in psychology rather than magic. The naturally gifted scryer is not someone in possession of supernatural abilities, but is more simply a 'good visualiser' who tends to think in images and produce 'mental pictures'. He supports these conclusions using the work of Miss X: her article for the *PSPR* and specifically her claim to experience 'every idea or recollection' as pictures filled with 'life and movement'.[143] One the one hand, crystal vision seemed to present a disenchanted form of divination, a democratic means of uncovering information about the self; but on the other, once knitted into the idea of psychical constitution, it came to resemble older magical or folkloric understandings of seership.

Over the course of the Highland investigation, crystal vision came to delineate something of a cultural boundary. To Lord Bute and the London-based researchers it comprised a method of subliminal research, but to the Gaelic speakers they interviewed it was said to be perceived as an 'exercise of magic and witchcraft'.[144] Here the question of how to classify divination—as a tool for exploring the deeper regions of the self or as a route to the supernatural—helped to bolster psychical authority over the kinds of folkloric knowledge still circulating in remote communities. Yet rather than dismiss the Gael as superstitious and uneducated, during the investigation Freer identified the Highlands as a 'place of study', where 'traditions' and 'practical teachings' create an 'atmosphere' that is most conducive to the work of the 'Sensitive'.[145] Characterising herself as an 'adept in their own line', she often described the second-sighted islanders, fishermen and crofters she encountered on her travels as akin to visionary mentors.[146] In doing so, Freer drew on the imaginary of the Celt as spiritual, poetic and romantically inclined, which established the subjects of the Enquiry into Second Sight as in some way more refined than the poor of England's towns and cities. The average Highlander, she observed, possesses an 'inherent' nobility that is derived from their having historically lived on close terms with those of the 'higher ranks'; an historical proximity to the aristocracy that means the activities of the second sighted must be distinguished from the type of work performed by spiritualist mediums.[147] This distinction was drawn primarily along class lines, so that where the Gaelic peasant was poetic and high born, the mediums typically investigated by the SPR were feckless, ill educated and disreputable. In remote northern communities, Freer reported approvingly, the 'suggestion of Spirit Return' is rejected with 'strong expressions of dislike', and the typical seer views the spiritualist movement with a healthy mix of distrust and disdain.[148] Mapped onto questions of supernormal experience, it is this clear differentiation of the prophecies of the second sighted from passive channelling of mediums that makes identification with the former possible for the psychical. Just as the learned magic of the Golden Dawn was aimed at excluding the kinds of plebeian experimentation associated with spiritualism, so too was the framing of the second-sighted Celt as noble, even aristocratic, and beyond the reach of commercial temptations, a means of reinstating visionary abilities as a form of expertise.

It is significant that both magicians and psychical researchers privileged second sight over other expressions of supernaturalism, as in the closing decades of the nineteenth century these discourses worked together to transform a tradition associated with folkloric, oral, peripheral culture into the substance of privileged knowledge. This project reflected a growing interest in arcane, learned, textual approaches to the occult over more populist expressions of the magical or the uncanny. On the founding of William Stead's *Borderland*, for instance, Henry W. Massingham at the *Daily Chronicle* remarked derisively that 'If I am to study mysticism, I will have it from the great masters—from Blake, from Swedenborg and the rest, not from lisping spooks and stuttering clairvoyants [...] I do not want a short cut to the supernatural.'[149] The magical practices of the Golden Dawn and the scientific aspirations of the SPR shared in this desire for a more scholarly approach to the supernatural, and each worked to reground numinous authority within the purview of educated elites. The revivalist 'rediscovery' of the Celt set the same alchemical process in motion by placing the stories and histories of marginalised communities in the service of dominant culture. Though this excavation of folklore and myth was envisioned as part of a revolutionary project, the conversion of the local/oral into the universal/literate still constituted a form of appropriation. The traditions associated with second sight proved particularly vulnerable to cultural seizure. At the *fin de siècle* the second-sight tradition emerged as a site of contestation, with psychical researchers claiming it as a function of the subliminal consciousness, occultists recasting it as an active power capable of shaping reality and revivalists binding it to an ascendant and collective 'Celtic spirit'. [150] These transformations were enacted in spaces from which the Gaelic Highlander was excluded, scientific institutions, urban temples and publishing houses, sites in which second sight was remade and reconstituted. This trajectory is a familiar one, as questions of ownership and appropriation thread through the history of second sight, but the patterns of rapport sought by figures such as Macleod and Freer mark a point of departure. In their creative self-fashioning and shifting authorial persona, these writers exemplified a new approach to the study of folklore that moved beyond observation toward a more active participation. In the reports of the SPR, the literature of the Celtic Revival and the magical experiments of the Golden Dawn, the power of second sight was recast, to varying degrees and in different ways, as accessible.

––––

In her discussion of second sight on the island of Iona, Ada Goodrich Freer wrote of the testimony she had collected that, though such stories 'may not be evidential of the latest theory of science', they remain as 'testimony to the inherent beauty of human life, they are immortal, because they are fragments of the divine life with which one day is as a thousand years'.[151] Juxtaposing the timelessness of second sight with the faddish affectations of modern science, Freer asserted the hermeneutic superiority of the former. While understandings of what constitutes 'truth' are historically constituted, the prophetic narratives of the Highlander precede and exceed such shallow temporal concerns. Writing three years after the inquiry and her acrimonious break with the SPR, this passage is justificatory in tone. It was not that the investigation failed, but rather that psychical research, 'the latest theory of science', had asked the wrong questions of a complex visionary experience. Though never directly affiliated with the Celtic Revival, Freer's characterisation of the 'immortal' and 'divine' seer connotes aspects of this literary renaissance. In an essay on the 'Gael and His Heritage', Fiona Macleod said of the relation of Gaelic to English in the Highlands that when a people is forced to 'speak in two tongues the native speech naturally remains that of the inward life, the inward remembrance, the spirit'.[152] For Macleod and other revivalists, the power of second sight remained bound to this 'inward life', one aspect of a collective 'Celtic spirit' formed from a shared history and a common folkloric heritage. Mapped onto the magical practices of the Order of the Golden Dawn, the prophetic tradition could be recast as a state of mind, a means of comprehending the supremacy of the symbolic over the illusion of the real; or as William Sharp had it, the 'imagination is in truth the second-sight of the mind'.[153] Driving the three projects examined by this chapter—the psychical, the revivalist and the occult—was a desire to claim ownership over second sight. The same charge could, of course, be levelled at all the supernatural investigators, folklorists, anthropologists, spiritualists, stage magicians and novelists featured in this book, all of whom looked to the Highland tradition to test theories, bolster established epistemologies or substantiate new systems of knowledge. In short, these inquiries were grounded in appropriative acts and, as such, tended to reveal far more of the observer than the observed. What set figures such as Freer and Sharp apart from earlier investigators is that their treatment of second sight was based on a wish for proximity over distance. In their reworking of personal identity, in terms of literary and magical persona, both writers looked to embody the visionary power rather than simply witness it. Where previous readings had posited second sight as either an exclusive faculty/hallucination or a universally available power/delusion, in their embodiment of Celtic identities Freer and Sharp insisted on it as both these things. The prophetic vision of the Highlander might now be a common facet of the psyche or a magic facility of the imagination, but its accessibility remained predicated on the tropes and imageries of national mythology.

NOTES

1. 'Ghost Hunting in the Highlands', *Glasgow Evening News* 5 September 1896. ('Ghost Hunting in the Highlands' . . . 1896).
2. Lord Bute made an initial donation of £150 on the condition that 'an exhaustive inquiry into Second Sight in the Highlands might be instituted', 'Annual Business Meeting', *Journal of the Society for Psychical Research* 6 (February 1893) 19. (Bute 1893).
3. On the rise of the questionnaire and the psychological census as the basis for knowledge claims see: Kurt Danziger, *Constructing the Subject: Historical Origins of Psychological Research* (Cambridge: Cambridge University Press, 1990), pp. 75–80. (Danziger 1990).
4. 'The Schedule to Circular Letter No IV' cited in John L. Campbell and Trevor Hall, *Strange Things: The Story of Fr Allan Macdonald and Goodrich Freer, and the Society for Psychical Research's Enquiry into Highland Second Sight* [1968] (Edinburgh: Birlinn, 2006), pp. 29–30. (Campbell and Hall 2006).
5. Begun in 1889, the 'Census of Hallucinations' intended to bolster the conclusions drawn by Edmund Gurney, Frank Podmore and Frederic Myers in *Phantasms of the Living* (1886).
6. *JSPR* 7 (January 1895), 3.
7. Fr. Allan McDonald has been the subject of a recent biography, Robert Hutchinson, *Father Allan: The Life and Legacy of a Hebridean Priest* (Edinburgh: Birlinn Press, 2010). (Hutchinson 2010).

8. Andrew Lang, 'Last Words on Totemism, Marriage and Religion', *Folklore* 23.3 (September 1912), 377. (Lang 1912).

9. Studies like Alan Gauld's *The Founder's of Psychical Research* (1968) (Gauld 1968), Brian Inglis's *Natural and Supernatural* (1978) (Inglis 1978) and Renée Haynes's *The Society for Psychical Research* (1982) (Haynes 1982), deal with the subject fleetingly if at all. This is mirrored by nineteenth-century accounts like Frank Podmore's *Studies in Psychical Research* (1897), which contains no mention of it and William F. Barrett's *Psychical Research* (1911) (Barrett 1911) which gives time over to the phenomenon of second sight but again, makes no mention of the SPR's own inquiry into the topic.

10. In 'Powers of Evil in the Outer Hebrides', *Folklore* 10.3 (September 1899) 258–282 ('Powers of Evil...' 1899) Freer avows that 'I could never myself have accomplished such a collection, and have to acknowledge most cordially and fully the help of Rev. Allan Macdonald, Priest of Eriskay, to whose patience, erudition, and perhaps even more his friendship with these people, these records are mainly due' (256).

11. Trevor Hall claims that he 'had been told that in some circles an affair between Miss Freer and F. W. H. Myers, one of the founders of the S. P. R., had been suspected', John L. Campbell and Hall, *Strange Things: The Story of Fr Allan Macdonald and Goodrich Freer, and the Society for Psychical Research's Enquiry into Highland Second Sight* [1968] (Edinburgh: Birlinn, 2006), p. 96. (Campbell and Hall 1968).

12. Hilary Grimes, *The Late Victorian Gothic: Mental Science, the Uncanny and Scenes of Writing* (Farnham: Ashgate, 2011), p. 88. (Grimes 2011).

13. *Strange Things* p. 102.

14. In studies like *The Spiritualists: The Story of Florence Cook and William Crookes* (1963) and *The Strange Case of Edmund Gurney* (1980) Trevor Hall established himself as a vocal critic of the SPR's early members and the research aims of psychical research. Regarding his work on second sight, G. W.

15. Ada Goodrich-Freer April 1896, *Transactions of the Gaelic Society of Inverness*, vol. xxi, p. 106. (Goodrich-Freer 1896).

16. See Gregory Castle, *Modernism and the Celtic Revival* (Cambridge: Cambridge University Press, 2001) (Castle 2001), Stephen Regan, 'W.B. Yeat's and Irish Cultural Politics in the 1890s', in *Cultural Politics at the Fin de Siecle* ed. Sally Ledger and Scott McCracken (Cambridge: Cambridge University Press, 1995), pp. 66–83 (Regan 1995) and Michael McAteer, *Celtic and Irish Revival* (Oxford: Oxford University Press, 2015). (McAteer 2015).

17. *Cantrip* is a Scot's word denoting a magical spell or supernatural incantation.

18. 'Fiona Macleod', *The Academy and Literature* 15 May 1897, 525–526 (525). ('Fiona Macleod'...1897).

19. 'Fiona Macleod on W.B. Yeats, *The Academy and Literature* 25 October 1902, 444–445 (444). ('Fiona Macleod on...' 1902).

20. 'Ghost Hunting in the Highlands', *Glasgow Evening News* 5 September 1896.

21. 'Fiona Macleod', 525.

22. W. B. Yeats to Maud Gonne, 14 Jan. 1907, *The Gonne-Yeats Letters, 1893–1938: Always Your Friend*, eds. Anna MacBride and A. Norman Jefferes (London: Hutchinson, 1992), pp. 234–235. (Maud Gonne 1992).

23. Terry L. Myers, *The Sexual Tensions of William Sharp: A Study of the Birth of Fiona MacLeod, Incorporating Two Lost Worlds,* 'Ariadne in Naxos' *and* 'Beatrice' (New York: Peter Lang, 1996), p. 4 (Myers 1996) and see also Flavia Alaya, *William Sharp—'Fiona Macleod': 1855–1905* (Cambridge, MA: Harvard University Press, 1970). (Alaya 1970).

24. Miss X [Ada Goodrich Freer] 'The Art of Crystal Gazing', *Borderland* 1 (1894), 117–127 (127). (Miss X [Ada Goodrich Freer] 1894).

25. See R.A. Gilbert, *The Golden Dawn Companion: A Guide to the History, Structure and Workings of the Hermetic Order of the Golden Dawn* (Wellingborough: Aquarian Press, 1986) (Gilbert 1986) and Ellic Howe, *The Magicians of the Golden Dawn: A Documentary History of a Magical Order 1887–1923* (London: Routledge & Kegan Pall, 1972). (Howe 1972).

26. Alison Butler, *Victorian Occultism and the Making of Modern Magic: Invoking Tradition* (London: Palgrave Macmillan, 2011), pp. 173–174. (Butler 2011).

27. Butler, p. 163.

28. Deborah Fleming, *'A man who does not exist': The Irish Peasant in the Work of W.B. Yeats and J. M. Synge* (Ann Arbor: University of Michigan Press, 1995), p. 21. (Fleming 1995).

29. Joshua Landy and Michael Saler, *The Re-Enchantment of the World: Secular Magic in a Rational Age* (Stanford, CA: Stanford University Press, 2009), p. 6. (Landy and Saler 2009).

30. See Michael Hechter, *Internal Colonisation: The Celtic Fringe in British National Development, 1800–1997* (Berkeley: University Press, 1975). (Hechter 1975).

31. Freer, 'Saint Columba: The Father of Second Sight' in *Essays in Psychical Research* (London: George Redway, 1899), p. 299. (Freer 1899).

32. Ibid., p. 320.

33. Ibid., p. 298.

34. *Journal for the Society for Psychical Research* 7 (January, 1895), 2–5 (4).

35. The Schedule to Circular Letter No IV, reproduced in *Strange Things,* pp. 29–30.

36. *JSPR* 7, 3.

37. Ibid., p. 4.

38. 'Objects of the Society', *PSPR* 1 (1882–1883), 4.
39. Frederic Myers to Lord Bute 11 December 1892, quoted in *Strange Things*, p. 26.
40. Myers cited in *Strange Things*, p. 26.
41. *JSPR* 7, 184.
42. *Journal of Psychical Research* 8 (January 1896), 184.
43. Miss X [Ada Goodrich Freer] 'Second Sight in the Highlands', *Borderland* 2 (January, 1895), 56–59 (58). (Miss X [Ada Goodrich Freer] 1895).
44. On W.T. Stead and the New Journalism see Andrew Griffiths, *New Journalism, the New Imperialism and the Fiction of Empire, 1870–1900* (Basingstoke: Palgrave MacMillan, 2015) (Griffiths 2015) and Ann L. Ardis and Patrick Collier eds., *Transatlantic Print Culture, 1880–1940: Emerging Media, Emerging Modernisms* (Basingstoke: Palgrave MacMillan, 2008). (Ardis and Collier 2008).
45. Joseph O. Baylen, 'W.T. Stead's *Borderland: A Quarterly Review and Index of Psychic Phenomena* 1893–1897', *Victorian Periodicals Newsletter* 4.1 (April, 1969) 30–35. (Baylen 1969).
46. William T. Stead to Oliver Lodge 25 July 1893, SPR. MS 35/2518, Cambridge University Archives.
47. Miss X [Ada Goodrich Freer], 'Some Thoughts on Automatism', *Borderland* 3 (April 1896) and 'More About the Burton Messages', *Borderland* 4 (January 1897). (Miss X [Ada Goodrich Freer] 1896, 1897).
48. 'Some Thoughts on Automatism', 168 and *JSPR* (January 1897) 6.
49. W.T. Stead, 'Seeking Counsel of the Wise. What Think Ye of the Study of Borderland?', *Borderland* 1 (July 1893) 7. (Stead 1893c).
50. Stead, 'How We Intend to Study Borderland', *Borderland* 1 (July 1893), 5 (Stead 1893a).
51. See Roger Luckhurst 'Making Connections: W.T. Stead's Occult Economies' in *The Invention of Telepathy: 1870–1901* (Oxford: Oxford University Press, 2002). (Luckhurst 2002b).
52. *JSPR* (January 1897), p. 7.
53. Miss X [Ada Goodrich Freer], 'Second Sight in the Highlands', *Borderland* 2 (January 1895), 56–59. (Miss X [Ada Goodrich Freer] 1895a).
54. Ibid., p. 5.
55. 'Second Sight in the Highlands', *Borderland* 3 (January 1896), 58. (Goodrich Freer 1896).
56. G.W. Lambert, 'Stranger Things: Some Reflections on Reading 'Strange Things' by John L. Campbell and Trevor H. Hall', *JSPR* 45 (June 1969), 43–55 (44). (Lambert 1969).
57. Miss X [Ada Goodrich Freer], 'On the Apparent Sources of Subliminal Messages', *PSPR* 11 (1895), 114–144 (Ada Goodrich Freer 1985b)and 'Recent Experiments in Crystal Vision', *PSPR* (10 May 1889), 486–521.

58. Henry Sidgwick's comments on 'The Apparent Sources of Supernormal Experiences' as delivered at Westminster Town Hall 8 June 1894, *JSPR* (June, 1894), 261.

59. Trevor Hamilton gives a detailed account of the investigation and ensuing scandal in *Immortal Longings: F.W.H. Myers and the Victorian Search for Life After Death* (Exeter: Imprint Academic, 2009) pp. 229–244. (Hamilton 2009).

60. 'On the Trail of a Ghost', *The Times* 8 June 1897.

61. *The Times* 10 June 1897.

62. Frank Podmore, The Alleged Haunting of B—House, Including a Journal Kept During the Tenancy of Colonel Le Mesurier Taylor, PSPR 15 (1899), 98–100 (99). (Podmore 1899).

63. Ibid., p. 57.

64. *JSPR* 8 (January 1896), 184.

65. 'Second Sight in the Highlands', *Borderland* 3 (January 1896) 57–61 (59). (Goodrich Freer 1896).

66. Freer, 'Hobson Jobson', *Nineteenth Century* (April 1902), 585 (Freer 1902).

67. Miss X [Ada Goodrich Freer], 'Second Sight in the Highlands: A Provisional Report', *Borderland* 2 (January 1895), 57. (Miss X [Ada Goodrich Freer] 1895a).

68. Freer to Bute 8 August 1894 cited in *Strange Things*, p. 54 and 'Second Sight in the Highlands', 57.

69. *JSPR* 7 (January 1892), 186.

70. Ibid.

71. Freer, *Outer-Isles* (Westminster: Archibald Constable & Co., 1902) p. 319.

72. Malcolm Chapman, *The Gaelic Vision in Scottish Culture* (London: Croom Helm, 1978), p. 132. (Chapman 1978).

73. Roger Luckhurst, *The Invention of Telepathy: 1870–1901* (Oxford: Oxford University Press, 2002), pp. 166–167. (Luckhurst 2002a).

74. *Oban Times* cited in *Strange Things*, p. 86.

75. Fiona Macleod, 'Iona', *Fortnightly Review* (April 1900), 692–709. (Macleod 1900).

76. Ibid., p. 698.

77. Ibid.

78. Ibid.

79. Fiona Macleod, 'The Sunset of Old Tales', *The Winged Destiny: Studies in the Spiritual History of the Gael* (London: William Heinemann, 1904) p. 3. (Macleod 1904).

80. Macleod, 'Iona', *Fortnightly Review* (April 1900), 692–709.

81. See Alexander Carmichael's, *Carmina Gadelica* 6 Vols. (1900–1971), Rev. James McDougall, *Folk Tales and Fairy Lore in Gaelic and English Collected from Oral Tradition*, ed., Rev. George Calder (Edinburgh, 1910) and Rev.

John Gregorson Campbell's *Superstitions of the Highlands and Islands of Scotland* (1900) and *Witchcraft and Second Sight in the Highlands and Islands of Scotland* (1902)—the data for which was actually collected in the 1860s and published posthumously.

82. This term was first popularised by Patrick Geddes in 'The Scots Renascence', *Evergreen: A Northern Seasonal* 1 (Spring, 1895). It is distinct from the 'Scottish Renaissance', which refers to the later modernist movement, running from the early to mid twentieth century, associated with writers like Hugh MacDiarmid, Violet Jacob and Neil Munro.

83. *The Irish Independent* cited by Elizabeth Sharp, p. 6.

84. William Sharp to Edmund Clarence Steadman, 27 September 1895 (ALS, University of British Columbia Library, Special Collections), *The William Sharp Archive*, ed. William F. Halloran. Available at http://www.ies.sas.ac.uk/research/current-projects/william-sharp-fiona-macleod-archive/william-sharp-fiona-macleod-archive [as accessed 25 May 2016]. William Sharp to Edmund Clarence Steadman, 1895.

85. Elizabeth A. Sharp, *William Sharp*, p. 252 and 256. The Highland stories appeared in two of collections, *The Gipsy Christ and Other Tales* (1895) and *The Sin-Eater and Other Tales* (1895) and in a series of novels, *Pharsis* (1894), *Mountain Lovers* (1895), *The Laughter of Peterkin* (1895), *The Washer of the Ford* (1896), *By Sundown Shores* (1900) and *The Divine Adventure* (1900).

86. William B. Yeats, 'The Washer of the Ford', *The Sketch* April 1897. (Yeats 1897).

87. Macleod to Grant Allen July 1895 (ALS, Pierpoint Morgan, Morgan Library and Museum, Special Collections), *The William Sharp Archive*, ed. William F. Halloran. Available at http://www.ies.sas.ac.uk/research/current-projects/william-sharp-fiona-macleod-archive/william-sharp-fiona-macleod-archive [as accessed 25 May 2016].

88. Macleod, *The Washer in the Ford* (1895), (London: William Heinemann, 1910), p. 144.

89. Macleod, 'The Sight', *The Dominion of Dreams* (London: Heinemann, 1910) p. 86.

90. Macleod, 'The Sight', p. 89.

91. Find footnote for this.

92. Sharp, *Lyra Celtica, An Anthology of Representative Celtic Poetry* (Edinburgh: Patrick Geddes, 1896) (Sharp 1896a) was edited by Elizabeth Sharp and is divided into 13 parts covering Irish, Scots, Welsh, Breton, Cornish and Manx poetry ancient and modern.

93. Fiona Macleod, 'Iona' in *The Works of Fiona Macleod* vol. iv ed. Elizabeth Sharp (London: William Heinemann, 1912) pp. 93–205 (175). (Macleod 1912).

94. Andrew Lang, '*Green Fire*', *Blackwood's Edinburgh Magazine* (February 1897), 189–190 (189). (Lang 1897).

95. This is not comparison that William Sharp would necessarily resent. He was responsible for editing and introducing the centenary edition of *The Poems of Ossian*, trans. James Macpherson (Edinburgh: Patrick Geddes & Colleagues, 1896) (Sharp 1896b).

96. Lang, 'The Celtic Renascence', *Blackwood's Edinburgh Magazine* (February 1897), 181–191 (187, 188, 191) (Lang 1987). See also 'At the Sign of the Ship', *Longman's Magazine* (Dec. 1896).

97. Murray Pittock, *Celtic Identity and the British Image* (New York: Manchester University Press, 1999), p. 71. (Pittock 1999).

98. Pittock, p. 71.

99. Tania Scott, 'The Fantasy of the Celtic Revival: Lord Dunsany, Fiona Macleod and W.B. Yeats', in *Bordercrossings: Narration, Nation and Imagination in Scots and Irish Literature and Culture*, ed. Colin Younger (Newcastle: Cambridge Scholars, 2013) pp. 127–141 (134). (Scott 2013).

100. Sharp to Horace Scudder January 2 1895 (ALS Harvard Houghton Library) *The William Sharp Archive*, ed. William F. Halloran. Available at http://www. ies.sas.ac.uk/research/current-projects/william-sharp-fiona-macleod-archive/william-sharp-fiona-macleod-archive [as accessed 25 May 2016]. (Sharp to Horace Scudder 1895).

101. *On the Study of Celtic Literature*, p. x and William Sharp quoted in Elizabeth Sharp, *William Sharp (Fiona Macleod): A Memoir* (London: Heinemann, 1901), p. 1.

102. Patrick Geddes, 'The Scots Renascence', *Evergreen* 1 (Spring 1895), 131–139 (139). (Geddes 1895).

103. Lady Augusta Gregory, *Visions and Beliefs in the West of Ireland* (London, 1920), p. 214. (v 1920); Marie Trevelyan, *Folk-Lore and Folk-Stories of Wales* (London: Elliot Stock, 1909), p. 191. (Trevelyan 1909); see Donald James Gordon, *W.B. Yeats: Images of a Poet* (Manchester: Manchester University Press, 1961), p. 37. (James Gordon 1961).

104. Penny Fielding, *Writing and Orality: Nationality, Culture and Nineteenth-Century Scottish Fiction* (Oxford: Clarendon Press, 1996), p. 4. (Fielding 1996).

105. Yeats, *Essays: Ideas of Good and Evil* (London: Macmillan, 1924), p. 219. (Yeats 1924).

106. W.Y. Evanz-Wentz, *The Fairy-Faith in Celtic Countries* (1911), (New York: New York University Books, 1966), p. 477. (Evanz-Wentz 1911).

107. Ibid.

108. Yeats, *Fairy and Folk Tales of the Irish Peasantry* (London: Walter Scott, 1890), p. xiv. (Yeats 1890).

109. Yeats in reply to Rev. Percy Myles in John P. Frayne and Colton Johnson eds., *Uncollected Prose by W.B. Yeats Vol. II: Reviews, Articles, and Other Miscellaneous Prose* 1897–1939 (London: Macmillan, 1975), p. 174. (Rev. Percy Myles in John P. Frayne and Colton Johnson, 1975)

110. Yeats, 'The Body of the Father Christian Rosencrux' in *Ideas of Good and Evil* (London: A.H. Bullen, 1907), pp. 308–311 (310). (Yeats 1907).

111. Yeats to William Sharp/Fiona Macleod 3 May 1898, *The Collected Letters of W.B. Yeats, vol. 11 1896–1900, eds. Warwick Gould, John Kelly and Deirdre Toomey* (Clarendon Press: Oxford, 1997), p. 220. (The Collected Letters of W.B. Yeats, 1997).

112. Yeats to Sharp 7 May 1898, *Collected Letters,* pp. 222–223.

113. Robert Fitzroy Foster, *W. B. Yeats: A Life* (Oxford: Oxford University Press, 1999), pp. 196–206. (Fitzroy Foster 1999).

114. William Sharp to W.B. Yeats, 30 April 1898, *Letters to Yeats,* 35–36.

115. William Sharp/Fiona Macleod to W.B. Yeats, 5 May 1898, *Letters to Yeats,* 35–36.

116. W.B. Yeats to Maud Gonne January 14 1907, *The Gonne-Yeats Letters, 1893–1938: Always Your Friend,* ed. Anna MacBride White and A. Norman Jeffares (London: Hutchinson, 1992), pp. 234–235. (W.B. Yeats to Maud Gonne 1992).

117. W.B. Yeats, *Autobiographies* in *The Collected Works of W.B. Yeats* Vol. III, eds. William H. O'Donnell and Douglas N. Archibald (New York: Scribner, 1999), p. 257. (Yeats 1999).

118. Ibid.

119. R.A. Gilbert, 'Mathers, Samuel Liddell (1853–1918)', *Oxford Dictionary of National Biography* (Oxford: Oxford University Press, 2004). (Gilbert 2004).

120. W.B. Yeats, 'Magic' *Monthly Review* (September 1901), 144–164 (153). (Yeats 1901).

121. Richard Kaczynski, *Perdurabo: The Life of Aleister Crowley* (Berkeley CA: North Atlantic Books, 2002) pp. 50–60. (Kaczynski 2002).

122. Tobias Churton, 'Revolt in the Golden Dawn 1899–1900', *Aleister Crowley: The Biography: A Spiritual Revolutionary, Romantic Explorer, Occult Master and Spy* (London: Watkins, 2011). (Churton 2011).

123. Joscelyn Godwin, *The Theosophical Enlightenment* (New York: SUNY, 1994). (Godwin 1994).

124. Butler, pp. 173–174.

125. Yeats, 'Ireland After Parnell' in *Autobiographies* [1922] (London: Macmillian & Co. 1955), p. 204. (Yeats 1922).

126. Macleod, 'The Later Work of Mr. Yeats', *North American Review* (October 1902), 473–485 (476). (Macleod 1902).

127. Sharp quoted in Flavia Alaya, *William Sharp—'Fiona Macleod': 1855–1905* (Cambridge MA: Harvard University Press, 1970), p. 181. (Sharp quoted in Flavia Alaya 1970a).

128. V.H. Fra. Resurgam [Dr. Berridge], Flying Roll No. 5 quoted in *The Place of Enchantment,* p. 151.

129. Sinéad G. Matter, 'Yeats, Fairies, and the New Animism', *New Literary History* 43.1 (Winter 2012), 137–157 (138, 152). (Matter 2012).

130. Yeats, 'Magic' in *Ideas of Good and Evil* (London: A.H. Bullen, 1903), pp. 29–69 and Fiona Macleod 'Maya' in *The Winged Destiny*, pp. 153–163 (159). (Yeats 1903, Macleod).

131. Yeats, 'Swedenborg', 311.

132. Ibid.

133. Myers, 'The Subliminal Consciousness', *PSPR* 7 (1891–1892), 306.

134. Alex Owen, *The Place of Enchantment: British Occultism and the Culture of the Modern* (Chicago and London: University of Chicago Press, 2004) p. 142. (Owen 2004).

135. Rhodri Hayward, *Resisting History: Religious Transcendence and the Invention of the Unconscious* (Manchester and New York: Manchester University Press, 2007) (Hayward 2007).

136. *JSPR* (January 1896), p. 184.

137. 'Second Sight in the Highlands', *Borderland* 3 (January, 1896) 57–61 (60). (Goodrich Freer 1896).

138. Miss X [Ada Goodrich Freer] 'Recent Experiments in Crystal-Vision', *PSPR* 5 (May 1889). Cited in William James, 'What Psychical Research Has Accomplished' (1892) in *Essays in Psychical Research* (Cambridge MA and London: Harvard University Press, 1986), p. 97 (James 1986) and Charles Richet 'Experimental Cryptesthesia' in *Thirty Years of Psychical Research* (New York: Macmillan, 1923) pp. 201–203. (Richet 1923).

139. William F. Barrett, *Psychical Research* (New York: Henry Holt, 1911) p. 141. (Barrett 1911).

140. 'The Art of Crystal Gazing', *Borderland* 1 (Jan, 1894) and Freer to Frederic Myers quoted in *Strange Things.*.

141. Lang introduction to Northcote W. Thomas, *Crystal Gazing: Its History and Practice, with a Discussion of the Evidence for Telepathic Scrying* Northcote W. Thomas (London: Alexander Moring, 1905), pp. xi–xii. (Thomas 1905). See also his experiments with 'Miss Angus' as detailed in *The Making of Religion* (1898) and 'Magic Mirrors and Crystal Gazing', *Monthly Review* 5 (1901).

142. Lang, *Cock Lane and Common Sense* (London, 1894), p. 217. (Lang 1894).

143. Miss X, 'Subliminal Messages' *PSPR* 11, p. 123.

144. Miss X, 'Second Sight in the Highlands', *Borderland* 2 (January 1895), 56–59.

145. Freer to Bute, quoted in *Strange Things*, p. 56.

146. Miss X, 'Second Sight in the Highlands', *Borderland* 2 (January, 1895) 56–59.

147. Ada Goodrich-Freer, *Outer Isles* (Westminster: Archibald Constable & Co., 1902) pp. 84–85 (Goodrich-Freer 1902).

148. *JSPR* 7 (January, 1895).

149. William T. Stead, 'Some More Opinions on the Study of Borderland', *Boderland* 1 (October 1893), 107. Stead 1893b.
150. William Sharp to Horace Scudder January 2 1895 ALS Harvard Houghton and Fiona Macleod, 'The Later Work of Mr. Yeats', *North American Review* (1902). (William Sharp to Horace Scudder, 1902).
151. Ada Goodrich-Freer, 'Saint Columba: The Father of Second Sight' in *Essays in Psychical Research* (London: George Redway, 1899), p. 299. (Goodrich-Freer 1899).
152. Fiona Macleod, 'The Gael and his Heritage', *The Nineteenth Century* (November 1890), 825–841 (827). (Macleod 1890).
153. William Sharp to Horace Scudder January 2 1895 ALS Harvard Houghton and Fiona Macleod, 'The Later Work of Mr. Yeats', *North American Review* (1902).

REFERENCES

Alan Gauld, *The Founders of Psychical Research* (London: Routledge and Kegan Paul, 1968).

Alaya, Flavia, *William Sharp—'Fiona Macleod': 1855–1905* (Cambridge, MA: Harvard University Press, 1970).

Ardis, Ann L., and Patrick Collier eds. *Transatlantic Print Culture, 1880–1940: Emerging Media, Emerging Modernisms* (Basingstoke: Palgrave Macmillan, 2008).

Barrett, William F., *Psychical Research* (New York: Henry Holt, 1911), p. 141.

Baylen, Joseph O., 'W.T. Stead's *Borderland*: A *Quarterly Review and Index of Psychic Phenomena* 1893–1897', *Victorian Periodicals Newsletter* 4.1 (April 1969), 30–5.

Bute, Lord, 'Annual Business Meeting', *Journal of the Society for Psychical Research* 6 (February 1893), 19.

Butler, Alison, *Victorian Occultism and the Making of Modern Magic: Invoking Tradition* (London: Palgrave Macmillan, 2011), p. 173–4.

Campbell, John L., and Trevor Hall, *Strange Things: The Story of Fr Allan Macdonald and Goodrich Freer, and the Society for Psychical Research's Enquiry into Highland Second Sight* (1968) (Edinburgh: Birlinn, 2006).

Castle, Gregory, *Modernism and the Celtic Revival* (Cambridge: Cambridge University Press, 2001).

Chapman, Malcolm, *The Gaelic Vision in Scottish Culture* (London: Croom Helm, 1978).

Churton, Tobias, 'Revolt in the Golden Dawn 1899–1900', in *Aleister Crowley: The Biography: A Spiritual Revolutionary, Romantic Explorer, Occult Master and Spy* (London: Watkins, 2011).

The Collected Letters of W.B. Yeats, 1896–1900, Vol. 11, ed. Warwick Gould, John Kelly, and Deirdre Toomey (Oxford: Clarendon Press, 1997).

Danziger, Kurt, *Constructing the Subject: Historical Origins of Psychological Research* (Cambridge: Cambridge University Press, 1990).

Evanz-Wentz, W.Y., *The Fairy-Faith in Celtic Countries* (1911) (New York: New York University Books, 1966).

Fielding, Penny, *Writing and Orality: Nationality, Culture and Nineteenth-Century Scottish Fiction* (Oxford: Clarendon Press, 1996).

'Fiona Macleod', in *The Academy and Literature* (15 May 1897), pp. 525–6.

'Fiona Macleod on W.B. Yeats, *The Academy and Literature* (25 October 1902), pp. 444–5.

Fleming, Deborah, *'A Man who Does Not Exist': The Irish Peasant in the Work of W.B. Yeats and J. M. Synge* (Ann Arbor: University of Michigan Press, 1995).

Frayne, John P. and Colton Johnson, eds, Uncollected Prose by W.B. Yeats Vol. II: Reviews, Articles, and Other Miscellaneous Prose 1897–1939 (London: Macmillan, 1975), p. 174.

Foster, Robert Fitzroy, *W. B. Yeats: A Life* (Oxford: Oxford University Press, 1999).

Geddes, Patrick, 'The Scots Renascence', *Evergreen* 1 (Spring 1895), 131–9.

'Ghost Hunting in the Highlands', *Glasgow Evening News* (5 September 1896).

Gilbert, R.A., *The Golden Dawn Companion: A Guide to the History, Structure and Workings of the Hermetic Order of the Golden Dawn* (Wellingborough: Aquarian Press, 1986).

Gilbert, R.A., 'Mathers, Samuel Liddell (1853–1918)', in *Oxford Dictionary of National Biography* (Oxford: Oxford University Press, 2004).

Godwin, Joscelyn, *The Theosophical Enlightenment* (New York: SUNY, 1994).

Gonney, Maud, *The Gonne-Yeats Letters, 1893–1938: Always Your Friend* ed. Anna MacBride White and A. Norman Jeffares (London: Hutchinson, 1992).

Goodrich Freer, Ada, 'Hobson Jobson', *Nineteenth Century* (April 1902a), 585.

Goodrich Freer, Ada, *Outer Isles* (Westminster: Archibald Constable & Co., 1902).

Goodrich Freer, Ada, 'Powers of Evil in the Outer Hebrides', *Folklore* 10.3 (September 1899), 258–82.

Goodrich Freer, Ada, 'Saint Columba: The Father of Second Sight' in *Essays in Psychical Research* (London: George Redway, 1899).

Goodrich Freer, Ada, 'Second Sight in the Highlands', *Borderland* 3 (January 1896), 58.

Goodrich Freer, Ada, *Transactions of the Gaelic Society of Inverness* Vol. xxi (Inverness: Gaelic Society of Inverness, 1896), p. 106.

Gordon, Donald James, *W.B. Yeats: Images of a Poet* (Manchester: Manchester University Press, 1961).

Gregory, Lady Augusta, *Visions and Beliefs in the West of Ireland* (Oxford: Oxford University Press, 1970).

Griffiths, Andrew, *New Journalism, the New Imperialism and the Fiction of Empire, 1870–1900* (Basingstoke: Palgrave Macmillan, 2015).

Grimes, Hilary, *The Late Victorian Gothic: Mental Science, the Uncanny and Scenes of Writing* (Farnham: Ashgate, 2011).

Hamilton, Trevor, *Immortal Longings: F.W.H. Myers and the Victorian Search for Life After Death* (Exeter: Imprint Academic, 2009).

Hayward, Rhodri, *Resisting History: Religious Transcendence and the Invention of the Unconscious* (Manchester and New York: Manchester University Press, 2007).

Hechter, Michael, *Internal Colonisation: The Celtic Fringe in British National Development, 1800–1997* (Berkeley: University of California Press, 1975).

Howe, Ellic, *The Magicians of the Golden Dawn: A Documentary History of a Magical Order 1887–1923* (London: Routledge & Kegan Paul, 1972).

Hutchinson, Robert, *Father Allan: The Life and Legacy of a Hebridean Priest* (Edinburgh: Birlinn Press, 2010).

Inglis, Brian, *Natural and Supernatural: A History of the Paranormal from Earliest Times to 1914* (London: Hodder and Stoughton, 1978).

James, William, 'What Psychical Research Has Accomplished' (1892) in *Essays in Psychical Research* (Cambridge, MA and London: Harvard University Press, 1986).

John L. Campbell and Hall, *Strange Things: The Story of Fr Allan Macdonald and Goodrich Freer, and the Society for Psychical Research's Enquiry into Highland Second Sight* (1968) (Edinburgh: Birlinn, 2006).

Kaczynski, Richard, *Perdurabo: The Life of Aleister Crowley* (Berkeley, CA: North Atlantic Books, 2002).

Lambert, G.W., 'Stranger Things: Some Reflections on Reading "Strange Things" by John L. Campbell and Trevor H. Hall', *JSPR* 45 (June 1969), 43–55.

Landy, Joshua, and Michael Saler, *The Re-Enchantment of the World: Secular Magic in a Rational Age* (Stanford, CA: Stanford University Press, 2009).

Lang, Andrew, 'The Celtic Renascence', *Blackwood's Edinburgh Magazine* (February 1897a), 181–91.

Lang, *Cock Lane and Common Sense* (London: Longman & Green, 1894).

Lang, Andrew, '*Green Fire*', *Blackwood's Edinburgh Magazine* (February 1897b), 189–90.

Lang, Andrew, Introduction to Northcote W. Thomas', in *Crystal Gazing: Its History and Practice, with a Discussion of the Evidence for Telepathic Scrying* (London: Alexander Moring, 1905).

Lang, Andrew, 'Last Words on Totemism, Marriage and Religion', *Folklore* 23.3 (September 1912), 377.

Luckhurst, Roger, *The Invention of Telepathy: 1870–1901* (Oxford: Oxford University Press, 2002a).

Luckhurst, Roger, 'Making Connections: W.T. Stead's Occult Economies', in *The Invention of Telepathy: 1870–1901* (Oxford: Oxford University Press, 2002b).

Macleod, Fiona, 'The Gael and his Heritage', *The Nineteenth Century* (November 1890), 825–41.

Macleod, Fiona, 'Iona', *Fortnightly Review* (April 1900), 692–709.

Macleod, Fiona, 'Iona', in *The Works of Fiona Macleod*, Vol. iv, ed. Elizabeth Sharp (London: William Heinemann, 1912), pp. 93–205.

Macleod, Fiona, 'The Later Work of Mr. Yeats', *North American Review* (October 1902), 473–85.

Macleod, Fiona, 'Maya', in *The Winged Destiny: Studies in the Spiritual History of the Gael*, pp. 153–63.

Macleod, Fiona, 'The Sight', in *The Dominion of Dreams* (London: Heinemann, 1910).

Macleod, Fiona, 'The Sunset of Old Tales', in *The Winged Destiny: Studies in the Spiritual History of the Gael* (London: William Heinemann, 1904), p. 3.

Fiona Macleod to Grant Allen, July 1895, ALS, Pierpont Morgan, Morgan Library and Museum, Special Collections, *The William Sharp Archive* ed. William F. Halloran. Available at. http://www.ies.sas.ac.uk/research/current-projects/william-sharp-fiona-macleod-archive/william-sharp-fiona-macleod-archive, accessed 25 May 2016.

Matter, Sinéad G., 'Yeats, Fairies, and the New Animism', *New Literary History* 43.1 (Winter 2012), 137–157.

McAteer, Michael, *Celtic and Irish Revival* (Oxford: Oxford University Press, 2015).

Miss X [Ada Goodrich Freer], 'The Art of Crystal Gazing', *Borderland* 1 (1894), 117–27.

Miss X [Ada Goodrich Freer], 'More About the Burton Messages', Borderland 4 (January 1897).

Miss X [Ada Goodrich Freer], 'On the Apparent Sources of Subliminal Messages', *PSPR* 11 (1895b), 114–44.

Miss X [Ada Goodrich Freer], 'Second Sight in the Highlands: A Provisional Report', *Borderland* 2 (January 1895a), 56–59.

Miss X [Ada Goodrich Freer], 'Some Thoughts on Automatism', *Borderland* 3 (April 1896).

Myers, Terry L., *The Sexual Tensions of William Sharp: A Study of the Birth of Fiona MacLeod, Incorporating Two Lost Worlds* 'Ariadne in Naxos' *and* 'Beatrice' (New York: Peter Lang, 1996), p. 4.

Owen, Alex, *The Place of Enchantment: British Occultism and the Culture of the Modern* (Chicago and London: University of Chicago Press, 2004).

Pittock, Murray, *Celtic Identity and the British Image* (New York: Manchester University Press, 1999).

Podmore, Frank, '*The Alleged Haunting of B—House, Including a Journal Kept During the Tenancy of Colonel Le Mesurier Taylor*', *PSPR* 15 (1899), pp. 98–100.

Regan, Stephen, 'W.B. Yeats and Irish Cultural Politics in the 1890s', in *Cultural Politics at the Fin de Siecle*, ed. Sally Ledger and Scott McCracken (Cambridge: Cambridge University Press, 1995), pp. 66–83.

Richet, Charles, 'Experimental Cryptesthesia', in *Thirty Years of Psychical Research* (New York: Macmillan, 1923), pp. 201–3.

Scott, Tania, 'The Fantasy of the Celtic Revival: Lord Dunsany, Fiona Macleod and W.B. Yeats', in *Bordercrossings: Narration, Nation and Imagination in Scots and Irish Literature and Culture*, ed. Colin Younger (Newcastle: Cambridge Scholars, 2013), pp. 127–41.

Sharp, *Lyra Celtica, An Anthology of Representative Celtic Poetry* (Edinburgh: Patrick Geddes, 1896a).

Sharp, William, *The Poems of Ossian* trans. James Macpherson (Edinburgh: Patrick Geddes & Colleagues, 1896b).

Stead, William T., 'How We Intend to Study Borderland', *Borderland* 1 (July 1893a), 5.

Stead, William T., 'Some More Opinions on the Study of Borderland, Borderland' 1 (October 1893b), 107.

Stead, W.T., 'Seeking Counsel of the Wise. What Think Ye of the Study of Borderland?', *Borderland* 1 (July 1893c), 7.

Trevelyan, Marie, *Folk-Lore and Folk-Stories of Wales* (London: Elliot Stock, 1909).

William Sharp to Edmund Clarence Steadman (27 September 1895), ALS University of British Columbia Library, Special Collections, *The William Sharp Archive*, ed. William F. Halloran. Available at. http://www.ies.sas.ac.uk/research/current-projects/william-sharp-fiona-macleod-archive/william sharp-fiona-macleod-archive, accessed 25 May 2016.

William Sharp to Horace Scudder (2 January 1895), ALS Harvard Houghton Library, *The William Sharp Archive*, ed. William F. Halloran. Available at http://www.ies.sas.ac.uk/research/current-projects/william-sharp-fiona-macleod-archive/william-sharp-fiona-macleod-archive, accessed 25 May 2016.

Yeats, W.B., 'The Body of the Father Christian Rosencrux', in *Ideas of Good and Evil* (London: A.H. Bullen, 1907), pp. 308–11.

Yeats, W.B., *Essays: Ideas of Good and Evil* (London: Macmillan, 1924).

Yeats, W.B., *Fairy and Folk Tales of the Irish Peasantry* (London: Walter Scott, 1890).

Yeats, W.B., 'Ireland After Parnell', in *Autobiographies* (1922) (London: Macmillan & Co., 1955).

Yeats, W.B., 'Magic', in *Ideas of Good and Evil* (London: A.H. Bullen, 1903), pp. 29–69.

Yeats, W.B., 'Autobiographies', in *The Collected Works of W.B. Yeats* Vol. III, ed. William H. O'Donnell and Douglas N. Archibald (New York: Scribner, 1999), p. 257.

Yeats, W.B., 'Magic' *Monthly Review* (September 1901), 144–64.

Yeats, W.B., 'The Washer of the Ford', *The Sketch* (April 1897).

CHAPTER 7

Conclusion

In 1998 *The Herald* newspaper reported on a remarkable research project under way at Edinburgh University. A psychologist based in the Department of Celtic and Scottish studies had been awarded funding of £60,000 to 'chart the tradition of "second sight" or prophetic visions', using questionnaires distributed to potential respondents around the country.[1] Shari A. Cohn-Simmen's long investigation into the phenomenon, originally undertaken as part of her PhD, yielded several journal articles and book chapters, as well as some attention from the Scottish press. The 65-point questionnaire requested information regarding not only the prevalence and experience of second sight, but also detailed personal and family histories. Using this data, the researcher conducted interviews around Scotland and gathered over 500 separate accounts of events forecast, marriages foreseen and deaths foretold. These registered a wide range of visual, auditory, olfactory and tactile experiences; examples reprinted in the newspaper article include that of a bus driver who had a vision of funeral procession on his route and two young siblings who foresaw the death of a child in a caravan fire on the Isle of Skye.[2] What made the study newsworthy and perhaps more than another example of academic eccentricity were the conclusions that it drew: as *The Scotsman* reported, this research apparently offered 'empirical evidence' that second sight runs in families.[3] Combining the methods of ethnology, psychology and human genetics, Cohn-Simmen observed patterns of inheritance, which

© The Author(s) 2017
E. Richardson, *Second Sight in the Nineteenth Century*,
Palgrave Studies in Literature, Science and Medicine,
DOI 10.1057/978-1-137-51970-2_7

indicated that the capacity to experience visions may be borne in the blood. Analysing these findings for the *Journal of Scientific Exploration*, she argued that we should examine second sight not as a superstition or a piece of local folklore, but as a 'creative mental ability' characterised by hereditary 'sensitivity'.[4] Regrounded in the language of modern genetics, the 'extra-sensory' ability could be attributed to an 'autosomal dominant mode of inheritance' and even narrowed, if the correct 'chromosomal region' were identified, to a 'single genetic locus'.[5] According to this research, the power is no supernatural aberration or credulous fallacy, but rather a sensory characteristic passed down through the generations.

The story this project tells is one of an unbroken connection between the past and the present. Heredity persists as the dominant explanatory framework: as *The Herald* enthused, the 'first detailed accounts of psychic communication date back three centuries' and these are now 'woven into the culture and oral tradition of Scotland'.[6] This modern take on second sight is similar to many of the others featured in this book: its findings might be framed by the lexicon of autosomes and chromosomes, but its conclusions do not depart far from those drawn by seventeenth-century demonologists, eighteenth-century travel writers and nineteenth-century evolutionists, spiritualists and eugenicists, many of whom also classified the faculty as in some way inborn. In this instance hereditary has a dual aspect: signifying both the inheritance of visionary powers and the passing down of a canon of writing devoted to cataloguing and explaining those visionary powers. Data used by the study, from which conclusions concerning the genetic makeup of gifted individuals could be derived, was gathered using a series of questions, some of which were 'drawn up in light of the historical literature from the 17th century onwards'.[7] In other words, contemporary instances of prophetic sight only become legible in light of the images, symbols and narrative patterns set by 'historical accounts and investigations'.[8] Respondents to the questionnaire were also asked to categorise their 'psychic' experiences in familiar terms: had they ever had a vision of 'a funeral procession', a loved one shortly before their death, or perhaps 'a person not recognized but later met'?[9] The study diverges from many of its forebears, however, in its division of 'genuine mental talent' from 'cultural phenomenon'. Where once the power of prophecy was confined to the Highlands and Western Isles, Cohn-Simmen now finds it in the histories of families around Scotland, with the residents of Edinburgh apparently just as likely to experience visions as the inhabitants of Lewis. From this distribution pattern the researcher concludes that because second sight is reported by people of 'diverse ages, occupations, and religious and cultural traditions', some hereditary force must be at work.[10] Underpinned by a common genetic component, second sightedness is no longer only a product of landscape, tradition or culture, because such gifts circulate in the genetic makeup of the nation.

This book opened with the Society for Psychical Research (SPR) and its ill-fated foray into the Scottish Highlands. Begun one hundred years after the first circular was drafted by committee, Cohn-Simmen's modern survey echoes aspects of the original 'Enquiry into Second Sight in the Highlands'. Partly funded with money from the SPR, its author makes use of the same techniques—questionnaire followed by fieldwork—employed by Ada Goodrich Freer, Lord Bute and the Reverend Peter Dewar. Beyond methodological congruity, affinities can be traced in terms of shared objectives. Like her psychical forebears who placed the prophetic tales of islanders in the service of subliminal psychology, Cohn-Simmen also looks to the example of second sight as a means of bolstering new theories of mind. After all, were it possible to prove that the fabled Scottish seer possesses a 'genuine mental talent partly hereditary', then the limits we ascribe to our sensory systems would be subject to radical renegotiation.[11] In common with the work of Frederic Myers and Andrew Lang, her research takes up the question of supernatural vision primarily as a way of interrogating the nature of human creativity; if the premonitory powers of the interviewees derive from 'creative inborn talent', might there be other 'genes for the susceptibility to have specific mental and artistic abilities'?[12] The conclusions drawn by this study reflect a way of thinking about second sight, observable at moments throughout the tradition's history, that interprets it as one element of a broader philosophy of the imagination. When, for example, Jane Carlyle wrote to a friend in 1851 of her 'second sight', she did not claim the power to see death shrouds or spectral funeral processions; rather she employed the term to connote the possession of a particularly vivid insight: 'It was nothing you said in your letter which made this impression on me, but what you did not say, which I seemed to read by second sight behind the outward visible words.'[13] As well as serving as a synonym for special intuition, from the Romantic period onwards, second sight was also put to work on the task of 'imagining the imagination'.[14] Merging the figure of the seer with that of the poet, the prophetic power was brought to bear on the theorisation of creativity; so that, as William Sharp had it, 'imagination' was 'in truth the second-sight of the mind'.[15] Under the gaze of early theories of the unconscious, magnetic interpretations of sympathy, subliminal under-standings of mind, the symbolist poetics of writers such as Sharp, the phenomenon of second seeing could be reconfigured as an expansive metaphor for the mysteries of artistic inspiration

One narrative that has threaded through this book concerns the trans-formation of second sight, a faculty or superstition associated with the geographically distant and culturally mysterious Scottish Highlands, into a supernormal facet of the psyche, potentially accessible and exploitable by all. We have noted how theories of magnetic influence established the groundwork for this change and how writers such as Catherine Crowe incorporated uncanny visionary experiences into new theories of the mind; how the plebeian experimentation encouraged by mesmerism was taken up by the spiritualist movement and how the Highlander's second sight became exemplary of the workings of a higher spiritual law manifesting in parlours around the country; how the SPR theorised instances of fore-knowledge as paradigmatic instances of telepathic communication and subliminally accessed memory; and finally, how the Hermetic Order of the Golden Dawn recast second sight as a technique for transcendental self exploration, one that might be obtained through the study of ancient texts and cultivated through a programme of magical training. Part of what allowed second sight to operate in these distinct generative contexts was the widely held perception of the power as involuntary and unsought. As we have seen, from the first investigations into the strange faculty, its evidentiary value has been founded on its seemingly involuntary character. Unwilled and largely unwelcome, the second-sighted vision was thus distinct from the diabolical work of seventeenth-century witches, quite unlike the staged performances of clairvoyants, separate from the deluded proclamations of millenarian prophets and unrelated to the activities of ghost-bothering spiritualists.

The question of volition continues to dominate discussions of the faculty, and in her recent study Cohn-Simmen once again presses the 'spontaneous' nature of the 'vivid' visions reported by her respondents. Spontaneity also endures as a measure of veracity and a means of distin-guishing reliable from unreliable witnesses: just as Miss X drew a sharp divide between the ignoble chicaneries of the drawing-room spiritualist and the artless prophecies of the Highlander, so too is Cohn-Simmen careful to exclude testimony from any respondents who 'professed to being mediums or had some other involvement with the occult'.[16] Alongside 'serious medical or clinical problems', dabbling in the mystical arts is deemed a disqualifying offence, one likely to impair the judgement of the witness.[17] The exclusion of certain voices from the survey helps to set the terms on which evidence will be judged as valid or invalid, and establishes the character of the seer as the primary measure of truth. Since the seventeenth century, English-speaking observers have wrestled with how to make sense of second sight and with how to transform super-natural and orally circulated narratives into usable scientific data. Told through the same citational structure as the rumour, the stories of the second sighted were not especially amenable to the empirical standards of evidence: usually recounted second hand, without outside verification and after the foreseen event had taken place, the 'truth' of these mun-dane prophecies was always subject to contestation. Claims to verity could be based, however, on the reliability of the seer rather than the veracity of his visionary experience, and this model of reliability came was tightly bound to an image of the Gaelic Highlander as by nature unknowing, simple and entirely without artifice. What is more, from the earliest written reports of the faculty, the guilelessness of the rustic seer was affirmed by the untutored nature of the gift itself, because unlike witchcraft or related methods of divination, second-sighted visions were said to be unsought and often unwanted. This way of thinking about premonitions and their veracity lives on in Cohn-Simmen's survey, where the testimony of mediums and occultists is omitted on the grounds that such witnesses engage in practices out of step with the spontaneous nature of the second-sighted vision.

If the 'awake visions' recorded by this survey derive not from conjuring or incantation, then some other force must be at work in their production, and for Cohn-Simmen that force is inheritance. Framing second sight as at once specific to certain family lines and as a 'mental talent' alike to artistic inspiration, her study works with a contradiction negotiated by many of the investigators featured in this book. Over the course of the nineteenth century, observers tried to make sense of the peculiar faculty by gathering first-hand accounts, translating oral testimony into written evidence and, importantly, converting customary knowledge into universal discourse. But their desire to shift the phenomenon from the local to the general was always held in tension with what attracted phrenologists, mesmerists, anthropologists, folklorists and psychical researchers to the strange phe-nomenon in the first place: its geographical specificity. Distinct from countless other prophecies and presentiments, second sight entered the cultural imagination as a Scottish faculty, a complex and contested marker of national identity. More specifically still, when tales of the visionary power first began to appear in antiquarian miscellanies, scientific studies, travel narratives and novels, it was established as the peculiar preserve of the Highlanders. The opening chapter of this book examined how the second-sight tradition was, from the beginning, demarcated in close proximity with a broader mythology of the Highlands as a preliterate, primitive culture, under imminent threat from the forces of modernity. Whether ascribed to the Celt's inbred credulity or poetic temperament, deemed the inevitable consequence of a savage mode of life or an ancient skill threatened by civilisation, regarded as a delusion encouraged by the barren terrain or as a gift bestowed by the sublime landscape, the idea of second sight was grounded in an image of a northern region and its people. We can think about this prophetic tradition in terms of its hybridity—the way it adapted to meet the demands of very different investigative cultures—but it is important to acknowledge how persistent its connection to the Highlands proved. Even in the final chapter, where psychical researchers and occultists recast the power as a creative facet of the psyche, this embodiment was still based on the cultivation of a Celtic identity one played out in the tartan theatricals of the Golden Dawn, in Freer's fabricated ancestry and in Sharp's creation of a Gaelic-speaking, croft-dwelling literary persona.

Though most starkly realised in the creation of Fiona Macleod and the forged heritage of Miss X, all the encounters described by this book rest on the performance of the same tropes negotiated by these writers: that long-established imaginary of tartan, romance, poetry and superstition. The second-sight tradition emerged as part of the same mythology of the Highlands, as delineated by artists, writers and politicians from the early eighteenth century onwards. Examining the place of these odd portents in the nineteenth-century imagination, this book has concerned itself with a vision of the Highlands as refracted through the eyes of English-speaking observers. We have seen how the figure of the seer was absorbed by popular culture, how he moved between press reports, literary texts, stage shows, scientific reports and religious sermons, shifting to meet the demands of these distinct formations. Detached from the remote communities in which they were said to take place, stories of second sight were put to work in forming new knowledge at the metropole. Whether taken up in support of the semi-legitimate claims made by mesmerists and phrenologists or used to bolster the emerging evolutionary theories of anthropologists and folklorists, the lore of the illiterate, the poor and the marginalised was always vulnerable to annexation. Bringing the language of colonisation to bear more directly on the study of peasant customs, it is possible to read the second-sighted Highlander as an object made and remade by imperialism in multiple guises.

What this story of hegemony and appropriation leaves out, however, are the myriad ways in which prophetic peasants frustrated and subverted the desires of dominant culture. Never wholly amenable to the magical beliefs of the elite, stories of eerie foreknowledge in Britain's northernmost reaches troubled the secular and self-consciously modern take on the supernatural being championed by a new breed of educated ghost-seers. Nowhere was the volatile status of second sight in bourgeois culture more apparent than in its relation to narrative and to history. Over the course of the nineteenth century, Scottish Highlanders were written into a teleological account of history, where they were called upon to exemplify pre-modern primitivism and evolutionary regression. Second sight, whether dismissed as a super-stition or praised as evidence of their innate spirituality, was used to shore up this developmental account. But the prediction of a seer, whether repro-duced by oral or textual formations, authored a version of history opposi-tional to the dominant stadial model. Refusing linear formations of time to conflate the present with the future, so that effects are ascertained before their cause comes into existence, premonitions unwhorl the threads of sequential narration. The alternative temporal patterns woven by prophetic sight make possible other ways of mapping history: the histories produced by the second-sighted privilege inner visionary experience over external observation, customary knowledge over written records, the local over the universal. Writing in the 1950s, the Italian Marxist Antonio Gramsci described folklore as a 'conception of the world and life' set in opposition to '"official" conceptions of the world' and ultimately 'fragmentary'. According to Gramsci, for radical social change to come about such 'contra-dictory' conceptions of life needed to be 'overcome' and the masses edified by superior cultural forms.[18] Though it is useful to think of folklore as existing outside 'official' discourse, to dismiss it as 'contradictory' is to overlook how far traditions such as second sight are rule-governed and operate according to their own internal logic. Far from being a passive recipient of random and 'fragmentary' information, the seer must engage in active processes of decoding and reconstruction, as it is only through the correct appreciation of a vision's peculiar symbolism that its significance can be ascertained. As Andrew Lang recognised when he cautioned that the 'tourist or angler who has no Gaelic' should not expect to learn much about it, second sight was rooted in a world to which English speakers had only limited access.[19] Against the sweep of evolutionary discourse and universalist historiography, second sight remains predicated on the possession of privileged, local knowledge.

NOTES

1. 'Focusing on Second Sight', *The Herald* 18 May 1998. ('Focusing on Second...' 1998)
2. Ibid.
3. 'A Second Sight for Sore Eyes', *The Scotsman* 23 February 2006. ('A Second Sight...' 2006)
4. Shari A. Cohn-Simmen, 'Second Sight and Family History: Pedigree and Segregation Analysis', *Journal of Scientific Exploration* 13.3 (1999), 351–372 (351). (Cohn-Simmen 1999b). See also Shari A. Cohn-Simmen, 'A Questionnaire Study of Second Sight Experiences', *Journal of the Society for Psychical Research*, 63.855 (1999), 129–157. (Cohn-Simmen 1999a)
5. Ibid., p. 370
6. Focusing on Second Sight', *The Herald* 18 May 1998
7. Cohn-Simmen, 'Second Sight and Family History' p. 354
8. Ibid., p. 353
9. Ibid., p. 355
10. Ibid., p. 353
11. Shari A. Cohn-Simmen quoted in 'Focusing on Second Sight', *The Herald* 18 May 1998
12. Cohn-Simmen 'Second Sight and Family History' p. 370
13. Jane Welsh Carlyle to Lady Airlie, 27 December 1851, *The Carlyle Letters Online* [*CLO*] ed. Brent E. Kinser (Duke University Press, 14 September 2007), accessed 22 September 2013. (Jane Welsh Carlyle to Lady Airlie 2007)
14. Peter Womack, *Improvement and Romance: Constructing the Myth of the Highlands* (London: MacMillan, 1989), p. 94. (Womack 1989)
15. William Sharp to Horace Scudder January 2 1895 ALS Harvard Houghton and Fiona Macleod, 'The Later Work of Mr. Yeats', *North American Review* (1902). (Macleod 1902).
16. Ibid., p. 354
17. Ibid.
18. Antonio Gramsci, *Selections from Cultural Writings* (Cambridge MA: Harvard University Press, 1991), p. 189. (Gramsci 1991).
19. Lang, *Cock Lane and Commonsense*, p. 247

REFERENCES

Jane Welsh Carlyle to Lady Airlie, *The Carlyle Letters Online* [*CLO*], ed. Brent E. Kinser (Durham: Duke University Press, 2007).

Cohn-Simmen, Shari A., 'A Questionnaire Study of Second Sight Experiences', *Journal of the Society for Psychical Research* 63.855 (1999a), 129–57.

Cohn-Simmen, Shari A., 'Second Sight and Family History: Pedigree and Segregation Analysis', *Journal of Scientific Exploration* 13.3 (1999b), 351–72.

'Focusing on Second Sight', *The Herald* (18 May 1998).

Gramsci, Antonio, *Selections from Cultural Writings* (Cambridge, MA: Harvard University Press, 1991).

Macleod, Fiona, 'The Later Work of Mr. Yeats', *North American Review* (1902), pp. 473–485.

'A Second Sight for Sore Eyes', *The Scotsman* (23 February 2006).

Womack, Peter, *Improvement and Romance: Constructing the Myth of the Highlands* (London: Macmillan, 1989).

INDEX

© The Author(s) 2017
E. Richardson, *Second Sight in the Nineteenth Century*,
Palgrave Studies in Literature, Science and Medicine,
DOI 10.1057/978-1-137-51970-2

CPSIA information can be obtained
at www.ICGtesting.com
Printed in the USA
LVHW080043241119
638297LV00004B/279/P

9 781137 519696